The Midwife Factor

A Lynn Davis Mystery

GIGI GOSSETT

Foreword by Nikki Giovanni

THE MIDWIFE FACTOR
A Lynn Davis Mystery

iUniverse books may be ordered through booksellers or by contacting:

iUniverse
1663 Liberty Drive
Bloomington, IN 47403
www.iuniverse.com
1-800-Authors (1-800-288-4677)

ISBN: 978-1-4917-4391-1 (sc)
ISBN: 978-1-4917-4392-8 (hc)
ISBN: 978-1-4917-4393-5 (e)

Library of Congress Control Number: 2014914111

Printed in the United States of America.

Publisher's Cataloging-in-Publication
(Provided by Quality Books, Inc.)

Gossett, Gigi.
    The midwife factor / GiGi Gossett ; foreword by Nikki
       Giovanni.
    p. cm.

    1. African American private investigators--Fiction.
2. Women private investigators--Fiction. 3. African
American midwives--Fiction. 4. Twins--Fiction.
5. Adoption--Fiction. 6. Cincinnati (Ohio)--Fiction.
7. Detective and mystery stories. 8. Suspense fiction.
I. Title.

PS3607.O855M53 2013   813'.6
                     QBI13-600092

iUniverse rev. date: 10/20/2014

This book is dedicated to my identical twin sisters who were the inspiration for this storyline.

Gwen and Gay Anderson, you are
gone but never forgotten.

"Precious Lord, take my hand."

Excerpt from E. E. Cummings's "i carry your heart with me (i carry it in)" (1920)

i carry your heart with me (i carry it in
my heart) i am never without it (anywhere
i go you go, my dear; and whatever is done
by only me is your doing, my darling)

Acknowledgments

IT TAKES A VILLAGE TO prepare a book for publication, and I have many to thank for their contributions to this one.

The story originates in Cincinnati, Ohio, but the case takes my heroine to Budapest, Hungary. I personally found Budapest to be a lovely and enchanting city during my visits there and felt it offered the perfect setting for this empirical story. Divided by the Danube River, the city is both old, especially in its style of architecture, and contemporary, with its popular public baths and restaurants. However, without knowing the language or immersing myself in the culture to fully understand its customs and conventions, I felt it was impossible for me to convey the true essence of the city without help. Thankfully, some of my associates, native to the area, gave me helpful perspectives and insights into this quaint city with its very rich culture and legends. While nearby Transylvania is more often associated with well-known mythical lore, I learned that beliefs and superstitions regarding the supernatural still have a solid place there. I appreciate all who provided me with greater insight into this beautiful city.

Marti Stafford provided valuable critique, input, and editorial advice, and I greatly appreciate her many contributions along the way. I also want to acknowledge Sharon Chapman for the thorough editing review she generously provided.

Every writer seeks feedback from his or her readers, and I offer my sincere thanks to those who gave me such encouragement after my first Lynn Davis novel *By Any Other Name*. Many even asked for a sequel. However, in this book, I did not continue the first story; instead I gave Lynn Davis a new case, one that was recommended to her by her client from my first novel. I want to thank those with whom I shared *The Midwife Factor* storyline and who, in turn, shared their thoughts with me about it. Many improvements were made as a result of their input.

And finally, I wish to thank the diligent and capable team at iUniverse that I had the pleasure of working with, including Traci Anderson, Sarah Disbrow, and Brian Hallbauer. They were encouraging, patient, and helpful to me in readying this book for publication. The editors were outstanding, and I cannot say enough about the valuable developmental edit conducted by J. McConkey, which resulted in my strengthening this work manyfold.

My heartfelt thanks to all.

Foreword

WOW! ANOTHER LYNN DAVIS MYSTERY ... and one addressing several very topical questions of identity. Who are we? Biologically conceived or birthed by love? What should a fifteen-year-old who finds herself pregnant do? To whom does she owe alliance? GiGi Gossett bravely goes where the heart leads, from Cincinnati to Paris to Budapest, in search of family.

What I love so much about *The Midwife Factor* is that we all *midwife* something. Some midwives are there at birth; some are there to stand against tragedy; and some are there to bravely show love and support. The most difficult thing Dr. and Mrs. Wellington must do is let their daughter seek her fate. Every mother, from Eve to the slave mother sending her child to journey the Underground Railroad, knows the fear knowledge has brought and the enlightenment freedom can bring. But Morgan Wellington isn't escaping—she is uniting.

What a thrilling and timely story. We all are seeking our destiny, our identity, our *reason*. GiGi Gossett has done it again. *The Midwife Factor* is a smooth read, an exciting mystery, and a loving look at one of today's most serious problems.

Nikki Giovanni
Poet

Prologue

Cincinnati, Ohio, May 11

FLOSSIE WALKER WIPED THE YOUNG patient's forehead. The girl was screaming with every new contraction, each coming with increasing frequency. Finally she had to put her to sleep. Soon afterward, the baby calmly made its way through the birth canal. It was a girl. Before Flossie could get the baby cleaned up, the young mother began to writhe and moan, and Flossie realized that another baby was coming out, one she hadn't even known was there. But the very life was being choked out of this second baby by the umbilical cord. Suddenly, with sirens blaring, the ambulance attendants burst in and carried away the young mother, who was lying in a pool of blood.

Flossie awakened with a jolt.

After her birthday celebration earlier, she had returned to her room with cake and gifts. Her dear friend Agnes had made her a lovely white afghan with red chevron stripes. "Honey, I hope you love this 'cause I certainly worked hard enough on it," Agnes had said. Beulah made her a pink-and-white shawl that would go nicely with her pink suit. After placing her cake in the cooler, she sat down in her rocker to rest. Before she knew it, she had dozed off. That childbirth dream had come almost immediately. Over the last nineteen years, Flossie had been visited off and on by the same dream, blood-covered sheets and all. It was a nightmarish reenactment of the day she delivered the Moldovan twins and made a decision she would live to question many times. While the dream was unwelcome and unsettling, the new one she had just last night troubled her the most.

In the new dream, the twins, who were now young women, were being chased by two evil-looking men with guns. They were running for their lives through the woods as faint light from the full moon above streaked through the trees. The dream had felt so real that Flossie was convinced that it was. She was certain it was a sign that those girls were actually in danger. She had awakened last night to find herself breathing hard and fast. Instead of basking in the joy of her upcoming birthday, she'd found herself filled with remorse and guilt.

Time was drawing near. She pulled herself up and went into the bathroom to wash her face. When she returned, she folded up her pink-and-white shawl and put it away. Then she sat down in her rocking chair and covered her legs with her new afghan. As if on cue, her three-year-old cat, Cinderella, leapt onto her lap, yawned, and stretched her long, lithe body contentedly. Flossie stroked Cinderella and began humming an old Negro spiritual. "Just a Closer Walk with Thee" was one of her lifelong favorite hymns. Cinderella looked into Flossie's eyes and purred.

Glancing up at the clock, Flossie noticed it was now 6:55 p.m. Just a few minutes more. Since she'd first awakened this morning, she'd eagerly awaited this time of this special day. She looked down at her cat and in a cheerful voice said, "It won't be long now." Her cat meowed softly. Flossie was so sleepy ... She went ahead and closed her eyes.

7:02 p.m.

SUDDENLY, CINDERELLA'S EARS PRICKED UP, and she jerked her head around. Flossie started, opened her eyes, and looked toward the door.

There she was.

Dressed as always in her traditional white nursing outfit—a crisp, long-sleeved white uniform, white stockings, and white nursing shoes—her neat pageboy hairstyle partially covered by a stiff white nursing cap. With a broad smile on her face she seemed to float into the room. Flossie stood up to greet her visitor, and Cinderella jumped onto the bed. Smiling, her guest walked over to her and said sweetly, "I'm here."

"Mossie Lee, it's you!" Flossie Walker squinted her eyes and exclaimed joyfully, "I have been waiting for this moment all day long. Happy birthday." Then the two gave each other warm and long-awaited hugs.

"Happy birthday to you too, my dear," Mossie answered. Then she sat down on the aged leather ottoman in front of Flossie and leaned forward, resting her palms on her knees. "I'm so glad to see you again. I've missed you."

"Girl, you don't know how much I've been looking forward to seeing you. I've missed you more than you know. I often think of all those years when you were here.

So long ago now. I'm telling you, Mossie, time certainly flies." She added with a smile, "Can you believe I'm sixty-seven today?"

"Plus twenty," Mossie corrected good-humoredly. "Don't forget I know exactly how old you are."

Flossie chuckled. "I sure know you do. But on a serious note, sometimes it does seem like the mind's just not as sharp as it used to be, you know. I've noticed it more since I've been living here."

"Well, I'm certainly glad you are living here. And your place still looks good," Mossie said, looking at the floral sofa and matching chair. Her eyes landed on the once brightly colored heirloom quilt folded neatly across the wrought iron bed. "I remember when Aunt Bea passed this on to you. All your antiques just get lovelier with age. They practically look as good here as they did in your home in North Avondale." She eased over to Flossie's antique mahogany sideboard and said, "I always loved this piece with all the beveled glass and inlaid ivory carvings. Remember, we were together when you bought it. You used to keep it in your big old dining room. I was wondering if you ever missed your home. After all, you were there for over fifty years."

"I don't miss it like I used to. After I got arthritis in my knees, I could hardly get up and down those three stories anymore. Coming here to Felix House was the best thing."

"It sure looks like you all have a good time here. The folks I've seen seem young at heart, like you. By the way, I've watched you line dancing during your monthly socials. You've still got all the moves."

A thoughtful look instantly replaced the smile on Flossie's face.

"There you go again. I can see you've been worrying about something. You know you shouldn't let things weigh your heart down," Mossie said.

"It's this heavy secret I've been carrying around all these years. I've never stopped agonizing over it." She shook her head and said, "Acting on the spur of the moment like that; I just didn't have time to think things out. So many times I've wished I could take it all back. I've never been able to discuss this with another soul, and I'm grateful that you've been here for me. It's been such a relief to be able to talk to you about it."

"You know I'll always be here for you, Flossie, so you need to stop fretting. You only did what you felt was right at the time."

"But it would be different if people's lives weren't involved. I have prayed so many times that everything turned out well for everyone concerned."

"And you know the good Lord answers our prayers."

"I believe that too. But why does He keep sending me these dreams?" Then Flossie told Mossie about the new one she'd had last night. "I do believe He's trying to tell me something. I believe those girls are in danger. Maybe they're already … oh, Lord." She shook her head, unable to make herself say what crossed her mind. She added, "What can I do?"

"I won't tell you they're not in danger, Flossie, but I will say this. If they are, it doesn't have anything to do with you or anything you did. You shouldn't feel responsible for everything that happens. But I believe things are all going to work out. You'll see."

"But that's just it, Mossie. How will I see? How am I supposed to know?"

"You'll know it in your bones. Trust me on that."

"But I feel like I should do something about it now," Flossie replied.

"Listen to me. I need to say something, and this time, you've got to heed my words. If that dream is of any real significance, it's time, more than ever, for you to write those letters."

"I knew that's what you were going to say, and I hear you. I know I should, especially now since I believe they're in trouble. But I'm afraid that's easier said than done." Flossie cocked her head and added, "Because even if I write this letter, just where am I supposed to mail it to, anyway? I know the Wellingtons' address, but I can't just up and write to them. Several years ago, I did get Mrs. Moldovan's new address. Her family moved from Romania to Hungary. I put it away somewhere. And I tell you, I've searched high and low for it, but for the life of me, I don't know what I did with it. Besides, for all I know they might have moved again by now. Who knows where these people are today?"

Mossie Lee walked over to the bookcase. When she returned, she handed Flossie a small slip of paper on which a name and address were handwritten. "Write the letter," she commanded softly.

Flossie glanced in surprise at the paper. "Lord, have mercy. This is just what I've been looking for. Where in the world did you find this?"

"You had put it away a little too well. But very little gets past me," Mossie answered, smiling broadly.

"You're certainly right, girl. Guess I'm gonna have to go ahead and write that letter now. Lord knows, I've run out of excuses."

"Believe me, it's the right thing to do. I won't keep harping on the fact that you should have written it years ago, because you already know that. Just remember that things always turn out right when your heart is right," her visitor said, and then she winked.

"What you say means everything to me, girl." Then Flossie stood and extended her arms, saying, "Now come and give me another hug."

As the two women embraced, Flossie said, "Just look at you. Thirty-seven years old and pretty as ever, even in that getup. Of course, you don't have to worry about anything anymore. I guess that keeps you young."

"Well, you look pretty good yourself, Flossie Mae. And look at your skin. I used to hear the white nurses whispering about you, 'You know what they say. Black don't crack.'"

Flossie beamed. She took pride in keeping up her appearance.

"I've even seen you outside, fussing with the flower garden. You can still stretch and bend good as any young girl. And shush that crazy talk about your mind not being as sharp as it used to be. Most young folk would love to have a mind half as sharp as yours. And if you feel even half as good as you look, you'll probably live longer than Aunt Beatrice, who made it past the century mark. No one else in the family lived that long. It's up to you."

"I'm not so sure about that. You know, it gets pretty lonely here sometimes. In a way, I feel like I have already lived such a full life. Whenever the end comes, I'll be at peace." Then Flossie furrowed her brow, and said, "I know I have asked you this before, but I'm starting to think about it all the time now. Tell me again. Just how is it over there?"

"Like I've told you before, they don't like us to talk about it much, but I know one day you and I will be able to spend more time together. For now, my dear Flossie, I just want you to get busy writing those letters." Then the two women read the Bible together and talked into the night about old times.

* * *

At five the next morning, Flossie opened her eyes and looked around. *Heavens, I've done it again—fell sound asleep in my rocking chair still sitting here in my birthday clothes.* Flossie's heart was filled with elation from last night's special event, one she could count on occurring like clockwork every year on her birthday at exactly 7:02 p.m. She glanced over and saw that Cinderella was now on the bed, purring soundly. The lamp on her nightstand was still on. She smiled to herself and stretched, glancing over at the ottoman, which she knew was empty. Except, that is, for her big, brown family Bible.

Flossie saw a small slip of paper peeking catawampus out of the pages of her Bible and reached over to pick it up. She looked down at the paper and saw Corina Moldovan's Hungarian address in Mrs. Moldovan's own handwriting. *Well, I'll be. Now I remember sticking it there for safekeeping years ago. Must have been walking in my sleep.*

She washed up and pulled out her fancy stationery and her quill pen she only used on special occasions. Flossie had promised Mossie that she would write the letters right away. She decided now was the time. It took nearly two hours that morning to put the words on paper. She spent another thirty minutes writing the second letter to the Wellington family of Cincinnati, Ohio.

After breakfast, her niece, Hazel, picked her up and took her to the post office, where she mailed her letters. *It's done,* she sighed. She felt the lifting of a heavy burden from her heart. As usual, Mossie had been right.

After the post office, Hazel drove Flossie to the florist's shop for fresh flowers. Hazel bought white roses, and Flossie bought lilacs. Their next stop was Spring Grove Cemetery for their annual visit to commemorate the death of Flossie's sister, Mossie Lee Jackson, Hazel's mother. Hazel wore a bright-yellow suit, and Flossie wore black. She and Hazel rode along in quiet contemplation, Flossie thinking about that terrible day fifty years ago when her identical twin sister, Mossie, was fatally injured by a hit-and-run driver while crossing the street on her way to the hospital where they both worked as registered nurses. This had happened at precisely 7:02 p.m. on their thirty-seventh birthday.

Flossie and Mossie had been exceptionally close. Flossie thought again about how for the past fifty years, starting the year after Mossie died, her twin sister had come to her in a warm and special dream like she had last night. It was uncanny how real those visits were—so real she could see the pores on Mossie's face, feel the warmth of her arms, and see the twinkle in her eyes when she smiled. Mossie would always be dressed in the nursing outfit she had on the day she died. These visits occurred at the exact same time on the evening of their birthday. Flossie would visit her sister's grave site the next day to acknowledge her visit, which wouldn't happen again until May 11 the following year. These dream visits were Flossie's own private secret. She treasured them and shared them with no one. She remembered her great-aunt Beatrice telling her and Mossie they would be connected to each other throughout eternity. They never understood what she meant until Mossie's first visit a year after she died. Flossie felt enriched by their connection and treasured having an identical twin with whom she shared a telepathic relationship.

Flossie and Hazel arrived at the cemetery and went directly to Mossie's well-tended grave site. Just being there, touching her sister's name on the headstone, knowing she was standing next to her dear sister's remains, brought tenderness to Flossie's heart. Hazel walked forward and kneeled down for a few minutes at her mother's headstone. Then she placed the roses near the headstone and stood up and took Flossie by the arm. She laid some plastic on the ground and placed a small pillow on it. Then she helped her aunt get down on her knees on the pillow. Flossie placed the fresh lilacs by the headstone and quietly whispered, "Thank you for your visit last night, sister. I know it was only a dream, but like every time, it felt like the real thing. I could even smell your Chanel No. 5. I can't begin to tell you how much I enjoyed seeing you. You know you're always with me, for I carry you in my heart."

She told Mossie she'd written and mailed the letters. "It's in the Lord's hands now." Then she told her she was still worried about that other dream, about the twins being in danger. "If there is any way you can tell me what to do, I promise I will do it. My heart will give me the message from you." After a few minutes more, she told her sister good-bye and looked over at Hazel who came and took her by the elbow and helped her to her feet, retrieving the pillow and plastic from the ground. The two women walked away from their loved one's grave, warmed by a sense of everlasting love.

CHAPTER

1

Budapest, Hungary, May 21

CORINA MOLDOVAN WORKED UNTIL NOON and had just arrived home as the mail delivery man was walking up to her door. He asked for her signature on a piece of mail, and Corina reached for the letter. The stamp on the floral envelope showed it had originated in the United States. This letter was both curious and unexpected, since Corina knew very few people in the United States. She went into the living room to open the letter.

It was a handwritten letter. She flipped to the last page and saw that it was signed by a Flossie Walker. *Flossie Walker!* Corina immediately remembered that this was the midwife who had delivered Ivona. *Why would she be writing me after all these years?* Corina remembered Miss Walker with fondness for taking care of Nicola and delivering Ivona. She had even been kind enough to take care of things while Nicola was at the hospital recovering from the complications she suffered during childbirth. Before reading the letter, that memorable day, May 11, flashed before her eyes exactly as it happened nineteen years before.

Corina saw herself rubbing Nicola's forehead; more beads of sweat surfacing with every contraction and every scream. When the midwife examined Nicola, she stood up and said, "The baby's almost here, Mrs. Moldovan. I have to give your daughter something to put her to sleep. I tried to get her to do the breathing technique, but she won't use it, and she's pushing too hard." Corina nodded and continued placing a cool facecloth on Nicola's forehead. The midwife quickly administered an injection, and within seconds, Nicola's eyes began to close.

Corina said, "Nicola, dear. The baby is almost here. You know I can't be in here with you during the delivery or I don't think I can go through with the adoption. The sight of my first grandchild being handed away would haunt me for the rest of my life." She looked at her daughter, who was now sleeping calmly, and went into the next room to wait. However, a few minutes after Ivona was born, all hell broke loose. Corina could hear the commotion in the delivery room. Miss Walker was calling out orders to her attendant. Corina stepped into the labor room door and asked, "What's happening?"

Miss Walker told Corina that her daughter was experiencing some uncontrolled bleeding and that she had just called the ambulance. Corina rushed over to her daughter's side. Nicola's complexion was ashen. She told Nicola, "Fight, baby. You'll be all right. Just hang on."

The midwife said, "I'm afraid she's lost a lot of blood. She needs to be in a hospital. Stat."

At that moment, her attendant led the paramedics, pushing a gurney, into the room. In less than sixty seconds, Nicola was strapped down, and they were ready to roll her out. Corina looked to Miss Walker.

"You go on," Flossie Walker said. "I'll take care of things here."

"I'm her mother. I'm going with her," Corina said to the paramedics.

That evening Corina noticed that Nicola's color had returned after a blood transfusion and a minor surgical procedure. She called Miss Walker, who assured her things were under control and that she would see them when Nicola was released from the hospital. She stayed by her daughter's side the entire three days of her hospital stay. Nicola improved each day. After she was discharged from the hospital, they returned to Miss Walker's place to collect their belongings.

"I can't tell you how sorry I am about what happened with Nicola," Miss Walker told Corina.

"Thank you, but her condition was not a result of anything you did wrong. We are grateful to you for acting quickly before she lost too much blood. Indeed, thank you for everything," Corina said.

"I have your things all ready for you," Flossie Walker said. Then, with a twinkle in her eye, she added, "And I also have a surprise for you. One I think you are going to be pleased with." Nicola and Corina looked at each other and wondered what the midwife had for them.

In a minute, she came back out carrying a bundle in pink in her arms. The baby was cooing contentedly. "Here is your little baby girl. And before you say anything, you need to know that the Wellingtons changed their minds. I know how much both of you hated to give up your baby anyway. She's all yours now."

Nicola's hand flew to her mouth. She shrieked with joy and reached for the baby. Corina said, "Honey, you shouldn't lift anything just yet. Let me take her." Corina took the baby from Flossie Walker's arms and looked down at the most beautiful face she had ever seen.

Corina smiled as that moment flashed before her eyes. Then she remembered the letter in her hand. She began reading the midwife's staggering revelations. She could hardly contain her shock when she learned that nineteen years ago, her daughter had twins. Not only was it shocking to know Nicola had another child, given the circumstances, it was also extremely heartbreaking. Corina slumped down in the nearest chair. She wondered what had happened to the other twin. Was she stillborn? She continued reading, learning that the Wellingtons had adopted the other twin. How could that be? The midwife had told them the Wellingtons had changed their minds. *She had told an outright lie!*

Reading the details of what had really transpired the night Nicola gave birth stunned Corina beyond belief. When she finished reading, she immediately called Nicola. The administrator said she was out of the office. "*Segélyhívó.* Please, find her now!" Corina said in near panic. Two minutes later, Nicola Palaki came to the phone.

"Reeni, what is it? I was on my way to a meeting. Is something wrong?"

"It certainly is. You must come home right away. I just received a letter. Our world has been turned upside down. You have to see this. Can you come now?" Nicola told her she would come straight home.

"Reeni, I'm here," Nicola called out when she walked in her front door a short while later.

"In the living room, Niko."

Nicola came into the room. "Who is the letter from?" she asked, looking at her mother quizzically.

Corina patted the sofa seat for Nicola to sit down next to her. Handing her the letter, she said, "This is from the midwife who delivered Ivona. Do you remember Flossie Walker?"

Nicola wondered what could be in the letter to make her mother call her home. She thought briefly, then said, "I do. It's been a long time. What did she say that could turn our world upside down?"

"Just read it."

Nicola began to read, and Corina watched her daughter's facial expression turn to shock, then rage. "This can't be true!" she exclaimed.

"I believe it is, Niko," Corina replied.

Nicola finished the letter. She plopped back in her chair and said, "I can't believe this." She was dumbfounded and couldn't quite fathom what she'd just learned. Dazed and confused, her emotions went crazy. She felt angry, hurt, even guilty, but mostly she felt betrayed.

"I thought the midwife was so nice. All along she was deceiving us. Why would she do that? She never even told me I was carrying twins. And the Wellingtons. They had to know. Why would they willingly separate them?"

"We don't even know that they knew about the twins either. Besides, would you have wanted them to take both of the girls?" Corina asked, giving her daughter something to think about.

Nicola thought that if she had known she was carrying twins, she might have reluctantly agreed to adopt both of them out. She was aghast at the notion that had she given up both of her daughters, she would never have had Ivona in her life. It occurred to her that the Wellingtons never spoke to her or Reeni about changing their minds. It was the midwife who had told them that. How could this nurse rob her of her child? Did the Wellingtons make some kind of deal with her?

The fact that she had another daughter in this world she'd never known about suddenly hit Nicola like a ton of bricks. She no longer felt anger. She felt a void in her heart that she was sure would never close. She had missed out on nineteen years of her other daughter's life, all the important phases: all the birthdays, all the long talks. For a long moment, she could not speak. When words finally came, she said, "I feel violated. My daughter was taken from me. It's so unfair and just plain wrong. I feel I will always pine for the daughter I never knew. As much as I would love to cry my heart out, I know I can't afford to dwell on this right now. We have to think about Vonni. How will she feel when she finds out she has a twin sister in America? If she feels as badly as I do, this will not be good."

"I know this will hit her hard. She always wanted a sister or brother. To find out she had an identical twin will be difficult for her to grapple with," Corina said.

Nicola couldn't imagine how Vonni was going to react. She could only pray that this would not push her back into one of those dark moods she'd experienced throughout her life. The conversation with Vonni would be tough, but she had to get it together so she and Reeni could show her this letter.

* * *

When Ivona arrived home from class that day, Nicola called her into the living room, where she and Corina were waiting. Ivona noticed the somber looks on both their faces and wondered what was going on. Her mother said, "Vonni, come sit down so we can tell you something important that happened today. Our lives are forever changed."

Ivona thought about the previous thing that had changed their lives forever: her father's death on the ski slopes eight years ago. *This had to be bad news.* Nicola then handed Ivona the letter and said, "This is a letter Reeni received today from the midwife who delivered you. We want you to read it. There is a lot in here, and there's no way to prepare you for what you're about to read. When you finish, we will talk."

Ivona found Niko's tone cryptic and strange. She began to read hurriedly, slowing down as she started to grasp what was on the pages. She found herself going over some parts of the letter over and over, including the part that made her gasp—the part that said she had an identical twin sister! And the midwife had separated them! And her sister was adopted by Reeni's former employers in America! When Ivona got to the end of the earth-shattering letter, she found it difficult to deal with what she'd read. It felt like she had been reading about somebody else. But she had to accept the fact that this wasn't somebody else. It was her own life and her sister's, her mother's, and her grandmother's.

Her reaction was quick. "I have a twin? I just can't believe this. And Niko, I can't believe you almost gave me up for adoption? Why? How could you?" She looked accusingly at Nicola.

Nicola saw the anguished look in her daughter's face. She felt terrible but had to explain, so she told her everything. Her answer sufficed for the moment, but Niko knew this was going to have to be revisited. Next, Ivona said in a near whisper, "And neither of you knew any of this?" She looked from Niko to Reeni, painfully waiting for an answer.

Reeni said, "Everything we learned in that letter today was news to us. Neither Niko nor I ever had a clue about any of this. We know how much of a shock this is to you. It is the same for us, but we have to accept it. This is our truth now. We're as torn as you are. We're excited on one hand but terribly upset on the other. We are just going to have to deal with this."

Ivona was stunned to learn she had a sister, but she was exceptionally happy. At the same time, she was sad that she never knew her. Never even knew *of* her. She felt confused, but strangely, it seemed like her life now had a whole new meaning, and she felt more excitement than she'd ever experienced in her life—even more excitement than when her father adopted her. Or when she took the third-place trophy at the Big Air ski contest last year. Much more excited than when she was awarded a full scholarship to Central European University. Receiving this news was by far the best thing that had ever happened to her.

"I want to see her," she told Niko. "Can we call the Wellingtons?"

Although Corina wanted to see her too, she replied, "We can't act hastily. We need to think this through. Miss Walker's letter did not tell us if she has also notified them or if they knew all along. Perhaps the best way to find out would be to contact Miss Walker, but that's a problem. Her letter didn't give a return address."

"We *have* to talk to her," Ivona said. "Niko, can we hire someone to locate her in Cincinnati, Ohio?"

"I believe we must try. I need to hear her explain why she would do such a thing as to separate my twins," Niko said. "Besides, we can't just let this information hang here. It would chip away at all of us. Nineteen years ago, I had another daughter. I am desperate to see her too."

"As am I," Corina said.

A couple of days later, Nicola and Corina were sitting in the office of a private investigator.

Adolf Felip sat behind his desk facing Corina Moldovan and Nicola Palaki. He took notes without looking down. He gazed admiringly at Nicola, who explained what they wanted. "And so, all we really need to know is how to contact Miss Flossie Walker. If we can get an address or telephone number, we will take it from there," she told him.

"I should be able to get you what you want," Mr. Felip said, looking into Nicola's eyes. "I will contact an agency in the United States I have used before. I am sure they can have this information in a day or two." He glanced at Corina and said, "I can probably have what you want by the end of this week. Shall I deliver it to your home?"

"No, thank you. Either my mother or I will pick it up from you here at your office," Nicola responded.

Two days later, Nicola and Corina sat facing Mr. Felip again. He said, "I have the information you requested. The US agency I contacted came up with the address where this Miss Walker is living and some telephone numbers." He handed Nicola an envelope.

Nicola opened the envelope and pulled out a sheet of paper. Flossie Mae Walker, The Felix House, 4861 Reading Road, Cincinnati, OH 45237. There was a telephone number for the Felix House and Miss Walker's private room number, along with some personal information, including her age, work history, and family details. "We cannot thank you enough, Mr. Felip," Nicola said. He walked them to his office door.

* * *

In her room that night, Corina thought about her and Nicola's lives in the United States. Life had been good until her daughter got pregnant at the age of fifteen. Corina remembered the day nineteen years ago like it was yesterday when her daughter came to her crying and just blurted it out.

"Mom. I think I am pregnant."

Corina could have passed out. "Honey, you can't be. You haven't even been with a boy." Then realizing she really didn't know that, asked, "Have you? I'm talking about in an intimate way."

Nicola looked like she was too ashamed to answer this question. "But we love each other, Mom."

A doctor confirmed Nicola's condition. At that point, Corina knew that life as they knew it would never be the same. She could see her daughter's education being halted as her own had been. She herself had had to leave school early to help the family. After her parents died, she got married and never finished high school. *Is my daughter doomed to suffer the same fate?* she worried.

She and Nicola discussed their options. Along with trying to figure out how they could manage with a baby, they had to also look at the options of abortion and adoption. Nicola refused to consider abortion, and at first neither she nor Corina could bear the idea that her child be given up for adoption. But neither could see how they could keep the baby. It took awhile, but they finally concluded that adoption was the best choice. Gratefully, the Wellingtons offered to adopt Nicola's child.

The Wellingtons were her employers, and it was in their maid's cottage that she and her daughter lived. Corina believed they could give her grandchild a life Nicola would be unable to provide. Nicola would leave her high school behind and attend a school where she was not known. After the baby was born, they would return to their homeland of Romania, where Nicola could continue her education.

The Wellingtons offered them financial assistance so they could relocate. They even set up an education trust for Nicola. They asked Corina and Nicola to meet one condition: that they never try to see the child. The condition was agreeable, for neither Corina nor her daughter wanted to know the child they were giving up. It would be just too difficult.

Corina often thought of how close they came to actually giving up Nicola's baby, and she recalled their talk when Nicola finally agreed to the adoption. Arguing against adopting out her child, Nicola said, "How can a person give away her very own baby? If you get pregnant, that baby is your responsibility, not somebody else's. Besides, no one can love my baby like I can. And if I love it, I know I'll find a way to take care of it."

Although she was proud of her daughter's strong sense of responsibility, Corina had to talk with tough love. "I know you mean that. But it is not necessarily true that adoptive parents could never love an adopted child as much as the biological mother would. I've seen situations where no one would ever know a child was adopted, because the parents were so loving and devoted. And another thing, young lady. It took two people to create your baby. Where is your child's father when you talk of responsibility?"

"He doesn't know, and I'm never going to tell him. I don't want to get married, and I know he doesn't either. Besides, he has dreams."

"And so do you. What about your dream of following in Dr. Wellington's footsteps and becoming a research scientist?"

Nicola began to soften. "I still have my dreams. I will just have to put them on hold for now. I believe my baby would always wonder where its parents were and why we gave it away. I wouldn't want it to go through that. Even if we are poor, I think it would rather be with me than to be apart."

Corina said, "Niko, you know I want this baby as much as you. But remember, you will have to sacrifice your education, and I know how much college means to you. I didn't get a chance to even finish high school, and I always regretted it. We were fortunate to be able to come to America, where you've been able to get a good education. If you keep your baby, you will probably have to drop out of school; I will have to work to take care of you both. These are just the cold, hard facts."

"Mom, I know you want me to go to college. And I do too. Until a few weeks ago when the baby started moving in my stomach, it felt like I would be able to sign the adoption papers. But now that it moves, I can picture it. And I can't wait to play with it."

They continued to talk, and Nicola began to come around to the idea that it might be better to give the baby up. Then one day, a teary Nicola said, "Reeni, I know what you said is right. I will do what you suggest and sign the papers. I promise not to bring it up again."

Corina often relived the tremendous relief she and Nicola had both felt when, at the last minute, the

Wellingtons changed their minds. They named the baby Ivona Kay. Nicola finished high school in Bucharest and went on to attend Central European University in Budapest. They'd been there ever since.

And now, learning of another granddaughter, Ivona's twin, left them all with much to think about.

Cincinnati, Ohio, One Week Earlier

GRETA HOOPER, SARA WELLINGTON'S HOUSEKEEPER, arrived at the Wellingtons' house just as the mailman drove up and handed her their mail. The pool-service man had also just arrived. Before going inside the house, Greta walked to the back to show the pool man the problem with the pool sweep. As she leaned over to point out the problem area, some of the mail fell from her arms into the deep end of the pool.

"Oh my goodness!" she exclaimed. She threw everything else down on a table and raced to get the net. The service man beat her to it and began raking the mail out of the pool. He got the last piece out and handed it to Greta, who thanked him profusely. She hurriedly took the mail into the kitchen and tried to towel it dry before it became completely unreadable. One of the letters appeared totally undecipherable; the ink had run together or was washed off the envelope. Greta felt terrible. She hoped the pages on the inside weren't as badly ruined.

Sara Wellington listened to Greta's explanation and said, "Sometimes these things happen, Greta. I'll see what I can salvage. Some of the mail is okay. This one piece is completely gone. It looks like a handwritten letter." Sara pulled out the sheets and stared at the blurred pages.

"I can hardly remember the last time I received a letter written by hand. I wish I knew who it was from so I could contact them. Let's just hope there wasn't anything too important in it."

CHAPTER
2

Cincinnati, Ohio, May 24

"HOLD YOUR HORSES. I'M COMING, I'm coming," Flossie Walker said out loud, drying her hands as she came out of the bathroom to grab her telephone.

"Hello, Flossie here," she said.

"Miss Walker, this is Corina Moldovan and my daughter, Nicola, is on the other end."

Flossie nearly dropped the phone. She had been thinking all day about those girls and was still afraid they were in harm's way. And now Mrs. Moldovan was on the telephone. "Yes, Mrs. Moldovan and Nicola. It is wonderful to hear from you after so many years. I'm sure you're calling about the letter I sent you."

"Yes, I am."

"Of course," Flossie said tentatively, wondering if Corina Moldovan was calling to tell her something had happened to the girls. "Is everything all right?"

"Yes, everything is fine, except we are all still in shock. Your letter came several days ago. I have to tell you that none of us can understand how you could separate Nicola's babies like that."

"I know, and I'm so sorry. I tried to explain it, but I can still understand how upset you must be."

"Still, we want to thank you for enlightening us. If you had not done so, we could have lived out our lives never knowing about the twins. As you must imagine, this information caught us completely off guard, and we are still trying to make sense of everything you told us. My granddaughter, Ivona, pleaded with us to call you so we could get more information. She wants to contact her twin sister right away. We hired an investigator to find your phone number so we could call you."

Flossie imagined herself in her callers' shoes and realized how distraught they had to be. "My Lord. I've been praying this was something you could deal with. Of course, I've also prayed that you could forgive me for what I did. I know how hard it had to be to hear about it. How can I help you?"

"It is very hard. Ivona desperately wants to meet her sister, and Nicola is also desperate to meet her other daughter. And I am practically beside myself with anticipation. Ivona has truly been a joy in our lives. And to now know that there is another girl just like her is almost beyond our wildest dreams. We want to call the Wellingtons. Ivona wants to talk to her sister. We need to know if they know about their daughter's twin sister. Did you write them the same letter you wrote us?"

"Oh yes, I wrote them too, the same day," she said.

"We haven't heard from them, so we wondered if they knew about Ivona. We were afraid to call and drop this on them."

Flossie was at a loss for words. "Why, I gave them your address and thought for sure they would get in touch with you right away. Maybe you should contact them."

"I'm sure we will," Nicola answered, and then said, "Do you mind my asking why it took you so long to contact us?"

"That's definitely a fair question. Of course I regret waiting so long. Over the years, I kept putting it off by talking myself into letting sleeping dogs lie. I wondered if the truth would cause more harm than good. But my soul finally got the better of me. As I said in my letter, I am an identical twin, but my twin has been dead for fifty years. Yet, in spite of her death, we share an extraordinary relationship and a powerful spiritual connection. So often I've worried about depriving your twin granddaughters of that same powerful connection with each other.

"On top of that, I was eighty-seven on my last birthday, and while I'm still pretty healthy, I didn't want to go to meet my Maker without doing right by you and your girls."

"I appreciate your sentiments and we're grateful that you finally did contact us. At first we were very upset at what you did, but since you did explain what happened in your letter and how you made your decision, at least we understood."

Flossie was glad they understood, but she wondered if they would ever forgive her. Her heart was laden with guilt and still heavy with fear over the twins' well-being. Before they completed their call, Flossie needed to know if her fears were warranted. She asked, "Now tell me. How *is* your granddaughter doing?"

"Exceedingly well. Thank you for asking. She's in college and wants to be a scientist like her mother."

"It's wonderful hearing that. Like I said, I think about both of those young ladies all the time. Just tell her to be very careful."

When they hung up, Corina and Nicola wondered if there was a hidden warning in Miss Walker's last comment. Flossie pondered why the Wellingtons had never contacted the Moldovans.

Budapest, Hungary, June 10

AFTER THE PHONE CALL WITH Miss Walker more than two weeks earlier, Ivona would rush home from the university each day to find out if they'd heard from the Wellingtons yet. They were all at a loss to understand why Sara Wellington had not called them; they could not come up with a reasonable answer. Nicola was perplexed and hurt. But Ivona suffered the most. She could not accept that her sister wanted nothing to do with her. One evening, she grabbed the telephone and said, "I'm calling them."

Corina felt it was time to contact them too. Nicola said, "Vonni, hand me the telephone. Let me call them. How dare they ignore this matter? I'll call now."

The Wellingtons had an unlisted number, but Nicola was able to obtain the numbers for both Dr. Wellington's medical research office and his private practice. "I'll start with him," she told Vonni.

"Advanced Research Corp," the telephone operator answered.

"Hello, this is Dr. N. René Palaki. I am calling from Budapest, Hungary. May I speak with Dr. Horace Wellington, please?"

The operator probably assumed the caller was a colleague of Dr. Wellington's. She replied, "Oh, perhaps you haven't heard. I am sorry to tell you that Dr. Wellington is still in the hospital." She added, "You are aware he recently had a stroke."

Nicola was stunned by the news. "Is he going to be all right?" she asked.

"Oh yes, he is expected to make a complete recovery. It will just take some time. Would you like to speak with his partner, Dr. Evan Owens?"

"Unfortunately Dr. Owens cannot help me. I must speak directly with Dr. Wellington."

"Then I will be happy to take your information. When Dr. Wellington is able to start taking business calls, I am sure he will call you back. Please also give me your name again, your telephone number, and the reason for your call." Nicola gave only her name and telephone number. Of course she could not tell a stranger why she was calling. This matter could not be handled in a message. She said only that it was a personal matter.

She realized she had gotten more information than she was probably supposed to have gotten. But still, she felt let down. Given the current circumstances, it could be weeks before they could gain some clarity on why the Wellingtons had not contacted them, especially in light of such major news as their daughter having an identical twin sister.

She told Vonni and Reeni what she learned.

"Then that must be why we haven't heard from them," Corina said. "Dr. Wellington's stroke undoubtedly took precedence over our personal situation. I am sorry for his illness, but I feel like they should still have contacted us. How much time would it take to make a telephone call?"

"We could hire Mr. Felip to get the Wellingtons' home number, but I am not so sure I want to call Mrs. Wellington about this now. When Adam died," Nicola said of her late husband, "I was so distraught. I don't think I could have handled something as significant as this at that time. I'm afraid I prefer to wait just a little longer."

"At least now I don't feel so much like they were just rejecting me. They had other pressing priorities," Vonni said. "I'm glad you called. Now we know something. Do you think we can call again soon?"

Corina said, "I think we can. But for now, let's just hold off a little while longer."

"She did say that his stroke was serious and he would be recovering for a while," Nicola pointed out, wondering how long they should wait.

Cincinnati, Ohio, June 15

SITTING IN HER ROOM AT the Felix House, Flossie thought about the first time she dreamed the twins were in danger. She had been having premonitions that danger was imminent, and that dream came again last night. Today had been particularly bad. At times, she could almost sense an evil presence intent on doing the girls harm. Recently she'd gotten a strong feeling that the young ladies were close to connecting with each other. If so, that probably meant they were either both in the United States or in Hungary. Wherever they were, she prayed that they were safe from harm.

After writing the Wellingtons last month, she had thought that everything was in place for the twins to finally come together. But she couldn't get over the fact that shortly after she wrote those letters, Mrs. Moldovan had called to ask if she'd written the Wellingtons too. Then, not long afterward, she'd telephoned her a second time. Flossie recalled that phone call.

"Hello, Flossie Mae here."

"Hello, Miss Walker. This is Corina Moldovan." Corina quickly explained, "When we spoke before, you told us you mailed the Wellington letter when you mailed ours."

"Why, yes. They should have received my letter within days after I mailed it."

"But," Corina said, "we never heard from them."

"Land sakes! I was sure Mrs. Wellington would have contacted you by now."

"Miss Walker, are you absolutely sure you mailed that letter?" Corina asked.

"I absolutely, positively am. I mailed it, and it never came back. So I figure it was delivered. I knew it was going to be a big shock to the Wellingtons, but once they had a chance to digest everything, I was sure they would contact you. It's a mystery to me that they haven't. I would have thought the Wellington girl would want to know her identical twin sister. Is there anything you want me to do?"

Corina said, "Not at this time. Maybe the Wellingtons have to wrestle with this situation more than we know. Although, it's all I can do to keep Ivona from taking matters into her own hands and calling them up directly."

"Whatever you want from me, just let me know. I will be glad to do it."

"Thank you. I do have another question."

"Certainly," Flossie replied.

Mrs. Moldovan said that she and Nicola were trying to figure if Miss Walker was giving them a hidden warning of some kind when she had said to be sure their girl was careful. Flossie had to think about how to answer the question. She didn't want to frighten the living daylights out of Mrs. Moldovan by telling her about her dream, so she told her, "Well, it's just something I usually say to everyone.

It's a pretty crazy world out there. You never know who is sitting around trying to figure out how to do you harm. I just wouldn't want anything to happen that would get in the way of those twins getting to know each other."

That recent phone call still troubled Flossie. She'd not heard from Mrs. Moldovan since and hoped the Wellingtons had contacted them by now. But she still wondered if the girls were safe.

* * *

A couple of weeks later, when Nicola called Dr. Wellington's office again, she was told that Dr. Wellington was recovering nicely but was still undergoing intensive rehabilitation therapy and was unable to take a call. *We're not waiting any longer,* Nicola thought. She immediately contacted Mr. Felip. A few days later, she had the unlisted telephone number for the Wellington residence.

Corina and Ivona hovered around the phone as Nicola dialed the number. Ivona said, "I'm so excited!"

"Wellington residence," a voice said.

"Hello. May I speak with Mrs. Sara Wellington, please? She will know me by the name Nicola Moldovan."

When Sara came to the phone, she said, "Nicola, to what do I owe this unexpected surprise?"

Nicola said, "Mrs. Wellington, it's been nineteen years since we have spoken. I hope and trust you and your family are doing well."

"Well, Dr. Wellington is recovering from a stroke, but he is coming along quite nicely. Our daughter is in Paris this summer, taking part in a special program."

Our daughter. The words hung in the air.

"It is very nice to hear from you. How are you doing? And how is your mother?"

"We're doing fine, thank you. And I'm glad Dr. Wellington is recovering from his stroke. But the reason I am contacting you now is to ask if you recently received a letter from a Miss Flossie Walker. She is the nurse-midwife who took care of me during my delivery."

Sara Wellington said, "I remember her. But no, I did not get a letter from her. What is this about?"

Nicola didn't know what to say. She never expected Mrs. Wellington to deny receiving the letter. Miss Walker had insisted she'd mailed it. *Was Mrs. Wellington lying? And if so, why?*

Nicola told her she wanted to look into something and get back to her later.

After she ended the call, Corina said, "This is just too much. Maybe Mrs. Wellington is playing games with us."

Nicola said, "If she was telling the truth, I wasn't sure how to tell her about the twins. I guess I lost my nerve. Maybe we should ask Miss Walker to send another letter."

"At this point, I'm wondering who we can trust," Corina said sadly.

Paris, France, Mid-August

MORGAN WELLINGTON WALKED BACK TO her dorm room alone around nine-thirty p.m. She was in Paris participating in a fashion design program. Her roommate, Bela, had asked, "Are you sure you want to walk back by yourself?" and Morgan told her she felt comfortable because there were several students walking in her direction. As she approached her building, she became aware that a dark-colored car with two men in it appeared to be keeping pace with her. When she glanced over at the car, she noticed the men were looking her way. She looked away and stepped up her pace, jumping when the car braked suddenly when it nearly rammed into the back of another vehicle. Then it sped up and turned the corner and was soon out of sight. *What was that all about?* Morgan was relieved that the car was no longer in view.

She had left Bela at the coffee shop with some friends, and now she wished she weren't walking the two blocks alone. Thankfully, the bright campus lights brought some comfort. When she was within two minutes of her door, she still felt like eyes were trained on her. She pictured the two men in the car, both staring at her as they drove by, and even though she couldn't see them now, she felt the pierce of staring eyes. Could anyone really be following her? Morgan reached her dormitory, raced up the steps, and hurried into her building. She walked down the empty corridor to her room. Still feeling a little paranoid, she glanced in both directions before unlocking the door and entering.

Plopping down on the edge of her bed, Morgan took a deep breath. She chewed on her nails as she tried to figure out why she was feeling so peculiar. Was she overreacting? That car *did* slow down, and those imaginary eyes had felt very real. *But why would anyone be following me? And who could it be?* She thought about it for several minutes and suddenly remembered that this was actually the second time she'd felt spooked like this since she'd been in Paris. The first time was just two weeks ago while she was walking across campus in broad daylight. She felt like she was being stalked. It was odd; she'd never felt unsafe here before. But two such occasions in as many weeks was unsettling.

Suddenly Morgan wondered if the misgivings she was experiencing weren't about Paris at all. Immediately, her parents came to mind. It bothered her that her father had suffered a stroke while she was out of the country. He was doing much better now, but if anything happened to him while she was here ... She picked up her mobile phone and dialed her parents in Cincinnati.

Her mother answered.

"Hi, Mom," Morgan said, trying to sound upbeat.

"Morgan! What's up, honey?" her mother asked.

Morgan almost blurted it out. *I think someone was following me tonight.* But she refrained from saying anything that would worry her mother. As an adoptee, this was one of those times when she yearned for her biological mother. *I would be able to tell her anything, and she would give me assurances.* Instead, she said, "I was just thinking about you and Dad."

She and her mother talked for a few minutes before hanging up. Morgan hoped her voice hadn't given away her anxiety. Furthermore, that crazy idea about wishing she could talk to her biological mother made her feel guilty. She was very fortunate to have wonderful, loving parents. Why would she want more than that?

That night when she went to bed she had a very strange dream.

Although her father was a well-known physician and researcher, Morgan, had never had any interest in science, nor had she ever worn a lab coat in her life. But in her dream she found herself in a scientific laboratory, white coat and all, mixing up some concoction in a test tube. Patients were waiting for the outcome as she blended the chemicals and then looked at the results under the magnifying glass. Voila! She had discovered a cure for cancer! The dream woke her up. The thought of herself as a scientist almost made her laugh. But it had felt so real, and she still remembered every vivid detail. *Why would I dream about being in a laboratory and not at a sketch table?* But Morgan had had nonsensical dreams before, so she chalked this one up to mere dream-time fancies. Still, she couldn't help but wonder: weren't dreams the mind's way of revealing secrets? If so, what was this one trying to tell her?

Sitting quietly on her bed now, her unease began to let up. Her thoughts turned to that astonished look that had crossed Bela's face when the two had first met. "Oh my gosh, it's you!" Bela had exclaimed. "I didn't know you were into fashion design too. I'm Bela Hamza, by the way. I've seen you back home, but we've never met."

Morgan was completely taken aback by this strange greeting from the person who was to be her roommate. Did she have a problem? With a puzzled look on her face, she replied, "I think you've got me mixed up with someone else. I'm Morgan Wellington from the United States."

"Oh, I'm sorry," Bela exclaimed. "Now I'm embarrassed. But you look so much like a girl back home in Budapest I've seen many times."

Morgan had always heard that everyone had a twin somewhere, so at first she thought nothing more about it. However, after their first meeting they became friends, and Bela brought up the resemblance frequently. Morgan started getting curious. Eventually, she became intrigued by the fact that she had a look-alike in Hungary. As an adoptee, she craved to one day meet her biological family. Soon she started wondering if the girl might be a relative.

Oddly, it was after Bela mentioned this girl to her a second time that Morgan had first experienced the sensation of being followed. Tonight, before she left the coffee house, Bela had again invited her to come to Budapest with her for a couple of weeks before she went back to the States. She really wanted Morgan to see that girl, and now Morgan really wanted to see her too. With the Paris program nearly over and a few weeks still to go before she had to be back in Rhode Island, Morgan had told Bela tonight that she had decided to accept her invitation. Bela was thrilled with her decision. As Morgan thought about it, she made a bizarre connection. Her feelings of being followed seemed to have begun after she'd started hearing about her look-alike. *Do these vibes have something to do with Budapest? If they do, does danger lurk there? And if it does, what was this all about tonight, here in Paris?*

CHAPTER
3

Budapest, Hungary, Earlier That Summer

PISTA VLADÚ WAS AN INVETERATE criminal. A solidly built man of medium height, he had long, black hair that he kept slicked back in a ponytail. The skin on his pale face was blotched and oily. He usually had a toothpick dangling from his mouth, and he always kept a spare cigarette tucked behind his right ear.

Pista Vladú was not a nice man.

His mother ran off when he was six months old, and his father's permanent home had been the penitentiary, where he was killed when Pista was nine. In his teens, Pista had found school to be a major waste of time, especially when he knew he could be making real money. He lived with a drunken uncle who never knew or cared what he did. The few times Pista didn't play hooky from school were enough to bore him to tears. He quit school at thirteen. His uncle told him he'd have to pay his keep or get the hell out. His first job was digging ditches. He worked hard for little pay. It didn't take long before he discovered an easier way to earn money. To Pista, being a law-abiding citizen was like taking a rapid road to nowhere. He started picking pockets, something he learned from his more experienced buddies. While that was exciting at first, it proved to be only moderately successful, since most of the people whose pockets he picked were as poor as he was. He advanced to muggings, which got him by for a couple of years. He'd even been able to buy his first vehicle. It wasn't much, but owning his own car made him one of the big guys on the block. Then he got careless and was sent to juvenile detention.

When he got out, his uncle had torn up his car. Naturally, Pista had to beat the crap out of him. Then he went right back to his old ways. The next time he got locked up, it was in an adult prison. That was where he acquired the essential survival skills to either conquer or be conquered that men behind those walls required. He'd fight till the end before he let anyone get the better of him. Early on, Pista took up weight and strength training and became a tough fighter. During the years he spent in prison, he also established his reputation as a mean *töki* who fought often and dirty and did whatever it took to win. In fact, he'd made it through his last period of confinement by bullying other inmates. To stay on his good side, they plied him with cigarettes and extra food; so all in all, he pretty much had it made. Pista had just completed his second prison term. He intended it to be his last. There was too much life to live outside those walls, mostly girls. And man, had he missed them. The alternative, while it served the purpose, just wasn't the same. Today, Pista pretty much lived off the streets of Budapest, picking off easy marks to get by.

He and Fane Dobos had shared a cell for a few weeks during his last stint behind bars. Talk about the odd couple! Fane couldn't fight his way out of a paper bag. Tall and skinny, with dirty straw-blonde hair and sickly pale skin, Fane was a follower. Not only that, he was dumb and green. He had no family and was excited to hook up with Pista, who, after taking his turn with him in prison, protected him from the lechers behind those prison walls who saw Fane as easy prey.

While behind bars, Pista had cooked up a plan to score big when he got out. He happened to run into Fane on the streets of downtown Budapest shortly after Fane was released, and he let Fane hang out with him. Pista needed a good lackey, and he knew that Fane Dobos would do anything he told him to do. He told Fane about his big game plan, and Fane was proud to sign up. But Fane Dobos would soon learn that Pista had done him no good deed by inviting him to join in with him.

While spending the majority of his adult life behind bars, Pista had developed a fondness for libraries. Although he never gave a damn about school, libraries were something different. There, he could read about whatever he wanted and not have to worry about junk like calculus and archeology. Who used crap like that? It was in a library that he'd first hatched his plan. Today, while sitting in the National Széchényi Library trying to do a little research, he remembered when he'd first run across an article about a Dr. N. René Palaki in a magazine in the prison library. The picture was what caught his eye. The photograph was small, but he recognized her from his childhood neighborhood back in Bucharest. This N. René Palaki was none other than Nicola Moldovan. *I'll be damned,* he thought. She'd changed her last name to Palaki. *Old girl must've gotten married.* The article said she was being honored by the International Scientific Association at some dinner due to her work in microbiology. He didn't know what the hell microbiology was all about, but it sounded important. Better than that, the article pointed out that she had previously received numerous monetary awards for her breakthrough research. Since seeing that first article a year ago, Pista had continued to follow her accomplishments; she'd had many.

Although he never saw her picture again, he'd run across several articles. The main ones that interested him told how she'd been awarded substantial cash prizes for her work. The way he figured, the doctor had to be loaded. *Which is all the better for me.* He would just come up with a way to separate her from some of that money.

Pista thought about his prison mentor. Alphonse was one of the toughest inmates at the federal penitentiary. He was one of the few men Pista never tried to bully. Not only that, Alphonse had to whip Pista's ass every now and then to make sure everybody knew who was really running things. This made Pista respect him and look for ways to impress him. He decided that one way to do that was to tell Alphonse about his plan.

"Yeah, I've known her since she was a kid. Now she's rich and famous, and the good thing is, she's right here in Budapest. And she's got a little sister."

"So?" Alphonse said, unimpressed.

"So I'm going to kidnap the sister. Nicola's loaded, so I know I can make a killing in ransom."

"Kidnapping someone ain't as easy as you make it sound," Alphonse said. "You gotta know what you're doing. If you get caught, you could be doing life."

"You ever kidnap anyone?" Pista asked skeptically.

"I kidnapped a young lady once, and I made a lot of money off her wealthy folks. Some of it's still put away."

"So you got away with it?" Pista asked.

"Sure, but I had to knock her off. She caught a look at my face. I couldn't let her live to ID me."

"Was it hard to pull off?" Pista asked.

"What, killing the woman? Hell no. Of course, I had intended to screw her some more first."

"No, man. I mean was the job hard to pull off?"

"Well, I had to do my homework. Everything had to be precise. I had to track her and study her patterns until I knew them like the back of my hand. I probably followed her around for a couple of months. She was always with some guy. Guess they lived together. They went everywhere together. But one day, I got lucky. She came out of her place alone, and I followed her. She went to a department store. I parked right beside her in the parking garage. I waited till she came out, and she was mine."

"That sounds easy enough. Did her folks pay right away?"

"Well, let's just say they met my deadline. You gotta give them time to come up with the money. See, not everyone is sitting around with money in the bank. Sometimes they gotta unload some of their assets. I originally gave them forty-eight hours but had to increase it another twenty-four. I kept the girl bound and blindfolded, and I fed her myself."

Pista took it all in.

Alphonse continued. "While I was getting a little action, the woman managed to yank off her blindfold, and she saw my face. This scar is what got me." Alphonse pointed to the deep scar on his cheek that was a dead giveaway. "Well, the money was delivered right on time. But on the way to the drop, I had to strangle her. Then I picked up the money and told them where to find the car with her in it. They got to the car in time to see it roll into the river. Naturally, when they got her out and examined her, they discovered she'd been strangled, but the main thing was she couldn't make me."

"Damn, man. That took balls," Pista said.

"Well, I got 'em. That's for damn sure."

"So, were they ever able to pin the kidnapping on you?"

"Hell no. I got away clean on that job. I'm in here now because of another job. That damn store manager hit a silent alarm. Police burst in while I was cutting him into little pieces. How well do you know this doctor?"

Now it was Pista's time to impress Alphonse. "She went to school in Bucharest with my young cousin, who's also a doctor now. She attended the university here. She was always the brainy type, always getting special awards and crap like that. I could tell she liked me, but I never gave her the time of day," he lied. "I had women lined up at my door and no time for a skinny little nerd."

In reality, Nicola had been a gorgeous teen, and she certainly wasn't skinny. Pista thought she was stuck up as hell. In fact, she never looked his way, even though he was constantly checking her out, looking for the right time to hit on her. But the main reason he was targeting her now was because he didn't personally know anyone else who had made it big. Well, his cousin Vilmos had done pretty good, but Vilmos was family. And family was off limits. This made Nicola the perfect target. He knew she had a younger sister because he remembered the toddler who used to tag along behind her.

Alphonse said, "Since your Nicola is so rich, when I get out of here I may get some of her for myself." He was slated to be released within the year.

"Do what you gotta do, man," Pista shrugged. He figured Alphonse was just talking big. After all, the man didn't even know Nicola's full name or how to find her, and he wasn't telling. The truth though, was Pista didn't give even a rat's ass what Alphonse did, just so long as he got to N. René Palaki first.

* * *

Pista's original plan had a major flaw. The articles he had read said Nicola lived in Budapest, but he had no clue where. She wasn't listed in the telephone directory like normal people. And he sure didn't have a clue about where to find the little sister. Where would he even start? He tried the library and telephone directory assistance. He even called the newspaper and asked for Dr. Palaki's information, but they refused to give it out. One day when he was waiting for Fane to come out of the drug store, he happened to spot Nicola and the girl leaving a department store. Pista did a double take; he couldn't believe his luck.

Fane was getting in the car, and Pista told him, "There go my girls, right there. Hurry up. I'm following them. If you hadn't gotten out here, I'd be gone."

"Man, that's lady luck at her best," Fane said. "How'd you spot them?"

"I told you I grew up with her. I'd know her anywhere."

Nicola and her sister got in a car parked directly up the street from the store. Nicola was grown now and she looked more mature. She still looked good. She was wearing high heels and still had that same quick step when she walked, like she had some place important to get to. Same hair, same face. It was her, all right. Of that Pista was certain. And her sister looked like a younger version of her. "She looks hot—even better than she did twenty years ago. That younger one's a hot number too."

"They're both good-looking, that's for sure," Fane said, grinning shyly. He added suggestively, "I see why you want to grab the girl."

Pista followed the two women to the campus of Central European University. Nicola parked in the teacher's lot, and they got out of the car and went into different buildings. Now they knew how to find the girl. And it looked like they knew where to find Nicola too. They even knew her car. *She must be a teacher here.* Pista figured the girl must be in summer school. Following Alphonse's advice, they started driving to the school every day to learn her patterns. After awhile, they were pretty confident at predicting where she would be at any given time. They noted that occasionally she drove, but other times she caught a ride with others. She was almost never alone.

Pista and Fane had been running all over town, looking for an abandoned building or house where they could hold the girl. Finding nothing suitable, they started looking on the outskirts of town. If they could find something in a rural area, that would give them more privacy. Each time they spotted the girl, Pista realized that once they had their place, they could pick her up anytime they wanted.

Finally, they secured a place to operate out of, an old abandoned house on the outskirts of town. It was located in a rural area among some other dilapidated houses that, according to the sign posted near the highway, were slated for demolition in the spring. The house was practically invisible through the tall weeds and trees that had overtaken the area. They'd found the place after turning off the main road onto a dirt path that had a sign that read *NEM NA GYON*. It was boarded up and deserted. They had originally gained entrance to the house by breaking a rear window. They figured that from the look of things no one had been out there in years and that since it was out of the way on an unpaved side road no one would be coming by anytime soon.

Inside the house was a meager collection of crappy, bedraggled furniture. Of course, there was no electricity, but they brought candles. The place was old as hell inside, and although there was a potbelly stove and plenty of wood around, they couldn't take a chance of using it in case someone noticed smoke coming out of the stack. But, they were good. They brought extra layers of clothing. They also bought several gallons of bottled water and figured they'd only need the place a few days.

* * *

Morgan had now been in Budapest for several weeks. When the two weeks she was planning to stay were up, she hadn't been ready to leave. She and Bela had not even caught a glimpse of her look-alike, and that *was* why she'd come here, after all. Morgan had wanted to go to the Rhode Island School of Design since she was fourteen, and she still loved the school, but right now, she wanted to see this girl who could possibly be her kin. That was more important. So she registered for one semester at CEU. She liked it okay but looked forward to getting back to her own school next semester.

She left the school and walked to her favorite café to wait for Bela. Morgan was getting pretty discouraged over not finding the girl. Earlier that day she asked Bela, "How will we possibly ever locate her? We've been looking for weeks, but with two million people in this city, where do we even start?" So far, they had been everywhere they could think of: dance clubs, eateries, bookstores, coffee shops. "I'm almost ready to give up. Why did you even invite me here?" But even as Morgan expressed doubt, something was compelling her to continue the hunt.

"I'm doing everything I can think of, going every place I think she might be. I'm sorry we haven't found her yet. But it's not my fault," Bela had said, making Morgan realize she was coming across a little harshly. Morgan apologized.

Morgan was sitting inside the café before Bela arrived; some guy walking by saw her and did a double take. In Hungarian, he said, "Hi there, I haven't seen you around in a while. Where've you been?" Morgan looked at him in surprise, and he said, "I see you changed your hair." Then he looked her up and down and said, "And everything else. You look good."

"I'm sorry. I don't know what you just said. Do you speak English?" Morgan asked.

He looked disbelieving but repeated what he said in English.

Morgan's first thought was that this was a corny attempt to hit on her. It wasn't working. She said, "I'm afraid you're mistaking me for someone else."

"Oops, sorry, you're right. I can tell by your accent you're American, aren't you?" he said.

"Yes."

"What's your name?"

"Bethany." Morgan wasn't ready to give this total stranger her real name.

"I'm Dominik," he said.

"Nice to meet you."

As Dominik turned to walk away, it suddenly occurred to Morgan that this guy may have been mistaking her for the very girl she and Bela had been trying to find. "Dominik, wait a minute!" she called out.

He turned around. *"Igen?"* Then he quickly said, "Yes?"

"You said you thought I was someone else. Do you happen to know her name or what she looks like?"

"No, I've just seen her out at some clubs, that's all. But she's from this part of the world."

"Can you tell me what she looks like?" Morgan said.

"She looks like you, except she's blonde."

Morgan felt excited. This could be the one she was looking for. "If you don't mind my asking, when was the last time you saw her?"

"Probably several weeks ago. That's why I was so surprised to see you. What's all this about, anyhow?"

"Well, other people have also mistaken me for someone else. Might be the same person. I would just like to know who she is."

Dominik replied, "Curious about the competition, huh?"

"This isn't about competition, but I am curious."

He said, "If it's all that important to you, why don't you give me your telephone number? If I ever see her, I'll try to find out her name and give you a call. How's that?"

"Sure." Morgan wrote down her telephone number.

"Okay, Bethany. See you around." He turned to walk out.

"Oh, by the way, the name's Morgan. I only go by Bethany sometimes."

"Like when you're trying to hide your real identity from some strange guy? I get it," he said, grinning.

"Listen, Dominik, maybe you can give me your telephone number too. Just in case I want to call you sometimes to check."

"So *that's* what this is all about," Dominik said, smiling. He wrote it on a napkin and gave it to Morgan. "So all along you were just after *my* telephone number. Very clever," he joked.

Morgan smiled. Going along with the joke, she said, "And it worked; I got it. But look, I hope to talk to you soon."

"No problem. Maybe I'll see you around." He turned and walked away.

After this encounter, Morgan's confidence was bolstered. She now believed it could simply be a matter of time before they ran into the girl. *I can't wait to tell Bela. This is as close as I've gotten since I've been in Budapest. Dominik has to be talking about the same girl. He also said she's a blonde.* Morgan remembered Bela had told her the main difference between her and the girl was the color of their hair.

When Bela arrived, they grabbed a seat by the window where they could watch the world go by. Bela was thrilled when she heard what Morgan reported about what Dominik said. "I am so confounded. I used to see her often. Then you come here, and weeks go by. Nothing! Maybe this Dominik will bring us good luck. I hope he calls you soon with information."

In her excitement, Morgan never noticed the old car that drove up and down the street, cruising slowly, as if looking for a place to park. Bela noticed it first. What drew her attention was how beat up the car was. Both the man driving and his passenger were staring toward their café window. "I wonder what's with them," Bela said. "That's the second or third time that car has gone by. By the way, what did this Dominik look like?"

Morgan said, "He's pretty plain-looking; good build though." She glanced out the window just in time to see the car passing by. She too noticed that the driver was looking in their direction. She suddenly turned ashen and said, "Omigod."

"What's going on, Morgan? Do you know those guys? Was one of them the guy you just met?"

"No, that definitely wasn't Dominik. I don't know them. But for some reason, they give me the creeps."

"Do you suppose they were looking at us?" Bela asked.

"I don't know. It's just weird, that's all. I never told you this, but while I was in Paris, I felt like someone was following me a couple of times. Really spooked me out. It's happened here too. One day while I was on campus, I saw a car with two guys in it pull into the parking lot, and they appeared to be watching me."

Bela was shocked. "You should have told me. We could have gone to the campus police."

"With what?" Morgan asked. "I didn't see their license tags. And I didn't even see what they looked like. It was just an eerie feeling I get sometimes."

"Can't be the same ones you saw in Paris, because now you're eight hundred miles away from there. This might just be a coincidence or your imagination."

Morgan said, "I agree. I don't know why someone would be following me anyway."

"Now I wish you could have stayed with us longer."

Morgan thought about the weeks she'd stayed with the Hamzas when she first came to Budapest. Bela's family was prosperous. Her father, Berti, was a builder and her mother, Alexa, a judge. They had freely welcomed her into their home. When classes resumed that fall, Bela moved to her dormitory. Because Morgan was going to be at CEU, she took an apartment. "I appreciated your parents' hospitality, but I like having my own place," she said.

"Well, just make sure you don't go out alone," Bela said, adding, "I wouldn't take chances with anyone except me and György. It's not that I believe someone *is* after you, but I'd feel terrible if anything were to happen to you—you're here on my invitation."

"I'm not really the scaredy-cat type. It may have just been my imagination playing tricks on me. Those guys could have been looking at anything. But I promise not to take chances."

In another part of the city, Ivona Palaki got a sudden case of the chills. Again, as had happened many times before, it seemed like someone was watching her. Following her. But the crazy thing about this time was that she was safe at home, sitting at her desk in her bedroom.

CHAPTER

4

AFTER BELA DROPPED HER OFF at her apartment, Morgan put on her bed clothes and prepared to study for an upcoming exam. But she found it impossible to concentrate. Dominik had confirmed what Bela had said when they first met: "She looks exactly like you. I mean, if I didn't know any better, I'd think she was you." What if this person was the key to learning her true identity? Her adoptive parents were both fair and blond, which contrasted noticeably with her olive skin tone and dark brown hair. Finding family members, especially ones she resembled, would provide her a sense of connection she'd never felt before.

Over the years, Morgan had heard tidbits from her parents. They had adopted her from a fifteen-year-old pregnant girl from Romania, and after giving birth, the mother moved back to her homeland. Morgan's interest in her real family had been bottled up for years. Now that she was free to think about them, that seemed to be all she thought about. Knowing she had a look-alike here in Budapest excited Morgan more each day, and she fantasized that she and this girl could be related. She thought about how young her mother was when she was born. That would make her just thirty-four years old now. Morgan couldn't imagine being a mother, even at nineteen. *I've got to find her.*

As she thought about her biological family, memories from earlier years flooded her mind. There was her childhood make-believe friend, Eva. Her mother always thought she chose that name because Eva was her maternal grandmother's name. Maybe so, but the real truth was that name just felt right. She remembered telling a doctor about her make-believe friend when she was a little girl. Later, after hearing her mother and father painfully discussing a girl who renounced her adoptive parents, she decided not to speak of family matters again. Morgan never wanted to cause her parents such grief. Even though the doctor asked about her imaginary friend many times, Morgan had remained tight-lipped.

She removed a piece of jewelry from around her neck, a little gold pendant shaped like half a heart cut zigzag down the center. Before putting it away in her jewelry pouch, she gazed at it with fondness. Morgan treasured this little inexpensive piece of jewelry as much as she did anything in her collection, including her more costly pieces. She had received it ten years ago on her ninth birthday. Today, it was showing serious signs of wear. The lettering on it had become smoothed down and harder to read. Morgan always had this necklace with her. She remembered the day she received it.

"Happy birthday, darling," Sara Wellington said, handing Morgan her final gift.

"Thank you, Mom. What is it?"

"It's something special, dear. Open it and see."

Morgan tore the wrapping paper off and then gently opened the box and removed the contents. "It's a necklace!" she exclaimed joyfully, holding it by the clasp and gazing at the little pendant she held in her other hand. She studied the writing on it. "I love it, Mom. But what does it mean?"

"I really don't know. This necklace was given to you when you were first born. It was a gift from the midwife who delivered you into the world. I saw the words inscribed on both sides, but I never knew what they meant."

The words seemed abstract and made no sense to Morgan, but it didn't matter. This little necklace was a gift from the woman who had known her real mother. She wished she could talk to her. She was convinced the necklace held some kind of special message about her heritage. "I don't care. It's beautiful, and I love it very much."

"I thought you would. I've held it for you all these years until you were old enough to really appreciate and take care of it."

"Thank you for saving it for me, Mom. I'll take care of it forever."

As Morgan put her pendant away in her jewelry pouch, she wondered for the umpteenth time what the words meant. She believed there was a matching half somewhere. If only she knew where it was, maybe then she could know the meaning. Morgan believed this small piece of jewelry connected her to something very important, and she hoped that while she was here in Budapest she might somehow find some long-awaited answers.

The last thing on Morgan's mind before falling asleep that night was the mysterious words on her pendant. *One day, I hope I find out what they mean.* Moments later, she was dreaming a dream she'd had before. In the dream, she stepped up to the edge of a steep mountain wearing a blue ski outfit. Her helmet and goggles were bright yellow. Far below, scores of people waited for her to appear. When they saw her, they cheered and chanted something. Her name? But it sounded like Bonnie. *Bonnie?*

She glided around trees as if she had wings, steering perfectly, hearing the wind as she soared effortlessly through the cloudless sky. When she finally stopped, she was standing in front of her home, a yellow two-story frame house, holding her winning trophy. In previous dreams, Morgan walked into the house and realized it was not her home. The people in the next room were strangers. That was the point when she usually woke up.

This time, her dream had a twist. Two ominous-looking men stood away from the crowd at the foot of the hill, pointing at her. They began chasing her on foot. Holding on to her trophy, she ran for her life into the yellow two-story frame house. And who was waiting inside but the two men! They grabbed the one thing she treasured the most, her little pendant, and ran off. She awakened with a start, her heart aching at the thought of losing her prized necklace.

Maybe it was seeing those two men at the coffee house that made me dream about that, Morgan thought. Still, she felt the need to get up and check her jewelry pouch. Thankfully, her treasured pendant was still there.

Cincinnati, Ohio

FEELING SENTIMENTAL, FLOSSIE WALKER SAT in her rocker and studied the photos in her picture albums. She came across some childhood pictures of herself and Mossie, taken in Eden Park. Boats and barges on the river below looked like small toys. Their parents were sitting on a bench overlooking the river and had taken pictures of them while they played. Her mind wandered to another time in Eden Park, the day she and her sister came up with the idea for her favorite piece of jewelry. That was two weeks before their thirteenth birthday, seventy-four years ago.

Their parents had taken them to the park on a warm afternoon after school. Dr. and Mrs. Walker took a seat on a bench.

"Can we take a walk around the park?" Flossie asked. Her mother told her that was okay.

"Can I go too?" eight-year-old Hampton asked.

"No, you have to stay here with Mom and Dad," Mossie answered.

"You just want to talk about boys," Hampton whined.

"Girls, if you want to walk around, then your brother can walk with you," Gertha Walker said.

"Oh, all right. Come on, little whiny baby," Flossie said, and the three of them took off.

While they meandered through the park, Flossie said, "So you aced my math test today."

Mossie said, "And you aced mine too. But I almost got caught in your music class. Your teacher wanted me to play your flute."

Flossie laughed, "What did you do?"

"I made myself start coughing like I was choking or something, and she just told me to go out to the water fountain and get a drink."

Listening to his big sisters, Hampton was all ears. "I'm gonna tell it," he announced.

"And we'll never take you anywhere again," Mossie said.

"And I was going to give you half my Baby Ruth. But not if you're a tattletale."

"Oh, all right," Hampton said, reaching for his half of the candy bar. "You all aren't any fun. I want to go back and look at my comic book anyway." The girls gladly took him back to their parents' bench.

Sitting on some swings and eating their candy bars, Mossie said, "Brendon likes you." Brendon sat behind Flossie in math class.

"No way," Flossie said, laughing.

"Oh, yes he does. He kept tugging on my braids, like Phillip in my English class always does. Marsha Martin says that's how you know when boys like you."

"Marsha doesn't know anything," Flossie said. "He mostly tries to copy off my test papers, but I don't let him. Boys are so silly. Brendon Sykes needs to study for his own tests." They laughed and teased each other about boys some more. Then the twins talked about their last babysitting job, when Mrs. Ragsdale's two-year-old toddler had tried to yank the tail off the family cat.

An occasional barge floated down the river. The warm spring breeze was filled with the fragrance of lilacs from the bushes near the edge of the bank. "I love the smell of lilacs!" Flossie said, taking a deep breath. "They're my favorite."

"They're my favorite too. You know, we always like the same things. See, we're not just twins; we're plain old two of a kind." Then as if thinking about it some more, she pointed to Flossie and then to herself, saying poetically, "I am like you, and you are like me."

Flossie chimed in, "And together, we will always be." Then she added jokingly, "I'm a poet, and I know it."

"You're so corny," Mossie said. "But we did just make up a poem. Let's say it again." Together, the twins repeated their poem, and both decided they liked it. Mossie looked sentimental. She said, "One day, let's get our poem inscribed on a plaque or something."

Flossie said, "Or on an expensive piece of jewelry that we'll wear forever."

"Oh, sure—where're we going to get some expensive jewelry?"

"We may not have any now, but one day we might," Flossie said.

Two weeks later, they received money for their thirteenth birthdays. "Remember what we said," Mossie reminded Flossie. "We're supposed to have our poem inscribed on a piece of jewelry. Now we can." They asked their mother to take them to a jewelry store. With their money, the twins bought a plain gold heart. Then they gave the jeweler their poem and asked him to inscribe it on their heart and to cut it into two jagged pieces. He did so but had to use both sides of the heart. The lettering was so tiny, they practically needed a magnifying glass to read the words. But the words were there. When the jeweler finished, he cut the pendant in uneven halves like they wanted, smoothed the edges, and put thin gold chains through each half, creating two separate pendants.

"I love these! Let's never take them off," Flossie said, and her sister agreed. For the next several years, only rarely did either of them remove their pendants. Years later, when Mossie was killed in that hit-and-run accident, Flossie removed her pendant for the last time. Mossie's husband presented her with her sister's half. She put the two halves together in a little padded white box that she deposited in her jewelry box on top of her dresser. The pendants stayed there until she knew it was time to pass them on.

The sound of the dinner bell startled Flossie from her musings. She had enjoyed reliving that special time when she and her sister had designed their pendants. *Today, they're antiques. I hope the twins have loved them.*

CHAPTER
5

Budapest, Hungary

IVONA PALAKI AWAKENED WITH A sense of anticipation. It felt like something was in the air. Whatever it was, she felt eagerly expectant. At breakfast, she said to Reeni, "It feels like something special is going to happen today. I know this sounds unusual coming from me. I'm usually so stoic."

"I wouldn't say you're stoic. You are a scientist, that's all. But you are equally a creative girl who believes in that pot of gold at the end of the rainbow. I think that's quite wonderful, Vonni. What do you think this is about?"

"I don't know, Reeni. It just feels like a wonderful kaleidoscope of dreams keeps running through my head."

"What a nice description! Like I said, you are very creative. Sometimes I think you should be a writer, not a scientist," Corina said.

Ivona dressed in a long-sleeved cream-colored top, dark slacks, a waist-length black leather jacket, and black flat-soled boots and left for school. All day long, a tingly sensation stayed with her. However, nothing out of the ordinary happened at school. She was beginning to think that nothing was going to come of the feeling after all. She had a couple of hours to spare before meeting with her study group, and one of the members invited her to go to Carrefours Department Store with her. Ivona thought that maybe that was it; she would find those boots she loved and they would be on sale! They arrived at the store and split up. Her friend Frida went to look at jewelry, while Ivona headed to the shoe department.

Ivona tried on the long black boots she'd been looking at for a while. They were not on sale, however, but she wanted to see if she still loved them as much as before. She walked over to a full-length mirror in the shoe department to admire them and was about to return to her chair to try on another pair when her attention was drawn to a man's voice. He was walking down the aisle speaking with an American accent. Then she heard a woman answering him. She too had an American accent. Americans always caught her attention; she had a special interest in her birth country. Since learning she had a twin sister, she'd developed an even stronger reason for this affinity. The two Americans were walking toward her.

When Ivona looked up, at first she was confused. She thought for a minute that she was looking in the mirror, but Ivona knew she wasn't moving. She studied the girl who was coming her way, still talking to the guy, and in that instant, she realized she was not looking at herself. It was someone else who looked just like her! They were the same height and had the same complexion. And this girl's hair was the same color as hers used to be before it was bleached. They were even similarly dressed.

Ivona could have fainted. She gasped. *That is my sister! I know it is.* Too excited to think, Ivona left her purse on the loveseat and, still wearing the black boots, she took off after the girl, who was now a ways up the aisle. The sales woman noticed Ivona leaving the area in a hurry and ran after her, exclaiming in Hungarian, "Pardon me, madam. You cannot leave this area in those boots until you purchase them."

Ivona froze, realizing the saleslady may have assumed she was a shoplifter. As the American girl turned to head down another aisle, Ivona cried out in desperation, "Helloo. American lady, please wait!" The saleslady stood there impatiently, her eyes pinned on Ivona, arms crossed, tapping her fingers and her foot. Ivona turned back to her and said, "*Nagyon sajnálom.* I am sorry. I'll be right there." She waited for a second, and someone else who had turned down the aisle backed up to see who was yelling in the store. The girl, her sister, did not come back.

Ivona hastily returned to the shoe department, pulled off the admired boots, and threw on her own. Then she picked up her purse and rushed out into the store. Hurrying to the aisle where she saw the girl turn, she looked in both directions. She wasn't there! Ivona quickly moved up and down the different aisles looking for her, but she never spotted her again. After searching all over the store, she had to conclude that the girl was gone. Suddenly hopeful, she realized her sister might have gone into the restroom. Ivona rushed to the women's lavatory and waited until the two occupied stalls emptied, hoping one of the people coming out would be her sister. Each time the stall door opened, she studied the woman expectantly. In neither case were they the girl she hoped they'd be.

Ivona had never been more disappointed in her life. She had searched the entire store and never found who she was looking for. She was sickened to the core that she might have just missed her chance of a lifetime to meet the sister she'd thought about every day since she learned of her existence. *She is here in Budapest! In this very store! And I missed her!* The magical feeling she'd had all day, still present until a few minutes ago, was gone. *That's what that feeling was all about. I was to see my sister.* The reality that she'd missed a golden opportunity hit her hard. She believed her sister had probably come to Budapest looking for her too. Ivona felt the tears come. She cried until they were all out.

A lady came into the restroom and found Ivona leaning over the basin. "Are you all right, miss?"

Ivona thanked her. "Yes, *Köszönöm,* I got something in my eye." After splashing water on her face she reached for a paper towel and dried off. The tears had helped her settle down. Now, the very idea that she had just seen her twin seemed almost unbelievable. Still, in the deepest part of her heart, she knew she wasn't wrong. That *was* her twin sister. She was gone now, and Ivona had to make herself accept that fact.

Frida, her study partner, was still in the jewelry department when Ivona caught up with her. Frida said, "I saw you over there looking at coats. Did you find anything?"

"Oh no, you are mistaken. I wasn't looking at coats. I was trying on boots in the shoe department."

"Ivona, have you forgotten? Just a few minutes ago, you were right there," Frida said, pointing adamantly.

Ivona realized Frida had seen her twin sister. She hurried over to the coats and looked all around before returning. "Apparently, it was someone who looked like me. That's all," she said.

"If you say so," Frida replied, sounding unconvinced. Then she turned abruptly to Ivona and said, "Of course, you are right! The girl I saw had brown hair. It was the same color you used to have. But you two could have been twins." Then she looked at Ivona and asked, "What's the matter with your eyes? They look all puffy."

"Oh, I got something in my eye and had to go to the lavatory to get it out. It's okay now."

Ivona wanted to tell someone what had just happened, but she was not ready to confide something so personal to Frida. Besides, Ivona was feeling so emotional over losing her sister in the store, she believed she would probably burst into tears again if she started talking. She told Frida, "We'd better get going. The rest of the gang will be in the parking lot in thirty minutes." She couldn't wait to tell Niko and Reeni what happened, though. *They will be as shocked as I am to learn she's here in Budapest.*

As they left Carrefours, two men sat in a car across the street watching the store entrance. They had followed the girls from the campus to the department store. "Isn't that our girl?" Fane said, pointing to a woman wearing a short black leather jacket, gray slacks, and black boots coming out of the store.

"Hell!" Pista exclaimed. "Who's the guy, and where'd he come from?" He was pissed. While they could have grabbed both the girls, he wasn't prepared to deal with a guy. For a minute, Pista just sat there. When he started his car, about to take off, out she came again!

"Look there!" Fane said pointing toward the entrance. It was their girl, but now she was with the same woman she went into the store with. Scratching his head, he said, "Did she just double back through the side door?"

"I don't get it!" Pista said. "Maybe I need to quit drinking." They watched as the two women got in the car that was parked on the street in front of the store. They drove off. Pista told Fane, "This is it. Let's get 'em. We may just have to grab 'em both." They followed the two women for a few blocks and stayed with them as the car pulled into the student parking lot at CEU, where a group was gathered. Ivona and Frida got out and joined them. Pista was close behind. When he saw the girls get out of their car and join the group, he came to a stop.

"Wonder who those guys were who followed us?" Frida questioned.

"We were followed?" Ivona asked.

"Yes." Frida pointed to the car that had pulled into the parking lot. "I noticed them a few blocks back. They have been behind us for a few minutes. I don't see a university parking sticker on their windshield."

When Pista noticed the girl pointing at them, he backed up and began pulling away. Ivona caught a glimpse of the two guys in the front seat. She couldn't see their features, nor did she notice what make of car it was, but she did see the car itself. Fear shot through her. She'd seen this car before. One day she thought she was being followed, so she turned and looked at the car. It was pretty beat up and easy to remember. The men had taken off in a hurry, like they did just now.

* * *

Morgan Wellington and György left Carrefours. Morgan had stopped in to look for a pair of leather gloves and an overcoat. About ten minutes later, they were grabbing something to eat. All at once, Morgan froze.

"Morgy, what's wrong?" György asked. He noticed that she had abruptly stopped chewing and was looking off into the distance. "Morgan?"

She started. "Oh, darn it, I just had that feeling again."

"What feeling?"

"You know. That someone is watching me or something. I don't really know how to describe it, but it doesn't feel right."

György looked around. Then he said "Well, I don't see anyone who looks like they were following you. I would have noticed. But you can believe one thing. I'm not letting you out of my sight. And whenever you need to go anywhere, be sure you're with me or Bela. I don't know what's going on, but I'm definitely not going to let anything happen to you."

* * *

Corina was in the kitchen preparing a potato soup called *krumplileves* and chicken *paprikash* when the telephone rang.

"Reeni!" Her granddaughter was out of breath. "A few minutes ago in Carrefours, I saw my sister!"

"What did you say?" Corina had heard Ivona, but she thought her granddaughter had to be joking. Ivona repeated what she'd said, adding that she'd searched the store high and low afterward but never saw her again.

"I'm just devastated that I missed her."

As much as this shocked Corina, she couldn't bring herself to believe that her other granddaughter was right here in Budapest. Still, Vonni sounded convinced that she had actually seen her. *Is it possible?* Corina had to wonder. At the same time, she was worried that Vonni wouldn't easily get over her disappointment if it turned out that she was wrong. But how would she ever know? Throughout her life, events not nearly as significant as this had sent Ivona into a blue funk. This time could actually be worse. Corina didn't want to upset her. She said, "Ivona, I hear you, but how can you be so sure? Even if this girl did look like you and had an American accent, you know that could just be a coincidence. I know how much you want this, but don't you think this could just be wishful thinking on your part?" Corina could hear Ivona's sigh of disappointment.

"Reeni, you always told me there are just some things you know in your heart, and this is one of those things. Besides, it felt like an electric current shot through me when I heard her voice. Even Frida saw her and thought she was me. Don't you believe me?"

"Darling, I truly believe that *you* believe it was your sister you saw. And it is certainly possible that it was your sister. Although for the life of me, it is hard to imagine that she is here in Budapest."

"Why not? If the midwife told them about me, she probably came here looking for me."

"True, but we know Mrs. Wellington claims she never got a letter from the midwife. Besides, Miss Walker had our address and telephone number. If your sister knows you are here, it seems like she would have known how to contact you."

"I know it sounds crazy, but I know I saw her," Ivona said earnestly.

"But what if you don't see her again? How would you ever know for sure it was her?"

"I *will* see her again, Reeni. You need to believe me. I know now that that's what I was feeling excited about this morning. The minute I saw my sister, something told me, 'This is it!' That feeling vanished afterward. It was not some fantasy. Even though I have thought about her every day since I learned about her, I didn't dream her up. Seeing her in the flesh today felt like destiny. I know

I will see her again. I have to." In her enthusiasm, Ivona didn't even think to mention the two men who followed her and Frida earlier this evening.

When Ivona and Corina hung up, Corina continued to think about their telephone call. Vonni had said she *had* to see the girl again. *But what if you don't, Vonni?* Corina worried. *Will you be able to deal with that?* Still, the thought that her other granddaughter could be in Budapest excited her, and she thought about how wonderful it would be if the girl had actually come here in search of her biological family. Questions flooded her mind. *If this person actually is Ivona's twin sister, is that why she is here? Will the girls ever meet? Does she want to have a relationship with her twin sister? With her mother and grandmother?* Corina realized from the questions that she actually believed the person Ivona saw could have been her twin.

Ever since she received that letter from Miss Walker, Corina had felt that unforeseen developments awaited them. Could this be the beginning of those developments? These past six months, as the three women tried to come to terms with their newfound reality, plus the fact that the Wellingtons never tried to contact them, had been difficult. Corina had had many talks with Nicola and Ivona on the subject. Although the talks were therapeutic, none brought them any closer to answers. Corina knew they could not go on like this indefinitely. Their curiosity and desire to know Nicola's other offspring would drive them all crazy, especially Ivona.

CHAPTER
6

ALL AFTERNOON, NICOLA PALAKI, PROFESSOR of physics at Central European University, had been meeting with the university president. As she returned to her office, she pondered the question he had just posed to her about her future aspirations. Her answer to the president was that she wanted to be the head of the Department of Microbiology. He had sat back, laced his fingers across his stomach, and smiled.

Today, she was a world-renowned scientist. She expected to continue in that line of work for years to come. Although science had been an early dream of hers, she had nearly let the dream go when she found herself pregnant at the age of fifteen. Fortunately, in spite of her pregnancy, she never lost her passion for her studies. She'd finished high school in Bucharest, and her academic accomplishments won her a partial scholarship to Central European University. Along with the Wellington trust, the cost to cover her bachelor of science and PhD degrees in microbiology and physics were fully covered.

In the years since completing her education, Nicola had made many important contributions to her field. Consequently, she was frequently featured in the international media. A few years ago, after seeing her picture in a magazine, someone began stalking her. He even wrote several cryptic messages to her at her job. The harassment had persisted for some weeks but eventually ended when the person, a student, was caught and jailed. After that unpleasant development, she did not allow her picture to be published again.

Nicola usually spent her weekends grading research papers, reading scientific journals, and writing. She had little social life. Though she was only thirty-four years old and very attractive, she rarely dated. Ivona often urged her mother to stop working so hard and have some fun once in a while.

"Niko, look at you. You're still young and great-looking Yet you sit here night after night reading those papers. Why don't you come out with us? I think you'd have a great time," her daughter had said recently. Although Nicola treasured the special relationship she shared with Vonni, she always declined to take her up on her offer to socialize with her and her friends. The idea of spending an evening at a night spot for young people held little appeal. She was what they used to call "old school" in the States.

Nicola admitted feeling some guilt for not having raised her daughter herself. Indeed, she had practically grown up alongside Ivona under the watchful eyes of her stern but caring mother. She was grateful to Reeni for the time she spent taking care of them both. And she was thankful that her mother was now able to devote some time to herself.

She thought about how it was Dr. Horace Wellington, her mother's former employers back in Cincinnati, who encouraged her in her field, and for a few moments, Nicola became deeply engrossed in her memories of a carefree time in America. She had loved school and handled her courses with ease. Then she met Randolph Parks, one of the most popular boys in school. In her young mind, life could not have been better. Although she was thoroughly infatuated with him, she stayed focused on her education and continued to make excellent grades.

Nicola thought about why she had never told Randy she was pregnant. She'd been determined to take full responsibility for her condition even though she believed she might have to postpone her dreams of attending college. But in part because of her selfless act, he had been able to fulfill his dream of becoming an astronaut.

She thought about how much she'd enjoyed her studies and remembered a particular afternoon long ago. She had sat, studying, on a bench near a pond on the Wellington property. "Good afternoon, Nicola. What are you studying today?" It was Dr. Wellington. She had not heard him approach. She told him she was studying for a chemistry quiz. "Your mother tells us your grades are quite good and that you love science," he said with a smile.

"I do," she told him shyly. "Science and math are my favorite subjects." Then she explained where she was in her current studies.

"I am impressed, young lady," Wellington told her. His impressions meant a lot to her. "I assume you intend to study science in college?"

"Yes, sir, microbiology and physics."

He commended her for her choices. That day was a turning point in her life, for that was when she committed herself to following in his footsteps.

After that day, Dr. Wellington chatted with young Nicola about her studies from time to time, and he always encouraged her. Her fondness for him grew with every contact she had with him. On one occasion, he told her, "My dear, you may know that I am a research scientist." She'd nodded. "Then I'm sure you know that science holds the key to the future, just as it continues to unlock the secrets of our past. One day, through the work you or I and other scientists do, cures will be found for diseases that now kill thousands of people each year." He'd looked her in the eyes and spoken seriously. "Never let anything stop you from pursuing your studies. You could be the one to find the cure for breast cancer. I am going to read about you one day."

Nicola liked that Dr. Wellington took time to encourage her about her studies. She was proud of the interest he showed in her and was inspired by his words.

Many years later, when the Nobel prizes were awarded, she was happy to learn that Dr. Horace Peterson Wellington had been awarded the prize for his breakthrough discoveries in the medical field. Along with her mother, he had encouraged her to pursue her dreams. His encouragement continued to inspire her even now.

When Nicola had returned to her office earlier after her meeting with the dean, her secretary hurried over to hand her some phone messages. One marked *sürgős* was from her daughter. One message was from her mother. She immediately phoned Ivona but got no answer. She wondered what could be so urgent and tried again to reach her, unsuccessfully. Next she called Reeni. Her mother asked if she had spoken with Ivona yet. When Nicola said she hadn't, Reeni told her, "Vonni claims she saw her twin today at a department store here in Budapest."

"What!" Nicola exclaimed.

"She is convinced it was her." Corina relayed the details to Niko.

Stunned, Nicola asked, "What do you think, Reeni? Do you think it's possible that it was my other daughter?"

"I found it hard to believe at first. But mostly, I didn't want to see Vonni get her hopes up too high, so I told her it may have just been a look-alike. However, there was no doubt in her mind who she saw. In my heart of hearts, I hope she was right."

Nicola couldn't wait to talk to her daughter. Like her mother, she hoped her other daughter was in Budapest and even had reason to feel she might be. She recalled the day just recently when her heart had nearly stopped beating as she walked across campus to teach an afternoon class. She'd happened to spot a young woman heading into the library. At first she thought it was Ivona, but she realized after awhile that it was not. Still, this person so resembled Ivona that Nicola had to stop and stare. Her heart had been racing. Ever since that letter from the midwife, she had visualized the moment she would face her other daughter. Still, this particular woman's striking resemblance to Ivona made her feel the moment of their meeting was imminent. The young woman had vanished into the building, and Nicola took a deep breath and walked on.

She remembered that face all day long. Although the woman was wearing a hat, the long, thick hair that hung beneath it was dark brown, the same color as hers. And Ivona's. The woman had a walk that bespoke privilege. Could she possibly have been her daughter? And if so, how could this be happening?

Nicola had not mentioned to Vonni that she had seen a girl on campus who looked like her. Ivona seemed so desperate to meet her sister that Nicola hadn't wanted to set her up for more disappointment. She picked up her telephone and tried Ivona's number again. This time, Ivona answered. She was just finishing up with her study group. Nicola listened attentively as Ivona told her excitedly about the girl she had seen today. Nicola wasn't completely disbelieving, for in her heart she thought it might very well have been the same person she herself had recently seen. *I saw my daughter?*

Ivona was her immediate concern. After talking to the midwife, they had waited to hear from Mrs. Wellington, who had never called or written. Ivona's heart was already broken about that. They agreed to talk later at home.

* * *

That phone conversation with her granddaughter had been astounding. Vonni actually believed she'd seen her sister. Corina hadn't known what to say, so she treated the episode as if it might merely have been a look-alike. But Vonni had been insistent, and Corina now believed she was right. Vonni told her that this girl had not just resembled her; she *was* her. They were even dressed alike. While the idea that her other granddaughter could be in Budapest seemed improbable, it was not out of the realm of possibility. Especially for Vonni's sake, she hoped it was true and they would meet soon. Vonni's early years ran through her mind and stopped at her fifth birthday.

"Vonni, come on down. Your friends are here for your birthday party," Niko had called up to her daughter.

Five-year-old Ivona heard her mother and yelled, "Coming, Mother." Before her guests arrived, she'd gone back upstairs to play with the one playmate she loved the most: Margo.

"I'm sorry, Margo. I have to go downstairs now. You have to stay here so the others won't see you."

"Can't I go to your birthday party too?" Margo asked sweetly.

"No, because my mother does not believe that you are real," Ivona answered forlornly.

"That's okay. I will talk to her. Then she will see that I am real," Margo pleaded.

"Ivona," her mother called again.

"Here I come," she yelled. Then she quietly consoled Margo and told her she would bring her some ice cream and cake later. And they would play together with her new birthday toys. "Next time, I will try to bring you to my birthday party," she told her best friend. Then, with her pink handkerchief, she wiped a tear from Margo's eye and one from her own and left her room, closing the door behind her.

Corina had a pretty good idea what Vonni had been doing in her room: playing with her little imaginary friend, Margo. "Vonni, darling, are you ready for your party?"

"Yes, Reeni. I was just ..." Her voice faded.

"It's all right, Vonni," Reeni said. "I will check on Margo for you."

Vonni's eyes lit up. "You will, Reeni? Thank you. Tell her I will be back soon." *Reeni believes Margo is real.*

Corina had found herself near tears too. Even though her little granddaughter had her share of friends, she was still lonely. She'd often asked Niko to bring her a new sister or brother like most of her other friends had. "We'll see," was how Niko always answered. Vonni never got her new baby sister or brother, so she'd created her very own make-believe friend. Margo was more like a sister. Vonni would sometimes play in her room with her for hours. Corina and Nicola wondered if it was normal for a child to spend so much time with an imaginary friend, but after Vonni was adopted by her father, she no longer talked about Margo.

There was that period after Adam died, when Ivona became terribly depressed. He had treated her as if she were the second most important person in the world, and she had loved him very deeply. Her depression had gotten so out of hand that she had to see a therapist. The counseling worked, and after several months Ivona began to thrive. Today they could say she was a well-adjusted young adult.

The period last summer had been the exception. It happened shortly after she'd learned about her identical twin sister. At that time, Ivona seemed to go through some sort of identity crisis, transforming herself from a dark-haired scholar into a blonde-haired Goth girl. Corina and Nicola both considered this pretty extreme. They couldn't have been more relieved that the phase was relatively short-lived. It was gone by fall, all except the blonde hair.

Ivona rushed into the house, bringing Corina out of her reverie. She was at the kitchen table sipping tea. Ivona fixed herself a plate and sat down at the table to eat.

Corina said, "That was some news you dropped when you called. The idea of seeing my other granddaughter gives me the *meleg fuzzies.*"

"I can't get her out of my mind, and I really don't want to. I even hope I can see her in my dreams tonight."

"I'm not sure we can plan our dreams," Corina said. "But you've certainly had some interesting ones—some that seemed to come straight out of the blue. I remember the first time you told me the one about following me around my shop, pestering me to teach you to design and sew. That one made me laugh, for you've never shown any interest in sitting behind a sewing machine."

"And then there was the scary one I had several times," Vonni said. "I was very young when I first dreamed it." Ivona recounted the dream.

Someone called out to her, "Come away from the edge, Vonni," during a family outing on a boat.

"It's okay. I just want to see the fish," she'd said, sliding across the dock of the boat, moving closer to the edge. She leaned across the rail and peered over as far as she could. A sudden wave hit the boat, and she went over.

"Help, help!" she'd screamed.

Ivona said, "I don't know how I managed to keep my head above water. When I woke up I was even gasping for air."

Corina added, "And then a hand reached down and pulled you to safety, but you could not see her face at first."

"And when I did, I was seeing myself. It was me, saving myself. Very puzzling," Vonni said. "But you'd always told me that if one tells someone their dream, it will not come true. I'm sorry I woke you up so many times," she said with a smile.

Corina remembered the first time Vonni had that dream like it was yesterday, for her granddaughter had awakened her in a panic that night. She remembered Vonni's terrified description of nearly drowning. After that, she and Niko had tried to coax her into taking swimming lessons. "And you never would agree to learn how to swim," Corina said.

"I've just never been a water person. The only time I spent around it was when my friends and I skipped rocks across the Danube. But I wonder if this dream was symbolic of something else. I've always believed that dreams could have other meanings. I now believe with all my heart that these strange dreams have something to do with my twin sister."

As if reading her mind, Reeni said, "You know, as odd as it seems, when I think about that now it seems possible that it was your sister you were dreaming about, even though you didn't know about her at the time. They say identical twins can be unusually close."

"Seeing the face of my rescuer who I thought was me in my dream, reminds me of how I felt today when I saw my sister. It was like looking in a mirror."

When Nicola arrived home from a late meeting, she stepped into the kitchen, where Corina and Ivona were still sitting, and greeted them both warmly.

"How are you feeling, Vonni?" Nicola asked. "Are you all right? You've had quite a day. Do you want to talk some more?"

"Still excited. Just emotionally spent. I almost feel too exhausted to talk about it anymore."

"I understand. But sometimes talking helps," Nicola said.

"I know. First of all, I know what I told you was unbelievable, but I desperately want both of you to believe me. Because I know what I saw."

Corina said, "Vonni, when you first called me, I was too stunned to think. But I knew you really believed that it was your sister you saw. After I thought about it some, I realized that I believed it was possible too. Wish I could tell you how she ended up here in Budapest, but I believe somehow she did."

"I'm even thinking it might be her," Nicola said. "Because I actually saw a girl on campus this past week who I thought was you."

"What! You saw her, Niko? When? Why didn't you tell me?"

"I wasn't a hundred-percent sure. But now ..."

"I bet it was the same girl!" Ivona said excitedly. "I'm glad you saw for yourself, Niko. So now you can see why I'm so insistent and excited."

Corina stared at her daughter almost in disbelief. She asked, "Are you sure, Niko? Where? When?"

"Yes, I'm pretty sure now. I saw her on campus—she was walking away from me. At first I thought she was Ivona, but then I figured it was just wishful thinking. I didn't want to get our hopes up just in case it turned out not to be her. I should have told you. I wasn't positive at the time, but now I'm thinking it was her."

Nicola continued, "You know, Vonn, when we talked to Mrs. Wellington, she said her daughter was in Paris. If she is now in Budapest, I have to believe it's because she knows you are here. She may have come here looking for you."

Ivona's face lit up. "I hope she's as interested in seeing me as I am her."

"It just might be time to call the Wellingtons again. If their daughter is here, maybe they will be receptive," Corina said.

"Maybe we *should* call them again," Nicola added. "Now's probably good."

"Are you ready to tell her what the midwife told you?" Corina asked.

"I think so."

When the housekeeper said Mrs. Wellington was not home, Nicola was slightly relieved. When the housekeeper asked to take a message, Nicola just said, "No, thanks. I'll call back." Something about Mrs. Wellington's telling them she had not seen the letter from the midwife still troubled Nicola. What if she really didn't know about her daughter's twin? Nicola wondered what she could say to her. She wasn't sure she really wanted to phone her back.

* * *

Ivona was filled with hope after the discussion with her mother and grandmother. When she'd first called Reeni, she'd been half afraid that her grandmother would not believe her and think she'd just seen a doppelganger. But now Ivona knew Reeni *had* believed her. And after talking to Niko, she was excited to learn that she did too. And the amazing thing was that Niko had even seen the same girl!

Ivona was thrilled to have a sister. Although she'd wished for additions to her family, she'd accepted that her mother and grandmother were all the family she had. She'd been elated when Adam Palaki became her father and proudly bragged about him to her classmates at school. When he died, she was crushed. Her small family had been reduced by one. She recalled that terrible period of mourning for him; it seemed like forever.

Ivona thought about how, after learning she had a twin, she finally understood why she'd always felt like something was missing in her life. Before then, she'd had no idea why she'd felt this way. Now, for the first time, the missing piece of the puzzle was at hand. Ivona knew with every breath she took that she would see her sister again. *I've known from the start we would meet one day. I am positive I just came close.*

She was exhausted. Her grandmother had picked up her favorite ski outfit from the cleaners, and it was laying across her bed. The outfit was royal blue with yellow stripes on the sleeves. As she put the outfit away, she thought about the last time she'd worn it. She had participated in an annual competitive event and finished third. She remembered with pride how the people cheered her on and how exciting it was to take home her first-ever trophy.

Feeling satisfied now that her earlier frustration had been replaced with positives, Ivona dressed quickly for bed, turned out the lights, and slept soundly.

CHAPTER
7

Late October

A FEW DAYS AFTER HER encounter with Dominik, Morgan was sitting at the bar with György during his break. He said, "I really dig you, Morgan. But I've got a confession to make. I used to see you with your people, and I didn't think I'd ever get a chance to talk to you myself."

Morgan was confused. She usually only went out with Bela. Once in a while, there might have been a couple of other girls along, but most often it was just the two of them. So who were _her people_? "György, what are you talking about?" she asked, puzzled.

György looked surprised. "You know. I'm talking about when you used to be with Tibor Varga, the guitar player at the Lite House," he answered. "I mean, that dude's my idol. If our band could ever get the kind of breaks he's had, we'd be on our way. His group is going to be big, real big. Believe it!"

"Wait a minute, György. Who's this Tibor Varga? I've seen a group perform at the Lite House, but I don't know their names."

György stared at Morgan for a moment and then smiled. "Morgan, what's up? You're joking with me. Right? I used to see you with Varga lots of times. In fact, until a couple of months ago, I thought the two of you were pretty tight. Why are you saying you don't know him? Are you mad at him or something? Everyone could see you two were together. Remember the night his band manager gave the big party to celebrate their new record label? I was there, and I was secretly checking you out. Yeah, and, Morgy, you looked really good too. You were a blonde then, but to be honest, I like this color better."

In the back of her mind, Morgan was getting excited. Even György knew this look-alike of hers. But right now, she had to deal with her exasperation. She said, "György, listen to me. You've got the wrong person. I don't know Tibor Varga. I've never been to any label party. Remember, I've only been in Budapest a few weeks. And I have never been a blonde."

György finally heard her. He sat upright and gazed at Morgan quizzically. Then he frowned and scratched his head. "You're serious, aren't you? So who *are* you?" He was completely bewildered.

Morgan was too. She snapped her fingers and said, "Earth to György. It's me. Morgan Wellington. I'm the girl you met right here, remember?" She fleetingly remembered the night she first saw him playing in his band and he came over to say hello. The rest was history.

"Morgan, okay I'm gonna take your word for it. But believe it or not, if what you say is true, you have a twin right here in Budapest. I mean, this is a serious case of body double."

Here it was again! First Bela. Then that guy named Dominik who had mistaken her for someone else. Mom's friend, Mrs. Coleman, and now György. He had to be talking about the same girl she and Bela had been looking for.

"Look," she said. "Bela also told me there is a girl in Budapest who is my spitting image. I really want to see her, so whenever we go out, we look for her. So far, though, we've never run across her. Bela said she used to see her out occasionally. I am very curious about her."

György was still looking at Morgan incredulously. It seemed he didn't believe her, and suddenly, she became very upset with him.

"Stop staring at me like that, György. Can't you see I'm serious? I want to see this girl. It's important to me. I never mentioned this before, but I'm adopted. I'm an only child, and I've always wondered if I had siblings. And I even wonder if there is a chance this girl and I could be related. I believe it's possible. I think my biological mother came to Europe after I was born. I always thought she went to Bucharest, but she could have come here. As unbelievable as it sounds, I believe my real mother could be living right here in Budapest. Somehow, I feel like I am close to finding her, and I need to know for sure. That's what I came to Budapest for." Morgan dabbed her eyes.

György could see that Morgan was hurt. And he also realized he had touched a sore nerve with her. He put his arms around her to comfort her and said, "Morgan, I'm sorry. Obviously I didn't know any of this. Maybe this other girl *is* related to you. I can help you find her, and then you'll know for sure. Okay, Morgy?"

Morgan nodded and let György console her. She was glad to hear him say he could help.

Something suddenly dawned on her. She sat up, looked at György, and said, "Wait a minute. Let me get something straight. You thought you were hitting on Tibor Varga's girl. And all this time I thought you were interested in me. But now I know it was someone else. I'm not this other girl. So you might as well take your infatuation for her and go find her for yourself."

György's face turned red as a beet. He hadn't meant to upset Morgan like this. "Morgan, you're wrong," he said. "Yeah, I admit, I thought you were someone else at first. But you're the one I want to be with. Don't be angry. Okay?" He heard his band beginning to tune up and said, "Shoot, I've got to get back to the band in a minute, but I want you to be okay. I want us to be okay too. Deal?" Morgan just stared at György with a pouty look on her face. He held out his arms to her, which she ignored. He said, "I hate to leave you like this, Morgy, but I've got to get up there. Just think about what I'm saying to you. You're my girl, and you're the person I want to be with. I'll call you tomorrow, okay?" He leaned over and planted a kiss on her cheek.

Morgan watched György trot back up on stage. He turned and waved to her. *I guess I shouldn't be too upset with him. He wasn't trying to hurt my feelings.* She waved back, thinking, *Besides, maybe he can help me find this girl. He has seen her, after all. He knows people she used to go around with. I only have a few more weeks in Budapest. Together with Bela, we might be able to find this twin of mine.* When Morgan and Bela left the club, she realized she wasn't angry at György anymore. Just hopeful.

* * *

György knew he had messed up tonight and that he had to make things right with Morgan. He had mistaken her for the other young lady, and she had not liked that one bit. He thought of a way he might be able to make amends. He knew that Varga's band had been on tour; when they were in town, they played at the Lite House. After György's gig was over, he headed over there to see if they were playing. If so, he hoped to talk to Varga about that other girl. Maybe he could get some information for Morgan. Then hopefully she would understand where he was coming from. Besides, he wanted to meet Tibor Varga anyway.

He was in luck. Varga's band was playing the late set. György sat at the bar and watched the band, daydreaming about getting a label deal like Varga's group had. *Maybe Tibor will put me in touch with his contacts.* He sat and waited. At the break, Tibor Varga jumped off the stage and headed quickly for the side door. György followed him out the door. When he spotted Varga, he was standing outside facing the building, one arm bracing his body against the wall. A young blonde woman was facing him, her back against the bricks. They were sharing a cigarette.

"Nice set, dude," György said, walking up to Tibor, who glanced over his shoulder at the intruder.

"Yeah, thanks, man," he said in an irritated voice.

György asked, "Got a minute?"

Tibor, sounding very annoyed, said, "Do you mind? I'm busy here." György got the message. There would be no chatting during this break, so he decided he would try again during the next one, forty minutes from now.

György stood by the stage as the next break was about to start. When Tibor jumped off the stage, György said, "Say, man, can I ask you something?"

Tibor grunted and then said, "You again? Walk with me, man." They ended up at a booth. A waitress brought

Tibor a beer. György stood. "You got one minute, buddy," Tibor said.

György told him who he was and where his band played. He was proud when Tibor said he had heard him play. "I wanted to ask you about a girl who used to be with you," he said.

Tibor looked up and studied him for a minute as if he were nuts. But he asked, "What's her name?"

"That's what I wanted to ask you." Then György described the mystery woman.

"That description could fit any one of my ladies. Didn't you see Sonya earlier? I don't know who you are talking about. Anyway, your time is up," he said as an attractive blonde walked up and joined him in the booth. She was the one who had been wrapped up in Tibor during the earlier break. Frustrated, György walked away. He realized he wouldn't get any information from Tibor Varga about Morgan's double. He'd just have to be on the lookout for her himself. Surely she'd show up. A thought dawned on him. *Maybe I can bring Morgan over here sometime and let Varga see her. Then, he will know exactly who I'm talking about.* What György didn't know was that this was Tibor Varga's final night at the Lite House before embarking on a six-week tour across Western Europe.

November 1

PISTA VLADÚ AND FANE DOBOS sat on the faded old sofa smoking cigarettes and drinking beer in Pista's tiny, run-down flat. The twin bed in the studio was unmade, and the crumb-filled sheet covering a lumpy mattress was uninviting. Pista joked to Fane that one day when he struck it rich, he would get a fancy place, one that cost three or four times the few forints a week he paid for this place. The threadbare sofa and small black-and-white television were the major pieces of furniture. Orange crates substituted for a coffee table and TV stand. The place smelled like stale beer, the toilet like it hadn't been flushed in weeks. The little kitchenette where roaches scampered about freely was small and dingy.

Fane said, "I'm still hoping we thought of everything. I mean, this is serious business. We could get locked up again if we don't get it right."

God, Pista Vladú was so tired of listening to this whiny *balfasz*. He flicked his cigarette at Fane. "*Kuss!* Just shut the hell up!"

Fane batted the cigarette aside. It landed on the couch next to an old vomit stain and sat there for a moment. A lick of flame sprouted. Fane jumped up and swatted at the couch.

What a douche. Pista let out a deep laugh.

"That ain't funny. Smells like poop," Fane said, his nasally voice managing to climb an octave.

"No?" Pista said. "It's frickin' hilarious."

The flames refused to die, so Fane snatched a beer can from the table and emptied the contents onto the fire. The warm Bud transformed the tiny blaze into a curl of black smoke. Fane slumped back down, his face revealing the ordeal he'd just been through.

Pista shook his head and thought, *This guy. Oh, well, if things go south, although they better not go south, but if . . . Fane's ass will take the fall.* But he'd kick the little *lúzer's* ass first. The guy was several quarters short of a roll.

Fane was blonde and in his late twenties, a soft-spoken guy who'd gone to prison for going along with his buddies during a robbery. On the other hand, Pista, thirty-five, was a habitual small-time criminal with a serious nasty streak. He'd killed a guy in prison with his bare hands but got off on a self-defense ruling.

Pista swept a strand of greasy black hair out of his face. He thought about his plan for a moment and then decided he was too on edge to figure this mess out. A bit of weed should take his nerves down a notch. He pulled out some papers, rolled a joint, fired it up, and took a long drag. This crap tasted worse than his old lady's *bun*, but it was all he could afford. Despite the taste, it would get the job done. He released a long cloud of smoke.

Fane reached over for the joint, and Pista swatted his hand away. *"Mia fasz!"* Fane exclaimed.

Pista waved him off. Fane had several inches on Pista's five-foot-eight frame, but the retard was a big coward. Actually, Pista preferred that trait in a lackey. "This is mine," Pista told Fane. "You earn some money and buy your own."

Fane's brown eyes flashed a sad, puppy-dog look. *Probably how the lúzer survived in the joint when I wasn't around.* Pista thought about getting rid of him, but this was a two-man job. He decided to throw Fane a bone. "There's some beer in the fridge." The fridge was a dorm model with a frayed cord. Sometimes it worked, sometimes it didn't. Right now, Pista couldn't care less.

Fane got up and trudged over to the refrigerator.

"Get me one too," Pista called after him.

Fane grunted. A moment later, he returned with two sweaty cans, handed one to Pista, and then cracked the other open and took a long swig.

Pista cracked open his can and took a huge gulp. "This has taken long enough. We grab her the next chance we get."

"I don't know," Fane said. "What if the police get involved?"

"The cops ain't gonna get involved. You gonna tell 'em?"

"No way, man. I'm just saying."

"Well, don't say nothin' else," Pista said. *God, there's he goes with that pathetic whipped-dog look again.*

Then Fane noticed some strange markings on Pista's arm. "What's that?" he asked, pointing.

Pista's eyes fell on his freshly tattooed arm, and he pulled up his sleeve and gazed at his masterpiece—a long, slender snake, the head of the snake on the back of his hand. It traveled all the way up his outer arm. The snake was green and black with red eyes. Taking a deep puff from his cigarette and flicking the ashes into the air, he pointed to the art and added, "King cobra. Deadliest snake in the world. Ain't she a beaut? Alphonse has one on his upper arm. Stung like a *szuka*, but she was worth it."

"Yeah, man. It's real cool. I might just get me one like that one day."

Looking up from his tattoo, Pista added, "Yep, this is going to work out fine." Fane grinned, glad to be treated civilly for a change. Pista continued. "Like I said, you'll get your cut. I'm thinking 10 percent."

"Wait a minute. You said twenty, man, like we talked before," Fane said, uncomfortable challenging his leader but trying to sound firm. He knew he would settle for 10 percent if he had to.

"Oh, yeah, I forgot our deal," Pista said, pissed that his little flunky remembered his first ramblings. One thing was for damn sure. He wasn't about to give this punk 20 percent. *He'll be lucky to get anything at all.* "But, listen to me. We might have to go all the way on this. See, I'm gonna give the good doctor forty-eight hours to meet my demands. If she doesn't produce, we're getting rid of the baggage. Alphonse always said never leave loose ends. You with me?"

The droop in Fane's face showed that he didn't like that response. He knew his partner meant he might have to kill the girl if her big sister didn't cooperate. He didn't like that part, but he hoped the guy was drunk and talking out of his head. He just said, "Yeah, sure, man."

Pista finished the last drop of beer and crushed the can with his bare hand. He tossed it onto the pile spreading across the matted orange carpet. Then the two passed out, sprawled across the dingy sofa.

When Pista woke up, he was feeling pretty disgusted that they hadn't finished with this months ago, and they would have been if that crazy drunk hadn't made him beat the crap out of him and get locked up back in August. Now it was already November. He thought about that day late last August and got mad all over again. He and Fane had dropped by Sándor's for a beer. Sándor's was a little neighborhood joint in Pest that catered to the working class. He'd been sitting at the bar watching the boring crowd, trying to spot an interesting woman for the night, when suddenly some drunk had materialized by his side. "You the punkass been talkin' to my lady?" the drunk slurred in Hungarian. He grabbed Pista by the shoulder and swung his bar stool around. Without hesitation, Pista, who never minded a good fight, hauled off and knocked the guy to the floor. Then he jumped down from his stool and kicked him hard in the stomach and went back to his stool, taking a large swig of beer.

Fane touched Pista on the arm and said, "Come on, man. We better get out of here."

Pista jerked his arm away from Fane's touch and scowled. Meanwhile, the drunk lay on the floor, dazed for a moment. Then he staggered to his feet and, surprisingly, came at Pista again, uttering a host of obscenities. This time, Pista jumped down and pummeled the guy, breaking his nose and a few ribs. He continued beating him until the guy's buddies pulled him off.

Just when he thought he ought to hightail it out of there, the ambulance arrived. So did the police. The ambulance took the drunk away, and the police carted Pista off to jail. Fane disappeared. Too broke to make bail, Pista learned he would have to sit in his rotten cell until his trial date, which was set for late October. Over the next few weeks, he'd had plenty of time to think. He realized he should have just stomped the guy in the head and got the hell out of Sándor's when he had a chance. His plan was now on hold.

He wondered what that weasely little *lúzer*, Fane, was doing? The guy didn't know his own sorry ass from a hole in the ground. Since he now had a place to hold the girl, Pista decided he might go it alone when he got out of there. He hoped like hell they would give him an early trial date. Didn't happen.

In late October, Pista was found not guilty of assault. A witness testified that he'd acted in self-defense. The weeks he'd spent locked up had been a brutal reminder of his former life, and he hoped to God to never have to spend another night in a cell. Out on the streets again, he'd soon found Fane, who had been spending his nights at the old boarded-up house. Riding around the day he was released, Pista asked Fane if the old house was still stocked.

Fane answered, "I had to use some of our stuff. We need to get some more water out there and some canned food. Stuff like that."

"Then you'd better replace what you used."

"I'll replace the stuff. I got cash. I've had some day work."

Pista's retort, "You got so damned much cash, why the hell didn't you bail my ass out of jail?"

November 6

NOW THAT THEY WERE BACK on the case, Pista and Fane had been riding around the last few days, checking for the girl. Problem was she was no longer where her schedule said she should be. Pista was frustrated and getting more so by the minute. Then, by some lucky chance, they happened to spot her earlier coming out of an apartment building in an upscale area. She got in a car with some dude, and Pista exclaimed, "What the hell! This isn't where she's supposed to be today either. I've been away so long she's changed up her schedule on me. We'll just have to get it again. I'm getting sick and tired of messing around. It's her luck that she was with that guy today, but we'll see her again."

"I wonder if she's on to us," Fane said.

"How the hell could she be? We haven't even been around for a couple of months. No, I guess she must have changed her class schedule. That's all. We'll watch her a few days to get her new schedule. If we see her by herself, she's ours."

Then Pista told Fane, "You need to get out of here tonight. I got plans," Fane had been hanging out at Pista's place since Pista got out of jail.

Fane said, "Don't worry, man. I'll disappear."

That night, Pista was in an unusually bad mood. Tired of waiting and ready to be done with this, he picked up a prostitute and brought her to his flat to relieve the tension. They spent time rolling around in the sheets. It was good; Pista was getting his money's worth tonight. Afterward, he sat up and lit a cigarette. She pulled herself up, her large bosom hanging out over the sheets, and reached for his cigarette.

Pista jerked his hand away and ordered, "Fix me something to eat." After working her over pretty good in bed, he'd decided he was hungry.

Ilka said sexily, "That's not what you hired me for."

"Comes with the job, baby. Get your ass in the kitchen!" When Ilka didn't move, Pista took his heel and kicked her out of the bed.

She fell hard. "Hey, damn you! Who do you think you—"

In an instant, Pista jumped up and slammed his fist into Ilka's jaw. Blood flowed from the side of her mouth. Her hand went to her jaw to wipe the blood, and she cursed and glared at him with rage.

"Now do what I said."

She grabbed her skirt and top and began to put them on.

"Don't bother with those. You'll just have to take them off again."

Ilka looked as if she was trying to decide if she could get the hell out of that dump before he struck her again. Unfortunately for her, Pista had recognized the look. He showed her his fist and said, "If you want to see tomorrow, get in the kitchen before I get mad."

Ilka dropped her clothes on the floor and hurried to his refrigerator. She took out a couple of eggs and some *szalonnás.* "I like my bacon crispy," Pista told her.

Within minutes, she had fixed him a plate. He ate while she hurriedly dressed behind his back. After she'd got her stilettos on, grabbed her handbag, and headed swiftly toward the door, Pista heard the movement and jerked around, jumping up. He crossed the room in a hurry, grabbing her by her upper arm. "Where do you think you're going?"

Ilka jerked her arm away and shouted, "I know about creeps like you. I'm out of here. Where's my money!"

"What money? For what it was worth, you need to pay *me* for touching your used-up ass." Then Pista spit in her face. She wiped his sputum away with her arm.

"You're a low-down *korhadt*. You know that?" Ilka said in disgust.

"Get your sorry ass on out of here, and don't let me see you on the streets again."

Ilka managed to get the door open, but before she was completely out, Pista slammed it against her fingers, breaking off several two-inch nails. She screamed and ran down the hallway, cursing and holding her left hand.

Pista sat down on his old sofa and lit another cigarette. He had gotten laid, and it hadn't cost him a single forint. Spending time with that low-class *kurvával* had helped relieve his tension, but the best part was knocking her around. It felt good. Reminded him of old times. Pista knew she wouldn't report his actions to the police. Still, he knew he'd better be careful. After all, his last fight had landed him behind bars for two months.

Tomorrow he'd find Fane, and they would work on getting the girl's new schedule. He hoped they would luck out and catch her alone. He was ready to make his move.

CHAPTER
8

Cincinnati, Ohio, November 18

ON MONDAY MORNING, LYNN DAVIS ran her usual three miles in the crisp November air. Later, on her way to work, she stopped at Busken's Bakery for a bagel and cream cheese and arrived at her office in Carew Tower at seven thirty. She was looking forward to being on a flight to Hawaii later this week, where she would give the keynote address at the annual Private Investigator's Conference in Maui. She intended to spend all morning working on her speech. Lynn was excited at all the potential new business the presentation could generate.

She had no idea those plans would be changed.

Lynn finished steeping her tea just as Ella stepped into the lobby. Lynn greeted Ella warmly. Ella was one hell of an associate. It was why Lynn had brought her along when she left the Billingsleys and struck out on her own. She loved Ella's easy, reliable manner.

Ella flashed her dazzling smile. "Chamomile so early? It's going to be one of those days, is it?"

Lynn smiled and nodded. "I've got to finish my presentation for the conference."

Ella tossed her bag across the back of a chair and slid behind the receptionist's desk. "Janet won't be in today, so I'm sitting out here." Ella always stepped in where needed.

"Good," Lynn replied. "Since you'll be close by, you can help me with this talk when I get stuck."

"How far have you got?"

"Five, maybe six ..."

"Five pages aren't bad," Ella said encouragingly.

"Words," Lynn said. "Five words, not pages."

Ella grimaced. "Ouch."

"Tell me about it." Lynn took a sip of tea and watched as Ella's eyes followed her. "Want some?" she asked. Ella nodded and reached for her mug, which she handed to Lynn. Lynn filled it. After handing it back to Ella, she headed into her office. "Hold my calls this morning."

"No can do, chief. You've got that eleven o'clock with Sara Wellington."

Lynn's shoulders sagged. "Who is Sara Wellington? Can't I cancel?"

"Sure. But you may want to know that Elizabeth Remington gave her your name."

Lynn's face lit up. After successfully handling the Remington case earlier that year, Mrs. Remington had taken Lynn under her wing, inviting her to several prestigious events and introducing her to many of Cincinnati's elite. *This should be interesting. What could Mrs. Wellington want?* "Elizabeth Remington, you say? Oh, well, never mind."

"I thought you'd see things my way," Ella quipped.

"What did she want?" Lynn asked.

"All I know is she said it was very important."

Lynn groaned. "I'll never get this doggone speech done."

"Buck up, chief," Ella said. "Things are always darkest before the dawn."

"They say that, but somehow that little cliché doesn't always hold up. You might have to write my speech for me. Oh, and Ella, before she comes, can you bring a fresh pot of tea. And use the good china," she added with a wink.

Lynn thought about Sara Wellington. She knew of a prominent family named Wellington here in Cincinnati, and knowing this was an Elizabeth Remington referral, she figured this woman was probably from that family. She googled her and found this was the person she was thinking of. She also found several images. Sara Wellington was very attractive. Lynn recalled seeing her picture often on the society pages of the *Cincinnati Enquirer.* She learned that Mrs. Wellington was fifty-seven years old and that at twenty-one, she had represented the state of Ohio in the Miss America pageant. After college, Sara had married Horace Wellington, a budding research physician. The city of Cincinnati was proud that one of its own citizens, Dr. Wellington, had won the Nobel Prize in medicine a few years ago. The Wellingtons were one of Cincinnati's most prominent couples. Sara was active in the community, serving on several boards, including the Remington Foundation.

Just before eleven o'clock, Ella buzzed and announced, "Mrs. Wellington is here." Lynn told Ella to show her in and rose to greet her. Sara Wellington was above average height and had a neat, slender build. Lynn noted that her photographs didn't quite show how stunningly attractive she was in person. Dressed stylishly in a steel-gray wool suit and matching pumps, a bright multicolored silk scarf gracing her neckline, she walked into the office and reached out to shake Lynn's extended hand. Lynn invited her to sit down, and Mrs. Wellington lowered her body into the chair.

Smoothing her dress over her knees, she said, "I'm pleased to meet you. Thank you for seeing me. My friend Elizabeth has spoken well of you. She knows our situation and felt you might be of help to us."

Lynn acknowledged the reference to Elizabeth Remington and then offered Mrs. Wellington a cup of tea.

"No, thank you." She took a breath and continued, "I'm here about our nineteen-year-old daughter, Morgan." Mrs. Wellington appeared pensive.

Lynn prepared to take notes. "Please go on."

"First, let me give you some background. In June, Morgan completed her freshman year of college at the Rhode Island School of Design. She's wanted to go there since she was fourteen. This summer, she was among a small group of design students from around the world selected to participate in a summer co-op program at the Paris Fashion Institute. She studied in Paris during her sophomore year of high school and loved everything about her Parisian experience.

"The reason I called you is because after Morgan finished her summer program in August, just before she returned home, she phoned to tell us she would be going to Budapest instead."

"Budapest?" Lynn replied. "Vacation?"

Sara waved a hand, like the question was an inconsequential fly she could shoo away. "Her roommate in Paris was from Budapest. I understand she invited her."

Lynn nodded. "Sure she wasn't chasing a boy?"

Sara furrowed her brow and said adamantly, "No, nothing like that."

Lynn wondered if there was something more. Whatever it was, it bore looking into.

"Did this strike you as odd?" Lynn asked.

"Yes, Budapest was completely out of the blue. Not to say that Morgan hasn't surprised us before. But that was totally unexpected."

Lynn listened for more.

"She's not been difficult. She just usually goes after what she wants."

"Would you say she is spontaneous? Makes hasty decisions?"

"You could say that. The next surprise came when she phoned to say she had registered for a semester of study at Central European University there. Frankly, we didn't know what to make of this sudden development."

"Why would she want to leave Rhode Island this semester to attend school in a former Communist bloc country?"

"Morgan only told us she wanted to stay in Budapest a little longer."

"Is she usually forthcoming, or is she secretive?" Lynn asked.

"She's usually pretty open. However, I'm sure there are many things she's never told us. I believe that is typical of teenagers."

"What's happening with her program at Rhode Island?" Lynn asked.

Sara Wellington replied, "Well, it turns out all her courses were transferable, so she didn't lose anything. The next thing we knew, Morgan got herself an apartment. At this point, that is basically what we know.

"It seems to her father and me that Morgan has been rather preoccupied since she's been in Budapest. However, she did come home for a week last summer when he got sick."

Lynn had read about Dr. Wellington's stroke. "I hope he is doing well," she said.

"Thank you. Since Morgan began classes there, we speak with her less frequently than before. The truth is, Horace and I are convinced there is something she's not telling us. We would have gone to Budapest to see for ourselves what's going on. However, we simply cannot travel at this time."

"Oh?"

"Yes. Horace's doctors have advised him against long plane rides, and I won't leave him in his current condition. He is still recovering from his stroke. We were trying to wait it out, but we decided last night not to wait any longer."

"Did something happen?" Lynn asked.

"Yes, as a matter of fact," she responded. "A family friend, Celia Coleman, is in Budapest on business. She phoned to tell me that she saw Morgan the other evening. She said Morgan was walking into a dance club with a rambunctious group of young men and women. Of course, I was quite surprised that she had spotted Morgan, and even more surprised to learn of the rowdy people she was with.

"Celia said that one of the men was wearing black boots and carrying a guitar case. As they walked, he had his arm slung around her neck. And he appeared to be intoxicated, judging from the way he was weaving. The whole group was dressed in all black, Gothic style, including Morgan, who had a big fur hat on her head. Our daughter's not been into fads, certainly not Gothic, nor is she the rowdy type."

"What did Ms. Coleman do when she saw Morgan?"

"She had her driver stop the car, and she called out to Morgan. She said Morgan looked up and gave her a blank stare but did not return the greeting. Celia noticed that she looked as though she didn't recognize her. Then everyone in the group laughed and they went into the club."

"So Morgan did not speak to your friend? Does she know her well?" Lynn asked.

"She absolutely does. We've spent time in each other's homes since Morgan was a child.

"Celia said at first she wondered if she had made a mistake, taking someone else for our daughter. But she was convinced she was not mistaken.

"After receiving Celia's phone call, I called Morgan. She told me she had not seen Celia Coleman the evening before and that she'd been at an evening lecture. I didn't understand why she would tell me that. On the other hand, if she was telling the truth, then who did Celia see? It's a little frightening to think there could be another girl over there who looks so much like our daughter that people are mistaking her for Morgan. Horace and I cannot help but be concerned. We believe Morgan may not be telling us the entire truth. So after thinking about everything, we decided we needed to do something."

As Sara Wellington spoke, Lynn thought about the Gothic lifestyle. From what she understood, Goths were into the darker side of life, but they weren't particularly known for being criminals. *Drugs, possibly?*

"Mrs. Wellington, what do you know about Goths?"

"Other than that they dress in all that black—black lipstick, heavy eyeliner—not much. Why do you ask?"

"I was actually wondering if the Gothic group Mrs. Coleman saw was into more than just music."

"What are you suggesting?"

"Has Morgan ever gotten into any trouble with the law?"

Sara Wellington frowned at the question. "Morgan has never been in any trouble."

"I understand," Lynn said. Then she shifted to another question. "If your daughter wanted to change schools, why not the Paris Fashion Institute?"

"Apparently, this roommate convinced her to go back to Budapest with her."

"What do you think about that?" Lynn asked, wondering if Morgan could possibly be in a romantic relationship with her roommate but didn't want her parents to know.

"This seemed like another of Morgan's spontaneous actions."

Lynn sat back in her chair and thought about what Mrs. Wellington was saying. She asked, "Do you believe it was Morgan your friend saw?"

"I frankly don't know what to believe," Mrs. Wellington replied. "I want to believe my daughter, but I don't think Celia would have told me this if she weren't certain."

"But it could possibly have been someone else."

Mrs. Wellington sat for a moment pondering that question, her chin resting on her thumb and forefinger. "No, it had to be her. Celia knows Morgan too well to have made a mistake."

"Then why do you suppose Morgan didn't reply?"

"That, my dear Ms. Davis, is what I'm hiring you to find out. All I can say is that if what Celia told me is true, I don't think our daughter would want us to know she was involved with such a group.

"Frankly, we don't know what Morgan may have gotten herself into. So you can understand why we need someone to find out what is going on over there." She paused a moment, looked directly at Lynn, and said, "We need your help."

"What exactly do you want me to do?" Lynn asked Sara Wellington.

Sara Wellington took a deep breath and sighed. "We want you to go to Budapest to find out what is going on with our daughter. And we hope you can escort her home."

Lynn looked perplexed.

"Horace and I would be devastated if anything were to happen to our daughter in a strange land. We are hopeful that you can do this."

It took a minute for Mrs. Wellington's words to register with Lynn. "You're asking me to go to Budapest to check on your daughter and bring her home?"

Mrs. Wellington did not falter. "That is precisely what I am asking you to do. And we'd want you to leave right away, of course. No later than tomorrow."

Lynn was dumbfounded. Sara Wellington was asking her to go to Budapest to do something almost any investigator could do. She said, "Mrs. Wellington, I realize how important this is to you and your husband, and I appreciate your confidence in me. But there are agencies in Budapest that can easily check on your daughter for you. I could provide you with some names—"

Sara Wellington waved her off. "Don't bother. We don't want just any stranger involved in our lives. That's why I'm talking to you."

What about the conference in Hawaii? I'd have to miss giving my big speech. Why does it have to be me?

Mrs. Wellington seemed to read Lynn's mind. "Elizabeth was certain we could count on you for this. Are you unable to go to Budapest?"

Lynn thought quickly. Taking this job could be very lucrative, and with the costly renovations being made to her downtown building, she could certainly use the extra cash. Of course, it wasn't every day one got to handle a case for a Nobel laureate. But, to be honest, the main reason she would consider this request was because the referral had come from Elizabeth Remington. The Remington case had represented her foray into the circles of the wealthy elite, and success with this case could easily mean more referrals. She decided at that moment to take the case.

"Miss Davis?" Sara Wellington waited impatiently for a response.

"Of course, Mrs. Wellington," Lynn replied. "I will go to Budapest. And I will arrange to leave tomorrow."

"Thank you." Relief showed on Lynn's new client's face as she took a deep breath and exhaled. "I was hoping you would say yes.

"So let me give you some information about Morgan, including the university contact I have been in touch with." Sara Wellington took an envelope containing photographs of Morgan and other pertinent information from her purse. She described the contents: photos, address, telephone number, university contact, and the like.

Looking at Morgan's picture, Lynn said, "May I ask, is your daughter an adoptee by chance?"

"Why, yes. Why do you ask?"

"I didn't quite notice a family resemblance."

"Morgan is such an integral part of our lives that we never think of her as anything but our daughter." Mrs. Wellington then went on to explain how her former housekeeper Corina Moldovan came to the United States from Eastern Europe as a young widow with a small daughter. "Corina was an attractive woman who had Mediterranean features—long black hair and dark, deep-set eyes. I remember she once said people referred to her as a gypsy in her native country. Her daughter Nicola looked a lot like her mother. She gave birth to a baby girl with the same lovely features. That's our Morgan."

Lynn replied, "I see. And where is your housekeeper now?"

"After the baby was born, she took Nicola back to Bucharest to make a new start."

Hearing that, Lynn immediately thought about Budapest being in relatively close proximity to Romania. She didn't know if that had any relevance.

Mrs. Wellington continued. "When her daughter got pregnant at fifteen, she decided to put the child up for adoption. Horace and I had talked of adopting. However, there was so much to consider at our ages, including the ethnic difference."

Lynn glanced up from her notepad for an explanation. Mrs. Wellington said, "Corina was half Indian, and Morgan had her olive complexion. We did not want her singled out for that reason. However, we decided that with love for this child, we could overcome any challenges. Thankfully, they accepted our offer to adopt."

As their discussion was winding down, Mrs. Wellington said, "I will talk to Morgan and tell her to expect you. I want to stay in touch with you on a regular basis while you are there."

Lynn told her she would call whenever she had something to report. "And I'll let you know when I arrive in Budapest. My cell phone number is on my business card. Feel free to use it whenever you need to."

Mrs. Wellington stood to leave. Lynn stood too, and observed the poised and elegant demeanor of her client. Mrs. Wellington picked up her handbag and clutched it in one hand as she extended her right hand to shake Lynn's. "Thank you. This means a great deal to us." She walked to the door and stopped to make a final comment. "Miss Davis, we obviously do not know who the people are that Morgan may have taken up with. We can only ask that you be very careful. Keep our daughter safe."

Lynn watched Sara Wellington walk out of her office. Then she sat at her desk and pondered the case, wondering what she would find in Budapest. Did Morgan tell her mother the truth? If not, who were the people she was seen with, particularly the guy? Was he her boyfriend? That might rule out the notion that she and her roommate were an item. What were Goths into?

Lynn jotted down these and other questions and impressions as they came to mind. She was pleased to take this case. Representing a family of this stature could only be good for business. She wrote a quick card to Mrs. Remington to thank her for the referral.

"Ella," she said into the intercom. "Can you step in here right away?"

"Be right there, chief," Ella replied. When she entered Lynn's office, she said, "What did she want?"

"Believe it or not, she wants me to go to Budapest tomorrow."

"What! So what'd she say when you told her no?"

"Are you kidding? I couldn't turn her down. This is a big case."

"Maybe so, but what about the PI conference and your big speech?"

"I'm going to need you to get a replacement for me, which shouldn't be difficult. Start with Brad or Tracy." Lynn still stayed in touch with the Billingsleys at the firm where she and Ella both started. They all still referred cases to one another from time to time.

"I know one of them will jump on it. Heck, I'd go myself if I didn't have to handle things here. That's a bummer."

"There'll be other opportunities," Lynn said. Then she filled Ella in on her meeting with Sara Wellington.

"With what she wants me to do, I don't know how long I'll be over there. We need to consider that I could be gone at least a week, maybe longer. You'll have to take my appointments or reschedule if necessary. Also, I'll call Harvey. I know he'll help if you need him."

"Gotcha," Ella replied. "Guess I'd better get out there and look at our calendars and start doing some rearranging."

"And Ella, I need you to get me a flight to Budapest tomorrow evening. I'd like to be there early Wednesday."

"Sure thing," Ella replied, and she turned and headed out to the desk to answer the telephone.

A little while later, she ducked back into Lynn's office. "You've got a seven o'clock flight tomorrow evening. It'll get you into Budapest late Wednesday morning."

"Excellent. Thanks, Ella. That means I can come in for a while tomorrow."

"Good. Oh, and you're right," Ella said. "Tracy was delighted to step in to give the speech. She said to tell you she owes you one."

CHAPTER
9

Budapest, Hungary, November 20

DURING THE LONG PLANE RIDE, Lynn caught only a few hours' sleep. Instead, her mind was filled with thoughts about the recent developments. She reflected on how quickly things had changed since the day before. Instead of being on a flight to Hawaii, here she was on her way to Hungary on a mission to bring home Morgan Wellington, daughter of a Nobel laureate. In the back of her mind, she was wondering if Morgan Wellington would willingly come back home.

When the plane was descending for its landing, Lynn got the perfect bird's-eye view of the city. Her initial observation was how classical and medieval everything looked, even from the sky. The landscape was dotted with spire-topped cathedrals, and she could see wide expanses of stained-glass windows. Lynn noted the distinctly intricate Gothic-style architecture of the buildings.

She saw the Danube River snaking through the terrain, separating one part of the city from another, and she saw a huge regal-looking structure sitting at the edge of the river. The captain announced that it was the Parliament Building. *Lovely*, she thought. Even from this vantage point, Lynn could easily see why Budapest was considered one of the most beautiful cities in the world. And when she stepped off the plane in Hungary's capital city, finding herself surrounded by its world-famous architecture, she felt like she was stepping back onto the pages of European history. Little did she know she was stepping into the arms of danger.

Lynn made her way to Immigrations and stood at the back of a very long line. She glanced over at a magazine being read by someone who was standing in the next aisle. On the cover was famed actor Bela Lugosi, known for his portrayal of Count Dracula. Seeing his image reminded her of her uncle's warning about this particular trip. "Watch out over there, Lynn," Uncle Ed had cautioned. "You're going to a foreign country, and people everywhere prey on foreigners. Besides, they say that's vampire territory, you know. Werewolves too." He'd made that last comment with a slight grin.

She'd told him, "Don't worry. I'll be careful. Besides, I don't believe in those characters."

"That's good. All I know is that when I was stationed in Europe, I ran into an awful lot of people who did believe in them," he answered. "After seeing how seriously some people took that stuff, I learned they had a right to believe whatever they wanted to." Lynn wondered if her uncle really believed in those creatures too, but at that moment, he pointed upward and told her, "But me, I believe in only one supernatural being. And He resides up there."

"Miss ... Miss!" the immigrations agent repeated sharply. Lynn hadn't realized how engrossed she was in her thoughts. She quickly stepped up to his counter and handed him her passport. The agent looked from her to her passport photo, eyed her sternly, and then stamped her passport and passed her through. After getting through immigrations and customs, she looked around for a driver holding a sign bearing her name. Spotting him, she waved, and they approached each other.

The driver, Jozséf Balog, wore a gray and black uniform. Jozséf gathered her bags, and they headed out to his limousine. The crisp, bright fall sun warmed the air, which was fresh and clear. In English, he began making small talk. "First time in Budapest?" Lynn indicated that it was. "I hope you enjoy it here. Are you here on business or pleasure?" She told him business. Lynn saw that he was trying to be friendly, but she hoped she didn't have a talker on her hands. Soon they were on their way to the Hilton Hotel.

Along the drive, in spite of the lovely scenery, Lynn found she could not really appreciate the view; she was completely focused on why she had come. She wanted to figure out how to expediently accomplish her mission and then be on her way back home. Lynn also thought about being away from her office, but she knew she'd left things in good hands. Ella Braxton was quite capable of running things in her absence. On top of that, her good friend and fellow private investigator Harvey Chapman was there if Ella needed him.

"Did you know," Jozséf was asking, "that Budapest was formerly two separate cities called Buda and Pest?" He went on to explain that Buda represented the working class and Pest was where the elite class lived. Lost in her thoughts, it suddenly dawned on Lynn that the driver was speaking to her. She glanced up.

"I'm sorry. What were you saying?" When he repeated himself, she responded that she had not known and asked when they united as one city.

"In 1872, Buda and Pest became Budapest. Even though it is now one city, the notion of separate cities lives on," the driver droned on. "You will hear parts of the city referred to as either the Pest side, or the Buda side."

Lynn nodded and returned to her thoughts. When Jozséf apparently realized his passenger was preoccupied, he remained silent for several minutes. Lynn appreciated his silence.

A short time later, the driver told Lynn they were almost at her hotel. As they approached their destination in the heart of the city, she noticed that the relatively uniform height of the buildings and medieval architecture were just as she'd observed from the plane. Noticing that Lynn was now looking at the sights as they drove through certain districts, Jozséf pointed out some of the quaint residential areas and historic buildings.

After they reached the hotel, Lynn told the driver she wanted to use him whenever she needed transportation while she was here.

"I am at your service, miss. I will take you where you need to go anytime."

Lynn told Jozséf she wanted to go somewhere right away and asked him to wait while she checked into the hotel. Inside, she was welcomed by friendly staff and was glad that, like her driver, the hotel employees spoke English. It was two in the afternoon. Back in Cincinnati, it was eight in the morning.

She phoned Mrs. Wellington to tell her she'd arrived in Budapest. Mrs. Wellington said, "I've tried to reach

Morgan. She has not answered the phone, and I've left her several messages. I can't imagine why I have not heard back from her, and I am a little worried. I'm afraid she does not yet know you are coming."

Lynn was concerned. "I was about to go over to her apartment to see her. It will definitely help if she knows why I'm here."

"Of course, I will try her again," Mrs. Wellington replied.

Lynn ended her phone call with Sara Wellington and then phoned Ella. "I've been thinking about what I can say to Morgan to convince her to come back to the United States with me. Now, after speaking with Mrs. Wellington, I find out that she hasn't been able to tell her daughter that I'm coming. I'm about to go over to her apartment now. Wish me luck."

"That's not so good," Ella said. "But maybe the element of surprise will work to your advantage. You'll get a chance to see her without a mask."

"Let's hope you're right," Lynn said. After she hung up with Ella, she dialed Morgan's cell phone. There was no answer. Lynn wondered if she might be in class. The voice mail came on, but she decided against leaving a message, especially since Morgan probably didn't know about her yet. She changed into a dark pantsuit. Within fifteen minutes she was back outside.

Jozséf was waiting at the curb. Lynn gave him Morgan's address, and he took off. Along the way, they passed several large buildings. Lynn saw the sign for Central European University, where Morgan was studying. She noticed that the campus buildings seemed to be a mix of old and new. After passing the university, they drove by some newer dormitories, continuing past individual student apartments.

After driving by what appeared to be efficiency housing, they came to some apartment buildings in a more upscale area. A few minutes later, the driver stopped in front of Morgan's building. He jumped out and opened the door for Lynn, and she asked him to wait. "I could be awhile," she told him. She walked up the pathway past a well-manicured courtyard that led into the building. There were tall, neatly trimmed hedges on both ends of the building. Inside the lobby, Lynn spotted the attendant sitting behind a desk. He was a college-age, dark-haired man whose name tag read Zaka. She handed him her calling card and asked him to buzz Morgan Wellington's unit.

"I will try the room, ma'am, but I do not think the young lady is in," he said politely in a thick Hungarian accent.

"Did she say where she might be?" Lynn asked.

"No, but she takes classes at the university. I will phone her apartment."

Lynn waited while he tried to reach Morgan on the intercom. There was no answer. "Do you know what time she usually returns?" Lynn asked.

"Well, today is Wednesday, and on Mondays, Wednesdays, and Fridays, she usually arrives back here around two thirty."

Lynn looked at her watch. It was not yet three o'clock in the afternoon. She decided to wait a few minutes, but by 3:20 p.m. Morgan had still not arrived, so she wrote her hotel number on her business card and gave it to Zaka. She asked him to tell Miss Wellington that she had come by to see her and would phone her later. Lynn knew that if Mrs. Wellington had gotten a chance to explain why she was there, it would make the conversation go easier.

Joszéf was waiting in his limo to drive Lynn back to her hotel. On the ride back, Lynn wondered if Morgan would return her call. She figured it probably depended on whether or not she had spoken with her mother, or at least listened to her mother's message. Lynn decided that if she didn't hear from her, she'd keep trying to reach her every thirty minutes or so until she did. "Here we are, ma'am," Lynn's driver said as he stopped in front of her hotel.

The first chance she got, Lynn called Harvey. They spoke awhile about her case. She enjoyed the first real break she'd had since Mrs. Wellington walked into her office on Monday at eleven o'clock. Talking to Harv relaxed her.

* * *

After speaking with Lynn Davis, Sara wondered whether or not Morgan might be going through another of her *mood swings*. Could that be why she had gotten into the Goth lifestyle? Lynn Davis had asked about Goths, and Sara had researched it when she returned home. What she read distressed her even more. She learned that Goth practitioners were into such things as bats, death, and cemeteries, and sometimes sacrificial rituals. The thought that her daughter could be involved in such morbid activities was extremely alarming.

Sara wondered why these things were happening to her family now. Overall, they were an influential and well-respected family. Sara herself had never worked outside the home, but she was civically active. She'd certainly never had to deal with complications like the ones she was facing now. Horace's stroke had devastated her. He had always enjoyed excellent health, so to see him down was very difficult. Thank goodness, he was recovering nicely. But now their daughter was off in a foreign country doing who knew what.

After the recent Remington Foundation board meeting, she'd found herself pouring her heart out to her friend Elizabeth Remington. She told her about Morgan's sudden decision to go to Budapest and then to transfer to a university there. She also told about her moods that, although far less frequent than when she was younger, could sometimes last for long periods of time. She discussed Morgan's stubbornness and impulsiveness. Elizabeth immediately recommended that she contact Lynn Davis to look into this for her. She felt Lynn could find out what was really going on with Morgan.

Sara had made note of Lynn's name, but she'd hoped it wouldn't have to go that far. She had never had any dealings with a private investigator and, frankly, never thought someone of her ilk would ever require their services. Her notion of a private detective was a stereotypical one: cigarette smoker, store-front office, old car. However, after Celia called to tell her about seeing Morgan, Sara decided that Elizabeth Remington would never recommend someone untoward. After all, she'd used Lynn herself. That's when Sara decided to call Lynn Davis. And after meeting her on Monday and seeing how competent and savvy she seemed, in addition to being a graduate of an Ivy League school and having an office in the prestigious Carew Tower, it was now a different story. Sara was grateful she'd not let her prejudgments get in the way of hiring her. She was pleased that Lynn was willing to leave the country on short notice. She could now see why Elizabeth Remington thought so highly of her, and she suddenly felt much better about her family situation than she had for a while. With Lynn on the ground in Budapest, she would soon have some answers.

She went to tell her husband about Lynn's phone call. He was with his physical therapist in the exercise room of their home. Horace Peterson Wellington was a managing partner in a successful medical research organization. His expertise was often sought by top officials across the scientific community and even by influential government leaders. Fortunately, he was able to work, and he spent many hours in his home office each day. Dr. Wellington was doing difficult leg exercises and the excruciating look on his face quickly changed to a pained smile when Sara came in. He excused his therapist, who left the room. Sara leaned over and gave her husband a peck on the cheek.

"Lynn Davis just called from Budapest. She was about to go over to Morgan's apartment. She'll call back to let us know if she met with her and how everything went." Her husband nodded. "The problem is I tried Morgan's number again, and this time I couldn't even leave a message because her voice mailbox is full. So she still doesn't know about Lynn. I get more worried each time I can't reach her. Horace, where is our daughter?"

"I wouldn't worry that much, honey. I'm sure she's all right. Morgan's got a good head on her. Probably just busy with her classes. That's all. She could just be having fun with friends."

"You're probably right. I just don't want Lynn's surprise visit to affect her emotionally."

"You worry too much. Let's just wait to hear what Miss Davis has to say."

Sara returned to her office and sat at her desk looking out the window. Again Morgan crossed her mind. She hoped she'd hear from Lynn soon. With the cold wind whistling and blowing the snow around outside, she studied the lovely family photo on her bookcase taken just two years ago. Morgan was flanked by her parents. She thought of how blessed she and Horace were to have Morgan, especially after their frustrating early efforts to have a child. After three miscarriages, she had needed help healing, both physically and emotionally. A friend recommended a private duty nurse to stay with her. Nurse Flossie Walker had been a godsend. She pictured her feisty nurse.

"Young lady, what you have been through is hard, and I know that. But you've been in that bed for two weeks. It's time for you to think about yourself now. See, you won't be any good to yourself or your husband if you don't get up from that bed and take your life back," Flossie Walker had told her in her no-nonsense style. Miss Walker had successfully coaxed her back to herself, and Sara had a great appreciation for her.

Over time, she also came to have a great deal of confidence in Flossie Walker's nursing skills. Knowing she was a certified midwife too, she thought Miss Walker might be able to deliver Nicola's baby and suggested this to her housekeeper, Corina Moldovan, who accepted her recommendation. Thus, midway into Nicola's pregnancy, Nurse Walker became Nicola's caregiver. Sara smiled, remembering how sweet was that day in May when the midwife handed over their new baby girl wrapped in a soft pink blanket—a bundle of joy. Throughout it all, Morgan had brought her and Horace a great deal of happiness. Sara looked out at the snow. Still thinking about Morgan being halfway across the world, she dialed her daughter's number again.

CHAPTER
10

BACK AT HER HOTEL, LYNN phoned Mrs. Wellington to tell her she went to Morgan's apartment, but Morgan wasn't home, so she left a message for her to call.

"Unfortunately, I haven't been able to speak with my daughter yet either. I have left several messages for her to call me," Mrs. Wellington said. "In fact, I am getting pretty worried. She always returns my calls."

That didn't sound right. If Morgan hadn't yet talked to her mother, Lynn was doubtful she'd return a call from a stranger. Because Mrs. Wellington was worried, Lynn wondered if anything had happened to her daughter. "What would you like me to do?" she asked.

"In the papers I gave you was a telephone number for Bela Hamza's family. She's Morgan's friend. After we spoke earlier, I tried to call them to see if they knew how I could reach Morgan. I figured they could have Bela get a message to her for me. But they did not answer their telephone. I left a message for them, telling them what I wanted. I'm still waiting to hear back.

"If you don't hear from Morgan in a couple of hours, I would like you to go back to her apartment and see if she is there or learn whatever you can find out. If she isn't, please check in with the Hamzas. Morgan's friend now lives in a dormitory, and I don't have her number. However, if I should happen to hear from Morgan in the meantime, I will call you."

Lynn told Mrs. Wellington she would call her as soon as contact had been made. She had been hoping this matter could be resolved with just a conversation or two. But now she wasn't so hopeful. Morgan hadn't called her mother, who'd left several messages, and she hoped nothing had happened to her.

While waiting to return to Morgan's apartment, Lynn caught up on phone calls. She called her parents to let them know she had arrived in Budapest. Then she remembered to call Mr. Smith, the general contractor in charge of renovating her downtown office building. Lynn was very proud to own a piece of Cincinnati's most prime real estate. After receiving a handsome bonus from a case earlier in the year, she had been able to begin her remodeling project in earnest. In fact, the bonus came from Elizabeth Remington, the woman who had referred the Wellingtons to her. Lynn's parents had always advised her that real estate was the key to personal independence. When she'd acquired her hundred-year-old building a few years before, it had little value and needed a complete refurbishment. Located near the Cincinnati's new Horseshoe Casino, its value had since increased many times over.

After speaking with Mr. Smith, Lynn checked in with Ella.

"What's it like over there?" Ella asked.

"From what I've seen, it's a very lovely old city. But to tell you the truth, I'm too busy with this case to notice." Then she told Ella she had not been able to reach Morgan yet, but she'd be heading back out to her apartment again in a few minutes.

"You say her mother's been leaving messages for a couple of days? I don't know, but I feel like you could have a problem on your hands."

"I'm about to call her friend's parents; see what they can tell me."

"You'd better go ahead and do that. Catch up with me later," Ella said.

Lynn called the Hamzas. When Mrs. Hamza answered, Lynn identified herself as calling on behalf of Morgan Wellington's parents and asked how she could get in touch with Bela.

Mrs. Hamza said, "I'm sorry. Our daughter is not here. I returned home a little while ago and just listened to a message from a Mrs. Wellington. I phoned her back and told her I would try to reach Bela."

"Have you reached her yet?" Lynn asked.

"No. She is in a late class. However, she should be calling me in a few minutes. If you would like to leave your telephone number, I will pass it along to her. Either she will call you, or she will reach Morgan. I expect you will receive a call from one of them very soon."

Lynn thanked her and decided to head over to Morgan's apartment. She called József, who said he would pick her up in ten minutes. She got downstairs as he was pulling up to the hotel, and he drove her back to Morgan's apartment. When she went in, Zaka, the attendant, was still there. Lynn asked if Miss Wellington was back yet. "No, madam. I do not believe she has returned, but I will call her apartment to be certain." Lynn waited while he made the call. After a minute, he replied, "She does not answer."

Lynn decided not to wait around this time. She still expected to receive a call from either Bela or Morgan. She called to tell Mrs. Wellington where things stood and had her driver return her to her hotel.

As she walked out of the building, Fane tapped his partner on the forearm and asked, *"Ki ez?"* Fane and Pista had arrived at the apartment a few minutes ago in hopes of catching the girl coming or going. It was damn unusual to see a black woman in this town. *Maybe she is from Africa,* he thought.

Shortly after Lynn got back to her hotel, her telephone rang. Hoping it was Morgan, she answered.

"Hello, this is Bela Hamza," a young woman with a Hungarian accent said. "My mother said you are trying to reach Morgan Wellington."

"That's right. Do you know where she is?"

"She is here with me. Well, actually she is in class. I'm waiting to take her home."

Lynn breathed a sigh of relief. "Her mother has been trying to call her for a few days, but she hasn't heard back from her. So she is pretty concerned."

Bela said, "Oh, that is because Morgan lost her telephone on Sunday. She just happened to find it this morning. It had fallen out of her purse under the passenger seat of my car. Of course her battery was run down, so she has not played her messages yet. I believe that may be why she has not called home."

"I'm certain her mother will be relieved to know that. After she talks to her mother, will you tell her to call me too?"

"Certainly," Bela said, and she and Lynn ended their call.

Cincinnati, Ohio

Sara Wellington disconnected the telephone after speaking with Lynn Davis and immediately dialed Morgan's number again. Morgan's voice mailbox was still full. *Morgan, where are you? Is everything all right?* Sara was worried. She'd always been able to reach her daughter. Not being able to do so was very distressing, particularly now that Lynn Davis was there to encourage her to come home.

She prayed that Lynn would be successful in discovering what was going on. Morgan could be headstrong at times. She had called it spontaneity, but now she wondered if she should have mentioned Morgan's occasional mood swings? At times when Morgan was younger, these moods had been so severe she'd had to see a counselor. In fact, there was a time when her daughter's mood could literally darken a room, just as, conversely, her smile could brighten it. No one ever knew the reason she had those mood changes. Thankfully, they were usually short-lived. Lynn Davis had asked if Morgan was secretive, and Sara had answered her truthfully, except she hadn't mentioned Morgan's refusal to discuss whatever it was that created that dismal moodiness. Morgan's mind was like steel when it came to her determination not to talk about it.

Thank goodness, these phases had long since passed. Probably the worst time she could remember happened when Morgan was about eleven. She went through a brooding period and seemed to be in mourning. During that time, which had lasted several days, she could barely eat or sleep. She often looked on the verge of tears, and she never wanted to talk about it. It got so bad Sara finally took her to see her old therapist, Dr. Helene

Stern. Dr. Stern told Sara that Morgan told her she'd had a horrible dream that her father had died. The trauma of losing a father who loved her enough to adopt her as his own weighed her down. Dr. Stern reasoned that the dream, coupled with the loss of her biological father too, was more than Morgan could deal with. Thankfully, with the therapist's help, they got through that difficult time, and soon Morgan was back to her normal self.

During the period of Morgan's brooding, across the pond, unbeknownst to all, an eleven-year-old girl named Ivona Kay Palaki was mourning the death of her father, Adam Palaki. He'd had a serious accident on the ski slopes and never regained consciousness. Ivona had felt so proud and honored when he'd adopted her five years earlier, and he'd been an awesome dad. Until her adoption, she'd never had a father. And now the only one she'd ever known was gone. She'd pined for her father for weeks.

* * *

A couple of hours after Lynn returned to her hotel from Morgan's apartment, she decided to order dinner. Before she could call for room service, the telephone in her room rang. She answered. An impatient voice said, "Hello, is this Miss Davis?" Lynn responded affirmatively. "This is Morgan Wellington. My friend Bela Hamza gave me your number. Plus, I have the business card you left for me at my apartment today."

"Yes. Thank you for returning my call. Did you speak with your mother yet?"

"Yeah, I just spoke with her. But I'm afraid I don't understand. She said you are here to see how I am doing?"

Lynn detected what seemed to be hostility in Morgan's tone. "That's right, but there's more to it than that. Is it possible for us to meet soon, perhaps tomorrow? I can meet you wherever is convenient."

"I just don't get why my mother would send someone all the way to Budapest just to see how I was doing."

"Did you ask her about this?" Lynn asked.

"Well, yes, but she really didn't tell me anything. What more does she want you to find out? This is nuts. I don't understand it."

"I can explain better in person. Like your mother said, she wanted me to see how you were doing."

"Then I can save you some time. I'm doing just fine. Is that good enough?"

"Actually I'd rather speak with you face-to-face if you can schedule it," Lynn said calmly.

Morgan sighed. "I have classes in the morning until eleven, and then I have to go downtown for an afternoon class. There's a little restaurant on the corner near the university where I go sometimes. It's called the Pierrot Café. Is twelve o'clock okay? If you want, we can have lunch and talk. I'll only have half an hour."

Lynn got the address and agreed to the time, and Morgan said, "By the way, how will I know you?"

"I'll be wearing a gray pantsuit. And I am African American." It occurred to Lynn at that moment that she had not seen another person of color in this city. Interestingly, this was the first time she had even thought about it.

Now that she had finally spoken with Morgan, she decided to eat and get a good night's sleep. She had no idea what tomorrow would bring. First she called Mrs. Wellington to tell her about her conversations with Bela and Morgan.

Sara Wellington said, "Yes, Morgan called me a little while ago. Losing her phone was the only thing that made sense for her not returning my calls. We had talked the day before I tried to reach her, so I guess she probably hadn't expected to hear from me again on Monday. I look forward to hearing about your lunch meeting with her tomorrow."

"Morgan seemed very confused about my being here to see how she was doing. She said she asked you about it but you didn't really explain. I'm afraid she sounded annoyed."

"She didn't really like the idea of me sending you over. I didn't tell her you were there to bring her home."

"I can understand that. Well, let's just see how our meeting tomorrow goes," Lynn said. They ended their conversation.

While eating dinner, Lynn realized she was more tired than hungry. She prepared for bed, read for thirty minutes or so, then went to bed and slept soundly. The alarm woke her at six-thirty. Lynn called the front desk and asked the temperature and learned that it was nine degrees Celsius. She did a mental conversion. *Forty-eight degrees Fahrenheit is good running weather.*

Lynn wasted no time getting into her jogging outfit. Running always got her days off to a good start. She put some emergency money, a copy of her passport, and her hotel key in her waist belt. Then she clipped on her cell phone and went out to the lobby where the hotel clerk helped her map out a two-mile course. Outside, daylight was just beginning to break. Traffic was sparse. Lynn breathed in the crisp fresh air while she stretched. From the corner she would run a few blocks east, then south. Then she would turn west and finally loop back to the hotel.

Checking her runner's compass, she started jogging. As she ran, she took in the sights. The downtown area looked historic and well-preserved. The structures appeared to be a mix of office buildings, apartment buildings, and restaurants, and many looked like they had been renovated. Lynn couldn't tell whether the style of the intricate architecture of the stone and marble facades was art nouveau, Gothic, or Renaissance. She decided they might be a combination of all those styles. Mature trees and automobiles lined both sides of the street. She saw no other runners and only a few pedestrians on the street.

Turning south, she came upon a scenic old church. Next to its neatly tended grounds, Lynn saw an expanse of freshly cut grass surrounded by a tall black wrought iron fence. She thought at first that it was a park. As she got closer, she could see it was a cemetery. Inside the iron fence, the park-like grounds were lined with huge trees. Life-size statues adorned many of the mausoleums and tombstones. Tree branches overhung the sidewalk, giving the area a look of enchantment. Lynn noted that some of the tombstones were covered with ivy. Some were slightly tilted. They looked very old, and, in fact, she noticed some headstones dating back to the nineteenth century.

The sun had not yet fully risen, and the early morning mist cast an eerie haze. The cool air smelled fresh and damp, but there were no dark clouds in the sky. Lynn jogged in place as she stopped to read the bronze plaque on the tall, ornate gate. The cemetery had been founded in 1847. She read that it was the most well-known cemetery in Budapest and that many famous Hungarians from the nineteenth and twentieth centuries were interred there. It was no longer open for new burials.

Startled by a rustling sound inside the gate, Lynn looked up and spotted an old man stooped over one of the nearby graves. A gray hat reminiscent of the old 1940s movies covered his long white hair. He was wearing a long gray wool cape and appeared to carry something in his hands. Was it a shovel? When the old man spotted Lynn, he stopped what he was doing and watched her with interest. Then he stood erect. When he did, Lynn noticed that he was still hunched over. It made her think of the Hunchback of Notre Dame. The old man said something and she jumped.

He may have only been speaking to her, but suddenly this whole scene, the cemetery, the haze, the caped man, was giving her the creeps. Realizing that she was beginning to let her imagination get the better of her, Lynn backed away from the cemetery entrance and started jogging again. When she looked back, the old man was no longer in sight.

Lynn turned east at the next corner and was glad to see the sun coming up. When she returned to her hotel, she asked the front desk clerk about the cemetery. He told her, "You got to see our historic burial ground. It happens to be a major tourist attraction. There are many notables, including statesmen, artists, and composers, buried there. Some of their remains are in huge, elaborate mausoleums you may not have seen from the street."

"I actually did see some very impressive-looking mausoleums. Who was the old man tending the graves?"

"Oh, that was Jacob. He has been the caretaker of the churchyard for over fifty years."

"My goodness," Lynn said. "Well, from what I could see, he does a good job."

"People say caring for that cemetery is his life. He lives on the grounds in the old caretaker house, alone—no family. Pretty eccentric, but harmless. Old Jacob is always out early, piddling about, and you're right, he does a wonderful job taking care of the grounds. It looks like a park. Sometimes he's out there as late as the bewitching hour, or *bűvös óra*. You are not the first person to ask about him. We think he gets a kick out of startling people."

Lynn returned to her room and smiled at the alarm she'd felt seeing the old man bending over the grave site. She showered and dressed, put her digital camera in her purse, and went down to the hotel restaurant and had breakfast. It was nine o'clock. With an hour to spare after eating, she decided to walk through the medieval ruins of St. Nicholas Dominican Monastery near the hotel. She walked around in the seven-hundred-year-old church admiring its finely tuned craftwork until it was time to go meet Morgan Wellington.

CHAPTER
11

Budapest, Hungary, November 21

LYNN ARRIVED AT THE PIERROT Café several minutes early. She took a table by a window with a view that also faced the front door and looked around, noting the trendy atmosphere of the restaurant. The dark hardwood floors, modern furniture, large hanging plants, bright lighting, and colorful paintings gave the place an artistic flavor. Soft music added to the ambience. The clientele were mainly young and casually dressed. They appeared to be a mixture of tourists and locals. Through a side window, Lynn could see a lovely garden area for outdoor dining in warmer weather.

She ordered a bottle of Naturaqua Mentes, which she sipped while waiting for Morgan to arrive. Just before twelve, she noticed a petite, dark-haired young woman crossing the street with purpose, coming toward the restaurant. She was wearing sunglasses, a tan leather jacket, brown slacks and boots, and a plaid beret. Lynn recognized Morgan Wellington at once from her pictures.

Morgan entered the café and began looking around. Lynn stood and waved her over. Morgan approached the table looking tentative. She removed her gloves to shake Lynn's hand. "Hello, I'm Morgan Wellington."

Lynn sensed the attitude. "Hello, Morgan. It's nice to meet you. You picked a good place for us to talk."

Morgan removed her glasses, looked around, and said, "It caters to the university crowd."

Lynn noticed that Morgan glanced nervously at two men standing by the bar. The men, who were average-looking, did not appear to be paying any attention to Morgan.

"Sorry, thought I recognized someone," Morgan said. "You said my parents sent you to see how I was doing?"

"Yes."

"To be honest, I really don't understand why they needed to send a private investigator all the way over here to see about me. I've told them over and over I am doing just fine. What exactly did they want you to investigate?"

Their waiter appeared and took their order. After he walked away, Lynn noticed Morgan looking at the two men, who were now leaving the restaurant.

"So, just what are you supposed to investigate here? Me?"

"Morgan, your mother and father are very concerned about you. So much so, they would have come over to see how you were doing for themselves had they been able to travel. They asked me to come instead. Apparently your dad can't take long flights."

"I know," Morgan interjected. "I was in Paris when he had his stroke. But I went back home to see him. I would have stayed home, but my parents are the ones who insisted I return to Paris to complete the program."

"But instead of going home when your program ended, you came here to Budapest."

"Yes, but I knew my father was expected to fully recover."

"So, what brought you here? I have to tell you this is the thing your folks don't understand."

Morgan's response was quick. "My roommate, Bela Hamza, is from here. She invited me. Didn't my mother tell you that?"

"Yes, she did. But she also wondered if there was another reason."

"What other reason could there be?" Morgan asked defensively. "I wanted to visit my friend. That's all." When she finished speaking, Lynn noticed that she began biting her fingernails, remaining defensive. Undoubtedly, she knew that whatever she said would be relayed to her parents. However, because her words seemed guarded, Lynn felt there was more that was left unsaid. She figured she probably wasn't going to find out more today; it was unlikely Morgan was ready to confide in a complete stranger. It was going to take some time to build trust.

When Lynn didn't comment, Morgan continued. "At first I was just going to stay a couple of weeks, but once I got here, I decided to stay longer. I registered at CEU for one semester; that's all. They have a good school of fashion design here. I like their program." Morgan shrugged.

"Your mother said that for years, you'd wanted to attend Rhode Island School of Design. Did you ever think about coming back to Budapest over the Christmas break instead? That way your program of study wouldn't have been interrupted."

"It's not exactly interrupted. In other words, I can transfer my credits back to Rhode Island. Honestly, it isn't as if I haven't explained all this to them before."

"Your parents don't understand how someone you met for the first time last summer was able to influence you to leave your classes in Rhode Island."

Morgan sighed. "Bela didn't influence me. She only invited me. I made the decision myself to register at CEU," she said, sounding irritated.

Their lunch arrived and they ate and talked, although Morgan barely ate. Lynn saw that she frequently touched a gold pendant hanging around her neck on a long gold chain. She seemed to rub it unconsciously. It appeared to be a nervous habit. That and her nail biting.

"Morgan, I believe your mother asked you about a family friend, Ms. Celia Coleman, who was in Budapest recently on business." Morgan acknowledged this. "You realize, this friend told your mother she saw you. But you told your mother you never saw Ms. Coleman, even though she stopped her car and called your name. Your parents are having a tough time with that. They don't believe Ms. Coleman would deliberately tell them something that wasn't true. But when you said you had not seen her, they wanted to believe you too."

Morgan fondled her pendant, looking upset. "Then they should believe *me*. I'm their daughter, after all. If I had seen Mrs. Coleman, I would definitely have spoken to her. I know her, and she knows me. But it wasn't me she saw. I was never out with a loud group of musicians."

"May I ask you this? Have you ever dressed in Goth attire?"

"What! No way," Morgan said, frowning. "Oh, brother. Why are you asking me that?"

"Well, because that's what your mother's friend thought she saw. She said you had a black fur hat covering your head."

Morgan sat up straight. "It's not true! I don't even own a fur hat. I have never dressed Goth. Ms. Coleman is definitely mistaken."

Morgan sounded convincing, and Lynn said, "Morgan, it's possible Ms. Coleman did make a mistake. But you can imagine how your mother felt when she heard about it—this is a person who's known you all your life." Frankly, Lynn couldn't understand it either. Was there someone here who looked so much like Morgan that a long-time family friend couldn't tell the difference? She supposed anything was possible.

Morgan was wondering if it was her long-lost look-alike who Ms. Coleman saw.

"Listen, I'm going to tell your mother about our meeting today. I'm sure she'll be pleased that we talked. I'll tell her that I believe Ms. Coleman made a mistake." Then Lynn decided it was time to tell Morgan the rest. "I need to let you know something else. Your parents want you to come home with me."

Morgan looked shocked. "What? They want me to come home? Now? Why? I can't just walk away from my classes. I really don't understand why they need me to come home now. I'm not a child, and I certainly don't need an escort to travel back home."

Lynn could tell that Morgan didn't like being told to come home, and she was definitely offended at the idea of having a chaperone. "After your mother heard from Ms. Coleman, both she and your father became very worried about you."

"I think they should have trusted me before hiring someone to come over here to spy on me."

"It's not spying. As an investigator, my job is to find out the truth. I'm here because your parents love you and are concerned about you. And when they were unable to reach you, they were feeling pretty helpless, as any parent would under the circumstances. Remember, your mom has been trying to reach you since Monday."

"Oh, I get it. If you can't reach your kid, call a private detective. Listen, I told my mother I lost my phone." Morgan looked at her watch and said, "If we're finished, I've got to get somewhere." She'd taken no more than a few nibbles of her food.

For Lynn, the brief lunch visit was only the beginning of the investigation. If she wanted to get to the truth, she would have to spend more time with Morgan. She told her, "I'm going to be here for a few days, and I would like to get together again. Can we schedule a time?" Lynn noticed Morgan didn't appear too eager to set up another conversation with her.

"Is there something more we need to talk about?"

"I want to get a better sense of why being here is so important to you and talk more about returning to Cincinnati."

Again Morgan sighed. "I explained that already. I don't know what else to tell you. What I've already said is basically it."

"Still, can we go ahead and set up a time?" Lynn asked.

"Well, I guess. Probably Saturday, but I can't say what time yet. I have classes tomorrow and a date tomorrow night. I'm meeting with Dr. Pálfi, one of my professors, on Saturday, but she hasn't given me a time yet. So Saturday might work, but I'll have to call you tomorrow to give you the exact time."

"That will be fine with me."

Lynn and Morgan walked out of the restaurant together. Lynn noticed that Morgan got into a car with a young man in the driver's seat. In the back window of the car was a guitar case.

* * *

"No way!" Fane Dobos had been watching the door to the restaurant when he saw their girl come out. But she was with that woman they saw at the girl's apartment last night. "Hey, boss. You'd better check this out."

Their car was parked in the parking area of an eyeglass store across the street from the restaurant. The inside of the car was filthy—it was where the two ate, drank, and sometimes slept. Pista had been slouched in the front seat, head down, hat pulled over his eyes. He jerked his head up and looked toward the door. "What the hell is *she* doing with our girl?"

"Who do you suppose she is?" Fane asked.

"How am I supposed to know who the hell she is?" Pista said. Then he checked her out. "But my hunches tell me she's trouble."

They watched as the girl got in the car with the same guy who dropped her off there thirty or forty minutes before. Pista started his car. "She's trying to move in on our territory. We're putting a stop to this right now."

The woman got in a limousine that then took off. Pista began following.

"I don't think we should waste our time chasing her. She looked harmless enough," Fane said. "We need to see where that guy is taking Sis."

"Obviously, I know what I'm doing. If you don't have anything intelligent to say, just shut the hell up!"

After a few blocks, Józséf said, "Miss, I don't want to alarm you, but I think we are being followed."

Lynn resisted the temptation to turn around and look. "Are you sure? Who is following us?"

"I'm afraid I don't know, but yes, I am sure. They have made every turn I've made and even changed lanes when I did. I can see two men in the car."

"Can you see their faces?" Lynn asked.

"No, their heads are covered, and hats are blocking their faces. I've noticed they are managing to keep a few cars back."

"Do you think you can make them pass us so you can see who they are?"

Józséf said, "I will try."

He slowed down enough so that the cars behind him began to pull around him. The car tailing them dropped back. "Looks like they're not going to go around. I think they realize that we've spotted them." He tried a few more maneuvers, but the two men stayed back. "Apparently they know we are on to them. They ducked around the first corner they came to. I think they're gone. But I wonder who they were."

"Do you know of anyone who would want to follow you?" Lynn asked.

"No, madam. Not at all."

Pista cursed up a storm. "They spotted us. Let's hold up for a bit and try to pick them back up in a few blocks." When he turned the corner and saw that the car was on a straightaway, they were able to double back. He spotted the limousine dropping the woman off at the university. The woman got out and walked toward the administration building, and the driver drove off.

After the men who were following them turned off, Lynn was puzzled. *Wonder why someone is after Joszéf? He sounded sincere when he said he had no idea who it was.* She certainly didn't need to get caught up in some local feud. Lynn wondered if she should use a regular taxi the next time she had to go somewhere, just in case he did have enemies.

When she got out of the limousine, she told Jozséf she would be in touch when she needed him again, and he left.

While walking across the campus toward the administration building, Lynn called Mrs. Wellington and told her about her meeting with Morgan. It was early morning in Cincinnati. "We just met for lunch. Your daughter seems to be doing fine," Lynn told her.

"Thank goodness. Did she look well?" Mrs. Wellington asked.

"She looked and sounded fine to me, but I will tell you that Morgan was adamant about not having seen Mrs. Coleman. I believed her."

"I hope you're right. Celia must have made a mistake."

"Also, I need to tell you that Morgan doesn't seem to have any desire or intention to come home before she completes her semester."

"I was hopeful she would be willing to return to Rhode Island. But I shouldn't forget Morgan can be very headstrong. Maybe you can talk to her again. She just might be more agreeable the next time."

"I already told her I would like for us to get together again. I didn't get the feeling Morgan told me everything. I expect there is more to learn. This was just our initial contact. We're going to meet again on Saturday, and I'll let you know what happens. I must tell you, however, that Morgan seemed none too pleased about my being here to check on her. I think it's going to take some work to get her to open up to me."

"I was afraid she might be disagreeable. Just stay on it. Please don't get discouraged. I believe she will come around," Sara Wellington said.

"Morgan's reaction was probably not unusual, given the situation. In the meantime, since you gave me a contact at CEU, I'll go over there and see what I can find out." Lynn had no idea what to even look for at CEU.

* * *

"Didn't mean to keep you waiting so long. That's why I was going to take the metro," Morgan told György. "It comes right by here."

"No problem. Since that thing at the coffee house, I'm not taking any chances with you being alone. Remember, when Bela can't take you, I'm your man. By the way, what was that all about?" he asked as they drove away from the restaurant.

"It's a long story, and I'm upset about it." Morgan's parents wanting her to come home really bothered her. And she didn't appreciate that woman's soft pressuring her to think about it. There was no way she was leaving here. She said, "My parents sent someone over here to see how I was doing. They're concerned about me and want me to come home."

"You're joking, right? What brought that on?"

"One of my mother's friends was here in Budapest, and she told my mother she spotted me out with a group of Goths. Her description of what she saw disturbed them."

"Heck, you're no Goth. What was she talking about?" György asked.

"I know exactly who Mom's friend saw. It was my look-alike girl. You remember, you told me she used to dress in all black. The sick thing is it seems like everyone has seen her but me."

"We're going to find her one day. I know we are. Did you tell that woman about your look-alike?"

"No. I still haven't even mentioned her to my parents. I've never wanted to tell them that's why I really came here. And I wasn't about to tell a stranger who would only run back and tell them anyway. I'm just mad that they don't trust me enough to make good decisions. I don't like being checked on as if I'm a baby or something!"

"I wouldn't get too down on my parents if I were you," György said. "My folks and I have gotten much closer since we left the United States because we spend so much more time together than before. They trust me now, but before that, I was pretty rebellious."

"What changed?"

"We started talking more. The more we talked, the more I understood them and they understood me. Have you thought about telling your folks about the girl?"

"Nope. How could they understand about me coming to Budapest searching for a look-alike? Anyway, I'll just be here a few more weeks. If I don't find her by then, I'll put it all behind me."

György studied Morgan for a long moment and said, "Are you sure you could do that, Morg?"

* * *

Morgan couldn't wait to call her mother. She was still disturbed about meeting with that private detective. She placed the call the minute she got back to her apartment that afternoon.

When Sara Wellington answered, Morgan said, "Mother, you'll be happy to know I met with your private investigator today."

"Morgan?" her mother said, hearing her daughter's curt tone. Lynn Davis had said Morgan seemed perturbed by their meeting. "I was planning to call you to see how things went today, but you sound upset," Sara Wellington said.

"Well, things didn't go well, if you want to know the truth. I feel rotten. I can't believe you and Dad thought I needed to be investigated. What did you expect her to find?"

"Honey, it's not that we expected her to find anything besides a reasonable explanation."

"An explanation for what? What have I done that's so wrong?"

"Dear, no one said you did anything wrong. Your going there is certainly curious, though. You have to understand that we were worried about you."

"But why? I'm not the only girl who's traveled to a foreign country before. All I'm doing over here is going to school and hanging out with my friends. Why is that so worrisome?" Morgan knew that she was not telling her mother the whole story. That didn't feel very good, but she thought they should have trusted her anyway. After all, she was only trying to protect them from knowing the real reason she was there.

"We did not expect you to suddenly enroll in a university in a foreign country after your first year of college. Your father and I never knew what to think. And then when Celia said she saw you ..."

"But, Mom, I told you before—it was not me she saw. This is so unfair. Ms. Coleman needs to buy herself some new glasses. She never saw me, and I never saw her. And I have never dressed Goth. I can't believe that's why you sent that woman over here."

"Granted, Celia might have made a mistake, but that was not the only reason," Sara Wellington said, distressed by the conversation.

"Then what was the other reason?"

"Your decision to go to Budapest was one thing, although it did seem rather abrupt. Your father and I feel that you haven't been very open with us. In fact, if there is something you've not told us, now would be a good time, because your actions have been difficult to understand."

Morgan didn't know what to say. She *had* been withholding something very important from her parents. Her being here was all about finding someone she hoped might hold the key to her true heritage. How could she tell her mother that? She mumbled something and managed to find a way to quickly end the call. When she hung up, she felt terrible about her emotional outburst because she knew full well her mother was right.

CHAPTER
12

Cincinnati, Ohio

AFTER DINNER, FLOSSIE RETURNED TO her room, thinking about her conversation with her friends Agnes and Beulah. Agnes's oldest daughter had the flu and wouldn't be able to pick her up this week. Her friend was very disappointed. She had so been looking forward to spending Thanksgiving with the family.

"You girls are both lucky to have family. My Ben died when he was fifty-four, and I never had any children. So my sisters were about the only family I had. Their children live in other states. Both of my sisters passed away, and I've been the only one left for the past ten years," Beulah told them. "Thank goodness I've got you two."

Flossie began thinking about her own family. It used to be pretty large, and they had family reunions every year. Now they were spread out all over the country, and they didn't have reunions anymore. Flossie thought about the day when she was just a child that she and Mossie learned about their special connection as twins. Twin telepathy, their father had called it. It was only as they got older that the twins came to appreciate what she meant. Aunt Bea first told them about it during the family reunion back in July 1935.

"You girls, hurry up now. Aunt Beatrice is getting ready to tell her story," Gertha Walker told her daughters as they scurried along to the meeting hall. The Walker family reunion, held every year in North Carolina, was in full swing. They'd had a fish fry that Friday night, and now, after a typical family reunion Saturday morning breakfast of scrambled eggs, bacon, sausage, cheese grits, biscuits, and pancakes, they were all headed to meet with the oldest member in attendance, ninety-two-year-old Beatrice Johnson, Flossie and Mossie's great-great aunt.

"Can't we just stay outside and play, Momma? We heard that silly old slave story before," eight-year-old Flossie declared. She thought slavery was make-believe, since no one could actually own real live people. "I know I sure wouldn't be anybody's slave."

"Now you shush your mouth," her mother admonished. "You don't know what you would be. Besides, if it weren't for the slaves, none of us would be here today."

"But slavery's wrong. Why didn't our ancestors just fight back?" Mossie asked.

"Honey, they not only fought, but many of them died trying to be free. I want you girls to appreciate your history and stop turning up your nose at it. And there's no better way to learn than from someone who lived through it," Mrs. Walker said.

"Yes, ma'am," Flossie replied.

"Yes, ma'am," Mossie repeated.

Beatrice Johnson's skin was black as coal and smooth like silk. Her hair, which she wore in a short Afro, was as white as snow. She had fierce dark eyes that could peer right through you, and few ever saw her smile. Aunt Bea's demeanor was stern. Still, everyone flocked around her. Whenever she stared at the twins, it frightened them. She always looked angry and spoke gruffly.

"But why's she so mad all the time?" Flossie asked.

"Now listen, little girl, stop being so contrary. And you too, Mossie. Aunt Bea's not mad; that's just her facial expression. Besides, she's been through an awful lot in her lifetime. Now you all come on in here and listen, and be on your best behavior." Flossie and Mossie just looked resignedly at each other and marched into the meeting hall, where fifty or so family members had already gathered. They spotted their ten-year-old cousin Scotty sitting by himself.

"Pssst, Scotty," Mossie whispered. "Come sit over here with us."

Scotty came over. "What's up?" he asked the girls.

"We don't want to hear that stupid old slave story again. We already heard it last time," Flossie whispered.

"It's not stupid. Maybe you all just don't understand what it was all about," he replied. "Slavery was a very bad time in our history. My daddy told me our ancestors were on the very first ships that came to America."

The girls looked wide-eyed. "They were?" they both exclaimed in surprise. "We thought they didn't get here until much later," Flossie said.

"A lot of them did. And a whole lot, like millions of them, died on the ships before they even got here. Many of them died of starvation. Some even jumped overboard to avoid being enslaved. After awhile, the evil slave traders started chaining them up during the entire trip from Africa. That had to be pretty horrible since they had to eat, sleep, and everything else chained up like that. These trips were called the Middle Passage. You should read about it."

"And once they got here, it was real bad too. My momma said Aunt Bea told them that when she was thirteen, she got beat with a whip because while she was babysitting the slaveowner's baby, the baby started crying."

The girls looked shocked and horrified. "But why? It wasn't her fault. That's real mean."

"That's just the way it was back then," Scotty said. "The slaves even got beat if they were caught trying to learn how to read."

"Ooh wee, that is so horrible. I'm glad there aren't really any slaves anymore," Mossie said. Flossie agreed.

Scottie continued, "But did you all know that slaves made hundreds of inventions, like the vacuum cleaner and the lawn mower? My dad said they even made a machine that could dry your clothes. And did you know a Negro invented the elevator right after slavery ended?"

"No. Wonder why we never learned about that in school," the twins exclaimed, wide-eyed. They continued to be all ears as Scotty rendered his history lesson. The twins were in such awe, they were suddenly very interested in hearing what their aunt had to say. Just then, their father escorted Aunt Bea into the room. He had one arm through hers, her huge frame leaning forward, supported by a staff held in her other hand. Seeming larger than life, she took a seat.

Dr. Walker introduced his great aunt to the ninety or so who had arrived by then. "Few Americans today are fortunate enough to ever be in the presence of someone who actually experienced slavery. We are lucky that Aunt

Bea is still here with us. I hope you all listen and learn as much as you can from her, for unless we know our history, we are doomed to repeat it."

Aunt Bea then told her family the fascinating story of her early years in the days of slavery.

She told about being born in Galveston, Texas, several years before President Lincoln signed the Emancipation Proclamation; thus, she'd lived the first twenty or so years of her life in slavery. Although she worked hard picking cotton, she said that once in a while as a child she got to have fun with the other kids while the grownups did the work. "Our family worked from sunup to sundown and our clothes were threadbare, but my momma and daddy used to say everything was gonna be all right one day. And they were so right."

Although they'd heard it many times before, many members of the family were especially intrigued by the part about when slavery came to an end in Texas. "The first day of January, eighteen hundred and sixty-three, was just another day to us. Us Texans didn't have no idea that slavery was over, so we went on with our lives as slaves for another two and a half years. Then one day, on the nineteenth day of June in the year of Our Lord eighteen and sixty-five, we got the word," she said. "Union soldiers came marchin' into the city, bringing news that we was free. This was real important. Freedom was what we'd dreamed about and prayed for." Aunt Bea smiled when she added, "And my, oh my, how we all celebrated. We danced and sang and got happy." Aunt Bea smiled! Flossie, Mossie, and other family members looked at one another in awe. They'd just witnessed a rare sight.

"June 19 was a blessed day. Juneteenth, they call it these days. It was all over. Ya'll don't know how thankful we were. Master Johnson gave our daddy two acres of land in payment for the extra time our family was enslaved. Wasn't much, but we was free. We could live." The family sat spellbound, hearing Aunt Bea's description of life during those times. Then Aunt Beatrice raised her hand in praise and looked up to the heavens at the wonder of the Lord. Everyone applauded her story and *Amens* were shouted. Someone started humming "Go Down Moses." Family members picked up the chorus: *Way down in Egypt land, Tell old Pharoah, Let my people go.* Flossie and Mossie knew that song and they sang along too, proud to now know more about their family heritage.

When the session ended, Flossie and Mossie got scared when Aunt Bea pointed to them and told them to stay while the others were leaving. They wondered if they were in trouble for talking about the slaves before. *Did someone tell her what we said?* They wished their mother would wait, but she told them she had to go to the kitchen and help prepare lunch.

"Yes, ma'am," Flossie and Mossie both said, sitting on their knees on the floor in front of Aunt Bea with their hands resting on their thighs, their fingers laced. *What does Aunt Bea want?*

Aunt Beatrice looked directly into the eyes of one twin and then the other. Then she looked again. "I look into ya'll's eyes and I see deep into your soul. I see that you two are of *one mind.* I seen it in you last year. Got that special thing b'tween identical twins." The girls looked perplexed.

Their aunt explained what *one mind* meant. "You know what the other one's thinking; you know when she's in trouble, and when she's happy. You have dreams about things you never experienced. These just might be your sister's dreams. When one of you hurts, the other will hurt too. When one of you has a question, the other one will probably have the answer. You're both responsible for what the other one experiences, so you owe it to each other to be good to yourselves."

The twins understood some of what she was saying, but they didn't know how that could be. They asked if other twins had this special thing. Aunt Bea said not all of them did. "Out of thirteen kids, my momma had two sets of twins. Me and Leatrice, and Joseph and Jonathan. Now me and Lea, we had it, so I know what I'm talking 'bout." Flossie hadn't known Aunt Bea had a twin. She wondered where her twin sister was just as their aunt said, "The good Lord called Leatrice home twenty-two years ago. I still miss that girl, but she's with me at all times. Still speaks to me to this day. Steers me in the right direction. That's the thing about having this one mind.

"Now my brothers, they was close, you know, but not like me and Leatrice. You two won't ever be separated—not even when death calls. One day you'll understand what I'm telling you. What ya'll got is a mighty precious gift." Then Aunt Bea fanned herself, wiped her forehead with a handkerchief, and said, "Now y'all run along. Tell ya' daddy to come back and get me so he can take me to the lunch room."

"Yes, ma'am," they both chimed.

A few years later, when Aunt Beatrice died at the age of 102, her picture was featured in *Jet Magazine* as having been the oldest living former slave in the country. Everyone in the family got copies of *Jet* and framed the little picture of Aunt Beatrice Wilomena Johnson. Her father's copy of that framed picture still sat today on the console in Miss Walker's sitting area, flanked by pictures of her and Mossie, her brother Hampton, and their parents.

Back when Aunt Bea had first told them about this gift they shared, the girls really hadn't understood what she was talking about. They asked their father, and he told them that sometimes twins could communicate with each other telepathically. "Telepathically?" they questioned.

"That's when you can speak to each other without words. You speak through your thoughts. And you don't have to be together when it happens. Your aunt Beatrice is right. Your mother and I always realized you girls had that special quality. You're very fortunate."

Flossie had felt extremely fortunate to have had such a relationship with her beloved Mossie. Like Aunt Bea had observed and their father explained, they shared many telepathic experiences, including, as Aunt Bea had said they would, each other's dreams. Furthermore, when one of them was sad, the other felt it too; when one was happy, the other was ecstatic. What they never understood was how they would not be separated by death. Did it mean they would both pass away at the same time? It took until the first birthday after Mossie died that Flossie finally understood. Those yearly visits with her sister on their birthday got her through life, and she treasured them with all her heart.

Everyone needs family. Thinking about her own made Flossie pull out her old photo albums. She made herself some sassafras tea and pored over her old photos. The memories contained in the albums were precious and dear to her. She found herself studying a photograph of her and her sister's nursing school graduating class. It so happened, they were the only black women in their class. The sixteen women graduates wore identical white nursing outfits, complete with little securely pinned white caps on their heads. An emblem of Bethesda Medical Hospital was proudly displayed on each uniform.

Flossie studied the picture, remembering that when the photograph was taken, her sister had been trying to decide whether or not to accept a plum job in a Chicago hospital. Flossie didn't want her to leave, but she didn't have to try to convince her not to because she knew Mossie would turn that job down. Flossie always knew when Mossie was going through something, even when she wasn't around. It had happened many times in their lives. Like when Mossie was pregnant. She knew her sister was expecting a baby before Mossie knew it herself. Flossie herself had been experiencing morning sickness for no apparent reason. And the smell of certain commonplace fragrances suddenly made her nauseous.

Twin telepathy. What about the Wellington girl and the Moldovan girl? She had often wondered if those twins she'd separated nineteen years ago also had *the gift*. Because if they did, she knew in her bones that neither of them would ever be complete until they connected with each other. No sooner had the girls crossed Flossie's mind when the nagging sense of dread and danger encompassed her all over again. She could only pray that they were all right.

CHAPTER
13

Budapest, Hungary

WHEN LYNN ARRIVED ON THE campus of Central European University, she stepped out of her limo and looked around. The campus had the typical feel of academia; a sense of learnedness and critical thinking filled the air. Students were walking in every direction. Others milled about in the square.

Lynn spotted the administration building and went inside; she checked the directory for the Office of the Registrar. She followed the signs to the office. "Good afternoon," the receptionist said. The name plate on her desk said Anastasia Simón. In well-spoken English, she asked, "How may I help you?"

"Good afternoon. My name is Lynn Davis," Lynn said, handing the receptionist a business card. "I would like to verify the registration of one of your students."

The young woman eyed Lynn with interest. "May I see your university ID, please."

Lynn explained that she was not affiliated with the university.

"Then I am sorry, madam. Our records are only available to people affiliated with the university. If you would like to fill out a request form, our registrar will review it. Unfortunately, she is out of the office until next Wednesday."

Lynn hoped to be back in the States by next Wednesday. She told the young lady, "I'm in Budapest on a business matter and need to get information for a client in the United States." She pulled a piece of paper out of her briefcase and said, "I believe this form allows me to have access to the records. Is it possible to speak with Ms. Kalka Lenzyel of student records?"

"Miss Lenzyel?" Miss Simón said in surprise as she took the consent form from Lynn and looked it over. "Why, she *is* our registrar. And as I said, she is out until next Wednesday. But you are correct. She has already authorized you to have access to the records." She smiled at Lynn and said, "Give me the name you wish to verify. I will pull up the information for you."

Lynn gave her Morgan's name and year. Ms. Simón pointed to a seat at a small computer desk and said. "You may sit here while I look this up for you." Lynn took a seat. "This should take only a few minutes." Miss Simón said as she began searching for Morgan Wellington's records. After searching the records of all the sophomores with last names beginning with *W*, she was surprised that she did not find Morgan's name among the list of regular full-time students. "Could she possibly be listed under another name?" she asked. Lynn answered no. Miss Simón looked at her watch and turned back to the computer. She searched the *W*s again to no avail. Then she scrolled through the *W*s one by one. "Unfortunately, her record has probably been misfiled. I do not know how I would locate it without searching through every record."

"Why don't you check the first-year student files?" Lynn asked.

Anastasia Simón was happy to oblige. But again, she didn't find Morgan Wellington's name. Lynn asked if she would mind checking the records for the junior and senior students. Ms. Simón's telephone rang. She looked at her caller ID and said, "Please excuse me. I must take this call." When she finished her call, she told Lynn. "I am sorry. I have to pick up my daughter; that was her sitter. I must leave now. Our office closes in thirty minutes. Could you possibly come back tomorrow?"

"Unfortunately, I have plans for tomorrow. Is there someone else who can help me?"

Ms. Simón looked toward the back corner where another woman was working, and said, "Ursola is here. She's new, but I believe she may be able to find the record for you." She called Ursola up to the desk and spoke to her in Hungarian. She showed her Lynn Davis's authorization and handed her Morgan Wellington's name to look up. Then she left the office. Ursola looked at Lynn and smiled and sat down to do what was asked of her. After looking through the records she'd been told to search, she turned to Lynn Davis and shook her head. In tentative English, she indicated that she could not locate the file.

Lynn tried to ask Ursola to do what she had asked of Ms. Simón—to search the entire file for each year. Ursola only shrugged and shook her head, not understanding. Lynn reached over to take the mouse so she could show her what she meant. Ursola didn't understand. Then, as if she just had a brainstorm, she made a gesture Lynn took as an offer for her to conduct her own search. When she stepped forward, Ursola smiled and stood, offering her seat to Lynn. Then she took Ms. Simón's place behind the receptionist's desk.

This will be easier. Lynn had no reason to believe Morgan was not enrolled here. Morgan's parents had obviously checked on this already. Still, Lynn wondered if there was something else to be learned on campus. She suddenly remembered that Morgan was only registered for one semester, so there was a chance she might be found under a different classification. Lynn searched a few odd categories, including one labeled REGULAR PART-TIME, and there she was, Morgan Alana Wellington.

Lynn copied Morgan's registration page onto her flash drive. It included her photo. Since Ursola had given her the computer and it was still a few minutes before the office closed, she decided to see what else she might find; all she had done so far was verify something that was already known. She felt it was possible that somewhere on this campus, something might explain Morgan's strong attachment to Budapest.

Lynn closed the student enrollment files and decided to look at the professors. At Yale, she'd had one professor in particular who'd mentored her, and she wondered if possibly Morgan had one such professor, possibly someone who had participated in her summer program in Paris. Morgan had mentioned having a meeting with a professor, P-something. She began scanning the *P*s. As she reviewed credentials, she noted that the school had an impressive professorial staff. Photographs were included with each record, and Lynn glanced at the names and faces as she scanned each name, one by one.

All at once, Lynn released the mouse and froze. She stared at the computer screen and could not believe her eyes. Lynn was captivated by a photograph of a professor named Dr. N. René Palaki. She was shocked that this professor had the face of none other than ... Morgan Wellington! Indeed, Dr. Palaki and Morgan Wellington looked like they could be sisters. Lynn proceeded to read her biography. The holder of several degrees, Dr. Palaki had studied at CEU, obtaining an undergraduate degree in microbiology and a PhD in physics. According to her records, she was well-published and tenured. Her hobbies included reading and conducting scientific studies. Family: mother and a daughter. Dr. Palaki was not presently married.

Lynn drew in her breath. How was it that she was looking at the same face she had just seen earlier that day on Morgan? Sure, people sometimes look alike, but this particular likeness was uncanny. The two women had the same features: eyes, mouth, hair and skin coloring. Everything about them looked the same. This was incredible. She copied Dr. Palaki's photo and bio onto her flash drive.

Lynn remembered that Morgan's biological mother was not from the United States but from Bucharest, Romania. Could this woman possibly be Morgan's mother? Morgan was nineteen; her mother would only be thirty-four or thirty-five. Professor Palaki looked like she could be about that age, though Lynn really couldn't tell from the photograph.

Rachel Davis, Lynn's mother, always said, "There are no coincidences." If this was Morgan's mother, she wondered if Morgan knew about her. Had she seen her? Was she the real reason Morgan was here? Dr. Stern had said that as a child, Morgan got very upset when the topic of family came up. Had the two met? Of course, with her major being fashion design and Dr. Palaki being a microbiologist, their paths were probably not likely to cross. The two disciplines would be in different buildings. They might even be on different campuses.

When Lynn got back to her room, she called Ella to run it by her. She told her about finding a professor who looked enough like Morgan to be her biological mother. "If not her mother, they definitely look related in some way."

"That's interesting, Lynn," Ella said. "I guess you've already figured that if this is Morgan's mother, and if Morgan knows about her, it could explain why she doesn't want her parents to know why she's in Budapest or why she's not ready to return home right now."

"You're right. I want you to take a look at these pictures, Ella. See what you think. You should receive my e-mail in a few minutes. I sent you pictures of both of them."

Minutes later, Ella called back. "Lynn, in my opinion, there's no question about it. When I saw the pictures, like you, I was pretty convinced. I believe these two are related. My guess, too, would be mother and daughter."

"Thanks, Ella. I need to call Sara Wellington," Lynn said.

Ella replied, "I bet she won't be expecting anything like this."

"I'm sure you're right. Morgan is calling me tomorrow evening so we can arrange to meet again. I know there has to be more behind all this. I hope I can find out what it is. Check you later."

"Sure you will."

Lynn called Mrs. Wellington, who listened intently as Lynn told about her visit to CEU. Hearing Lynn confirm Morgan's registration gave her some reassurance. Then Lynn told her about the file on a Dr. N. René Palaki. "It was startling to look at her picture after just meeting

Morgan earlier today. Does that name mean anything to you?"

Mrs. Wellington said it did not. Still, Lynn heard the uneasiness in Mrs. Wellington's voice. Lynn continued. "These two people look so much alike, I couldn't help but wonder if they are related. I thought they could even be mother and daughter." Lynn could hear Mrs. Wellington take a deep breath. She continued. "If there is a connection, I was wondering if that is why Morgan's in Budapest."

"I think not. Morgan knows nothing of her biological mother's whereabouts. I can't believe she is there searching for her." Sara Wellington continued. "Morgan has never talked about her mother. I would be pretty surprised if she were there searching for her. She's never even seemed the least bit curious about her background. Besides, Morgan's birth mother's name was Nicola Moldovan. I don't know anyone named Palaki. None of this adds up for me."

"Mrs. Wellington, I'm going to e-mail the woman's picture to you. Her background information will be included."

"Yes, of course," Sara Wellington replied.

After hanging up, Lynn looked over her notes and waited to hear back from Sara Wellington. She was glad she had reconsidered sending the e-mail before speaking with Mrs. Wellington. The conversation seemed to have upset her. If this was indeed Morgan's biological mother, at least she'd prepared Mrs. Wellington in advance. While Lynn waited, she realized this could be a more complex case than either she or her client had first thought.

* * *

Sara Wellington waited at her desk for the e-mail message from Lynn Davis. Suddenly, the message arrived.

Sara gave a start. She had not realized how anxious she was. Fumbling at the keyboard, she opened the message. It read, "Here is the photograph of Dr. N. René Palaki." In a moment, the picture filled the screen.

Sara Wellington could not react immediately. Her gaze was fixed on the deep, dark eyes that stared back at her. Those were Morgan's eyes. As Lynn Davis had said, this face was, indeed, a replica of her daughter's. She was staring at the face of Nicola Moldovan. Dr. N. René Palaki was Corina Moldovan's daughter and Morgan's biological mother, whom Sara hadn't seen in nearly twenty years. The teenager she remembered was now a grown woman with features she recognized: long dark hair; deep, luminous eyes; thick eyelashes; full lips; rich complexion. With a jolt, Sara suddenly thought of something she had long forgotten. Nicola's middle name was René. She pictured the innocent face of the fifteen-year-old girl she once knew. This was that girl. She printed the picture. Sara was beginning to feel sick.

She had been so insistent that Lynn Davis was on the wrong track, she was not prepared for this. Now seeing the name Palaki, Sara Wellington assumed Nicola had gotten married. Reading the biographical information, she learned of Nicola's many accomplishments. Horace had always spoken well of the bright young girl who had such a passion for science. He had encouraged her to pursue the field. Sara herself had often wondered if Nicola had stayed in the scientific field, and she was impressed to see that she had not only continued in the field but had earned a doctorate in it as well. She noted that Nicola was now a full professor as well as a research scientist and that she was published in several international trade journals.

After thoroughly reviewing the file, Sara Wellington was hit with hard questions: Did Morgan know that her biological mother was at the same university? If so, how could she have known? Had the two met? What about the other child Nicola mentioned in her bio? Morgan's sibling. Was the person Celia Coleman had seen possibly a sibling? What about Morgan's grandmother, Corina? Sara considered phoning Morgan to ask her these things but decided against it.

Instead, she took the picture to her husband.

"What's this?" he asked.

"Horace, do you recognize this woman?"

Horace Wellington reached for the picture. He studied it for a few seconds and then said, "She looks an awfully lot like Morgan, doesn't she? In fact, this looks just like our former housekeeper's young daughter." His eyes lit up, and he said, "Nicola. Nicola Moldovan, the young scientist. Yes, her mother sometimes called her Nicola René. I see she got married. I've often wondered what ever happened to her." Sara remained silent. Her husband said, "Where on earth did you get this picture?"

"Lynn Davis found it while looking through records on the campus of Central European University. When she was going through CEU records and saw this picture, she found the resemblance striking, so she e-mailed it to me."

"Nicola is at CEU in Budapest?" he asked in surprise.

"Yes. She is a professor and a researcher there."

"And that is where our daughter is attending school this semester," he said pensively.

"Yes.

"Dear, do you suppose this is the real reason Morgan went to Budapest?" Dr. Wellington asked.

"I don't know. Lynn and Morgan met this morning for the first time. Lynn said Morgan never said anything about meeting Nicola or even knowing that her mother was in the same city, let alone at the same school. But I have to wonder. That would certainly answer a lot of questions. But it would also be terribly hurtful."

"I understand this would be shocking to you, because it certainly surprises me. But I wouldn't get too alarmed about it just yet. She's probably just been waiting for the right time to tell us about her. That is if they've even met each other."

"I have to call Lynn Davis back. She asked if there was a relationship."

"What will you have her do?"

"I don't think we want her to mention this to Morgan yet. I want her to keep trying to find out whatever else she can."

Dr. Wellington asked his wife, "Are you concerned that Morgan might want to stay in Budapest?"

"As a matter of fact, that has crossed my mind, Horace. I only wish she would tell us what she's really doing over there so we wouldn't have to guess. We've always been open with her about everything. Tell me why she cannot do the same."

"Dear, she's young. Still a teenager. It takes a lot more for them to open up. We just have to believe that we have laid a good foundation for her and that she will do the right thing."

"You have more confidence than I do at this point. This whole thing frazzles me. Sometimes I feel like I've been a complete failure as a mother." Her husband assured her she had been a wonderful mother.

Sara walked toward the door and turned around. She said, "From the biography Lynn Davis sent, Morgan and Nicola are in two completely different fields. I suppose it's possible their paths may not yet have crossed."

Lynn's phone rang, When she answered, as she expected it was Mrs. Wellington calling to tell her it was, indeed, Nicola Moldovan, Morgan's biological mother.

"And on the chance that Morgan does not know about her, I would like you not to mention it. You have already discovered much more than we ever expected. Let me know if you learn anything else. Horace and I need to discuss this."

"I understand. Morgan and I are going to speak again very soon. She's to call and let me know when we can get together again. I have to say, at my first meeting with Morgan it did not seem that she was withholding anything as significant as this."

"Thank you. I hope Morgan will be more open with you the next time you talk. Please let me know what she says as soon as you speak with her again."

When she and Lynn finished talking, Sara Wellington stared straight ahead, holding the receiver in her hand. It took a few seconds before she realized she had not hung up the telephone. In that few seconds, one question continued to crop up: Out of all the cities in the world, how could Morgan end up in the same city and at the same university as her real mother?

CHAPTER
14

Budapest, Hungary

AFTER ENDING HER CALL WITH Sara Wellington, Lynn decided to get something to eat at a nearby Hungarian restaurant that had been highly recommended by the concierge. The restaurant was on the opposite side of the street, a few doors up. She entered to find it practically empty. Lynn remembered that in Budapest, as in many places in Europe, people usually ate dinner much later. As time went on and patrons began to fill the place, she found herself people-watching and occasionally eavesdropping on conversations that were taking place in English.

She listened in on one entire conversation at a nearby table of four. Two couples were discussing the upcoming New Year's Eve, or, as Lynn learned, *Szilveszter* in Hungarian. It was a little more than a month away. Within minutes, she'd learned that many Hungarian customs and traditions dealt with bringing luck, fortune, health, wealth, and happiness in the coming year.

She also learned the importance of not leaving anything to fate but preparing a lucky meal to increase one's chances of having a good year. Eating pork on New Year's Day brought good luck, while lentils brought wealth. Lynn compared that tradition to the United States, where many prepared black-eyed peas for good luck. Lynn also learned that Hungarians avoided eating chicken and fish on New Year's Day. She found it interesting to hear about the traditional fireworks that heralded in the New Year, scaring off demons and evil spirits.

Before long, Lynn noticed two men come into the restaurant and take seats across the room. One was a burly guy with a thick black mustache. His oily black hair was pulled back in a ponytail. While the men drank their sodas, Lynn noticed that the muscular one kept staring at her. He had a rather menacing expression on his face. She could not figure why he was studying her so intently and thought perhaps he hadn't seen many African Americans. Lynn noticed that on the back of his hairy hand was some kind of dark-colored tattoo. After awhile, the men got up from their table and left the restaurant.

The waiter recommended *fogas*, a white fish from the waters of the Danube River. Lynn found it quite tasty and enjoyed her Hungarian meal. After eating she left the restaurant. The street was well lit, and she began walking briskly toward her hotel. Although there was not much traffic and the streets were quiet, she felt somewhat strange, as if eyes were trained on her. She casually glanced in all directions, but all she saw was an old man coming toward her. From his silhouette, she could see that he was wearing a hat and a cape. Old Jacob from the cemetery! No wonder she was feeling leery. Just up the street, someone started a car; it began inching its way down the street toward her. Lynn decided that rather than to have a face-to-face encounter with old Jacob, she would cross the street.

She had no more than stepped off the curb into the street when the driver of the slow-moving car accelerated and drove toward her from behind. Already in a mode of heightened awareness due to her feeling of being watched, Lynn was instantly aware of the approaching car. She turned and jumped up on the curb just in time to keep from getting smashed. The momentum from her fast evasion sent her to the ground. She immediately rolled across the sidewalk toward the building; then she saw someone stooped over her. The man grabbed her arm to help her up. She accepted his hand and turned to thank her helper. It was old Jacob!

As the car sped away, he asked in a deeply accented, raspy voice, "Are you all right, madam?"

"Yes, thank you. I don't know where that car came from," Lynn answered.

"Well, I do. It was parked just up there," he said, pointing up the street. "And when you started walking down the street, I saw it pull away from the curb. It looked suspicious because its lights were not on. Then the driver sped up and drove right at you."

"My goodness, you're saying this was deliberate?" Lynn asked in alarm.

"I certainly think so. At least it sure looked that way. You're lucky you weren't hurt."

A couple of people had come out of the restaurant just after Lynn left, and they stood at the door watching what happened. The lady spoke up. "I saw the whole thing, miss. The way that driver swerved toward you, it looked like he was trying to hit you on purpose."

"I'm calling the police," Lynn said.

"When I saw what was happening," the lady said, "I called them. They're on their way."

Shortly, the police arrived and took a report. The woman said, "I didn't get the license plates, but I could see that it was an old, dark-colored car. It looked pretty beat up. I saw two men in the car. After you fell, they sped away down the street."

Old Jacob also reported what he'd seen. The police asked if Lynn wanted to go to the hospital, and she declined. When they left, old Jacob told Lynn, "I recognized you from jogging past the cemetery yesterday morning. I am Jacob Danko. I tried to say something to you, but I don't think you heard me. I didn't mean to alarm you."

"I'm pleased to meet you. I'm Lynn Davis. And you're right. I'm afraid I didn't hear what you said."

"I said, 'Don't get lost,'" he chuckled. "I hadn't seen you run by the cemetery before."

Lynn had noticed that Jacob was saying something to her yesterday, and she now felt badly for thinking the worst. "I appreciate your concern," she said.

"You've got to be careful. You don't know if this was a random act, or if those lunatics were really after you. So I don't think I would go out by myself again, if I were you."

"You're very kind, sir," Lynn said and she turned to head to her hotel.

"I will walk with you," old Jacob said. He crossed the street with Lynn, walking surprisingly briskly.

"I appreciate your kindness. Thank you," she told him.

Once she was safely back in her room, Lynn had a chance to assess the damage. She examined herself and saw only dirt scuffs on her suit and coat. Her upper arm was sore where she'd fallen on it, but thank goodness it wasn't broken. She thought about what had just happened. It seemed pretty obvious that it had been a deliberate attempt on her life. But she didn't have a clue who might want to hurt her. Did someone know that she was here to see Morgan Wellington and wanted to prevent her from taking Morgan back to the States? If that were the case, who would be trying to stop her from accomplishing that? Morgan's boyfriend? Beyond that line of reasoning, Lynn was stumped.

She thought about old Jacob and felt bad for how she had misjudged him. He still looked rather creepy, but he had been very helpful and considerate. Plus, he was pretty agile on his feet; from where he was, he'd had to have moved pretty quickly to reach her as fast as he had. Finally, Lynn pictured the two men who had come into the restaurant and had kept her in their line of sight. Especially that dark-haired one with the mean look on his face. But they didn't know her, and she certainly didn't know them. Who were they?

Lynn called Harvey back in Cincinnati. When she told him what had happened, he was stunned and upset.

"Look, Lynn," he said, "I don't know what's going on over there, but you've just been there a couple of days and already someone has tried to run you down. There may be a connection between that incident and what you're doing there. Because if whoever it was wanted money, they'd have probably just tried to mug you and run. But to try to hit you—damn! As much as I don't want to say this, someone might be after you."

As much as Lynn didn't want to agree with Harvey, she did. "I've got to try to figure this out, Harv."

"Do you want me to fly over there?" he asked.

"Oh, no. I don't think it's come to that. I have a driver who takes me everywhere and—"

"And tonight, he took you to dinner, I suppose?"

"No, but the restaurant was just a few buildings up the street. The streets are well lighted, but rest assured, I won't be going to dinner alone again."

"Well, just keep me informed. Definitely let me know if anything else suspicious happens."

"Cool. I'll call you if anything else happens. Thanks for your concern. I feel better having spoken to you."

Lynn called Sara Wellington and told her what happened.

"Good heavens," Sara exclaimed. "Were you injured?" Lynn told her she was not. "Are you sure it was deliberate?"

"The witnesses seemed to think so. I was wondering if someone knew why I was here and was trying to stop me from doing my job."

"I can't imagine that," Mrs. Wellington said.

"Is there anything else you think would be helpful for me to know about Morgan that let me understand her better? Anyone else I can talk to?"

Sara Wellington thought for a minute and said, "I wonder if Dr. Stern could shed some light. She's a child psychologist who counseled Morgan when she was much younger."

Lynn got Dr. Helene Stern's number and decided to give her a call. It was late afternoon, Cincinnati time. She dialed the number, but Stern was not available. Her scheduler made an appointment for them to speak the next day at two in the afternoon, Budapest time.

* * *

"Hey, man, why'd you do that?" Fane asked as Pista sped away. Fane had thought they were just waiting for her to come out of the restaurant to see where she was going. Then, all of a sudden, Pista was speeding down the street toward her.

"Cut the damn whining," Pista said angrily to Fane. "Lucky bitch! Must have heard us coming up behind her, because if she hadn't jumped out of the way, her ass would be pushing up flowers."

"I didn't think she was any trouble," Fane added.

"You wouldn't know trouble if it kicked you in the teeth. Look, man, Alphonse said take no chances. If there's any doubt, take her out. And he obviously knew what he was talking about, so I'm not taking any chances. This was a safeguard move. We've seen her twice now, and once she was with our girl. That spells trouble. I don't need any interference from her."

Pista Vladú knew no more about that woman than he did before he followed her and tried to take her out of the picture. While he had no idea what her connection was to his girl, he believed that whatever it was, it wasn't good. That was why he had tried to run her down. He chewed on a toothpick and cursed the fact that he'd missed her. After following her to the university, they'd been lucky enough to see her come out and get in a taxi. This time, he and his boy had no trouble tailing her to her hotel, where they watched her enter. They parked on the street and ate candy bars and drank soda while waiting for her to come back out. He'd already decided what he was going to do to her. But when she came out and quickly crossed the street, he couldn't get his old car moving fast enough to catch her. He hadn't mentioned this to whiny-tail Fane because he was sick and tired of explaining every little thing to that moron.

He and Fane had gone into the restaurant and taken a seat where he could watch her. They had to send the waitress away when she first came up to take their order because they weren't about to eat at those prices. "Just wait and see," he had said to Fane. "Soon I'll be able to buy dinner for everyone in this damn place." Fortunately, Fane was able to spring for a couple of Coca-Colas. Pista noticed that the black woman looked at them funny, and he shot her back a look. Maybe she had the hots for him or something. *Not today, lady.* But he thought about all the fun he *could* have had with her.

Even letting his mind stray didn't ease Pista Vladú's mounting frustration. After all, he had intended to be done with this whole thing weeks ago. He had planned to be long gone by now, living on easy street instead of eating beans. But he had been invested in this plan since long before he got out of prison, and he wasn't willing to give up now. Pista had told Fane the reason he went to prison the last time was because he had been in too big a hurry. He'd gotten careless and hadn't done his homework. This time he was doing everything by the books. By nature, he was not a patient man, so playing by the books was hard. Here it was, November already, and they were just getting going again. His new goal was to get his money and get out of Budapest by Christmas.

When they arrived at Pista's flat, he and Fane sat on his sofa and ate beans and link sausage that Fane had heated up, and they talked about moving forward. They had figured out the girl's new schedule, which was confusing because sometimes she was on one campus and sometimes another. But they would have no problem finding her now they had her whereabouts written down on a piece of paper in the glove compartment of his car.

When Fane had first spotted her on the other campus, he almost didn't recognize her because she was no longer a blonde. Fane had said, "Hey, what happened to the blonde hair?" Had it not been for the red jacket that he'd seen before, they might have looked right past her.

"How am I supposed to know?" Pista answered, although he did wonder if the girl was wearing a wig. Was she trying to disguise herself? They had been watching her off and on for a while now. Was she on to them?

Bottom line, Pista was becoming impatient and bored. He was also sick and tired of spending all this time with Fane Dobos. He was ready to collect his money and get on with the good life. He hoped to meet a cute little honey and have a real relationship for a change, versus the kind he was used to that usually lasted only a few hours, or minutes. Although he had to admit, those kind had their place too.

CHAPTER
15

November 22

THE NEXT DAY, LYNN HAD an appointment to talk to Dr. Stern at two o'clock. Until then, she had a few free hours. Since her discovery yesterday at CEU, her mind had been totally consumed with this case. And she had to admit last night's episode at the restaurant with those two men had unnerved her. It had also left her with pain in her right knee and shoulder from when she hit the ground. That was the least of her worries when she considered what could have happened. She decided to clear her head for a few hours by taking a sightseeing tour. She remembered old Jacob Danko's admonishment not to go anywhere alone, but she felt a daytime excursion was safe. She ate breakfast in the hotel restaurant and bought a ticket from the concierge, who pointed her to a tour bus waiting outside. Lynn took the city tour and enjoyed seeing the historic sites and lovely neighborhoods and shops. When she saw a few young people walking down the street dressed as Goths, she was unable to picture Morgan Wellington in such a group.

As the tour was nearing its end, the guide pointed out a popular shopping area just blocks from the hotel. Lynn had read somewhere that Hungary had some of the best seamstresses in the world and that their bead and embroidery work were extraordinary. Many dresses that Paris couturiers sold for thousands of dollars were made from Hungarian fabric. If she could find some good deals, she and her mother would be able to whip up something quite fabulous. Several people lined up to get off the bus to shop. Lynn also got off and looked for fabric shops.

As she walked along the row of shops, she glanced around from time to time to make sure she didn't see anything out of the ordinary—such as two men following her. She spotted several shops that had interesting displays of Hungarian wares in their windows. When she found a dressmaker and fabric shop, she entered. A sign in the window advertised luxury remnants on sale. She saw many lovely beaded fabrics on display. When she told the shopkeeper what she was looking for, she was shown a table of remnants.

Lynn sifted through the remnants and found a two-yard length of off-white bugle-beaded fabric. In the light, she could see glimmers of gold reflecting off the pearlized beads. The price of this rich material would probably be a hundred dollars a yard back home. Here, the piece cost only a few US dollars. Then she found a yard of soft blue embroidered silk similarly priced. The third piece she found was large enough for a dress. It had small white seed pearls. It too was a terrific bargain. Excited with her finds, she had the clerk wrap the purchases. When she looked at her watch, she realized it was time to get back, so she hailed a taxi and was back at her hotel in minutes. Lynn was more than satisfied with her afternoon outing and her purchases. She'd had a chance to clear her head and was pleased with her purchases. Whatever was made from these fabrics would definitely have a couture look.

* * *

At two, Lynn placed her call. "Dr. Stern, my name is Lynn Davis. I am a private investigator working for the Wellingtons."

"Yes, Sara told me you would be calling. She gave me permission to discuss her daughter with you. How can I help you?"

"I'm presently in Budapest ..."

"I am aware of that. What can I tell you about Morgan?"

"Maybe *you* can answer that question, Dr. Stern. What can you tell me about Morgan?"

"Of course, she's nineteen now. She was around ten or eleven when I was seeing her."

"What kind of problems were you addressing with her?" Lynn asked.

"You're aware that Morgan is adopted. For reasons I could never penetrate, she suffered pretty dramatic mood swings."

"She was pretty young, wasn't she?"

"Yes, but her moodiness was not terribly unusual. Her mother told me she would often wake up in tears. Sara said she moped around but never explained what was troubling her." Lynn pictured Morgan's dark eyes and again wondered what was behind them. "Her mother told me that she had undergone a similar period when she was around six or seven. She said that even though

Morgan had lots of playmates, underneath she was an unusually lonely child. Morgan once told me about an imaginary friend who was very important to her, but for reasons unknown, I could never get her to discuss her friend with me again. In any event, adoptees are often driven by a strong need to know their biological roots. Sara said Morgan never once asked about hers. When I probed the situation with her, I couldn't get her to talk about it. The good thing was that after awhile she seemed to be doing much better, and our sessions stopped. Sara said she has done just fine since then."

"Dr. Stern, I am in Budapest trying to get to the bottom of why Morgan came here, seemingly out of the blue. She even transferred to a university here for one semester."

"Miss Davis, Morgan is strong-willed and somewhat impulsive, but not to the extreme. I believe there is an underlying reason for her being there. Frankly, I still feel that the root of all her emotional problems stems from a strong desire to know her true heritage. She dearly loves her parents, but on several occasions I could sense that need in her. However, she never expressed it. That's about all I can tell you."

"If you think of anything else that might be important, will you please call me?" Lynn said.

"Of course. I hope you're successful in getting to the bottom of this, for all concerned."

* * *

After her meeting with Ms. Davis, as much as it had bothered her, their conversation stayed on Morgan's mind. That and her conversation with her mother—she now regretted speaking to her so rudely. Originally, she'd found it off-putting that this woman had come to *escort* her home. After thinking about it, though, she understood her parents' concerns. They were worried enough to send someone all the way here to see about her. Until she had spoken with Ms. Davis, how they might be feeling about her being here had not occurred to her. She hadn't meant to give them reason for concern. Morgan was now wondering if she shouldn't go ahead and return to the States. After all, she'd never even caught a glimpse of the phantom girl and possibly never would. And even if she did, she might be spending all this time chasing after a dream that could end without relevance to her life. So what if the two of them resembled each other? She knew that people see look-alikes all the time. That did not make them automatic kin. Besides, if they were kin, they might not even care. They'd given her up when she was born. If they cared about her, they'd surely have found a way to keep her. *Is it finally time to give up?*

To top it off, again, while walking across campus today, she'd had the feeling that eyes were following her. She was going from one building to another, and a number of students were crisscrossing the campus. Coming from the direction of the parking lot, which was visible from where she was at the time, the sense became almost overpowering. She looked, but nothing seemed unusual. But Morgan knew what she felt. This feeling was occurring all too often now. It was so creepy it was beginning to scare her a little. She felt safe enough once she was almost in the building. But the idea that she might be on someone's radar was troubling. Suddenly, it felt like she could really be in danger, and being here didn't really make much sense anymore. *I probably should just go back home.*

She finished her last class at three o'clock and waited for Bela. They went to grab a bite to eat. While eating,

Morgan told Bela she was having second thoughts about finishing the semester in Budapest. She said, "My parents are worried about me, and besides, my dad hasn't fully recovered from his stroke. I should be home."

"Morgan, I understand that you're concerned about your parents. But don't plan to leave just yet. I bet they wouldn't want you to leave school in the middle of the semester. You were already away at college anyway. Why don't you just finish this term like you were planning to do. Besides, I know you'll want to see this girl. And I can't wait to see your reaction when you do."

"I haven't had a chance to tell you, but my parents actually do want me to come home. They're starting to worry about me."

"Parents always worry. When you get home, I bet they'll still worry every time you leave the house. Mine still do."

"Yes, but this is different. They actually sent someone over here to talk to me. And, well, to take me back home."

"What! Why would they do that?"

"You know, being adopted, I've have always been sensitive to my parents' feelings. I never wanted to make them feel insecure or anything by wondering if I would have preferred my biological family. I love them, but of course I'd have preferred my real parents. Who wouldn't? So anyway, I never told them that I came here to see someone who looks like me. I was afraid they wouldn't understand."

"I can't even imagine being brought up by someone else. My parents aren't perfect. No parents are. But they're mine, and I obviously love them. I can see how adoptive parents would always wonder if they were second best. But Morgan, just stay. You only have a few weeks left. And I think we *have to* run into her one day."

"It sure hasn't happened yet. The other thing is that a friend of my parents was in Budapest recently, and she thought she saw me going into a night club with a bunch of Goths. One was carrying a guitar."

"Well, then, there you go. This girl looks so much like you that even your parents' friend thought she was you."

"Yes, but she spoke to this girl, and the girl didn't speak back. My folks thought something was going on with me. They could have even thought I was using drugs or something."

"So you should just tell them it wasn't you and that you had heard there was someone here who looked like you and you hoped to meet her."

"I did tell them it wasn't me, but my parents would die if they knew I was here hoping to find my real family. They would probably think I wasn't planning to come home. I would never do that, but at least I would know where I came from. And why my real parents gave me up for adoption. It's been lonely being an only child. I guess you should know that too. But I always wanted siblings. I could have a dozen sisters and brothers, and I suppose they could be anywhere. Even here in Budapest. Who knows? This girl you've seen, for all we know, could even be my sister. Furthermore, you're not the only one who thinks we look just alike." Then Morgan told Bela that György had also mistaken her for a girl he used to see with a guitar player. "That's why György started talking to me in the first place."

"Well, he may have thought that at first, but I can tell he is absolutely crazy about *you*," Bela said.

"I know. He's a good guy. Even if I stay for the whole semester, I'll still hate to say good-bye to him."

"So think about it then, Morg. This girl looks enough like you that she definitely could be your sister. I want the two of you to get together, especially since I feel responsible for you coming here in the first place. Okay?"

"I haven't made my decision yet. I'm just getting frustrated. That's all."

After they finished eating, Bela drove Morgan home and set a time to pick her up later that evening so they could go out.

* * *

At five-thirty, Morgan phoned Lynn Davis. Lynn had been thinking about her conversation with Dr. Stern and wondered if any of what the doctor told her played into Morgan's decision to come to this part of the world. She hoped to find a way to explore this with her the next time they got together. Lynn thought about her discovery of Morgan's biological mother. The Wellingtons didn't want her to mention this to Morgan. But Lynn expected they could change their minds when they realized that Morgan and her biological mother could encounter each other by chance on campus at any time. Knowing about her mother, Lynn felt it was entirely possible that Morgan could very well be here in Budapest seeking family ties. While she'd gotten past her mood swings, it was unlikely that she had gotten over her desire to learn about her natural heritage.

Lynn asked Morgan about her day, and Morgan said, "I've been thinking about our conversation. To be honest, I never even thought about how my parents felt about my coming here on the spur of the moment. I never wanted to cause them so much worry."

Lynn noted Morgan's tone was much less defensive now. "Yes, they are concerned, which I think is quite natural. I'm glad you're giving our conversation some thought."

Morgan said, "I just wanted to know if you still wanted to get together." Lynn told her she did. "Then I'll be free by noon tomorrow, and we can do lunch again if you'd like." Lynn said yes and got the place and time, and they hung up.

A few minutes later, Lynn's phone rang again. Morgan said, "Miss Davis, I keep thinking about it. I'm actually prepared to leave Budapest. My parents want me home, and I'd prefer for my dad to focus on recovering from his stroke and not worrying about me. It's time to go."

Lynn hadn't expected this, given their first conversation or even their phone call a few minutes ago. From what Dr. Stern said about Morgan's biological family, meeting her mother could possibly resolve some of her lifelong issues. She would speak to the Wellingtons about that. They might decide that Morgan and her natural mother should meet before she returned home. Lynn concealed her surprise and said, "Morgan, are you sure about this?"

"Yeah, I'm ready to leave school and everything. I mean, what's the worst thing that could happen? It's no big deal."

On one hand, Lynn felt relieved at Morgan's decision, since that was what she'd come here for. However, on the other hand, she wondered if leaving Budapest now was the answer. This case had gotten more complicated now that Morgan's mother had been introduced into the picture.

Morgan continued. "Of course, my friend Bela doesn't want me to go. But I think I'm ready."

Lynn said, "Let's just make sure your parents are still on board with your leaving CEU and coming home right now."

"But didn't you say that's why you came here? To get me to come home?"

"I did, but I still think it's best to run your decision by them. I'll be talking to your mother shortly. I'll let her know your decision."

"To tell the truth, I'm ready to put everything behind me. But I suppose you're right. I'll call them now. But I think they'll be happy with my decision. I guess I'll see you tomorrow then."

CHAPTER
16

ON FRIDAY EVENING, IVONA PALAKI and her lab partner were working on their class project in the laboratory. After awhile, they took a short break. Ivona sat by the window and took a bite of her sandwich and a sip of tea. She watched an old car pass by, and her mind was instantly drawn to something that had happened the other afternoon. She and some friends had stopped for a bite to eat after class. While they were eating, Ivona noticed two men come into the eatery and take seats at the bar. One of them removed his black leather jacket, revealing muscular, hairy arms. The cuff of his shirt sleeve was rolled up, and Ivona noticed a tattoo on his left arm. She couldn't help but observe that the men kept glancing over their shoulders toward her group. When one of them turned around and stared directly at her, she looked away. Shortly after that, the men got up and left.

Ivona and her friends left the restaurant and got into her lab partner's car. As they drove away, she noticed the old car in the side mirror. Its driver seemed to keep pace with them, slowing down whenever Andre did, even though it could easily have gone around them. Twice, the car behind them turned the corner when they turned. When she mentioned the car to her friends, they all turned back to look. The driver must have seen them looking; at the first corner they came to after that, it turned left and drove down another street. Ivona hadn't noticed what kind of car it was or who was driving.

As she remembered that incident, it occurred to her that the two men in the restaurant may have been the same ones following them in that old car after they left. It gave her an unsettling feeling. *What could that have been about?* And now she wondered if the old car that just drove by her window the same one? The idea was unsettling.

Or was it just a coincidence? She wanted to think so. Obviously, she didn't know who the men in the car were after. But she couldn't just dismiss the incident; there had been other recent occasions when she had specifically felt that someone was watching her. It had started last summer. Then for a long time that feeling went away. However, it had recently started up again. It even happened once while she was walking across campus. Ivona didn't understand why she felt that way. She couldn't think of a single reason anyone would be following her. Still, she had felt staring eyes. Thinking about it made her quiver.

When she and Andre got back to work, they completed the last of several experiments and celebrated with high fives. For the past six weeks, they had been completely immersed in finishing the project. It had been so demanding; she literally lived with it day and night Even her weekends had been committed to it, so she rarely went out anymore. Today, they both breathed a sigh of relief. Except for a few minor details, their lab work was finished. It was Friday night, and she decided to celebrate. Tomorrow, they would put the finishing touches on their experiment.

As a child, inspired by her mother's interest in science, Ivona had been drawn to that field. She definitely had the aptitude for it. When she graduated at the top of her high school class and received a full academic scholarship to Central European University, her mother and grandmother could not have been prouder. In college, Ivona continued to make top honors. She was passionate about her field, and during summer months when her friends were on holiday, she worked at a laboratory. She liked having a good time as much as anyone else, but unlike some of her classmates, her studies came first. So she only occasionally went out with girlfriends and with guys even less frequently. She'd had only one semiserious relationship in her life, and that was during her second year of college. It had lasted only four months, ending when her boyfriend graduated and moved away. Calling it quits was a mutual decision. Relationships demanded too much of her time, which she preferred to devote to her education.

For a period of time, however, to many people around her, including her immediate family, Ivona had become something of an enigma. She began to hang out more than usual. Last summer, she started dating a guitarist who had his own band. She was never in love with Tibor, but to her mother and grandmother's chagrin, she often accompanied him to the club where his band played, and she hung out with him at after-hours parties. They were worried that all the partying would dim her focus on her education and were relieved that she'd remained focused on her studies.

Tibor's band and the others who hung around with them dressed in all black. Ivona had gotten into that look too, which came as a big surprise to her family. Goth girls either dyed their hair jet black or platinum blond. Ivona's hair was already almost black, so she decided to become a blonde. The drastic change had taken place a few months ago, around the time Ivona learned she had a twin sister. Her mother and grandmother were puzzled about the change in her behavior, and they wondered if she was experiencing an identity crisis. They asked her what was behind the new look.

Ivona was not really sure. She did know that after learning she had an identical twin, she had begun to feel confused and disconcerted. She told Niko and Reeni she just wanted to do something different. However, she assured them that nothing she was doing interfered with her main priorities. They accepted Ivona's answer, for it was true, she seemed to be as committed to her education as always. They decided to allow her to work it out of her system. Underneath it all, they trusted her to do the right thing. Before long, she had reverted to her old self.

For Ivona, the brief lifestyle change had been a welcome diversion from the tough rigors of academia. More importantly, it allowed her mind to escape the constant reminder that she had a twin sister in this world she had never even seen. And she'd never actually taken her relationship with Tibor seriously. She knew he had a string of female groupies, and when he wasn't with her, he was with one of them. After awhile, she tired of the whole scene, and Tibor Varga became mostly a thing of the past. So did the Gothic look. In fact, she had also tired of being a blonde and was planning to change her hair color back when she had the time. Her current class project had been so demanding, it had kept her away from the nightlife for the past several weeks.

Ivona had managed to get out a couple of weeks ago. Tibor had invited her, and she'd agreed to stop by his club. As she cleaned up the lab, something that happened that night crossed her mind. She and Tibor and his band were about to enter his club when a woman with an American accent stopped her car and called out to them. Ivona had not been certain who the woman was speaking to, but she had the impression it was her. The stranger had called out an American name. Morgan. She had been looking right at Ivona while speaking. Ivona assumed she had mistaken her for someone else and ignored the woman. She had not thought of that night since, until this evening as she prepared to go out. Now she wondered if the American woman who called out to her that night might have thought she was the very girl she'd seen the other day.

Ever since seeing her sister in Carrefours, Ivona hadn't been able to get her out of her mind. Even though she hadn't seen her since, she still felt warmed by the memory of having seen her. Now that her lab project was nearly finished, she would go home and change her hair back to its natural color tonight. The dark brown had looked great on the other girl. Besides, Reeni had always said that blonde did not become her. When she got home from the lab, she spent the next two hours coloring her hair.

When Ivona arrived on the club scene later that evening, she sported a new look. A dark-haired beauty, tonight she wore a red sweater with a black scarf slung around her neck and a short black skirt. Black knee-high leather boots completed her look. She and two girlfriends entered the Lite House and walked toward the bar to see if they recognized anyone. They spotted some friends on the dance floor and joined them.

The band played several more songs. While she was dancing, some guy she didn't know made a nuisance of himself. He kept calling her Bethany.

"So are you Bethany tonight? Or don't you remember me?" he asked.

"What? I don't know you, and I'm not Bethany."

"Well, I sure know you. You were all over me one day to get my telephone number."

"I think you're drunk," Ivona said and walked away, leaving the nerdy guy looking perplexed.

What was that about? she wondered. During the intermission, Tibor hurried over to Ivona, put his arm around her neck, and planted a kiss on her forehead. "You look fantastic!" he said, giving her the once-over. "Where've you been, kid?"

"I've been busy. You look pretty good yourself, Tibor. You guys sound great. It's good to see you."

"Say, where'd my blonde beauty go? Not that you don't look incredible, because you do. I couldn't take my eyes off you while I was playing. What's with the look?"

"Guess I was ready for a change," Ivona said.

"It's been a long time. I haven't seen much of you lately. Actually, I think I caught a glimpse of you last weekend, but when I looked up again, you were gone."

"No, I did not come out last week. Too busy in the lab, you know."

"My mistake," Tibor stammered. "Whatever you say. Look, gorgeous, can we get together after I'm finished here tonight?"

"Afraid not. We're meeting some friends at the Blue Diamond," Ivona said as she turned to walk away. Tibor winked, puckered his lips, and blew a kiss at her just when she turned to look back at him. Tibor had once told Ivona he dug her unique combination of brains and beauty. He said he'd certainly had his share of blonde lookers, but none of them had half the smarts she had. He told her she was too high-class for someone like him. But a man could try.

* * *

A little while later at the Blue Diamond, Ivona was waiting for the band to start playing when one of the musicians came over to her. "Hey, Morgy," he said. "I thought I'd see you later this evening. I'm glad you got here early. Me and the guys were trying out a couple of new songs. I wondered what you thought about them."

"Pardon me?" Ivona said, staring at him. "I'm afraid I don't know what you're talking about." She was surprised at the mistake, which reminded her of earlier at the Lite House, when some guy mistook her for someone named Bethany. This mistaken-identity thing seemed to be happening more and more lately. This one called her Morgy. She wondered if Morgy was someone's real name or a nickname. Practically everyone she knew had a nickname. She wondered if perhaps Morgy and Morgan were the same person. For the second time, she might be being mistaken for the other girl. Her twin sister? Although she didn't show it, she was getting excited.

At first, György thought Morgan was just fooling, but with the blank look she was giving him plus her accent, he realized that, although she was no longer a blonde, this was the girl Morgan had been looking for all this time. He couldn't believe his luck. He muttered, "You're that girl!" At Ivona's look of surprise, he said, "I'm sorry. But you look just like a friend of mine. I thought you were her. Oh my gosh, Morgan is going to be so excited."

Morgan! That's the name the American woman called me. Morgan has to be the one I saw in Carrefours. This guy also had an American accent. Maybe he was the guy with my sister that day.

György could not let this opportunity pass. He hadn't been able to get anything about her from Tibor Varga, but now here she was, in the flesh. Somehow, he had to get her and Morgan together. That shouldn't be too hard—he knew Morgan was coming here tonight. The encounter would be so important to her. Wouldn't it be something if this girl was her sister? Besides, if he could put the two of them together, it would put him back on Morgan's good side. He knew he had messed up when he told her he thought she was someone else. So he said, "You're Tibor Varga's girl, right?" he asked.

"I don't really see Tibor much anymore."

Back on stage, the band was warming up. György had to get up there and play. He had to move fast. "Listen, I gotta go back to my band. But I think you will want to meet Morgan. She should be here soon. In case she doesn't get here before you leave, give me your name and number."

She searched her purse for a pen and paper. "I want to know about the girl I look like. Is she American?"

György looked at his watch. He had to go. "Yeah, she is American. Look," he said. "Please, don't go anywhere. I've got to get back up there with the guys. The management has been getting tough with us. I'm György Novak. That's my band." He pulled a card out of his wallet and said, "Here, take my card. I know this girl I'm talking about would very much like to meet you. Just say you're interested and we'll make it happen. Like the hair, by the way." And he was off.

"What was that all about?" one of her friends asked. "You always seem to attract the musicians. After Tibor

Varga, this guy György Novak is the next hottest musician in town."

"With the change in my hair color, he mistook me for someone else," Ivona explained. She believed this guy was talking about her mystery girl. The name was right, the same name the American woman had called her. Was Morgan the one she had seen at the department store? If so, then who was Bethany? Although she was puzzled about that, she recalled that Tibor had mentioned seeing her last week at his club. He must have seen Morgan too. She was so close! She felt tingly with excitement.

CHAPTER
17

MORGAN WAS FEELING MIXED EMOTIONS. On one hand, she was relieved that she had made the decision to return home. On the other hand, she felt remorseful, knowing she would be leaving Budapest empty-handed. After her talk with Lynn Davis, she returned to her apartment and began to organize things for shipment prior to her trip home. She should be able to leave by the middle of next week. She called her mother, but the housekeeper told her she wasn't home from a board meeting. Morgan didn't want to leave something so special in a message, so she told the housekeeper to tell her mother she'd call her later.

Morgan tried to tell herself it really did not matter anymore whether she ever saw the girl or not. But, of course, that did not work. *What if she really is ...?* Morgan could not let herself complete the thought. To keep her mind off the notion of leaving Budapest, she began packing some of her things.

Afternoon turned into evening, and Morgan decided it was time to get ready to go out. She was looking forward to her last Friday night on the town in Budapest. She added special touches to her appearance, including a cute hairstyle with a part down the center and perfectly applied makeup. Then she put on a white mohair sweater, black leather pants, and black leather boots. Usually Bela picked her up, but tonight, because of their schedules, they were going to meet at the club. Morgan called a taxi, and the driver came into her building to pick her up. She looked terrific as she walked into the Blue Diamond about an hour later. She looked around for Bela, who was not in sight. *She'll be shocked when I tell her I'm leaving after all.*

She would also tell György tonight she was leaving; she knew he'd be disappointed. She liked György, but the two of them would soon be history anyway. Morgan looked toward the stage and saw that György and his group were just about to head up to play some more. While sitting at the bar sipping a Coke and waiting for Bela to show up, she watched the guys play and the dancers move and groove to the music. Strobe lights flashed, and everything looked real cool. György spotted her and waved. He quickly set his guitar in its stand, jumped down from the stage, and hurried across the dance floor, bumping into some dancers in his rush to get to her. The guys played on, never missing a beat.

"Hi, Morgy." György kissed her on the cheek. "You look great!" Morgan smiled radiantly. Then he added, "Listen, Morgan, I gotta tell you something. She was here tonight!" Morgan looked at him blankly, and György repeated, "That girl. She was in here tonight, Morgy. I talked to her. In fact, she just left about twenty minutes ago." It took only a second for Morgan to realize who György was talking about.

"The girl I told you about was in here tonight?"

"I tried to call you so you could hurry up and get over here, but you didn't answer. Maybe you were in the shower and didn't hear the phone."

Morgan was in shock. "You actually saw her, György? You talked to her?"

"You bet! And Morgy, at first I thought she was you! I mean, the two of you are flat-out freakin' identical. I even gave her a peck on the cheek." Morgan looked at him with a suspicious eye. "Seriously, Morg, it's uncanny. She even has dark hair now. She's not a blonde anymore. I swear I couldn't tell the difference until she spoke. I mean, she did have an accent and all, but I still thought she was you. You gotta see her, Morgy. I was so taken aback, I could barely take my eyes off her the whole time she was here." Before Morgan could say more, he quickly said, "Look, I gotta get back up there, but I'll see you at the next break. I can't wait to tell you everything then."

Morgan was too stunned to speak. Could it finally be happening? The girl had showed up here tonight and left just a little while ago. She tried to visualize the girl and pictured herself. After all, that's who everyone said she looked like. She was excited. György said they now had the same hair color; she found herself looking around the club, hoping the girl was still there. No luck.

Here she was, preparing to leave Budapest next week. She'd all but given up and was planning to go back to the United States in a few days. *Don't go!* a voice screamed in her head, loud and clear. How could she leave Budapest now? The girl had actually shown up here tonight. Furthermore, György had actually talked to her personally. Morgan wondered if she could possibly abandon her hopes now. *How can I go without seeing her?*

Now that I've made a decision to go home, she shows up. Mom always says timing is everything.

Just then, Bela arrived, and Morgan couldn't wait to tell her what György said. She told Bela the girl's hair was now dark like hers.

Bela was giddy with excitement. "Finally! You know, we've looked so hard to no avail, I was starting to think I had dreamed her up myself. Did György get her name? I mean, who is she? Where can we find her?"

"Hold it, Bela," Morgan said. "He didn't get to tell me everything yet. He ran down from the stage so he could at least tell me that much. I'm so excited. But all I know right now is that she was in here. Can you believe it? In fact, György even got to talk to her. Kissed her on the cheek and everything, because he thought she was me. He said she only left a little while ago."

Bela laughed. "See, I told you. You two *are* identical. Oh, Morgan, I am so happy. I can't wait for you to see her. And I guarantee she will be as shocked to see you as you will be to see her."

"I'll bet. György will be back during his next break. Then I'll know more. I can hardly wait either. In fact, I'm so excited I was tempted to go over and yank him off the stage. But they'll be stopping in a few minutes. Then I'll know more."

Morgan and Bela chatted until the band stopped playing. In an instant György was at their side.

"Hey, Bela, did Morgy Baby tell you we saw her twin? I nearly freaked out—they look so much alike."

"So what's her name, György?" Morgan interrupted. "Did you find out?"

"Actually, no, I didn't get a chance," he answered. "I asked her, but she hesitated. I figured she thought I was just putting the make on her or something. After telling her how much she looked like someone I knew, I could tell she was interested and wanted to know more. But the guys had already started playing and I had to get back up there," György told a disappointed Morgan. "I gave her my card and asked her to call me so I could get the two of you together."

"Great! What did she say?" Morgan asked.

"Nothing. Just took the card. It was all I could think to do at that moment. I kept hoping you would come in while she was here. Then I looked up, and she was gone. But she'll call, Morg. I feel sure of that. I mean, she seemed curious too," György replied earnestly.

"Gosh, I wonder who she is," Morgan said, disappointed that György didn't have more information.

"So do I," Bela said. "I've seen her plenty of times, but with her hair like yours now, I bet I wouldn't be able to tell you two apart either. You know, there's got to be some kind of connection. She could definitely be your sister, Morgan. If not, I know they say everyone has a double somewhere in this world. Well, this girl sure is yours."

"I want to tell you something," Morgan spoke again. "Tonight I was going to tell you guys that I made up my mind to leave next week. I was going back home."

"Next week!" György exclaimed. "Why so soon? What about school? What about us, Morgy? You can't just take off and leave like that. Anyway, what about the girl? You do want to meet her, don't you?" György didn't wait for answers. He said almost pleadingly, "C'mon, Morgan. You can't leave now."

Morgan just sighed and said, "Actually, I don't know what to do now, because I really do want to see her. I can't believe she was in this very club tonight. That makes me feel like we were supposed to run into each other. Or that I'm getting close. But even if I stay, you know it will only be until the end of the semester—just a few more weeks."

György looked hopeful; a few more weeks was a whole lot better than a few more days.

Bela said, "I knew you were getting tired of everything, and I can hardly blame you. No matter where we looked, we never saw her. But I hope you won't leave now. Besides, I think you should finish your semester. Or at the very least you should wait until you see the girl. You owe it to yourself. Don't leave now. Just think about what György said. You're so close. After all, she was right here tonight."

"I know, I know. And I can't believe it either," Morgan replied. "I can even feel her—maybe because she was just here. Now I think fate is trying to put us together. She left here a little before I arrived. I would have been here too, but I was starting to get some of my stuff ready to ship back home. You guys are right. I have to stay, at least until I meet my double. Or until the semester ends. Whichever comes first," she smiled resignedly.

"Atta girl," György said. "I'm proud of you, Morgy. I want to see you as much as possible while you're still here. Think I can do that?" Morgan gave György a *we shall see* look. He gave her a self-assured smile and walked away. Morgan was already thinking about telling her parents she had changed her mind. They had been so happy when she spoke to them earlier. Miss Davis was expecting them to travel next week. *Well, I just changed my mind back, that's all,* Morgan told herself.

Saturday, November 23

LYNN AROSE EARLY SATURDAY MORNING to check her e-mail. Among her new messages was one from a special client, Manning Witherspoon. Manning brought her up to date about a development in his Houston property case and told her he would have to go to Texas to follow up on it. After reading about the development, Lynn wrote back that given the gravity of the situation, she should accompany him to aid in resolving the matter expediently and that they could set a tentative date when she returned from Budapest.

Manning Witherspoon was a wealthy forty-six-year-old widower who lived in Cincinnati. A real estate mogul, he owned extensive property around the country: condos, apartment buildings, and strip malls. His diverse holdings included an orange grove in central Florida and vineyards in California. A management company handled his holdings. Through successful investments in real estate, he had attained wealth at an early age and at thirty-five had been written up in a national business magazine as one of the top five most successful African American real estate investors in the country. Manning had been a star football player in college. A knee injury kept him out of the pros, but he still had the athletic build of his younger days, which he maintained with daily workouts at the gym. He was also an avid racquetball and tennis player. Manning Witherspoon was widely known across the city of Cincinnati.

Three years earlier, his wife, Peggy, had passed away. Because of her untimely death, her biography was featured in the *Herald*, a weekly African American newspaper with a large readership. Like her husband, Peggy Witherspoon had been well-known in the city due to her many civic works. Their son was in law school and their daughter, her second year of medical school.

He had first contacted Lynn six months before about problems with a deal he was working on. From the start, Lynn was aware he showed more than a professional interest in her, but she made a practice of not mixing business and relationships. Therefore, their association had not become personal.

Lynn had successfully handled his first case. Manning valued and respected her expertise. Two months before she left for Budapest, he'd asked her to research a piece of property he was considering purchasing in Texas, a one-thousand-acre cattle ranch outside of Houston. They had met on several occasions, sometimes over lunch, and had been scheduled to go to lunch to discuss his case last Tuesday, the day after Sara Wellington came into Lynn's office and presented her with this case.

Manning was one of the most sought-after bachelors in the city, and Lynn was secretly flattered by his interest. She also appreciated his business. Although he was a serious businessman, he had a great sense of humor and was very pleasant to be around. Indeed, Lynn had enjoyed the few lunches they had shared while working on his case. When Manning came to her office for their meeting the day she left for Budapest, she had personally walked out to the lobby to pick him up. She'd greeted him with her hand outstretched, and he looked up from the magazine he was reading, smiled, and rose to his feet. The picture of suave elegance, he reached to shake her hand. His six-foot, two-inch frame was elegantly attired in custom-tailored tan slacks, a tan-and-white striped shirt, and a red silk tie. A black cashmere sport coat topped off his *GQ* look.

When they walked into Lynn's office, she took her seat behind her desk. Manning sat in a chair facing her. Lynn explained her change of plans, which meant there was no time to go to lunch because she had to leave for Budapest later that day. Their business discussion was short; twenty minutes later, they wrapped up. As he stood to leave, Manning said, "We'll do lunch another time then."

Lynn rose too and extended her hand, which he
graciously took and then continued to hold. He gazed
into her eyes and softly said, "As always, it was nice
seeing you, Lynn. You look great, by the way."

Although Manning's case was coming to an end,
Lynn had a feeling this would not be their final business
dealings. She hadn't dated since her former boyfriend
Donald Anderson took a job in London. As she thought
about Manning, she had to admit she was attracted to
him. *I may have to revisit my policy about not mixing
business with personal.*

The next e-mail message Lynn read was from Ella.
Lynn was pleased to learn that things were running
smoothly back at the office. Ella had attached an
update, and she told Lynn that she'd had to call Harvey
Chapman in on one case. Harvey was not only one of
Lynn's trusted colleagues; he was also a good friend
and one of the most talented investigators she knew. A
retired policeman, he occasionally did some freelance
investigating. Harvey no longer kept an office but
worked from home—that is, if he felt like taking a case.
Currently, he spent more time on his other interests,
especially restoring antique cars. Over the years, Lynn
had learned a great deal under his tutelage. Harvey
Chapman was reliable and dependable. She could always
turn to him when she needed help; he never failed to
come through. She found it extremely comforting to
have someone like him in her corner.

"Hey, Lynn, what's up? You calling to invite me to
lunch, kiddo?" he'd said when she'd phoned him before
she flew overseas.

"I do owe you lunch, as a matter of fact," Lynn told
him. "But the fact is, Harv, I've been asked to go to
Budapest. I have to leave tomorrow. Actually, my client

would probably be happy if I left today. I figure I might be gone as long as one or two weeks."

"No stuff!" Harvey exclaimed. "Say, wait a minute, Lynn. Aren't you supposed to give the big speech at the conference next Monday? You know, I was only flying over to Hawaii for your presentation. So what's this about Budapest?"

"Well, it just came up this morning," Lynn said. Then she told Harvey about her meeting with Mrs. Wellington. "So Tracy Billingsley is doing my keynote address at the conference. I'm glad she was available."

"Oh, yeah," Harvey said. "Lucky girl."

"She *is* happy about it, but Tracy and I are doing each other a favor. I sure didn't want to cancel and leave the conference planners high and dry, you know. I'll try to get on the program next year."

"Now, what about everything else? How're you gonna make this Budapest thing work?"

"Actually, Harvey, it's pronounced Budapesht."

Harvey snorted. "Actually, I thought you were mispronouncing it. I wondered, *When did Lynn get a lisp?*"

"If I had one, I'd be calling it a lithp," she said smiling. "Anyway, Ella can handle things here, but she might need to call on you from time to time. Like I said, I don't know how long I'll be away. Who knows, I might even have to call you from Budapest myself." Then she told him what her case was about and said, "After I find the young lady, I have to convince her to come back with me."

"You're gonna have your hands full. You know I'll do what I can."

"Harv, you realize you've got to cancel your plans to go to the conference," Lynn said.

"No problem. I've been going to that thing so many years, it's old hat to me."

"I'll make sure you don't lose your registration fee," she assured him.

"What registration fee?" he asked, laughing, and then added, "Girl, you know I don't bother with stuff like that. You got an interesting case. I know you'll work it out. Just watch your step over there in Europe. You don't know what kind of people you'll be dealing with. And oh," he added, laughing, "watch out for the vampires."

"Come on, Harvey. Be serious."

"Well, you know they say those characters are still running around over there."

"I don't believe that nonsense," Lynn said through her smile. "But thanks for the word of warning."

"You know I'm just joking. So tell Ella to be sure to holler if she needs anything," Harvey added.

"Thanks, Harv. When I get back, it's lunch or dinner on me. You name the place."

"Watch out, now," Harvey teased. "I haven't eaten at my favorite steakhouse in a while," he said, referring to Morton's, one of downtown Cincinnati's finest eateries.

Still thinking about Harvey and smiling about that call, Lynn shut her computer down. When it began to get light outside, she set out for her morning run in the clear, crisp air. Now that she had met old Jacob, her reservations about taking the route past the cemetery were gone. As before, she saw him tending the grounds. This time, Lynn waved at him as she passed by, and he waved back. During her hour-long run, she pondered the Wellington case.

Certain thoughts kept nagging at her. When she first saw the picture and bio of Dr. N. René Palaki, she remembered reading that Dr. Palaki was not married and that she had one child. Since her name was no longer Moldovan, Lynn assumed Dr. Palaki had been married at one time.

Lynn was also curious about the doctor's other child and wondered whether or not she was Morgan's look-alike girl. It certainly seemed possible, given the strong resemblance between Dr. Palaki and Morgan. It seemed like too much of a coincidence to ignore. Since Sara Wellington didn't want her to mention Nicola to Morgan until they figured out what to do, Lynn believed that if she could find out more information, it might help them determine how to proceed. She thought about the situation and wondered if she might learn anything more in Bucharest, since that was where Nicola and her mother were from. She would talk to Mrs. Wellington about going there.

Lynn's telephone rang.

"Hello, Miss Davis, this is Morgan Wellington."

"Hello, Morgan. I was just thinking about this whole situation. How are you coming with your packing?"

"Well, that's just it. I have something to tell you, but I'll discuss it with you when I see you for lunch," Morgan said.

"Sure thing. I'll see you at noon." *What could Morgan have to tell me?*

CHAPTER
18

Cincinnati, Ohio

FLOSSIE TRIED ON HER WOOL turquoise dress, but it hung loosely on her frame. When she first bought the dress some ten years or so ago, she remembered how she used to have to work to fasten it around her ample curves. At that time, she tipped the scales at around 145 pounds, but today, she weighed at least twenty pounds less. She changed into something that fit. Flossie still liked to look her best and never stepped out of her room without makeup on her face. Working in a uniform all her life had redoubled her love of dressing up. In fact, she always got compliments when she did, especially for church. She wore her hats cocked just right, and Agnes and Beulah would say, "You go, girl!" She enjoyed that. After breakfast, Flossie decided she would sort through her clothes and pull out the ones that no longer fit to give to Goodwill. That decided, she headed downstairs to eat.

She finished eating and returned to her room to look through her closet. *The Goodwill can use several of these outfits,* Flossie thought as she located a number of items she could no longer wear. Feeling nostalgic after searching her closets, she decided to rummage through a trunk full of keepsakes. After Mossie died, her husband gave Flossie several of her sister's good dresses; they wore the same size. Flossie came across a black dress that brought back precious memories. More than fifty-five years ago, her sister had worn it when she and her husband and Flossie had celebrated their thirtieth birthday. She pulled it out and held it up; her eyes became dreamy as she relived that evening.

"Flossie, hurry up," Mossie yelled. "Howard Eugene is ready to walk out the door. Let's go."

"I'm coming. I'm coming. Just give me one more minute. I'm trying to get my seams straight," Flossie said. "Come in here for a minute and help me zip up this dress."

Mossie went into Flossie's bedroom and exclaimed, "Ooooh, look at you, Miss Fine. That short red dress is definitely showing off those legs. Now turn around and let me zip you up."

"Thanks, girl. You always look good, but especially tonight in that black dress. Love that sexy fishtail."

Mossie twirled around and said, "Notice I'm wearing fishnet stockings too? Looks like we're both looking to have a good time."

"Well, I haven't been out since I don't know when. I'm glad you got me a ticket to this cabaret dinner-dance. Thanks for letting me tag along with you and Howard."

"Now you know you are always welcome to join us. I'm glad Howard found out about this dance. The Tri-County Queens put on really good affairs. It's a great way to celebrate our birthday. Now if you'd just give Earnest a chance, you'd probably be going out all the time. After all, you're thirty years old now. You can't stay a virgin your whole life."

"What makes you think I'm still a virgin?" Flossie asked.

"Cause you tell me everything, that's why. If you had ever done *it*, I'd know about it."

"Girl, you're crazy. No one knows everything about anybody."

"Wanna bet?" Mossie said and added with a wink, "You just don't know what you're missing."

"Well, anyway, Mossie Lee, you know I'm not studying Earnest Paul. Everyone says he's a womanizer. As far as I'm concerned, the other women can have him. I'll meet somebody who's right for me one day."

"I didn't say you had to marry the man. Just have some fun going out with him."

Flossie and Mossie walked into the living room, and Howard whistled. "Now there's two fine, big-legged foxes," he exclaimed, smiling.

They got into Howard's Persian gold Lincoln Continental and headed to Franklin Hall, where they found a table and enjoyed a delicious baked chicken and dressing dinner while the band played soft music. The moment the plates were cleared, the band started playing dance songs. Howard grabbed Mossie's hand to lead her out to the floor to dance the Boogie Woogie to Bill Doggett's popular "Honky Tonk." Flossie sat at the table, popping her fingers and patting her feet, and bobbing her head to the music, watching her sister and brother-in-law have the time of their lives on the dance floor, wishing she was out there too. Mossie and Howard returned to their seats breathless and sweating to wait the next few

songs out. *I feel like a wallflower sitting here by myself.*
The next song had everyone doing the Charleston, and
then came the Lindy Hop.

When the band began playing the "Stroll," Mossie told
her, "Now here's a dance you don't need a partner for, Flo.
Come on." Flossie joined them for the line dance of the
same name. She enjoyed every minute. The band slowed
the pace with Louie Armstrong's "What a Wonderful
World," and some good-looking guy walked over to Flossie
before she got back to her seat and asked her to dance.
She accepted, and it felt so nice to be held in someone's
arms, gliding across the dance floor. He held her firmly
enough that she could feel his strong body and smell his
aftershave cologne. She didn't want that song to end.
Flossie danced a few more times that night, including
another slow dance to Sam's Cooke's "You Send Me"
with the same guy. His name, she learned, was Quinton
Lewis. He asked for her name and number and if he
could take her home. Since she didn't know him, she
declined his offer to take her home, but she did give him
her telephone number and found herself hoping he would
call soon. All in all, she'd had herself a great birthday.

"Don't forget about me the next time you and Howard
get dance tickets," Flossie told her sister when they
dropped her back home.

"You know I won't. I'll let you know when something
comes up," Mossie told her.

Flossie had a great time that night. But as she thought
about the evening, her mind was flooded with another
memory.

Quinton Lewis had called her, and the two of them
started going out together. They dated for a few months.
She couldn't believe that she was finally falling in love

again. But too soon, Quinton broke her heart. One day, he told her he was getting back together with his wife. He said that when they separated, neither had known she was pregnant, and it just didn't feel right to walk away from her at this time. They were going to try to work things out. Another love lost.

She yearned for Quinton for a long time. Her relationships with men after that were few and far between, and none serious. Flossie sat for a while with her thoughts, caressing the dress. Then she wiped her eyes and folded it up tenderly and placed it back in her trunk.

Shortly afterward, the twins crossed her mind. *I wonder if they will ever have fun going out together like me and my sister did?* All at once, her dread returned. *Lord have mercy, what is happening to those girls?*

* * *

Budapest, Hungary

GYÖRGY DROPPED MORGAN OFF AT the Arcade Bistro. Lynn arrived at the same time. "Hello, Morgan," Lynn said, greeting Morgan with a handshake.

"Hello again."

They took a seat in a booth. Morgan seemed more relaxed than the first time they met—possibly because she had decided to go back home, Lynn thought. Practically before they got comfortable in their seats, Morgan blurted out, "I know what I told you last night, but I've changed my mind. I am staying here in Budapest after all. I've already told my parents."

Lynn was surprised. When they'd talked the night before, Morgan had seemed adamant about leaving

Budapest. In Lynn's mind, staying was probably a good thing since Morgan might get to meet her mother. That could no doubt fulfill her lifelong need to know her real identity.

"So you called your parents? That's good."

Morgan sat back in the booth and began biting her nails as she stroked her pendant. "Yeah."

"What did they think about your change in plans?"

"They were good with it. They accepted my decision."

"So what made you change your mind?" Lynn asked Morgan.

"I had my reasons."

Lynn could see she didn't intend to share them.

"Well, okay. I just thought about it and realized I'd made a pretty hasty decision. I really didn't want to leave, but I was worried about my parents. When I talked to my mom, she gave me their blessings to stay."

"That's good." Lynn wasn't surprised that the Wellingtons agreed with Morgan's decision. She had spoken with Mrs. Wellington yesterday and explained that Morgan had decided to come home. However, in light of the discovery of her biological mother, Lynn questioned if that was still the right thing. She'd also relayed what Dr. Stern had said, and Mrs. Wellington decided that Morgan should, indeed, have a chance to meet her biological mother. She said she would discuss it with Helene Stern herself and told Lynn she might want her to arrange a family meeting. Mrs. Wellington asked Lynn if she could stay in Budapest awhile longer, and Lynn agreed.

"You told them why you were staying?"

Morgan continued fondling the pendant. "Basically," she offered reluctantly.

Typical young response. Lynn said, "'Basically' tends to mean not at all."

"It means I told them enough."

Lynn said, "They have a right to know your reasons, since they never really knew why you came here in the first place." Lynn knew she was pushing Morgan, but the girl seemed determined to say only so much.

Morgan rolled her eyes. "I don't think they'd care. They're just glad I'll be home next month."

"No more second thoughts?" Lynn asked.

Morgan shook her head. "Nope. This gives me a chance to do what I really came here to do."

"Was there another reason you came to Budapest?" Lynn asked.

"Well, not really. I came because Bela invited me. But since you asked, there is someone here I want to meet. Is that what you want to hear?"

Is Morgan talking about her mother? Lynn said, "Someone at your university?"

"No, nothing like that."

"Is there something more you want to say?"

Morgan sat up. "What do you mean?"

"It just feels like there's more you want to tell me, that's all," Lynn replied.

Morgan gave a half smile. "Actually, there is and there isn't. I haven't told my mom about it yet, so I'll keep it to myself."

Lynn said, "Morgan, I'm not trying to force you, but if there's something you'd like to tell me in confidence, I will respect that."

"Cool," Morgan said as the waiter came up to take their order. When he walked away, she said, "Okay, so as I said, I haven't told my parents about this yet." Then she told Lynn about her alleged look-alike. "Since I've been here, I've run into people who thought I was her a few times, including my boyfriend, György."

"He thought you were someone else too?"

"Sure did. He told me when we first met, he thought he was talking to this other girl. He told me he used to see her around all the time."

So there is more behind Morgan's coming here. In light of the discovery of Morgan's birth mother, Lynn wondered again if this person Morgan wanted to meet could possibly be her sister.

"Anyhow, that's why I came here. Now can you see why I wouldn't want my parents to know about this?"

When their food came, they began eating and continued to talk.

"Morgan, this conversation is between you and me. But, I feel you should tell your parents about this. It would certainly help them understand why you're here."

Morgan said. "I can't tell them. They wouldn't understand."

"You might be wrong," Lynn said.

"I've known them my whole life. You've known them for what? Like a week?" Morgan replied.

It was a valid point, but Lynn knew something the girl didn't. God, she wished the family would just stop circling the darn tower and land already. "I'm just saying you'd be surprised."

Morgan sat back. "Whatever."

"So is that why you changed your mind so suddenly about staying here?"

Morgan's face came to life. She told Lynn that the girl finally came to the nightclub last night. But she left before she got there. "It's strange that I've been here over three months and Bela and I have never even caught a glimpse of her. I was beginning to feel like giving up. Then she showed up last night."

Lynn responded. "Too bad you didn't get to see her."

"Tell me about it; I was crushed. But György talked to her. He didn't get her name, but he did tell her about me and gave her his card."

Lynn wished she had a name. *If her last name is Palaki ...* "I understand how you feel," Lynn said.

"Well, I'm going home after this semester whether I find her or not, but I feel like it's about to happen. The thing is, the reason I want to see her is because my biological parents could be here. When I was younger, I accidentally heard my parents say that my mother was from Bucharest. That's so close to Hungary. This girl could even be my sister. And if she is, I am dying to know her. And of course, I'd love to know why my parents kept her but gave me up."

Lynn was struck by Morgan's last statement. Lynn was also struck by how open she was being now compared to a few minutes earlier. She wished she could tell Morgan her mother was, indeed, here. She hoped the Wellingtons would decide soon what to do about this situation. She said, "Can you tell me why you haven't discussed any of this with your parents?"

"They adopted me, that's why. I'm sure they wouldn't appreciate me trying to find my blood relatives. I know it would bother them if they knew I was searching for my roots."

Lynn countered. "Personally, I think they would want to know that you're interested in your biological connections. They may be surprised that you've kept this to yourself, but I think they'd understand. Your feelings are only natural. This may not bother them as much as you think. After all, they've had almost twenty years to prepare for it." Then Lynn told Morgan something that she never expected to hear. She told her that her parents already believed she was here in search of her biological family.

"What?" Morgan said. "Why would they ever think such a thing?"

Lynn said, "I suppose parents just have a sixth sense about things like this sometimes. If you would explain all this to them, it would very likely ease their minds. Especially since their friend Ms. Coleman said she saw you, and you denied seeing her. Now, I think it's quite possible Ms. Coleman saw the other young lady. So it won't be difficult to convince them there really is someone over here who looks just like you."

"Okay, I get it. Can we change the subject now?" Morgan said. Suddenly she gave a startled looked toward the door as two men came into the restaurant. One of them had a ponytail.

Lynn noticed Morgan looking up at them and said, "Someone you know?"

"No. But I was just thinking. György dropped me off here, and I was going to take the bus back to my apartment. I think I'll call a taxi instead."

Lynn said, "My limousine driver is right outside. He can drop you off."

"Thanks. I don't like using the bus much these days because I kind of think someone's been following me around. I've seen a couple of guys watching me."

Lynn was taken by surprise. "What are you saying?"

"Well, the thing is, it happened in Paris too. That's why it's probably nothing but my imagination."

Lynn immediately recalled her own experience Thursday evening when she walked to dinner from her hotel feeling eyes on her and the car that nearly ran her down. It was strange that Morgan had a similar experience. Even stranger was the fact that Morgan had also felt this sensation in Paris last summer. *Does she have a stalker? Is she in danger here? If these sensations*

started in Paris, did they follow her to Budapest from
Paris? Or even from the United States? She said, "You
shouldn't discount your gut feelings. It's possible someone
could actually be keeping an eye on you? Have you seen
anybody?"

"No, I haven't. I've just had a feeling. You know how it is
when you can tell someone is looking at you? Sometimes
those feelings have been real strong."

"Did you tell your parents about this feeling?"

"And give them something else to worry about. No,
thanks."

"Of course, they could change their mind and want
you to come home right away, but I think they need to
know."

"Oh, gee. So much for confidential."

"I understand how you feel, but you could be in
danger. This is definitely something they need to know.
I want to tell you something. Obviously I don't know
what's going on, but someone tried to run me down
Thursday night."

Morgan's mouth dropped open in shock. "No way!"
she exclaimed.

"It's true," Lynn said, and then she told Morgan what
happened. "I don't know if this has anything to do with
what's happening to you, but you're alone in a foreign
country. I don't need to tell you to be careful. I would
advise you not to go anywhere by yourself, especially at
night."

"I don't. I'm pretty careful. But now I'm getting a little
spooked."

"Just keep your eyes open."

They finished lunch, and József drove Morgan home
and took Lynn back to her hotel. As she rode along,
Lynn's mind took her back to the other day when József

said they were being followed. *Is it possible there could be a connection between these things and what Morgan has been going through?*

* * *

Late that morning, Pista and Fane drove over to the girl's apartment. Come hell or high water, this was the day. They planned to catch her coming out of her place sometime that morning and grab her. Not knowing her schedule, they waited for her to appear. Every time the door to her complex opened, they braced themselves. But she never came out.

"She must have done some heavy partying last night. Probably still laying up there in bed asleep," Pista said.

"That's what I would like to be doing," Fane murmured.

"What'd you say, asshole?" Pista exclaimed angrily. He was pretty damned tired of waiting himself, and he certainly didn't need to hear Fane whining like a wimp. Here he was, handing this dummy the chance of a lifetime, and all he could talk about was sleep. He said angrily, "Listen, this could be our big day. Apparently you're not serious about this. Tell you what, buddy. You want out, you got it!" Pista didn't much like Fane. Matter of fact, Pista didn't much like anybody. Period. But he needed Fane for a few reasons. One being to carry out this job, but the other was that Fane gave him someone to take out his antisocial behavior on. The only thing Pista wished was that this mild-mannered chump would fight back sometimes and give him a good reason to beat the shit out of him once in a while.

Fane spoke up quickly. "Oh, no, brother. It's not like that. I meant it would be nice to be in bed with her myself. She's such a hot little number. I was only joking."

"Well, this isn't the time for jokes," Pista scowled. "We both have to be up for this. This waiting is taking a toll on me. I'm not wired for this kind of shit. Been trying to be patient, and it's hard as hell. Far as you're concerned, you'll have plenty of time for fun and games after we do our thing."

After waiting about two hours and becoming hungry and bored, Pista sent Fane down the street to get some food while he watched the apartment. "Hurry up, 'cause if she comes out, I'm gone."

When Fane returned twenty minutes later, they sat in the car and ate their sandwiches, watching and waiting for another thirty minutes. "Who knows when she'll be out?" Pista said, just as a limousine rolled up in front of her door. It reminded him of the one they'd followed a couple of days ago.

Flicking ashes through a crack out the window, Pista couldn't believe it when the door opened and their girl climbed out and went into her apartment building. And who was sitting in the limo but that black *szuka*?

"What the ...?" he said. "See, I knew I should have run that bitch down the other night when I had the chance. I got strong vibes about her. I believe she could really mess things up."

"She might just be one of her teachers for all we know," Fane said.

"I told you to shut your stupid face. If you were so damn smart, you wouldn't be broke right now." Pista started his car. "I'm following her ass."

"Wait up, man. If we hang tight, our girl could come back out by herself. Doesn't look like her dude is around. Maybe we can still grab her today."

"Sometimes you actually put that brain cell of yours to work." Pista turned off the ignition.

The girl never came back out. The two men gave up after awhile and went back to Pista's place for a beer.

* * *

Lynn called Sara Wellington to tell her about her meeting with Morgan. Mrs. Wellington said, "Morgan already told us she's staying in Budapest. When she first told us she was coming home, Horace and I were thrilled, of course. We wondered how you'd managed to get her to change her mind in the first place. But after you and I talked, we decided it would be best for Morgan to meet her mother before she leaves. We'll work out the details and let you know our thoughts. At least her father and I aren't as worried now that you have seen and spoken to her."

Mrs. Wellington then asked Lynn to see what more she could learn. "We want to understand why Morgan ended up going to Budapest where her mother is. Furthermore, now she's staying, we can't leave it to chance that she won't run into her, especially since they're both at CEU. When they connect, we want it to be under the right circumstances."

Then Lynn told Mrs. Wellington about Morgan's feelings of being followed. "That is certainly a concern. I'm asking you to watch out for her. I do have to say this isn't the first time Morgan's had these notions. Even when she was very small, she could come up with the strangest ideas that had no basis in reality. I will talk with her about this." Mrs. Wellington sounded unusually calm, but her calmness did not allay Lynn's misgivings. As the call ended, Lynn was thinking that she wanted to tell Mrs. Wellington the real reason Morgan came to Budapest; however, she had promised confidentiality.

Besides, this really was something Morgan needed to do herself. *Such a dilemma.* Not being able to tell Mrs. Wellington what she needed to hear was as bad as not being able to tell Morgan about her mother being right there, at CEU. Lynn would be glad when all this was out in the open.

CHAPTER
19

EARLY THAT AFTERNOON, IVONA JOINED her mother for a leisurely brunch at home. Nicola had a folder full of papers and was marking one up. "Morning, Niko. What are you doing?" Ivona asked.

"Putting the final touches on my keynote address for the IBC dinner in Vienna tomorrow evening."

"Oh yes, the International Biophysics Conference. When are you leaving?"

"First thing in the morning. I also have to conduct workshops Tuesday and Wednesday morning, but I'll be back Wednesday afternoon." Then Nicola studied Ivona's look and said, "I see you changed your hair color back. I like it," Nicola said taking a sip of her tea.

"Thanks, Niko, I do too," Ivona said excitedly. She could hardly wait to tell Niko the latest development. "I must tell you—something amazing happened last night."

Nicola looked at her daughter. "What happened, Vonni?"

Ivona told her mother about the musician at the club who had mistaken her for another girl. "He was so convinced I was someone else, he didn't seem to believe me."

Nicola was getting excited. "Maybe he thought you were the girl you saw at the department store," she said.

"My thoughts exactly." Ivona then told Niko her plans to call the musician and ask him to set up a "date" so the two could meet.

Ivona could not tell that upon hearing her account of last night's developments, her mother's heart was racing.

Nicola said, "It's incredible to think that she could be right here in Buda. The good Lord knows I'd give anything to meet her myself. But like I told you before, I would hate for us to get our hopes up just to be let down if this young woman turns out not to be your sister."

"Well, we'll find out soon. I'm going to call him after I eat. He played the late-night set, so I assume he'll be sleeping late."

Nicola could feel Ivona's excitement. She thought about that young lady she saw on the campus the other day and wondered if she'd actually been looking at her own daughter. She told Ivona, "She could be a student at CEU. Just as soon as I get a chance, I'll check and see if I can locate her in our student files." *And if I find her?* she wondered. *If she is Vonni's sister, would she want to meet us? Dear God, I hope so.* Nicola tried to calm her emotions.

"That's great, Niko! Will you get a chance to check before you leave tomorrow?" Ivona asked.

"I'm afraid not. I won't even be going to my office in the morning. My flight is early."

"I wish I could go look myself, but my lab partner and I have to spend every waking moment finishing our term project. Besides, this guy I met last night might be able to get something set up before then."

"I hope so, but if not, I'll get on it the minute I return. It shouldn't take long to find her, especially if her last name is Wellington."

Ivona was breathlessly happy. If her sister was on campus, Niko would find her. She said, "Well, at least I can do something about it now. I'm going to call György Novak."

Nicola went into her study to finish preparing for her trip. But she found herself thinking about Vonni's great news. Her excitement was definitely contagious. Nicola's thoughts became filled with family matters. Her small family was very important to her. Even though her father had passed when she was young and she had no siblings, it was fulfilling to have a great relationship with her mother and daughter. Also, she still kept up with a few of her father's family members back in Bucharest. Learning that her daughter was an identical twin was admittedly Nicola's greatest shock ever. She still hadn't quite gotten over that, and the thought that her other daughter could be right here in Budapest was nearly too much to hope for. But she believed it could be so and desperately wanted it to be. But she wondered fearfully, *If this is my daughter, will she want to see me as much as I want to see her? Will she want to have a relationship with me? I pray so.*

In some ways, Ivona was like Nicola, especially given her fierce interest in science. Her daughter had always been serious about her education, and her behavior had been fairly predictable. However, earlier this year she had turned into a night owl, hanging out with a group of musicians and dating a band leader. For Ivona, who rarely dated and whose friends were typically students with similar interests, this had been a huge change. One thing Nicola had not cared for was the way Ivona dressed when she hung out with that group. She recalled one particular blowup.

"Vonni, all that black is very unbecoming on you. You've always looked great in vibrant colors. And you've practically ruined your beautiful head of hair. What's next? Tattoos?"

"Niko, you, of all people, have a lot of nerve criticizing how I dress. It's a style I happen to like. I sure wouldn't want to walk around looking like I'm forty years old, like you do."

"This is not how you used to dress."

"But can't you see I've changed? I am not the same person I used to be. Just let me do my thing!"

Nicola said, "I will not try to control what you wear, but you *are* still the same person you used to be. Maybe you're going through something right now, but I just don't think you should play down your looks to fit into a crowd."

"You wouldn't understand," Ivona snapped and walked out of the room.

Nicola had discussed the change in her daughter with Reeni, and they both believed that Vonni was just going through an adjustment to the fact that she was half a set of twins, the other half being someone she'd never met. The good thing was that Ivona only dressed that way when she went out at night. With the exception of that blonde hair, she looked pretty normal the rest of the time.

Fortunately, that phase didn't last very long. When classes resumed in the fall, Ivona was back to her former self. Nicola was grateful that through it all, her daughter's focus on academics had never changed. And now Nicola was thankful that Ivona had gotten rid of that horrid blonde hair! It was good to have the old Ivona back.

Nicola stared at her family photos and envisioned one with both Ivona and her sister together. How incredible that would be! Since the midwife's letter, she had dreamed of seeing her other daughter one day. That would no doubt be one of the major events of all time. For a moment, she let herself daydream about what it might have been like had she reared both girls. Picturing the two growing up together with her and Reeni tinted her heart with sadness. For they had not grown up together. In fact, at nineteen they had never been together for even a single day of their lives. That line of thought brought other major events to Nicola's mind, starting with the death of her father. She was so young when it happened that her memories of him were few but remained strong. She remembered when she used to ride on his shoulders and when he twirled her around and around or bounced her on his lap. Nicola knew her father's death was the reason her mother took her to America.

She remembered having a pleasant childhood in the United States and enjoying school. Her most treasured possession had been the microscope she received in the sixth grade. She'd loved viewing all sorts of things under that scope, although remembering that some of those things had been rather gross brought a smile. She thought about how her interest in science had been whetted by Dr. Wellington, who had encouraged her to pursue that field. Nicola credited him with fostering her love of science and instilling in her the determination to reach her goals. For that, she would always be grateful to him.

Nicola had been a popular teenager. Even though her mother was only a housekeeper, she had lots of friends whose parents were professionals. Her looks had attracted boys like flies. She started going steady with Randolph, the most popular boy in school, and at fifteen, she thought she knew what love was. Young love. She remembered how Randy had coaxed her and convinced her to go all the way. His words had been so special to her young mind.

"Nicola, you are everything to me. I love you." He caressed her body, and it felt magical.

When he started putting his hands where they shouldn't be, she tried to make him stop.

"I need you. Please prove that you love me. I promise I'll be careful. I'll go crazy if I can't have you."

Knowing she had the power to make a boy go crazy, who needed her as badly as he did, touched her heart. The most important thing was that he loved her so much. She finally gave in. After all, she loved him too.

Young love, she mused. *I'm glad my daughter got past that phase in her life. I hope both of my daughters have.*

In any event, giving in was a mistake she soon regretted when she found herself pregnant. That meant that she had to face the difficult choice of what to do with her life. The memory of that agonizing decision still made her emotional. She took a tissue from her desk and dabbed her eyes.

Once she'd agreed to give her baby up for adoption, she had been unable to overcome the emptiness she felt. When she learned that the Wellingtons were interested in adopting her baby, she felt better. At least that baby would have Dr. Wellington as a father. He was such a wonderful man.

As she sat in her den with soft music playing in the background, Nicola continued reminiscing. As happened often, she thought of her late husband. She replayed the scene when they first met.

It was many years earlier in Budapest, when Ivona was a mere toddler and she a teenager. Nicola witnessed a fortuitous scene. It was early evening, and the sidewalks were nearly deserted. She was on her way home from her after-school job when she noticed a well-dressed man carrying a briefcase. He was walking ahead of her. All of a sudden, he staggered and grabbed a chain-link fence for support.

Nicola ran over to the ailing figure and patted him on the arm. "Mister, mister, are you all right?" The man moaned softly.

Then he said, "Thank you, my dear. I'm better. I was just feeling a little dizzy is all." When he tried to stand up straight and get his bearings, he appeared to be disoriented. "I think I will be all right," he said, still appearing unsteady on his feet.

"Sir, why don't you just sit down a minute?" she suggested, helping him to a bench. After a moment, his complexion still looked pallid. A man passing by noticed and stopped to ask if he could help. Nicola said, "I think this man needs an ambulance," and the man on the bench did not protest. The passerby ran to the corner pharmacy to call for help. While waiting for the ambulance, Nicola stayed with the man, who turned out to be thirty-four-year-old Dr. Adam Palaki, a physician and researcher.

Nicola asked the ambulance attendants where they were taking Dr. Palaki and was surprised to learn they were taking him to the hospital where she worked after school. The next afternoon, she stopped by his hospital room. He told her the doctors said that he'd had a very mild heart attack but no permanent damage was done. He thanked her for coming to his aid and said that if she had not stopped, he was not sure what might have happened.

After that night, Nicola found herself stopping by Dr. Palaki's hospital room each day to see how he was doing. Somehow, she still felt responsible for him. Besides, since her after-school job was at the hospital, it was easy to look in on him. He told her all about his work; what he did reminded her a lot of Dr. Wellington. He explained that he was conducting medical research on a condition that typically led to loss of eyesight. He said he'd been working on the project for some time. It sounded like extremely important work, and she was very interested. The day Dr. Palaki was released he mentioned to Nicola how pleased he was to get back to his project.

During their visits while he was in the hospital, Adam Palaki talked to young Nicola like she was a friend. He was a kind man who in many ways reminded her of Dr. Horace Wellington. She had finally acknowledged to herself her childhood crush on Dr. Wellington, who'd seemed larger than life to her when she was a teen. She realized she was beginning to develop similar feelings for Dr. Palaki. Like Dr. Wellington had done, Adam Palaki recognized her potential and encouraged her in her studies.

The following year, when Nicola was accepted at Central European University in Budapest and her family moved there from Romania, she lost touch with him. However, during her fourth year of college, Adam Palaki accepted a position at a hospital in Budapest and contacted her when he arrived there. They resumed their friendship, and she began working with him on his research project. Before they knew it, their friendship had blossomed into a full-blown relationship. For Nicola, despite her and Adam's seventeen-year age difference, the seeds of this romance had been planted years ago. They were married following her graduation from college. Dr. Palaki adopted young Ivona and encouraged Nicola to obtain her PhD in microbiology. Her mother, Corina, continued to live with them to look after Ivona.

Nicola found that she was caressing her wedding photo as she held it in her hands. She dabbed her eyes again as she thought about the tragedy of his death. An avid sports enthusiast, Adam Palaki was a marathon runner and an expert skier. He even taught Ivona to ski. Although he'd had that heart incident, his physician told him that he could still participate in strenuous sports. Unfortunately, fate stepped in. Just five years into their marriage, shortly before his forty-fourth birthday, Adam Palaki suffered a fatal accident on the ski slopes. Like her mother, Nicola became a widow at a young age. She had loved, respected, and admired her husband. He was devoted to his work but also to her and Ivona, and he generously showered his affection upon them. She was devastated by his passing. It had been a very tough time for her. She had appealed to her mother for support. "Reeni, I don't know how to deal with this. I miss him so much. How did you handle it when Daddy died?"

"I know it is hard, dear. It was extremely hard for me too," Corina had answered. "I was grateful for the years your father and I shared. And I was very happy that I had you, but along with having a child came much responsibility. Life had been comfortable with Dimitri, but I was left with no money and no way to provide for you. Making a better life for us became my chief focus. At first when your father died, I mourned him every day and didn't know how I could ever get over his leaving me like that. Then one day, something hit me. I was feeling sorrier for myself than I was for your father, who had suffered the greatest loss of all—his life. I realized how selfish that was of me. After that revelation, I was able to let go and appreciate my memories with him. I could almost sense him smiling down at me when I released my pain. I love him to this day."

Nicola had listened to her mother's wisdom, which gave her the strength to go on with her life. Not long after her husband's death, she'd picked up the research project that had been his life's work. Studying her deceased husband's notes gave her solace. It also provided a much-cherished connection to him. Two years after Dr. Adam Palaki died, Nicola completed his project. It was published under both their names, with her husband receiving the greater credit posthumously. The Palaki research was groundbreaking for people who suffered from a certain type of vision problem. Because of that work, Nicola became a prominent figure in research circles.

As a proven expert in the field, she wrote, published, lectured, and taught, and she enjoyed a fulfilling life. All was going well. They had a lovely home. Her mother was in good health. Her daughter was following in her footsteps. But then came that fateful day just six months ago, when her mother received that letter from Miss Flossie Walker, the midwife who'd delivered Ivona, the letter containing life-changing information that had thrown their lives into chaos.

Since learning she had another daughter, even now Nicola was torn. She often wondered if she should try harder to contact the Wellingtons. But when she'd spoken with her, Mrs. Wellington had said she'd not heard from the midwife. But Ivona was sure her twin sister was in Budapest, and so Nicola had elected to follow Reeni's advice and wait. Still, it left her with a strong sense of guilt over not being proactive. After all, this other girl *was* her daughter. She had given birth to her. She had been misled. She had a right to know what happened.

The predicament she and her family were in was no fault of her own. Ivona had a right to know her sister, and she had a right to know her own daughter. That pattern of thoughts never ceased.

Since the midwife's letter last May, Nicola found herself haunted by frequent dreams about her other daughter. In one recurring dream, she saw her walking down the street; she would try to call out to her, but she didn't know her name. Nicola caught up with her, but just before she reached out to tap her daughter on the shoulder, she would wake up. Still, although she didn't know how, Nicola believed she would see her other daughter face-to-face someday. Now Ivona was about to meet her sister. Nicola desperately wanted to meet her too. Could *someday* be here?

The very idea was daunting. Between nerves and excitement, Nicola now wished she wasn't taking this trip tomorrow. Hopefully, the boy Vonni met would be successful in bringing them together. Because what she really wanted to do right now was search the academic records for her other daughter.

CHAPTER
20

After taking no more than a few bites of her food, Ivona picked up her mobile phone and dialed the number György had given her. After several rings, a sleepy voice said, "Hullo." György looked at the clock and saw that it was noon. He had slept in after his late-night gig. "Who's this?" he said, slightly irritated at having been awakened by the phone. He'd wanted to sleep at least another hour or two.

Ivona could tell by his voice she had awakened him, but her need to know was much too great to let this opportunity pass. She said, "Oh, hello, György. I'm sorry if I woke you. This is Ivona Palaki, the girl you met last night. Remember, the one you said looked like your friend."

György bolted upright. He was surprised she was calling so soon. He said, "Hey, no problem. Glad you called. Yeah, my friend Morgan came into the club last night after you left. She was really disappointed that she missed you. She definitely wants to meet you before she leaves. Like I said, Morgan's from America, but she's attending CEU this semester. She'll be going back to the States soon."

Ivona was thrilled to hear that her sister was a student at CEU. *I'll tell Niko.* But she was sad that she was going back to America soon. *I have to meet her before she leaves.*

György continued. "She tells me other people have also told her she looks just like someone here in Budapest. They had to have been talking about you. Like I said last night, I thought you were Morgan too. You're so much alike, you could be twins. By the way, what did you say your name was?"

You could be twins. This statement sent quivers down Ivona's spine. The possibility that it was really her sister was practically blowing her away. It was exciting to know that Morgan had heard about her and wanted to meet her too. She realized this guy had asked her name. "Oh, it's Ivona. And I also attend CEU."

"No fooling. I'm surprised you two haven't run into each other on campus."

Ivona took a deep breath. "Me too," she said. "I'm on the science campus. What does Morgan study?"

"Fashion design. Her classes are on the arts campus."

They talked a little longer. Ivona was aware that she was keeping him from his sleep.

György said, "I want to get you two together. Can you come by the club tonight? My gig is from nine to one, and if you can get there, I'll make sure Morgan comes by too."

"Definitely," Ivona said. "I have to work in the lab this afternoon, but I can come by after I finish up. What time do you think Morgan will be there?"

"She's usually there by nine. Can I take your telephone number? I'll let you know for sure that she's coming."

Ivona gave György her mobile phone number. She could hardly wait for his confirmation that Morgan would be at the club that night.

After hanging up the phone, György tried to reach Morgan, but his call went straight to her voice mail, so he left an urgent message. He decided to try again in a little while, but as it turned out, he fell back to sleep before he got the chance and woke up a couple of hours later. He reached Morgan, who told him her phone had been on the charger. György told Morgan about his phone call from Ivona. He explained that Ivona wanted to know if she could come to the club tonight and that he had told her Morgan would probably be there at nine o'clock.

Morgan was thrilled. "Of course, I'll be there," she exclaimed excitedly. "I can even get there earlier if necessary."

"She's waiting for me to call her back," György said. "I'll tell her you're coming. And Morgy, you're gonna be amazed. I know you will."

* * *

Ivona found Nicola and excitedly told her that she thought she'd be meeting Morgan tonight. "Be sure to wake me when you come in and tell me all about it," Nicola told her.

She waited more than an hour to hear back from György. She'd hoped he'd have gotten back to her right away. When he didn't call, she wondered if maybe he'd been unable to reach Morgan. Still, he could have let her know something instead of not calling one way or another. She knew she could have called him too, but fearing he might have fallen back to sleep, she was afraid of waking him a second time. Her lab partner had already called to remind her they had to finish up their project today. She called her partner, and they agreed to meet in thirty minutes in the laboratory.

Once Ivona and her partner got underway in the lab, they discovered a serious glitch in their project. To correct it, they would have to redo one of their lengthy experiments. It was going to take several hours to complete, but they could take their time to be sure they got it right. Her cell phone rang just as she had her hands full of test tubes and equipment, but she managed to answer. "This is Ivona." György apologized for calling back so late and explained what happened. He told her Morgan would be at the club around nine.

Now that Ivona and her partner were working on their project, she knew she couldn't possibly get to the club that early. She said, "When I didn't hear from you, I came over to the lab to work with my partner to finish our semester project. We ran into some snags, and now it's going to take several more hours." She glanced at the big clock on the wall and added, "By the time I get home and get dressed, the earliest I can get there is probably eleven."

György apologized again and said, "That's cool. I'll let Morgan know. Don't worry, she'll be there when you arrive. Good luck with your experiment. We'll see you tonight."

Ivona hung up, excited that she'd finally meet her sister. She set her telephone down at her work station and got back to work.

* * *

The Blue Diamond was jammed with a typical Saturday-night crowd. The dance floor was packed, and there was only standing room left in the club. Morgan and Bela had gotten there early, avoiding the line of people waiting to get in that gathered outside later.

A long line met her when Ivona arrived at ten-forty-five. The club had a capacity of four hundred people. Because of fire regulations, when that number was reached, the doorman had to keep newcomers waiting outside until other patrons left. "Sorry, people, I can't let you in until this crowd thins out," he told the waiting crowd. When one or two people came out, he let one or two in. Ivona was concerned about how long it might take. She decided she'd better call György's number. *Even if he is playing right now, the band will take a break long before I get in there.* She looked in her purse for her phone. Horrified, she suddenly remembered leaving it on her work station at the lab. What could she do?

Someone asked, "How long will we have to stand out here?"

"Don't know," answered the doorman. "It's anybody's guess when people in there decide to leave. The band is doing an oldies thing tonight. That's usually everybody's favorite. So I can't tell you. Sorry."

Ivona's heart sank. "Can I just go in and look for someone for a minute?" she yelled from the back of the group.

"Me too," someone else yelled.

"Sorry, miss, everyone uses that line."

Ivona knew there was no point trying to convince him this was not a line. She decided to try cash.

"Look, miss, I'd be rich if I took all the money you people offered me." He pointed overhead and said, "See that camera right there? After being out of work for six months, I'm not about to lose this job. Keep your money."

So she waited outside for the next forty-five minutes. During that time, only five or six people got in. *At this rate, it will be two o'clock in the morning before I get in there*, she estimated. After waiting another hour and making it only halfway up the line, Ivona asked the person behind her to hold her place. Then she walked around to a side door to see if she could get in. It was locked. Against her better judgment, she walked to the back alley. It was dimly lit and really scary. She conjured up the courage to go to the back door of the nightclub. It too was locked, and when a cat hissed nearby, she practically jumped out of her skin and hurried back to the safety of her place in line, considering herself lucky to be alive. At one o'clock, the doorman announced that the band was finished playing; another was scheduled for the late-night shift. He still couldn't let anyone else in until there was space. Ivona looked at the door every time it opened, hoping to see Morgan and György. By one-thirty, she was about the tenth person in line. Feeling extremely disheartened, she had no choice but to leave. She would just have to speak to György tomorrow. When she got home, she didn't have a reason to wake Niko, and when she got up the following morning her mother was already gone.

On stage with his band, György watched Morgan. He saw her constantly turning her head, looking in every direction, sometimes walking around looking for Ivona. He could tell she was disappointed, and he was upset that she was being stood up. He kept going over to assure her Ivona would show up. Knowing how much meeting Ivona meant to her, he'd wanted so badly to make this meeting happen. He didn't understand why Ivona hadn't called if she couldn't make it. György tried to call her but got no answer. He didn't know what to think. But he would call her tomorrow. Had she chickened out? *This is crazy.*

Inside the club, Morgan looked around, as she'd been doing since before eleven o'clock. Anytime someone moved near her, she jumped expectantly. She bit her nails and waited anxiously. Every few minutes she walked around the club looking for her sister. No Ivona. *What happened?* She couldn't contain her disappointment. She and Bela stayed at the club pretty late that night, not wanting to take a chance of missing her. Finally, around two o'clock she, Bela, and György left. Morgan noted the thin crowd waiting outside the club, but it never occurred to her that until thirty minutes ago, Ivona had been waiting in that very crowd. She was too preoccupied to notice that some of the people in line did a double take when she walked by.

When Morgan got home, she went to bed. For the longest time, she couldn't sleep. Her heart was filled with disappointment that Ivona had been a no-show. *Doesn't she want to meet me?* She lay awake wondering, heartbroken.

* * *

On Sunday morning Morgan called Lynn Davis. "Remember I told you about the girl I hoped to see here in Budapest?"

"Yes, of course."

"I almost met her last night. She was supposed to come to the club, but she never showed up. She told György that she'd be there, but I never saw her come in."

"Did you learn her name?"

Morgan told Lynn the girl's name was Ivona. "I'll have to ask him again what her last name was."

Lynn said, "It certainly sounds exciting. You could be meeting her sooner than you think."

"I feel that way too. I guess she had to change her plans last night. I'm so disappointed. That makes two nights in a row that I could have met her. When I got home yesterday I called my parents, and I did tell them about her."

"That's great, Morgan. Was telling them as difficult as you thought it would be?"

"Actually it went okay. We had a good talk, and they were understanding. They were surprised, but both of them thought it was natural for me to want to explore my roots. They did tell me they wished I had told them about this before. It would have spared them needless worry. Now I wish I had too."

"I'm glad it went well, Morgan. At least now they know the truth. I'll bet they're very relieved," Lynn said.

"They sounded like it. I'm glad you encouraged me to talk about it. They did have a right to know, and now everything is out in the open. I feel much better about the whole thing."

Lynn knew that not everything was out in the open. Besides, there were still some unanswered questions, and she knew the Wellingtons would want more answers. She was waiting for Mrs. Wellington to give her the go-ahead to arrange a meeting between Morgan and her biological mother. She told Morgan, "Listen, I'm going to stay in Budapest a little while longer. Be sure to call if you need to reach me. I'll be back in touch."

On Sunday afternoon, Sara Wellington called Lynn. She said, "I wanted to tell you about our conversation with our daughter. It turns out Morgan admitted to not having been totally open with us about why she went to Budapest."

"Yes, I am aware. She phoned me today and said she'd told you everything."

"I assumed she had already told you about this, and I'm sure you encouraged her to be frank with us."

"Well, I ..."

"Thank you, however you handled it. The girl Morgan is looking for must look quite a bit like her. My husband and I figured she was no doubt the person Celia saw. That eased our minds too. If we had only known the truth in the beginning, we might have saved ourselves and Morgan some angst and you a trip to Budapest. We think we understand why she withheld this from us. We believe she didn't want us to feel hurt by the fact that she was interested in the biological side of her family. This interest has probably been with her all her life. I wish she hadn't felt like she couldn't talk to us about this."

Lynn said, "According to Dr. Stern, people who are adopted are usually driven by a strong need to know their biological roots. This desire may have even been responsible for her mood swings when she was younger."

"Yes, Helene explained all that. But unfortunately, we were never able to get Morgan to speak about it. In any event, I have a call in to Helene. I want to get her thoughts about Morgan's meeting her biological mother. I'm sure she will agree, and when she does, I will ask you to set it up."

"Certainly," Lynn said.

"Horace and I talked about this girl who looks like Morgan. It's even possible that because Nicola is in Budapest, she could be the child mentioned in her file. But the age is what's curious. She would have to be younger than Morgan, which seems a little young to be going to night clubs and hanging out with musicians."

"Except it's hard to say about teenagers these days. Many of them dress and act like they're much older. I will tell you this. If this is Morgan's sibling we're talking about, Morgan came very close to meeting her last night," Lynn said. "In fact, it was scheduled, but the young lady never showed up."

Sara Wellington listened and contemplated what she heard. Then she replied, "It seems inevitable that they will run across each other. And it would seem that this person must be at least as old as Morgan, if not older. So that rules out being a sibling, since Morgan is Nicola's first child."

Lynn wondered silently, *But what if this is Nicola's other child? Certainly if they had met each other, all that have would come out.*

She discussed this with Mrs. Wellington, who agreed.

"Given her emotional reaction to her biological connections, we wouldn't want to leave such a meeting to chance. I'm beginning to wonder if there is anything to be learned about this family in Bucharest."

"I had been thinking that too. I thought there might at least be some census records I could look through to see the makeup of Corina Moldovan's household while they were there." By the time the phone call ended, Lynn had agreed to go to Bucharest the next day to see what she might find out.

"The next time I speak with you, I expect to have talked to Helene Stern," Sara Wellington said.

* * *

Late Sunday morning, György tried to reach Ivona again. There was no answer, so he left a message. He tried once more an hour later. Still she did not answer her phone. *Is she avoiding me for some reason?* He left a second message for her and decided to let it go. *Hopefully she will call.*

When Ivona picked up her telephone from the laboratory later that morning, she found the battery completely dead. When she got home, she put her phone on its charger and took a nap.

* * *

On Monday morning, Lynn took an early flight to Bucharest, Romania. An hour and a half later, she arrived and went by taxi to see the lawyer she'd located online in an international legal directory. She was also able to set up an appointment online. She went directly to his office on the sixth floor and asked for Marcel Puscasu. His was a small law firm that occupied one wing of the floor. Windows with a lovely city view lined the outer wall of his office, which was otherwise austere.

Lynn told Mr. Puscasu that she wanted to know about Corina Moldovan's family makeup. He listened, and when she finished, he said he was sure he could help her. Together they headed on foot over to the Civil State Office two blocks away, where a wealth of information awaited them. They spent a few hours together, and by the time Lynn caught the plane back to Budapest, she had what she came for, and even more. From information the lawyer obtained, she learned that Corina Ruvni had married Dimitri Moldovan in 1976, and in 1978 they had one child named Nicola. Dimitri died ten years after they were married; Corina and her young daughter moved to the United States six months after his death. Corina Ruvni's birth records showed that she was born in Bucharest, Romania, to parents of mixed ethnicity—Indian and Moldavian. Next, they looked up Nicola's birth records. Nicola René Moldovan was born in Bucharest thirty-four years ago.

Census records from 2000 identified Corina Moldovan as head of household with two daughters, Nicola and Ivona. *Ivona!* Morgan had said that was the name of her look-alike! And just this morning, Morgan had called Lynn before she left for the airport to tell her mystery look-alike's last name was Palaki. *They are related!*

Their ages were given. Ivona and Morgan were the same age. Lynn was puzzled. Were Corina and Nicola Moldovan pregnant at the same time? Could the young woman Morgan was looking for possibly be Corina's daughter? That would make her Morgan's aunt, not her sister. There was no mention of Ivona's father. So where was Nicola's other child?

Mr. Puscasu said, "There is one more thing I will look into when we go back to my office. I will check the public tax records to see how many people were in the Moldovan household when she returned here from the United States in 1994. That way, we will know if the child was born before the family returned to Bucharest or after they moved to Budapest." Lynn wondered if that would be a waste of time, since she knew the child could not have been born before they left the United States. Morgan had been born just a few days before they left. The child in question had to have been born after Nicola left the United States. She told the lawyer that.

He replied, "In this business, Miss Davis, it is best never to assume. Sometimes things are not as they seem."

Finally, marriage records cross-referenced Nicola's marriage in Budapest, Hungary, to Adam Palaki. It was the only record of marriage for Nicola. Lynn wondered where Adam Palaki was now. More importantly, Mr. Puscasu found no birth records for a child born to Nicola Moldovan or to Nicola and Adam Palaki. "What this means," the lawyer said, "is that Ms. Palaki's child was not born in Romania." Depending on its age, it might have been born in Budapest, or even the United States.

During the flight back to Budapest, Lynn's mind stayed on the things she'd learned in Romania. As she processed it all, she drew some significant conclusions. First of all, the easy one: Corina Moldovan was *not* Ivona's mother. Too many things had pointed to that not being the case. Secondly, and more importantly, while Lynn had believed that Nicola's second child was much younger than Morgan and born in Budapest, she'd been way off. Morgan and Ivona were the same age. Nicola did indeed deliver before leaving the United States. The only conclusion Lynn could draw, as surprising as it was, was that Morgan and Ivona were sisters. But they were more than that. They were twins! Pretty shocking. Lynn felt certain she was right, and she was sure the Wellingtons knew nothing about it.

She decided to have Ella find the twins' birth records. She caught Ella at her home in Forest Park before she left for work. "I need you to do something first thing this morning." She told Ella what she'd found out in Bucharest. "Before you go into the office, I need you to stop over at the Office of Vital Records and get a copy of Morgan Wellington's birth certificate. Her birth date was May 11." She told her the year. "It should be a multiple birth record. See what you can find under the name of Nicola René Moldovan, age fifteen."

"Will do. Man oh man! It's something—Morgan Wellington has been looking for her twin sister."

"You're right—all things point to that being the case," Lynn replied.

"I'm just leaving the house. I'll call you as soon as I find it."

"Good. Fax whatever you come up with to me at the hotel."

Morgan had said she felt a special connection with her look-alike and was determined to meet her. She also told Lynn that she learned she'd almost had an encounter with the girl at a department store. Lynn knew that Morgan had no knowledge that this was her own sister she was talking about, let alone her twin! Lynn wondered how she would have handled running into Ivona the past weekend. She felt it was more important than ever that she set up a meeting between Morgan and her biological family. The trip to Bucharest had been productive.

Back in Budapest, Lynn's driver picked her up from the airport. She called Mrs. Wellington from the limousine. "I just returned from Bucharest and have some very interesting news. I believe you're in for a huge surprise."

"We were hoping the trip was worthwhile. Tell me, what did you learn?"

"Quite a lot. Do you want the long or short version of what I found out?"

"Please, let's not draw this out. Give me the short version. I'll take the details afterward."

"Before I left, Morgan told me the name of her look-alike—Ivona Palaki. Long story short, Ivona Palaki is Morgan's twin sister."

Silence.

"Mrs. Wellington?"

"You should have told me to sit down. I'm afraid what you just said practically bowled me over. This is perhaps the biggest shock of my life. I've never had any knowledge of Morgan being born a twin. The midwife delivered her to us the very night she was born. She told us that Nicola had to be rushed to the hospital right after giving birth. She said nothing about twins. None of us knew this, particularly Morgan. I worry about how she will feel when she learns she has a twin sister?"

Lynn proceeded to tell her about the details of her findings in Bucharest. "My partner is researching the birth records just to confirm. I'll let you know what I learn, but I wanted you to know what I found out as soon as possible."

"Yes, do keep me informed," Sara Wellington said. She hung up and pondered the situation. Her daughter was a twin. Her twin sister was right there in Budapest! It was almost too much to fathom. She still wondered how this could be, and immediately she was flooded with memories of the night they'd received their baby. She relived the moment Miss Walker had rung her doorbell, the evening of May 11. "I have a beautiful surprise for you," she had said. Sara had beamed with joy at the bundle in the midwife's arms. Her husband thanked Miss Walker and told her that he and his wife had planned to pick the baby up.

"It's quite all right. My patient and her mother are gone. After I cleaned this pretty little baby up, I didn't want you to have to wait any longer." They invited Miss Walker inside, and she immediately handed the baby over to Mrs. Wellington. She set a diaper bag full of essentials on the hall table. Sara and her husband always appreciated that the midwife delivered the baby to them herself. Now she wondered who had withheld this important fact from her and Horace? Corina, Nicola, or the midwife herself.

She rushed to tell her husband the astounding news.

CHAPTER
21

Monday Afternoon, November 25

ELLA CALLED LYNN TO TELL her she had located the girls' birth records under Nicola Moldovan's name. The records showed that Nicola gave birth to two unnamed girl babies on May 11, 1994. Morgan Alana Wellington and Ivona Kay Palaki were confirmed twins. "I'll fax you the certificate," she said.

Lynn said, "Somehow the Wellingtons never knew this."

"Do you think Nicola and her mother knew Nicola had twins?" Ella asked.

"You'd think they'd have known. But what if they didn't? What if this is somehow unknown to them too?" While that was hard to believe, Lynn would soon find out. She expected to meet with Dr. Palaki soon.

Ella told Lynn she had also learned that the midwife who delivered the twins was named Flossie Walker. "She lives in an assisted living residence on Reading Road."

"She can possibly explain what happened," Lynn said. She suggested that Ella see if she could meet with Miss Walker as soon as possible.

"Will do. I'll let you know how it goes," Ella told her.

Lynn was glad Ella had found the midwife. Maybe Miss Flossie Walker could shed light on the circumstances of the twins' separation.

Lynn called Mrs. Wellington to tell her the birth certificate confirmed that Nicola gave birth to twins. Mrs. Wellington sighed but said little else. She seemed to have already reconciled herself to the fact. Lynn said, "We will need to talk about your daughter meeting her biological family. We already know she is itching to meet this twin sister, who happens to be the reason she came to Budapest in the first place. And we know they almost met two times recently. Right now Morgan has no idea who Ivona Palaki is. And we don't know if Ivona knows about Morgan either."

"Of course, you are right. I'm sure Morgan will want to meet them all. This is quite a lot for her to deal with on her own. In fact, I would like to hear from Nicola about why they never told us about twins being born. Horace and I want to be there when this meeting takes place. We have an appointment with his doctor this afternoon to see if he can make the long flight to Budapest.

"Meantime, I spoke with Dr. Stern about all this, including this newest development with the twin. Helene agrees that Morgan should be told everything and recommends that we do so right away. Horace and I feel this is too important to discuss with her on the telephone, but since we aren't there right now and can't afford to put it off, Morgan will have to be told by phone. We need your help."

"Certainly. What would you like me to do?" Lynn asked.

"We would like you to set it up. Helene feels that you should participate in the call, and I agree. Just select the earliest time you two can call us. I'll give you a number to call."

"I'll do that," Lynn replied.

"It doesn't matter what time you give us. We want Morgan to know everything," Mrs. Wellington said. "Of course, she'll have many questions that we can't answer. But I am hoping that with you on the case, we'll soon know the truth."

"I'm about to go over to the university to try to catch Dr. Palaki, or at least arrange a meeting time with her. While I'm there, I'll check student records to see if I can find Ivona Palaki. Morgan learned that she too is a student at CEU."

"My God, the coincidences never cease."

"Before I head to CEU, I'll try to reach Morgan to set up a time for the conference call. I'll call you with the time. Then, after I speak with Nicola Palaki, I'll let you know when the family meeting will take place so that if your husband can travel, you can reserve your flights."

Then Lynn called Morgan and explained that her parents had some very important information for her. She asked Morgan to give her a time when they could talk.

"You're going to be in on the call?" Morgan asked, perplexed. Lynn told her that she was. "Why you?"

"As an investigator, I have learned some things that I shared with them. They want me on the call to help fill in the details," Lynn answered.

"Can't you just tell me?" Morgan asked.

"I'm afraid not. This is a discussion your parents want to have with you."

"Then can we just call them now? I have two classes this evening, but I have a few minutes now."

"I'm afraid your mother was going with your dad to a doctor's appointment. I believe tomorrow morning will work best. They wanted to make it early if possible, even if it is in the middle of the night for them."

"Now I'm even more curious," Morgan said. "But it can't be bad, or they wouldn't make me wait. I guess we can meet at the Történelmi Café tomorrow morning at nine."

Lynn called Sara Wellington and gave her the time. "Morgan was extremely curious and wanted to make the call right now because she has classes this evening."

"I'm sure, poor dear," Sara Wellington said, "but Horace and I have to leave in ten minutes, and I wouldn't want to have to rush something like this."

Next, Lynn went over to CEU and found Nicola's office. Her administrator explained that Dr. Palaki was out of town until Wednesday afternoon. Lynn made an appointment to see her during her first available timeslot: four on Wednesday. Afterward, she walked over to the administrative office building to see if she could obtain the records for Ivona Palaki. Ursola, the young woman who helped her the other day, was there. Lynn showed her the authorization letter and told her what she needed. Ursola went into the student records and copied Ivona Palaki's file, placed it in a manila envelope, and handed it to Lynn with a smile. Lynn's driver drove her back to her hotel.

Lynn was exhausted. In one day, she'd flown to and from Bucharest, spending a few hours there in between. And she'd made some pretty surprising discoveries. Things seemed to be coming to a head. She would be glad when everything was out in the open. She plopped down on her sofa and kicked off her shoes. Then she opened the envelope to study Ivona Palaki's records. She looked at Ivona's picture and stared in amazement. The young woman did not simply resemble Morgan Wellington. Except for her blonde hair, Ivona Palaki was the very image of Morgan Wellington! Lynn's head practically spun at the likeness.

From the records, Lynn saw that Ivona was a year ahead of Morgan, so she must have skipped a grade. Science was her field of study. There wasn't much more personal information, but Lynn had seen more than enough. She went down to the front desk and faxed Ivona's file to Sara Wellington. She also faxed Ivona's picture to Ella to get her opinion. Then she phoned Sara Wellington to tell her to look for her e-mail with the picture of Ivona.

Ten minutes later, Lynn's phone rang. "Miss Davis, Sara Wellington. Horace and I saw the picture. You are absolutely right. There is no doubt this is Morgan's twin, and they're definitely identical. Still, seeing the girl's picture was sobering. When we talk in the morning, please bring both Nicola and Ivona's file photos to show Morgan. You have uncovered more than we ever dreamed."

When Lynn hung up with Mrs. Wellington, Ella called and told Lynn there was no doubt she was 100 percent right about the girls being twins. Then she told her she would be meeting with Miss Walker later today. "Let me know the minute you learn anything," Lynn said.

Cincinnati, Ohio, Monday, November 25

ELLA ARRIVED AT THE FELIX House on schedule and told the middle-aged receptionist, "I am here to see Miss Flossie Walker. My name is Ella Braxton. She's expecting me." The receptionist told Ella to have a seat in the large living room.

The room was comfortably decorated with an oversized sofa in yellow and beige floral print and assorted chairs. On the dark hardwood floor was a pale green carpet with red, yellow, and blue flowers. A piano sat in one corner of the room, the elderly man at the bench softly fingering the keys. A television set was turned to a talk show, and two ladies watched in earnest as youthful-looking older women talked about how their looks defied their years. A couple of women were reading, and two were knitting. A wooden sign on the wall read WALK EVERY CHANCE YOU GET! Ella found the atmosphere of the place charming.

After a few minutes, a male attendant wheeled a white-haired woman into the room. Her short hair was curled tightly. *That's Flossie Walker,* Ella knew at once. The woman looked around, spotted a person she thought was Ella, and pointed her out to the attendant. Ella said, "Miss Walker?"

"How do you do? I'm Flossie Walker, and you must be Mrs. Braxton." Ella shook hands with Miss Walker and handed her a business card, impressed with how youthful and spry Miss Walker looked in her gray, two-piece leisure suit. The other residents in the room momentarily stopped what they were doing to observe Miss Walker's visitor. Flossie waved to two elderly women who smiled and waved back.

After the attendant left them, Miss Walker said, "If you don't mind, we can talk in there." Flossie pointed to an empty drawing room. Ella pushed the wheelchair into the next room and sat in a chair facing her. "You've got to pardon this wheelchair. I can usually get around pretty good on my own, but today the arthritis in my knees has been beating me up. It does that every now and then."

Ella smiled. "You're fortunate you don't have to use it every day. You look like you're in pretty good shape."

"I do pretty good for a young woman," Miss Walker said with a smile.

"Well, I promise not to take up too much of your time," Ella said.

"Young lady, all I have is time, although I can't say how much I have left. Take whatever time you need."

Ella liked Miss Walker's warm, friendly style. She said, "I want to thank you for seeing me. I understand in your career you worked as a nurse-midwife."

"Yes, I did." Miss Walker proudly gave Ella a brief history of her work experience.

Ella explained, "As I told you on the phone, my firm is looking into a case involving a maternity patient you handled nineteen years ago. Do you mind if I ask you about it?"

Miss Walker had known in her heart what Mrs. Braxton wanted to talk about. She told herself, *Here it is,* and she told Ella she did not mind.

"Thank you," Ella said. "On May 11, nineteen years ago, you delivered twins to a fifteen-year-old teenager named Nicola Moldovan."

Miss Walker took a deep breath and leaned forward to speak. "Yes, I did. Honey, just tell me what you want to know, and I'll help you anyway I can." Then Ella and Miss Walker had a conversation that lasted two hours, during which Ella learned the amazing details of the delivery. She was surprised but pleased that Miss Walker was willing to talk about it openly. And she knew Lynn would find her story very interesting.

Miss Walker told Ella about the letter she'd written to Corina Moldovan and the telephone call she received from her and Nicola a few months ago. "Hadn't talked to them in nearly twenty years. I am pretty sure they had to be upset with me, but, thank goodness, they only wanted to know if I had written to the Wellingtons too. Which I had. I hoped those two girls would get in touch with each other. If they haven't yet, I feel in my bones their reunion is getting close."

"I can tell you it is getting close," Ella said.

Then Miss Walker leaned in and said, "I want to tell you something that's worrying me. Lately I've been having some strange dreams about those girls. They were born on Mossie and my birthday, and I've always felt close to them for some reason. But recently, I have been afraid that they were in trouble. Sometimes I see some men after them. It frightens me. I just pray that they are safe."

Ella told her, "My associate is in Budapest with the Wellington girl right now. I'm pretty sure they're just fine."

"Thank you, Lord," Miss Walker said. Then she complimented Ella's sharp beige suit and pumps and told her about how she and her twin sister used to dress. "Three-inch heels were as high as you could get. But Mossie and I both loved to wear them. You know how they make your legs look so long and pretty." She chuckled and said, "Listen to me. Old as I am talking like this."

"Well, I'm with you. Looking good is important at any age. I can see that you take pride in your appearance," Ella replied.

"I try." Then she giggled and said, "Sometimes, Mossie and I dressed alike. We both had the same curve-hugging and slinky red jersey dress. When we walked into a restaurant in those dresses, every head turned. Men stared. I guess it was as much about our being identical as it was our dresses." She smiled, and Ella did too.

They discussed other things, including the older woman's family, hobbies, and her knitting projects. Flossie Walker told Ella, "You probably saw my two friends Agnes and Beulah sitting out there knitting. We're all making

Christmas gifts. We usually get together every day to work on them and, of course, visit. They're pretty nice girls. We've been friends a long time."

When their visit was over, the attendant came to wheel Miss Walker back to her room. At the doorway, she turned and waved good-bye to Ella and smiled. Ella had found Miss Walker very likeable, and she had enjoyed their visit very much. But she couldn't wait to call Lynn so she could relay to her what she learned. *This is a real lulu.*

Ella reached Lynn and told her about her visit with Miss Walker and the astonishing events that had transpired when the twins were born.

"You did good, Ella," Lynn said.

"That's how I roll," her feisty colleague replied.

* * *

Flossie intended to collect her knitting basket and go right back downstairs and visit with her friends. But first she just wanted to sit in her room and bask in the freedom she felt after telling Mrs. Braxton about the Moldovan delivery. Other than her spiritual talks with Mossie and the letter she wrote to Mrs. Moldovan, she had never told another soul about it. That particular delivery had resulted in her ending her midwifery career. It had made her doubt herself roundly for the split-second decision she had made and acted on. Withholding the truth from concerned parties who had every right to know had plagued her with guilt. She remembered how cathartic it had been to put the truth on paper when she wrote those letters months ago.

Flossie found Ella Braxton easy to tell her story to. The young lady just listened and made no judgments. Although she'd had a strong idea which case her guest wanted to talk about when she called, when she first heard Miss Braxton say the Moldovan name today, her heart had skipped a beat. But she'd decided to just open up and talk about it. It felt as good talking about it today as it had when she wrote those letters six months ago. She'd had no idea how telling the story with her own mouth would release her from the burden of her self-imposed secrecy.

After lingering in her room, she gathered her things and went back downstairs.

"Who was that woman you were talking to?" Beulah asked when she joined them.

"Now, can't I have a visitor without your two noses in everything?" Flossie said with a twinkle in her eye.

"Flossie Mae, you know we already know everything else there is to know about each other, so this is no different. Now, that woman looked like a lawyer or something," Agnes added. "You got something legal going on?"

"Well, she was a businesswoman, but it was *my* business. Not yours. So now, let's see ... Where are we?" she asked.

"Woman, you just aren't right," Beulah said. The three laughed.

* * *

That afternoon a severe thunderstorm was brewing in Cincinnati. At six o'clock, Flossie Walker was about to go to dinner. It was strange to have thunder and lightening in late fall. To Flossie, everything felt surreal. Suddenly, a clap of thunder hit with such ferocity, it seemed to rock the Felix House. Miss Walker felt the jolt, but at that precise moment, she felt something even stronger that shook her to her very core. She remembered only one other time in her life when she'd felt something as strong as the feeling she'd just experienced. That was the somber occasion of Mossie's death, when she had experienced a powerful shockwave that practically dropped her to her knees. It was like being shaken by an earthquake. As hard as it was to accept, something told her, without a shadow of a doubt, that her dear, beloved sister Mossie was gone on the evening of their thirty-seventh birthday.

Since she and Mossie had to work the weekend of their birthday, Howard Eugene took them to a Thanksgiving concert the weekend before to celebrate. They went to the Taft Theater to see Roy Hamilton, Etta James, and Brook Benton. The twins both wore their most glamorous after-five dresses—Mossie's a deep blue satin and Flossie's a pink and black chiffon. Flossie always remembered how Howard smugly strutted into the theater with his wife on one arm and her on the other. He seemed to genuinely enjoy the envious looks and admiring smiles from men and women alike. When Etta James sang "I'd Rather Go Blind," Howard turned and whispered, "Not me. I gotta be able to see my pretty baby." They all chuckled. Brook Benton's "It's Just a Matter of Time" had them swaying from side to side. But it was Roy Hamilton's classic rendition of "You'll Never Walk Alone" that would play in Flossie's head from that night on.

When she'd felt that jolt fifty years ago, she'd known exactly what it meant. She had just experienced the greatest loss of her life. She remembered the painful details of her loss.

Mossie always arrived at work thirty minutes before her seven o'clock shift. That evening, she was late. Flossie called her sister's home and spoke with Howard Eugene. He told her, "It was hard for me to let her leave—after all, this *is* her birthday." Flossie felt momentarily hopeful that her sister was still home. But her relief was short-lived. Howard said, "But she left over an hour ago."

Flossie panicked. "Something has happened, Howard! I swear it! Something's happened to Mossie!" Flossie cried, her voice alarming Howard. He told her he would call the hospital and call her back after he talked to Mossie. Flossie hung up the phone, knowing she couldn't wait for him to call her back. She called the nurses' station on the ward where Mossie worked.

"She hasn't arrived yet," said Loretta, the head nurse.

"Look, Loretta. I believe something has happened to my sister. Her husband said she should have been there thirty minutes ago. Please see what you can find out. I'll hold."

Flossie prayed. All at once, she could feel Mossie's presence and sense her message, one she desperately hadn't wanted to receive. "Flossie, you know by now that I have departed this realm. But I know you'll be all right. Remember our poem and know that together we will always be. I promise to come back and see you every year on our birthday. You can look for me at this exact time: 7:02 p.m. Don't worry about me. I'm at peace. Just look after my family for me and know that I'll always be with you. *You'll never walk alone.*"

Loretta came back to the phone. "Dear God, Flossie. Something terrible has happened."

Flossie barely answered, "I know," before she passed out.

The night before she died, Mossie brought up the subject of Flossie finding a mate for the zillionth time, telling her she looked forward to being her maid of honor at her wedding. "Howard Eugene knows all these guys who want to meet you. Why don't you let him introduce you to someone?"

Flossie said, "You know I haven't had any real interest in anyone since Lonford died except Quinton Lewis. When that didn't work out, I figured it's hard for someone else to be a soul mate. I've always believed you only get one chance for that kind of happiness."

Mossie told her, "But it has been over ten years now. You have to understand that death is God's will too. He intends for us who remain behind to go on with our lives. You have to accept death, just as you accept life. It's part of the cycle that everybody will experience at some point. Look at our dear little Hampton. He's gone, and yet we were both able to move on with our lives. Our sweet mother had a hard time with his death and never got over it. But although it was difficult, we accepted our mother's passing too. So you see, we all have to go sometime, and when we do, the world keeps right on going."

She'd continued. "I may go before you, or, heaven forbid, you could go before me. And as hard as that sounds, the other one of us will go on. But in the meantime, my sister, I still intend to dance at your wedding one day—whether it's on this plane or the next."

Mossie's last words proved prophetic. Flossie always wondered if her sister somehow knew her time on Earth was nearing an end.

Together we will always be. Aunt Beatrice had once said she and Mossie would never be separated, even by death. *Aunt Bea, you were so right. I feel blessed that even across different realms, my sister and I remain as close as we have ever been.*

This afternoon, though, if Flossie knew anything, she knew that the jarring jolt she just experienced was an omen. Ever since she'd delivered those twins on her and Mossie's birthday nineteen years ago, she had

246 | GIGI GOSSETT

experienced an inextricable connection with them, just as she now believed they'd always had with each other, even across the pond. Now she knew with certainty that something seriously bad was happening in Budapest. The sense of danger that she'd been feeling was the strongest it had ever been.

The twins were in trouble. This was especially worrisome because she didn't know what she could do about it. How could she warn them? She had Mrs. Moldovan's telephone number, but it was two o'clock in the morning in Budapest, and she figured the worst thing she could do was frighten the living daylights out of the woman by calling about something that might not be. So how could she warn them? She agonized for a time, and suddenly the answer came to her. She knew how to get a warning to the twins. She picked up her telephone.

"Mrs. Braxton," she said when Ella answered. "This is Flossie Walker."

"Oh, hello, Miss Walker. So nice to hear from you so soon. What can I do for you?"

"You know how I told you I'd been worried about the twins and how I had been dreaming that they were in trouble?"

"Yes," Ella said.

"Well, it's no longer a feeling. Something is happening to those girls. I know that they are in trouble. I want you to get a message to your partner in Budapest."

"I haven't talked to my partner today, but when I last talked to her, she never mentioned any kind of problem. What kind of trouble do you think they're in?"

"I'm afraid I don't know. You just have to trust me on this. I have a way of knowing these things. And I know for sure that they are in danger. If it hasn't already happened, it's coming. Your partner can probably do something about it—get a message to them or something."

Ella was worried. Lynn wouldn't appreciate getting a phone call at two in the morning without something definite to tell her, but what else could she do? Miss Walker was certainly making it sound like this could be a life-or-death matter. She told her, "I will try to reach my partner. I wish I had something to go on, like what she should be looking for."

"Child, if I could tell you more, I would. All I know is that something has to be done, or it could be very bad."

When they ended the call, Flossie felt like she had done the right thing. Now she could go down to the dining room. She called for an attendant to take her.

Ella put in a call to Lynn, waking her up. She told Lynn she had to tell her about Flossie Walker's warning. Lynn listened and told Ella that some strange things had been happening, but she didn't know what to make of any of them. She told Ella she was meeting with Morgan in the morning to tell her about finding her mother and sister. "I'll let you know if anything happens," Lynn told Ella.

CHAPTER
22

Budapest, Hungary, Tuesday, November 26

TUESDAY MORNING, LYNN ARRIVED AT the Történelmi Café at eight forty-five and selected a secluded booth away from the other customers in the restaurant.

Morgan said, "Good morning," as she approached Lynn wearing a bright-red jacket and gray slacks.

"Good morning, Morgan. We have a few minutes. Do you want to order something to eat?" Lynn asked.

"No way. I could never eat before I know what this is about. I could hardly sleep last night for wondering. I just hope my parents don't try to insist that I come home now that I've decided to stay." She ordered a glass of juice. When it arrived, they both dialed the number and punched in the confirmation code for the conference call.

"Mom?" Morgan said questioningly when she heard her mother's voice. "Dad? What's this all about? I'm dying to hear what couldn't wait. What's so important at three in the morning? Is everything okay?"

"Morning, sweetheart, and yes, everything's fine here," Dr. and Mrs. Wellington said. "Good morning, Miss Davis." Lynn greeted them back.

"Morgan, we have just learned of something that you need to know about right away. Miss Davis has uncovered some very important information." Morgan glanced at Lynn, a puzzled look on her face.

Dr. Wellington said, "Honey, this is going to be a lot for you to take in. But there are some things you have to know. We have asked Miss Davis to be a part of this conversation."

"Just what is it?" Morgan asked.

"There's no easy way to tell you this except to come right out with it. When you were born nineteen years ago, you were born a twin. You have a twin sister," he said.

"What!" Morgan reached for her pendant and began breathing fast. "Daddy, can you say that again?"

Sara Wellington could hear her daughter's disbelief. She said, "You heard right, honey—you have a twin sister. In fact, the girl you went to Budapest to see—"

"What about her?" Morgan blurted out.

"She happens to be your twin sister, Ivona Palaki."

"Twin sister!" Morgan gasped and turned ashen. *Ivona Palaki is the name György gave me. The girl I almost met.* "Mother, what are you saying? How ... how is this possible?"

Dr. Wellington said, "Apparently, the two of you were separated at birth, and until yesterday, we never knew she existed. We were just as shocked as you are to learn about this. Unfortunately, that's all we know right now."

"We wanted you to know this before you came face-to-face with her. Ms. Davis said you just missed meeting her this past weekend," Mrs. Wellington added.

"Yes, it was supposed to happen, but she never showed up," Morgan said, shaking her head in disbelief. "This is incredible, but I don't get it." Turning to Lynn with a puzzled look, she asked, "You knew about this?"

Her mother answered, "Morgan, Miss Davis discovered this and told us about it. The first thing we did was schedule this call. We wanted you to know everything as soon as possible."

"Why couldn't you have just told me yesterday? Why the big, mysterious phone call?"

"Dear," Mrs. Wellington said.

"This is about me, Mother, yet it seems everyone knew about this but me. Of course, I am shocked to know I have a twin. I think I have a right to be shocked. I'm nineteen years old, and this is the first I've ever known about this!"

"Honey, we have known about this exactly twelve hours longer than you. That's why we're on the phone with you at this hour. We didn't want to just drop it on you and expect you to deal with it. That's why we asked Miss Davis to be involved."

"How can she help? I can't believe it," Morgan said.

Lynn pulled out the photo of Ivona Kay Palaki she'd received from university records and handed it to Morgan. "You can believe it, Morgan. This is Ivona," she said.

Morgan reached for the picture and immediately did a double take.

"This looks just like me." Then, holding the picture up, Morgan blinked and fixed her gaze on the image of her twin sister. She was speechless, her doubts erased the instant she saw the photograph. She shook her head in awe. Here in her hand was the realization of a dream. She had been hoping this girl might be related to her, and now she was getting far more than that. Everyone who had seen Ivona had said they were identical. Bela had said it. György had said it, and even Dominik.

Mrs. Wellington asked, "Morgan, are you all right?"

"Yes, Mom. I'm okay. I'm sorry I was rude. I think I'm just in shock. It's like I'm looking at ... me! It feels so strange. From never even knowing I had a sister to this. I'm actually happy, but I do have mixed emotions."

"I understand how you must feel, dear," her mother said.

"I can't believe that you and Dad never knew about this. How could someone do something like this? At least they could have told you."

"Listen, Morgan. People who decide to give up their children for adoption have certain rights. And one is a right to privacy. You're aware we knew your birth mother, but that's all we ever knew. We've not seen her since she and her mother left our home, although, oddly, we did talk to her a few months ago."

"You spoke to my real mother?" Morgan said in disbelief.

"Yes, dear. She called us when you were in Paris, asking if we had received some kind of letter from the midwife who delivered you. I told her we had not, and we ended the call."

"But you never told me," Morgan said.

"Morgan, we were dealing with your father's recovery at the time, and it skipped my mind. We know you want answers, and we do too. We do have more to tell you."

"There's more?"

"Yes. Miss Davis has also located your biological mother."

Morgan looked stunned. "My real mother. Where is she?"

Lynn explained that she was a professor at CEU.

"She's at CEU too?" Morgan's heart was practically beating out of her chest.

Lynn handed Morgan the photo of Dr. N. Rene Palaki. Morgan looked at her birth mother's picture as tears streamed down her cheeks. She finally knew where she had come from. "Wow," she uttered, shaking her head.

Her mother explained, "Dear, Miss Davis discovered information on a Dr. N. René Palaki. When we saw Dr. Palaki's picture, we knew immediately who she was, even though we hadn't seen her since she was fifteen. We knew her as Nicola Moldovan."

Morgan was beside herself with excitement at learning her mother had been located. But she was even more excited about her twin sister. "I have always known I had a birth mother somewhere. But I never, ever dreamed I had a twin. I want to contact Ivona so we can meet each other."

Mrs. Wellington told her she wanted her to wait until Miss Davis had talked to Dr. Palaki. "She needs to find out what she knows, and if Ivona already knows she has a twin sister. If she does not, it will be better if her mother breaks this news to her first."

"Since I didn't know about this, maybe Ivona doesn't know either. But how could my mother not know? Or her mother. They have to know she had twins," Morgan said.

Lynn said, "I'm afraid we just don't know that yet. I tried to telephone her, but she is out of town until next Wednesday. I have an appointment with her when she gets back."

"Morgan, I know it will be hard to do, but we really need to wait until we know for sure," Mrs. Wellington said. "When the meeting is set up, we will be there too."

They talked a few minutes more, and after everything had been said, the call ended.

Lynn and Morgan sat in the booth for a few minutes and talked about what Morgan had just learned. Lynn asked, "Morgan, how do you feel right now?" Lynn asked.

"It feels like you've been collecting a lot of information about me and things that pertain to me. And having these hush, hush conversations with my parents. I feel like no one thinks I'm grown enough to handle the truth. If you knew all this, why couldn't you just have told me?"

"This is a very sensitive issue. I discovered this information while working for your parents and was obligated to tell them what I learned. They wanted to be very careful how it was presented to you. They were very concerned that this might be upsetting to you. That's why they want to be here with you when you meet your biological family. That, and they also want some answers as to how this happened."

Morgan said, "I'm glad to know about this, don't get me wrong. It just feels like I'm always the last to know."

"I understand how you feel. Is there anything else I can tell you?"

"Maybe you can just tell me how to be patient and wait. I don't know how I'm going to do that. I can't wait to meet Ivona. After all, I've already waited my whole life for this."

"I know you're anxious. I'll get this scheduled for the earliest possible time," Lynn said.

Morgan mentioned her parents coming to Budapest and said, "I'm so glad my dad can travel. I'll be happy to see them."

As Lynn and Morgan were leaving the restaurant, Lynn insisted on taking Morgan to her next destination. "My driver is just around the corner. I'll call him." She pulled out her cell phone while wondering if Ivona Palaki was safe.

Morgan had decided she wouldn't wait to meet her sister. *How can they expect me to wait for something as important as this?* She decided to get Ivona's number from György and call her this afternoon. *After all, what harm can it do? I bet she'll be as excited as I am.*

* * *

The Történelmi Café was situated in between other businesses on a quiet, tree-lined side street. At the present time, there was no automobile or pedestrian traffic in sight. Outside the restaurant, an old car sat idling as Lynn and Morgan exited. After so many hits and misses, Pista and Fane decided this was finally the day. They had seen the girl leave her apartment with her man about an hour ago, so they followed them. The guy dropped her off at this restaurant and took off. He was nowhere in sight. They planned to simply grab her when she came out. Things were looking good, and Pista was more than ready. The restaurant door opened, and their girl walked out and turned toward their car.

Pista poked Fane, who was slouched down in his seat. "This is it!" Fane quickly sat up straight. In the next instant, a woman followed on their girl's heels. "What the ...? That looks like the same bitch I tried to run down." Pista couldn't believe his eyes, but he said, "No problem, bitch. I got you now. We'll grab the both of them. Let's go," he ordered.

Fane readied himself for action. Just as the two women were about to walk by their car, he stuck his head out the passenger door window. "Uh, excuse me, ladies," Fane said. "Do either of you know how to get to the Buda Castle from here? *Segíts minket?*"

Morgan's head was a thousand miles away after having just received the best news of her entire life. She and Lynn looked over at the man trying to get their attention.

"*Tudna segíteni?*"

"I think he's asking for directions," she told Lynn, who was thinking the situation didn't look quite right. However, before she could act, Morgan stepped toward the man's car to give him directions. Lynn stayed by her side.

Fane was wearing dark glasses and a black knit cap that covered his ears. The collar of his dark jacket was turned up, hiding much of his face. The old car was a rusty gray-black.

The man who asked for directions quickly jumped out of the car, nearly hitting Morgan with the door.

Lynn said, "Hey, watch it."

"Oops, excuse me." The man was tall and lanky; strands of straw-blonde hair hung from under his cap. He was wearing dark gray jeans and black sneakers. He opened his map and said, "We've been driving all over, looking for the right street. My brother and I are leaving town this afternoon, but we didn't want to get away without seeing the most famous landmark in Budapest."

Lynn thought they were two unlikely looking tourists. She leaned over and tried to get a peek at the driver; she noticed his hand on the door handle. Taking Morgan's upper arm, she said, "Morgan, we'd better go."

Morgan was studying the map and tracing the route with her finger. She said, "I've just about got it." In an instant, the driver was out of the car. Lynn noticed that, unlike his tall, lanky friend, this man was of average height and muscular build. The collar of a gray shirt peeked out from beneath the plaid scarf around his neck. He was wearing navy blue slacks and black shoes.

Lynn started nudging Morgan away, but the man was lightning fast. He was behind them in a flash, pressing something hard into Morgan's back.

He has a gun! We're being mugged! Morgan shrieked. It happened so quickly, neither woman had time to react. Immediately, it dawned on Lynn that they were not being mugged. It was far worse. They were being kidnapped! In a quick glance, she observed that the driver wore dark sunglasses and a knit cap that covered his ears and forehead. The wool scarf wrapped around his neck hid the lower part of his face. He reached to open the door, and for a split second, Lynn caught a glimpse of a tattoo, what appeared to be a green and black snake with red eyes running up the back side of his hand. She thought about Miss Walker's warning.

He pushed them and said, "Get in the car."

"Ouch," Morgan squealed as she bumped her shin while scurrying into the back seat.

Then the man pulled two pairs of plastic safety glasses from his coat pocket. The glasses had been painted completely black, including the side shields. He threw the glasses at them and said, "Put these on. Now!"

Before they donned the black glasses, Lynn noticed more than the oil-stained, weathered upholstery. A quick glance revealed a new spool of rope on the floor. Morgan stole a worried look at Lynn before she placed her dark glasses over her eyes. The one with the gun jumped in the back seat with Lynn and Morgan. The other man got behind the wheel and drove off. The whole thing had taken only seconds.

Around the corner, just out of sight, Lynn's driver waited patiently, unaware of what had just happened to his passenger. Later he would go into the restaurant looking for her, only to learn she had left an hour ago.

Lynn Davis was known for keeping her cool under pressure. She'd had many occasions to exercise this quality at Yale, and she had honed it during her years as a member of Cincinnati's finest. Although she didn't know how she was going to do it, she knew she had to get herself and Morgan out of this mess. These guys looked like bad news, and there was no telling what they had up their sleeves.

"What's this about?" Lynn probed.

"Shut up, lady," Pista said.

"Where are you taking us?" she demanded.

"I said shut the hell up!"

Morgan shuddered. Lynn felt her shaking and subtly patted her reassuringly on the arm. She could tell by the man's deadly tone that it was best to keep quiet for now. She and Morgan sat in silence during the rest of the ride. With the other man sitting next to them, they were hesitant to make a move of any kind.

Lynn could hear normal city sounds outside the car for the first few minutes. Then the noise diminished, suggesting that they were going through a residential area. Finally, except for the rumbling of the car's muffler, there was quiet. Lynn assumed they were in a rural area.

The car stopped after what seemed like about fifteen minutes. Fane turned off the motor, and he and Pista jumped out of the car. "Get out," Pista ordered. Lynn exited the car, but Morgan didn't move. Pista grabbed her by the arm to pull her out.

Morgan said, "You're hurting me."

"What are you doing? And where are we?" Lynn asked angrily. She tried to move her head discreetly to get a look at the guys. It didn't work. The black side shields did their job.

Ignoring her, the gunman said, "Okay, you two, come on." He and Fane guided them from the car across the grass to some steps. "Up you go," Pista said. Lynn and Morgan climbed the four steps tentatively and walked across a creaking wooden surface, which Lynn assumed was a porch. *They're taking us into a house?* She could hear a door being unlocked and opened. The same voice said, "Move it. We need to conduct some business."

Once inside, Lynn and Morgan were assaulted by a stale, moldy odor that made them gag. They were directed into a room, guided to two chairs, and told to sit. The leader laughed and tied blindfolds over their glasses to ensure they couldn't see anything. His hands crudely stroked Morgan's cheeks and caressed her back. His touch made her skin crawl. She squirmed. "I can tell you like this," he said and then let his hands begin to wander over her body. "Damned sweet," he said, and patted her thigh.

Morgan jerked herself away from his touch. "Don't!" she pleaded.

"Morgan, what's happening?" Lynn asked, worried.

"Don't lose your shorts, lady," the main guy said. "Maybe you want some of this too." But he stopped his pawing. "We'll get to that later. Count on it. For now, let's talk."

Although Lynn and Morgan had seen very little of the men before, with their eyes blindfolded, now they saw only blackness. Lynn wondered if these men planned to hurt them. The one guy had certainly scared Morgan. She assumed he was touching her. But so far, the men hadn't robbed them. *Are they serial killers?*

Pista and Fane took seats facing their hostages. Frustrated and afraid, Morgan said, "What do you want? Is it money?" Morgan and Lynn could hear them moving, but neither answered.

Lynn said quietly, "All right, guys, what's this all about? You want to let us in on your little plan?"

Finally the apparent ringleader spoke. With icy calm, he said to Lynn, "Lady, I don't know who the hell you are. As far as I'm concerned, you're just along for the ride. You're lucky to be alive. My business is with missy here. So do yourself a favor and keep your mouth shut. I'm dead serious."

The other man added, "Oh, he's serious all right. If you don't think so, I could give you the names of a few people who could tell you." Then he laughed and said, "Oh, that's right, they can't talk anymore."

"Enough!" the leader retorted angrily to his sidekick. He did not call him by name. Pista turned back to Lynn and Morgan. "Okay, little miss." He patted Morgan on the knee. "I've got a debt to collect from you."

"What are you talking about? I don't owe you anything. I don't even know you," Morgan said.

"Don't remember me, huh? That's okay. Here's the deal. I'm going to keep you here until your dear old doctor sister pays me some money. It's simple as that."

"Listen, mister," Lynn said. "You must have the wrong person. This young lady is American. In fact—"

"Shut up," Pista said, angrily cutting her off. "You're starting to annoy me with all that mouth. If I have to, I'll stick something in it to keep you quiet. And I've got just the thing in mind. So when I want something from you, you'll know it." Then he asked, "Who the hell are you, anyway?"

"My name is Lynn Davis. I'm here on business from the United States."

"Just what kind of business are you in, Miss Lynn Davis? Interfering in other people's business?" he said sarcastically. To his partner, he said, "She thinks we care that she is from the United States. Do we give a rat's ass about that?" The partner just laughed.

"Missy, what's your name?" the man said to Morgan. "Lynn Davis here says you are an American. I say she's lying."

"M-morgan," she stammered. "And I am from America. I've only been here a few weeks. I don't have any doctor sister."

At that very instant it dawned on Lynn that these guys were after Morgan's sister! They thought she was Ivona Palaki! The leader referred to Morgan's *dear old doctor sister.* This was probably someone from Nicola's past who thought Nicola's daughter was her sister. It meant Morgan's biological mother was also a target. These guys had taken great pains to keep her and Morgan from seeing their faces. It seemed that the one guy believed Morgan could identify them. But she also hoped that protecting their identity meant the men weren't going to harm them, or worse.

"By the way, I'm not buying the phony accent," he said. "You're her, all right. You got that hot-shot sister scientist who's always in the paper—her and all her important scientific discoveries." He mockingly drew the words out for emphasis. "I hear she has made a bundle of money selling her ideas to the big labs. So she'll pay up. If she ever wants to see you again, that is."

Morgan gasped at his words. The man continued talking. "In fact, I'm willing to make it a package deal. Maybe I'll throw in Miss American Davis for free. Two for the price of one," he said nastily, adding, "But don't tempt me. It wouldn't take much for me to off her right now."

Farie was busy going through the women's purses. The girl's CEU identification showed that she was telling the truth about her name. She had credit cards, but no driver's license. Morgan carried about two hundred dollars worth of Hungarian forints, which he removed. That and her iPod.

This other woman did have a US driver's license. She also had some credit cards, which Fane decided they could use. He was pleased to find a wad of bills amounting to at least five hundred dollars in US money. "These girls are loaded," he told Pista, who's eyes bugged when he saw the thick stack of bills.

"According to her ID card, the girl's name is Morgan Wellington," Fane said.

Pista eyed the money. "Fake-ass ID. Anyone can get one. Anyway, I figure there's more money where that came from."

This is madness. Lynn had to know the men's plan. Again she spoke. "What do you want from us?"

Pista put his index finger under Morgan's chin and held her face up. He tried to study it but she jerked her head away. To Lynn, he said, "Frankly, until this minute, I didn't need you. But you're going to come in quite handy."

"What are you talking about?" Lynn said angrily.

"I'm going to let you max out your bank account at an ATM in town."

"You're crazy. Why would I do that?"

Pista rose from his chair and delivered a powerful backhand to Lynn's jaw. Since she was blindfolded, she hadn't seen it coming. "I may be crazy, but you'll do it because I said so. Now that's enough of your smart-ass mouth. From here on, I don't want to hear another word from you. If you know what's good for you, you'll do whatever the hell I tell you. I should have finished you the other night."

Lynn's face stung from his blow, but she couldn't worry about that now. This man had just given her something else to think about, and she heard him loud and clear.

The creep just the same as admitted to trying to run her down last Thursday. Things just got scarier. She moved her jaw and was grateful it didn't seem broken. She heard Morgan squirm in her chair and start to cry. "Morgan, it's all right." *This fool has to be some kind of sociopath.* Lynn knew they were clearly in danger. *Somehow we absolutely have to escape.*

"Where's her mobile phone?" Pista demanded of Fane, who fished around and pulled it out of Lynn's purse. To Lynn he said, "What's the number for your bank? We'll just see how much you got put away."

Lynn knew that at five in the morning in the United States, her bank would not be open, but more importantly, her phone probably would not work out here. She said the number and he dialed it. "If this is the wrong number, you'll regret it for the rest of the little bit of life you have left," he said as he put the phone to his ear. He heard nothing. "What the hell is happening? It's not ringing."

"We may not be able to get a signal out here," Lynn said drily.

"Shit!" Pista said. He tried a couple more times and dropped her phone.

"Try your phone," Fane offered.

"If hers won't get a signal, why do you think another one will?" Pista barked at Fane. But then he pulled out his cheap prepaid phone and tried it, to no avail. He told Fane, "Find the girl's phone. Maybe hers will work. She's local." Fane pulled out Morgan's cell phone, but again there was no signal. "When we get into town, we'll call the good doctor. Give me your sister's phone number," he told Morgan.

"What are you going to do?" Morgan asked the man in charge.

"Don't try my patience. I have business with her. Let's have it."

Morgan must have realized it was futile to try to convince these two that they had the wrong person, so she said, "I can't remember her office number. Maybe you can just call the university."

"It's early. She might still be home. Give me her home number."

"She hasn't had a phone for a while. The last big storm knocked it out, and it still isn't working."

"No telephone? You gotta be kidding me," the leader said. Morgan shook her head. He cursed under his breath.

"Let's tie them up," Pista said to Fane. He told Lynn and Morgan, "We'll go into town later to use the phone. Just don't try anything stupid."

Then, using the rope from the back of the car, the men tied Morgan to an old wooden rocking chair and Lynn to a wooden chair across the room. The women's arms were tied behind their backs. They tied Lynn's ankles to the legs of her chair and Morgan's to the thick rockers of hers. Then they left the room. Lynn and Morgan could hear a key being inserted into a lock. Another door opened, and the ladies could hear muffled voices grow fainter. They heard a car start up and drive away. They hoped both men had left.

"Thank God. The first thing we've got to do is get these things off our eyes," Lynn said. "Morgan, talk to me so I can hear where you are." Morgan's voice guided Lynn, who struggled to maneuver herself the few feet across the room to where Morgan was tied up. When she finally got close, she said, "Now, I'm going to try to get near your hands so you can take this thing off my eyes. Then I'll get yours off so we can see what we're doing."

The next few minutes were agonizing. At one point, Lynn nearly toppled over but did manage to keep her balance. "Close call." The second time she did lose her balance and fell, hitting her head on the wood floor. "Oh brother," she said, but she realized right away that when she fell, the chair leg broke, enabling her to ease one of her legs free.

"Are you okay?" Morgan asked, and Lynn told her she wasn't hurt bad. Then Lynn inched around while Morgan's clumsy hands maneuvered about, awkwardly poking her everywhere. After several attempts, she finally succeeded in yanking off Lynn's blindfold. The room was totally dark, but slowly Lynn's eyes adjusted to the faint light that was coming through the sides of the boards over the windows. She still had to work with her hands tied behind her back and one leg tied to the chair.

She managed to stand up on one leg. Her hands still tied behind her back, she somehow managed to pull Morgan's blindfold off. Then they went to work on the knots. While they were attempting to get untied, Lynn asked Morgan why she had been moaning earlier.

"It was awful. He was feeling me up. I was afraid he wasn't going to stop."

"The sooner we get out of here, the better," Lynn said. "How are you coming?"

"I can tell they're getting loose," Morgan answered.

In a few minutes, Lynn was free. Then she finished untying Morgan.

"I can't believe we got all this stuff off," Morgan said, breathlessly.

"Thank goodness we did, but that's just the first thing. Now we have to figure out how to get out of this place before they return. I'm assuming both of the men left, because we've made so much noise getting ourselves free and no one came in." Lynn looked around the darkened room. Streaks of light shone through the cracks where the window was boarded up. As best she could tell, they were in what looked like a living room. Dusty sheets covered the meager furniture. What was not covered was drab and worn.

Lynn and Morgan tried the door. It was locked. They both pushed hard, but the door would not budge. Another locked door apparently led into the rest of the house. They tried to force it open, but it too did not move. Lynn looked at the front windows. Although they were boarded up, they might be their best bet. Looking for something to break the window with, she spotted a set of rusty old iron fireplace tools. She pulled out a coal rake and broke the window. Then she and Morgan beat down the board that opened onto the porch. The noise seemed deafening. If anyone was in the house, he would have come running a long time ago.

In the light of day, Morgan saw Lynn's face and gasped. "Your face, it's swollen. And you've got black and blue welts where he hit you. What an animal."

"He got me pretty hard. I can tell my eye is swollen, but I can still see. Let's get away from here."

Lynn and Morgan paused for a few seconds to listen. They heard only silence. They found a dusty old knit throw, which they used to pull out the remaining jagged edges of glass so they could climb through the window frame.

They found their phones and grabbed their purses. Lynn told Morgan to turn her red coat inside out. The black quilted lining made her much less conspicuous. Very carefully, they climbed out the window, noticing as they looked around that they were in a rural area. The only other houses in sight were also boarded up and deserted. *Now what?* Lynn wondered as she glanced around. They spotted the road and headed toward it. Tall grass and huge trees flanked both sides of the road. They looked right and left. Both directions looked the same. Lynn concentrated for a moment and then pointed left and said, "Let's go this way." They started running, staying off the road so they could quickly find cover in the event a car went by. They couldn't take a chance of flagging anyone down for fear it might be their captors. As soon as they were a safe distance away, they both tried their telephones again. Neither had signals.

"I wonder how those guys knew I was at that restaurant this morning," Morgan said, panting.

"Do you think you were followed when you left your apartment?" Lynn asked, breathing hard but steady.

"I'm not sure. But György picked me up this morning to bring me to the restaurant. If those guys saw me, I guess they didn't want to take a chance of bothering me when I was with him."

CHAPTER
23

IVONA WAS HAVING A LATE breakfast with Corina when she suddenly broke out in a cold sweat. For no apparent reason, she started trembling and breathing hard. "Vonni, what's the matter?" Corina said, frightened by the terrified look on Ivona's face.

Ivona stared at her grandmother. At first, she didn't speak. Then she wrapped her arms around her body and rubbed her arms is if she were chilled, rocking back and forth. "I don't know," she managed to say. "But something is terribly wrong."

Watching what her granddaughter was going through concerned Corina. She walked over to Ivona and reached for her hands, holding them consolingly. When Ivona stopped rocking, Corina looked in her eyes and said, "I'm calling the doctor."

"Wait," Vonni said breathlessly. "Maybe it was that dream I had last night."

"What dream?"

"I dreamed that some men were following me. I ran and ran, but they kept coming. Every time I thought I had gotten away from them, they were there again. It was horrible. When I got up this morning it all came back. Every single detail. And for some strange reason, I believe the dream is real. But it's not me who the men were after. I believe it was my sister." Ivona was still breathing hard. "She's in trouble, Reeni. I know it. What can I do?" she cried.

"Your sister? Honey, what are you talking about?"

"I know this sounds crazy, but I think someone is after her. It may be too late already. In my dream, they never caught me, but I know *she* is in danger."

Corina didn't know what to say. She noticed that Ivona was trembling. She grabbed a throw from the edge of the sofa and placed it over her shoulders. "Honey, if what you are saying is real, I don't know what any of us can do. What makes you think this is real?"

"I can't say how I know this, but I have a very strong feeling. I absolutely know my sister *is* in trouble. This is making me crazy. I have to do something."

"I don't know what you can do."

"I know what. I'll call her friend György. Maybe he can help. He may know how to reach her." Ivona began to calm down. Corina noticed her trembling had ceased. Ivona went to find György Novak's telephone number. She dialed him, and after several rings he answered. Ivona could tell that she'd awakened him again. "This is Ivona Palaki."

György livened up. "Hey! We were wondering what happened to you Saturday night," he said. "I called—"

"Look, I'll explain later," she said, cutting him off. "Right now, I believe that something bad is happening to Morgan. She's in trouble. Have you spoken with her?

"Not today ... What are you talking about? What makes you think she's in trouble?"

"I'm sorry to be so blunt. I know this sounds crazy—I haven't even met her yet. It's just a feeling I've had all morning that I can't shake it. When did you last speak with her?"

"I saw her first thing this morning. I'll tell you what— I'll call Bela. They're usually together. She'll know where Morgan is."

"Please do. Will you call me back and tell me she's okay."

"Certainly," György replied, worried.

Ivona told Corina about the call.

"I'm calling Nicola."

"Wait, Reeni, don't worry her. She's away at an important conference. At least let me hear back from György first. But what if he can't find out anything? I almost want to call the Wellingtons in the United States."

Corina said, "The problem with that is a call like that might just frighten them to death. Especially if they try to reach Morgan and are unable to. Plus, they're helpless across the pond. Wait and see what the young man says when he calls you back."

Corina thought of the emotional battles Ivona had suffered through in her earlier years. Her therapist had helped her work through an unusual fear of being separated from family. Back then, no one knew where those notions were coming from. Now, after the discovery of her twin, everything began to make sense. It seemed as though Ivona's emotions had somehow stemmed from being separated from a twin sister she had never even known about. Corina prayed a silent prayer: *Dear God, please don't let anything happen to either of these girls.*

Later, sitting in class, Ivona felt her phone vibrate. She read the text message from György Novak: "Morgan's not answering. Bela hasn't heard from her either. I'll let you know when I hear from her."

* * *

Lynn and Morgan trudged along. Based on her estimate of the time it took their captors to drive out to the old house, Lynn figured they had gone about ten or twelve miles. The driver probably hadn't wanted to attract police attention by driving too fast. It had felt like they were going no more than fifty miles an hour. At their current pace, it would probably take them about five or six hours to get back to the city. As Lynn and Morgan ran along, they talked about the conclusion they had both arrived at back at the house: the men believed they had captured Ivona Palaki; their plan was to extort ransom money from Nicola Palaki.

The two had been running for about an hour when they heard a car in the distance coming from behind them. They ran into an area with huge trees and thick underbrush and ducked. Lynn peeked out and saw their captors' car pass by. "This is bad," she told Morgan. "We don't know how long it will be before they come back this way. We really need to stay off the road for a while."

"But what can we do?" Morgan asked.

"For right now, we'll stay clear of the road but keep moving forward. I'll try to think of something."

They moved cautiously for several minutes. Cars occasionally passed them in both directions, but they stayed out of view. They came upon an area that was completely clear of trees or bushes. At the edge of the clearing was a gravel road that ran along the length of the trees. They both spotted a house that was set back off the highway, surrounded by woods. Its quarter-mile-wide front area had been cleared. Lynn said, "We'll run through the trees along this road, behind the house and down the other side along the trees that lead back to the road."

They got to the end of the road and turned to run along the wooded area behind the house. Suddenly, they heard a car turning onto the gravel path. They glanced back at the car. "It looks like them, Morgan," Lynn warned. From the back woods, they could see a cellar door protruding from the opposite side of the house. They made a dash for the cellar, grateful it was unlocked. Lynn held open the door and Morgan crept in. Lynn followed her. There was an inside latch; Lynn found a broom and stuck the handle through the lock. It was completely dark and cold in the cellar, but at least for now they were safe.

A car door slammed, and they could hear men talking. Moments later, they heard footsteps going by the cellar side of the yard. The men were still talking. Someone tried the cellar door. Lynn could hear the leader cursing that it wouldn't open. Shortly after that, they heard loud banging on the front door.

The door opened. Lynn and Morgan could make out a woman's voice. They also heard a dog growling. "Ma'am, we're sorry to bother you. But our car ran out of gas about a half mile up the road. We went to find some gasoline, and our wives must have gotten pretty cold in the car. So we think they may have gotten out of the car to try to find a place to warm up. You haven't seen two strange women around here, have you?" Fane asked humbly in Hungarian.

"Two strange women, you say?" the old woman answered in her native language. Her dog growled again.

"Yes, ma'am," Fane answered.

"I sure haven't seen them. I hope they're not still running around in the cold. It's probably no more than two degrees Celsius out there."

"Thank you, ma'am. We'll be moving on then," Fane said, tipping his cap. He and Pista walked back to the car.

"This is the only house for miles. Where in the hell are those *szukák*?" Pista said.

"Did you believe that old lady?"

"I think she was lying. So we're going to keep an eye on that house and anyone coming or going from it. I've worked too hard on this to give up now."

"I believed her," Fane said. "Those two could be long gone."

Waiting in the cellar, Lynn and Morgan heard the car drive away. A few minutes later, someone was pounding on the cellar door. "Come on out of there," an old lady yelled in Hungarian.

"Someone must have seen us come in here," Lynn said. "Can you tell what she is saying?" she asked Morgan.

"I think she wants us to come out."

They hesitated momentarily. "Here we come," Lynn responded.

Hearing Lynn's voice, the woman switched to English. "I got a shotgun. And I aim to start shooting if this door doesn't open soon," she said.

Lynn pulled the broomstick out of the lock and climbed out first. Then she held the cellar door while Morgan climbed out. The old lady stood there with a shotgun aimed at them and eyed them carefully, her dog waiting by her side. She was short with a small, wiry frame. She wore clear-rimmed glasses and had curly salt-and-pepper hair. Baggy gray slacks; a pale blue, yellow, and gray top; padded gray house slippers, and thick socks completed her look. She said, "If you're those men's wives, you sure weren't gonna find any warmth down there."

Lynn quickly explained what had happened to them. Morgan chimed in.

The old lady told them she accepted their story. "I see he busted you in the face pretty good. A man that will hit a woman is pretty low. If Zoltán ever put his hands on me, he'd be under the ground right now, full of pellets. At least they're long gone now. And I can tell when a car is within a mile of here."

"Do you have a telephone we could use?" Lynn asked.

"Don't have a telephone. Don't have a car. All I got is a sick husband up there in the bedroom and my dog, Farkas. But you can come in and get warm. I got a nice fire going in the fireplace and some sweetbread and hot tea." She told them her name was Piroska Groff; her sick husband was Zoltán.

As they followed Mrs. Groff through the back door into her home, the first thing Lynn noticed was its homey warmth. Although the furnishings were scant, a cozy stuffed sofa faced the delightful fireplace which emitted a warmth they hadn't felt since ten o'clock that morning. The enticing aroma of baked goods from the kitchen filled the air. Mrs. Groff invited the ladies to sit at the small kitchen table, and she brought them a plate of fresh, warm delights and fresh fruit, plus two mugs filled with a delicious homemade sweet-potato tea.

"I didn't realize I was so hungry," Morgan said, sitting in the woman's kitchen and eating ravenously, Farkas, the dog, at her feet.

"Remember, all we had this morning was juice," Lynn said. "This certainly fills the void."

Morgan asked Lynn what they were going to do next, and Lynn said that when they left, they would continue running toward town. "I believe we could be at the city limits in a few hours," she said, looking at her watch.

"Don't count on it," Mrs. Groff said. "First of all, there are large, wide-open stretches between here and town. I think you girls should probably wait a few hours. If you want, you can stay here until dark. Sun sets around four thirty. Then you won't be so easy to spot. You'll be able to see lights from the cars from a great distance away, and if there aren't any trees, you can always jump down in the gully on the side of the road to keep out of sight."

Lynn thought about Mrs. Groff's generous offer. "Maybe we *should* wait here until then. Are you sure it's all right?"

"I wouldn't offer if it weren't. Zoltán needs to eat every four hours, and I'm fixing stew for dinner. You can eat some before you get back out in the cold air. By the way, city limits are about thirteen kilometers from here. You'll come upon a drug store. Go in and ask them for a telephone. Call the police. Maybe they can round up those scoundrels."

Lynn spotted a telephone on the wall. When Mrs. Groff saw her looking, she said, "It doesn't work. Since Zoltán's been sick, it's all I can do to keep us fed and warm. Because he can't work, we couldn't pay our telephone bill." She pointed to the back of the house and said, "Next month, I'll sell some of those pine trees for Christmas. That'll get us through till spring. By then he'll be back on his feet."

As the hours passed, Lynn and Mrs. Groff chatted about many things; Morgan curled up in front of the fireplace. In the end, Piroska Groff told Lynn she understood the danger they were in and that she wished she had a way to help them. "I have an old computer." She pointed to the outdated desktop computer sitting on the sidebar. "It's old, but it still got the Internet—at least when we can pay for it. Truth is, we're isolated here. We got no kids, no family. We get a monthly delivery from the grocery store, but other than the folks who come by for the trees, we don't get much company. We'll be better off when Zoltán gets well. All I can do now is give you advice. Just be careful. I could tell that short one had a meanness about him. Try not to end up in their hands again."

After a few hours, Lynn and Morgan ate a hearty bowl of vegetable stew and some homemade bread. Mrs. Groff gave them some scarves she'd made of sackcloth and told them to cover their heads well against the chilled night air. Then, with Farkas wagging his tail good-bye, she bid them Godspeed. Lynn and Morgan thanked her and made their way up the gravel road to the highway, using the light of the moon to guide them.

A few minutes later, their warmth had worn off, but running kept their body temperatures up. Lynn and Morgan wondered how the kidnappers might have known to come to the Groffs' house.

"I wonder where they are now," Morgan said.

"It's anyone's guess. They seemed pretty determined. I bet they're still out there looking for us," Lynn said. At one point they passed a car pulled off on the opposite side of the road. It appeared to have been abandoned. Lynn eyed it suspiciously but noticing nothing untoward in the dark, she said, "Maybe some unlucky soul ran out of gas."

Anytime she or Morgan saw a car coming in either direction, they stepped away from the road, and if there were no trees around, they hid in the gullies. They were only about forty minutes away from the Groffs' house when they came upon a section of highway without trees or tall brush. All at once, they heard a vehicle rumbling nearby. When they turned to look, a car with its headlights off was coming toward them. Could it be the car they'd passed a few minutes before, parked off the road? Morgan asked, "Is it them?"

Lynn recognized the old car and confirmed it was their captors. They dove for the ditch, landing hard. Then they pressed themselves close to the ground, hoping to avoid being seen. They prayed the ditch and the darkness concealed them.

The car moved on by, but Lynn and Morgan continued to lay low for a few more minutes. Then slowly and cautiously, they raised their heads and looked around. Seeing no one, they got up. They were both muddy and sore from their quick drop to the ground, but it looked like they were safe. Their only feeling was relief.

Lynn noticed her right wrist had suffered a nasty gash, and she glanced down at the sharp boulder she had landed on. "Ouch," she managed to whisper. She removed her scarf and wrapped it around her hand to curb the bleeding. Morgan seemed to have sustained an ugly cut on her jaw. However, what had looked like blood under the moonlight turned out to be mud.

Then they both saw the flashlight.

"Hey!" a man yelled angrily.

"Dammit, he found us," Lynn said. She turned to see the man standing off the road. It was not too dark to see that he had a gun pointed at them. They could also see that a black knit ski cap covered his face.

"Get over here!" he shouted.

"We've got to run, Morgan!" Lynn whispered. She figured their chances were better running from these killers in the dark than giving up and letting the men kill them anyway. They took off toward a wooded area about a half a block ahead. A bullet whizzed past them. The man ran after them and fired again.

Running as fast as they could over the uneven terrain, Lynn and Morgan reached the woods. A bullet ricocheted off a tree just above Lynn's head; she and Morgan ducked and kept running. Moments later, another bullet hit a large dead branch above their heads. It fell directly in front of the women. Morgan tripped over the branch and fell. She couldn't get up. Lynn tried to help her, but Morgan writhed in pain as she touched her ankle. "Do you think it's sprained?" Lynn asked.

"I don't know," Morgan said, trying to stand. But her ankle gave out, and she nearly fell.

"Morgan, hang on to me. Maybe we can reach those big trees up ahead." Lynn helped Morgan struggle over to the nearest tree before they saw lights from a flashlight dancing behind them.

Out of breath, the man shouted at them. "If you don't stop, I'll put bullets in your backs." The voice sounded like it was only a few feet away. Lynn and Morgan froze.

Just ahead, running down from the highway toward them was the other guy, also wearing a ski mask. The man with the gun told his partner, "Let's get them back in the car."

CHAPTER
24

Tuesday Evening

PISTA CHECKED THE FLOOR OF his car for the blindfolds and realized the women must have left them back at the house. "I ought to give both of you the bullets I promised you." Then he started cursing, working himself into a rage about how they were trying to fuck up everything. "Turn around. If you try to look at either of us, I'll pop you."

Fane knew firsthand how angry Pista could get. He knew his partner might possibly even shoot these women. Then, if he and Pista got caught, they would both do hard time for sure. He didn't like that idea. "Hey, man, it's okay. We've got 'em now. Let's just get our money and be done."

Pista slid into the passenger seat. "Yeah, well, if they try anything else, I'll damn sure shoot their damned kneecaps out. You lousy bitches are more trouble than you're worth," Pista spat at Lynn and Morgan in the back seat. "I should've done your asses back there and left you to rot in the ditch." Then he put his gun against Lynn's forehead. "*Bam!*" he said. She didn't flinch. For the next few minutes, they rode in silence back to the old house.

When the car stopped, Pista got out first and ordered the women to get out. Morgan struggled to put weight on her swelling ankle, Lynn helping her. Lynn could plainly see the man had a violent streak. She was alarmed, and she could sense Morgan's fear. When they stepped onto the stairs, she noticed that the men had stuck the board back up to the window. The tall one took Morgan by the arm and helped her navigate the steps. Once they got inside the house, she and Morgan were led into another room, dusty and barren, except for a single table and three wooden chairs. A quick glance revealed that the room had two windows. "Sit down," the leader ordered.

"My ankle is killing me. Can I get an icepack?" Morgan said.

"What? She thinks this is some kind of apothecary?" the leader said sarcastically. To his partner, "Cover their eyes. I need to get this damn thing off my face." Then to Morgan, he said, "If you hadn't caused all that trouble, you wouldn't be hurt. So deal with it."

Lynn said, "At least you can let her prop her foot up. That kind of throbbing pain can be unbearable."

Fane looked at Pista to see what he wanted him to do. Pista said, "Tie their legs. Be sure you do a better job than before. They better not get loose this time."

The other guy proceeded to cover Lynn and Morgan's eyes. Then he tied their arms behind their backs and pulled the rope around their legs so tightly it practically cut off circulation. Morgan moaned. Next, he gagged them. Lynn squirmed as he tightened the rag around her bruised jaw.

"Where'd you two hole up, anyway?" Lynn and Morgan didn't try to respond through their gags. "You trying to protect that old hag who hid you? Doesn't matter. We'll take care of her," the leader said.

Lynn knew that if they managed to get away again, they'd need to warn Mrs. Groff and report this man's threat to the police. Helping them had put the old couple in danger. Mrs. Groff had a shotgun, and she had a dog. But this man would no doubt figure out a way to get to her anyway.

"You cost us a day, you know. So tomorrow morning we're taking you into town to do some banking." Next he looked to Morgan and said, "And you'll be delivering a message to your big sister." Then he checked the knots. He was still cursing when he and the other man left the room. Once again, Lynn and Morgan heard the padlock being clicked in place.

The women could faintly hear the men's muffled voices in the next room. Lynn and Morgan tried to make out what their captors were saying without success. Lynn could tell the head man was still angry. He seemed to be arguing with his partner. *Is there dissension between them?* If there was, she hoped it would work to their advantage. Maybe the tall one could possibly aid them if the opportunity presented itself. She would sure look for that opportunity.

The ladies squirmed and wiggled and found very little play in their bindings. Each time Lynn tried to move her arms, it felt like the rope was slicing right through the cut on her wrist. It was still wrapped in Mrs. Groff's scarf, and appeared to have stopped bleeding. Morgan was worse. Any movement of her legs resulted in intense pain to her ankle. Because their mouths were tightly gagged, Lynn and Morgan could only mumble.

Around eight, the door opened and one of the men entered the room. He untied their hands and then removed their gags. "I can finally breathe," Morgan said as she slowly dropped her arms and rubbed them. "Would you mind undoing these ropes around my legs? My ankle hurts crazy bad."

"Sorry. No can do," he said. "But I brought you something to eat." Lynn recognized the voice of the partner and was relieved it wasn't that maniac with the gun. "Figured you girls might be hungry. I got you some sandwiches and water. You gave us a scare earlier. We went into town to get you some food, but when we got back here, you were gone. You don't want to try anything like that again. My partner's real upset." He removed Lynn's gag and untied her arms.

Lynn's wrist ached, and her right hand, elbow, and jaw felt tortured. She uncovered her wrist and looked at the ugly gash. "Listen," she said, "I need to wash this wound and cover it with something clean." She pointed to her injury. "Suppose you could get me something for this?"

The man glanced at her hand and responded, "It don't look too bad to me."

"Look, mister, if you don't mind, I don't want it getting infected. And it hurts badly. So can't you just get me a bowl of warm soapy water and a towel?" He was uncertain what to do. While he seemed to consider it, Lynn asked, "What are you guys going to do with us?"

The guy mumbled something to himself and quickly retied their hands so they couldn't remove their blindfolds. "Wait a minute," he said and left the room.

Lynn asked, "Morgan, are you still blindfolded?"

"Yes. I wonder where he went. What do you think they'll do to us?"

"I don't know. At least this one brought us something to eat. I hope he went to get something for this cut. If he did, he may have a shred of decency in him. Let's hope so." Just then the door opened. Lynn and Morgan heard two sets of footsteps.

The one who had brought food came over to Lynn and said, "Brought you something for your wounds." He untied her hands and handed her a small sudsy terrycloth towel.

She felt heartened. If they were going to kill her and Morgan, he probably wouldn't care about a little cut. She said, "Thank you. Now can I get this thing off my eyes so I can see what I'm doing? Besides, I'd like to see what I'm eating."

"Y'all are pretty demanding, considering all the trouble you caused," he said while he removed their blindfolds.

Slowly, their eyes adjusted to the dim light from the candle he held. Both men were there, their faces concealed by ski masks. Looking around, they discovered they were in a dark dining room. The only light came from the single candle the nicer one had brought in. Faded blue wallpaper and a large raggedy tapestry might have once offered a bright touch to the walls of the now dismal room. They saw a platter of bologna sandwiches and two glasses of water on an old table. Lynn looked down at her towel and hoped it wasn't as dirty as it looked.

She began to gingerly clean the cut on her hand. Touching her wound hurt, but it looked like it might not need too many stitches. Next the man handed her a dry kitchen towel to wrap around her arm.

* * *

Pista leaned against the wall, his hands stuck in his pants pockets and his feet crossed. He thought about how easy this should have been. It had been easy enough to grab them. He and Fane had followed the girl and some guy from campus to an apartment building yesterday and watched them go inside. Was it the dude's place? Had she moved in with the guy? He knew it was not the girl's house because they had followed her home before. She lived on Galesbury Street.

Pista had decided right then to go back to that apartment early that morning and get this done once and for all. He'd hoped to catch her alone. He and Fane had been dozing when Pista heard a car start up. When he looked, he saw the couple driving away. "Shit! It's them," he told Fane. He started his car and took off after them, following them to a restaurant. The girl went in and the guy drove off. When she came out of the restaurant with the same black woman he'd seen her with another day, the one he tried to run down, they'd grabbed them both.

As hard as he had worked on this plan, he wasn't prepared to fail. And after the women had got away today, he would have torn up the whole city to find them.

He watched them eat their sandwiches and studied the girl. She was damned good-looking. It would be a shame to waste a freebie. He looked at Fane and said, "Whaddaya think, dude? Maybe a night with these two ladies would be fun."

Lynn didn't like that. She didn't know what she would be able to do if they decided to take Morgan into the other room. She knew that if they came after her, she would put up a fight as best she could. Her years on the Cincinnati police force had provided some pretty strong survival skills, but there were two men, at least one with a gun, and she was not sure how much she could do to protect herself. But Morgan did not seem to be a fighter. Was she about to be sexually assaulted?

She and Morgan had to get away. That was all there was to it. She tried to figure out how they might escape again. Apparently, the guys fully intended to keep them there through the night. *Someone will get worried when they don't hear from us. Mrs. Wellington surely will, but unfortunately, there's nothing anyone will be able to do about it.*

"Hurry up and eat so I can tie you two back up," the sandwich man ordered.

"Do you really need to do that? As you can see, there's not much we can do, locked up in this room. Besides, these ropes are very uncomfortable," Lynn said.

The guy looked at the big boss, wondering what harm it would do to give them some slack. The leader said, "When they finish, tie them. Tight. We'll be seeing them later." Then he left the room.

After they finished eating, Morgan asked if she could use the bathroom. The guy flung his arms in exasperation as if to say, "If it ain't one thing, it's another."

"I'm sorry," she said, "but I have been sitting here for hours. I really have to go."

"I'm afraid we both have to go," Lynn said.

He yelled, "Hey, dude, they gotta go to the toilet. All right if I let them go one at a time?"

The leader shouted back from behind a partially closed door in the next room. "They can piss on the floor for all I care."

"I think they really gotta go," the nicer one said.

"Well, you'd better keep an eye on 'em, or it's your ass."

He untied Morgan's legs and said, "It's across the hall. One at a time. The other one stays here until you get back. Don't try anything funny."

Morgan hobbled to the bathroom, where a small candle was burning. When she closed the door behind her, she searched desperately for something, anything that could help them. She found nothing. She was surprised to find that the toilet worked. Dirty water from a well poured into the sink faucet. Morgan let it run until it became a little less rusty. Even then, she couldn't make herself use it to wash her hands. She'd use bottled water.

While Morgan was in the bathroom, Lynn talked to their captor. "You don't have to do this, you know."

Fane jerked his head in her direction and stared at her without saying anything. She repeated her comment.

Softly, he said, "Look, miss, you'd better not talk anymore, or who knows what my friend will do to you."

Lynn was disappointed that he wouldn't listen, but she wasn't surprised. By now, she could tell this guy was afraid of the leader. "If you let us go, I will tell the police you helped us," she said softly. He didn't respond, and soon they heard Morgan's uneven footsteps coming back.

Lynn took her turn going to the bathroom. As she walked back into the room empty-handed, she glanced around anxiously. It looked like the old house had been closed up for ages. These guys were apparently free to use it as they pleased. She noticed the door where the other one's voice had come from. It was the kitchen which was dimly lit by a candle. If he hadn't been in there, she'd have looked for a knife. She came back to the holding room and asked the man, "Do we have to sit here all night?" He said he had no choice and proceeded to tie them the way they had been before. Lynn could detect a slight air of sympathy from him. *Maybe we can still get him to help us.* She made a last-ditch effort. "Listen, we appreciate that you are being decent to us. Remember, we will tell the authorities that you helped us. It should go well for you. I have some more money hidden in my purse. You can have it."

The man seemed troubled, but of course they couldn't see his face. He slowly backed out of the room and locked the door.

Lynn was too uncomfortable to doze. The room was cold, the chair hard, and her wrist still hurt. More than that, she was worried about the threat that the men would come back.

She guessed it was around midnight when she heard the door being unlocked. "Morgan, wake up," she mumbled through the gag.

"I'm awake," Morgan mumbled back.

Someone entered. "I see you girls are waiting up for me," the man said cavalierly as he aimed the flashlight at their faces. His words were slurred. "That's nice. I'm just going to take this little one in the other room with me. We have a little firewood burning, and it's much cozier in there. Nice warm blankets too." He began to run his hand crudely across Morgan's neck, and she squirmed.

Lynn tried to say, "Leave her alone!" She didn't sound coherent through her gag, but she figured he understood what she was saying.

He began to untie Morgan's legs. "Or you'll do what, exactly?" he smirked.

To Morgan, he said, "I've been pretty nice to you today. Time for a little payback."

Lynn could smell liquor on the guy's breath. *This is bad.* She wondered where the other man was. Was he sleeping? Would he help them?

Before the man finished untying Morgan's legs, the other one came to the door, opened it, and stepped inside "You'd better come have a look," he told the leader.

Pista was on his knees, trying to undo the knot. "Scram!" he yelled at his partner. "Can't you see I'm busy?"

"Man, you'd better get out here now."

Apparently, the leader heard the seriousness in his partner's voice. "This had better be good, you asshole," he said, standing up and then staggering out of the room.

Lynn and Morgan couldn't hear what they were saying. They heard them go to the front door. "There are some officers out here," Fane told Pista.

"What! What are you talking about?" They pulled off their ski masks and went to the door. Two policemen were circling their old car. The police vehicle headlights were on. When Pista and Fane stepped outside, an officer shined the flashlight in their faces.

"What are you two doing trespassing out here? Did you not know this is private property?" he asked in Hungarian.

Pista had no respect for the law and was about to let them have it.

Fane knew they could get in deeper trouble if his drunken partner said anything. He jumped in, speaking to them in Hungarian. "Yes, sir," he said. "We were just looking for a place to rest awhile. We've been traveling a long time, and we couldn't afford a hotel. We turned off the highway and saw these old places boarded up. This one had a broken window, so we climbed in and decided to hang out for a few hours."

"Well, you can't stay here," the officer said. "You'd better get moving."

"How about you let us get a little sleep and take off before dawn?" Pista said, thinking about what was waiting for him inside the house. "Would that be okay with you boys?"

The officer shone his flashlight in Pista's face and studied him a moment. "How about you show us some identification so we can make sure you two aren't wanted," the officer said.

"Hell, we aren't wanted. We're just law-abiding men traveling a long way."

Fane jumped in and said to Pista, "You know, we're supposed to be in Visegrad by six. We probably better get going."

"Oh, yeah. Officers, we were just getting out of here," Pista said, realizing Fane was trying to save their butts. He didn't want to pull out his ID, and he realized he definitely didn't want to give the policemen any reason to look inside and find the girls.

The police radio caught the other officer's attention. He listened for a minute and then told his partner, "We've got to get back to town. There's a robbery. They're calling for backup."

The one talking to Pista and Fane said, "Well, see you on your way. If you're here when we come back, we'll have to take you in."

Fane said, "I'll just go in and get our coats and keys." He ran back into the house and went straight to the kitchen, where he got their jackets and Pista's car keys from the rickety old table. Pista's gun was sitting there, but Fane thought it best not to be caught with it so he left it where it was. Next, he went into the room where their captives were tied up.

"I'm going to untie your hands. We have to leave for a while. If you're smart, you will be long gone when we get back. You don't want to be around him when he's drunk." He quickly loosened the knots around Lynn and Morgan's hands and then rushed out, leaving the door closed but unlocked.

"I'll drive," he said. Pista got in the passenger's seat, and Fane drove off. The police car turned and followed them out.

CHAPTER

25

LYNN AND MORGAN HEARD THE men's car start up and heard the tires rolling across the gravel yard. Then they heard police sirens. "What! The police were here?" Lynn exclaimed. She could tell by how faint the sirens quickly became that they were long gone; they both wondered if that's why the men took off.

They needed to get away from there fast, so she and Morgan got themselves untied. It was easier than before because of the gentler man's help. Morgan's ankle still ached and Lynn's left arm was sore, but they scrambled as quickly as they could. The guy had left his flashlight on the floor, and Lynn used it to look around. She stepped into the kitchen and spotted a bag of food. She also saw Pista's gun, which she took. She and Morgan quickly left the house.

Lynn told Morgan she had Pista's gun. Morgan was surprised. She asked Lynn if she knew how to use one. "I used to be a police officer. If we hitchhike a ride, at least we won't be defenseless if some wacko picks us up, or if our guys come looking for us." They made it to the highway and once again began the long trek into town down the dark, lonely road. Fortunately, they would be able to spot headlights long before they would be spotted themselves. After plodding along for about thirty minutes, they heard a car coming from behind them. Lynn turned around and waved her flashlight frantically, hoping against hope it wasn't the kidnappers. The car stopped, and a middle-aged woman with a concerned look on her face rolled down her window and asked where they were going. She spoke Hungarian. Morgan asked if she knew English.

"Some," she answered.

They told her they were going into town and she told them to get in. She saw Morgan struggle with her leg and asked what they were doing out on the highway on foot so late.

Lynn told her they had escaped from two guys who had abducted them and they wanted to get into town, where their mobile phones could get a signal so they could call the police. The driver told them she would take them into town. The ride took only ten minutes.

The woman pulled in front of the police station and told them, "We are here. I will come in with you." She went into the police station and explained in Hungarian where she had picked them up. Then she asked for an English-speaking officer and wished Lynn and Morgan good luck. "I'm glad you got away." They thanked her for her kindness.

In a few minutes, an officer came out to speak with them. He invited them to take a seat at his desk. In a strong Hungarian accent, he said in English, "Please tell me about your abduction."

Lynn told him what happened. She and Morgan described their abductors as best they could. They described their old car and the boarded-up house where they were held. They told him about the mistaken identity and said they believed Ivona and Nicola Palaki were the intended targets. When they mentioned the men's threat to the Groffs, the officer said they would put surveillance on their home. She told them that one of the men had helped them escape and that they heard police sirens outside before their captors drove away. The officer said he would check to see if the police who went out there were from his precinct.

Lynn said the men could be long gone by now. However, if they could, they would surely go back to look for her and Morgan and also to collect their belongings. The policeman assured them they would do all they could to find the men, including check for fingerprints at the scene. He said the description of the automobile might help to locate the pair. That reminded Lynn that she still had the gun. She pulled it out of her purse and said, "Maybe this will help. They left this behind."

Lynn and Morgan provided information on how they could be reached. They were asked how long they would be in the country and told to report the incident to the American Embassy. After the officer had finished taking his report, he called for a police vehicle to drive them to a hospital. The policeman stayed with them. Lynn received four stitches on her wrist, and Morgan's ankle was bruised and sprained, but fortunately it was not broken. She was given some pain killers, an icepack, and a pair of crutches and told to ice her ankle every couple of hours and to keep her foot elevated.

Lynn insisted that Morgan temporarily move to her hotel in case the kidnappers came back to try again.

She knew Morgan would never be safe in Budapest as long as they thought she was Ivona. The policeman drove them first to Morgan's apartment, where she packed a bag. Then he drove them to the hotel, where she took a room adjoining Lynn's. Lynn told Morgan not to even think about going to her classes tomorrow. She needed to ensure Morgan's safety and had decided the very best solution would be to get Harvey Chapman there to protect Morgan for the rest of her stay.

When Pista and Fane doubled back to the house some time later, the women were gone. So was the gun.

* * *

After Morgan got settled in her room, Lynn dialed the Wellingtons. Sara Wellington answered, and the first thing Lynn did was try to assure her up front that Morgan and she were fine. Then she calmly explained what had happened and how they had escaped.

"My heavens! Are you sure Morgan is all right?" In spite of trying to sound cool and collected, Lynn still heard fright in Sara Wellington's voice.

Lynn explained that Morgan was fine. "She's right here," she said, handing the telephone to Morgan, who talked to her mother before giving the phone back to Lynn. She told Mrs. Wellington, "Obviously Morgan is shook up, but it's as much because the kidnappers may still go after her sister as it is her own personal experience. But physically, other than her bruised ankle, she was not hurt or harmed. We were obviously very lucky to get away. Morgan now has a room in my hotel. In fact, we have adjoining rooms so I can keep a close eye on her. She's going to skip classes tomorrow and nurse that ankle."

Mrs. Wellington told Lynn, "This truly worries me. I told Morgan we will be bringing her home after she meets her biological family. In fact, I'm almost inclined to ask you to put her on the next plane to the United States. I had no idea she was in such danger over there."

"I understand. Just let me know what you want me to do. In the meantime, I will do my best to keep her safe. And that brings up another thing I wanted to talk to you about. If you decide to allow her to stay, I have an associate in Cincinnati I would like to bring over to be Morgan's bodyguard. His name is Harvey Chapman. We have worked together for several years. He is very competent, and I trust him completely. He's a retired Cincinnati police officer. If I can get him an overnight flight, he'll be here tomorrow, and he'll stay as long as he is needed here."

"By all means. In fact, I spoke too quickly. My comment about putting Morgan on the next plane was made out of fear. I do want her to meet her sister and her family. Do what you must. In fact, getting your Mr. Chapman over there would make me feel much better. I want you to know that you have our heartfelt gratitude for being there and looking out for our daughter."

Lynn ended the call and dialed the airline. She hadn't spoken with Harvey yet, but she was confident he would come. She wanted to set his flight up as soon as possible. The reservations desk confirmed that he could be in Budapest tomorrow morning. On the chance that he was available to travel, she reserved his ticket.

A former officer of the law, Harvey Chapman was a seasoned professional. He liked to say he'd seen it all in his twenty-five years on the force. Lynn considered him a dependable and trusted friend. Currently, he was overseeing renovations to her downtown office building, as he did whenever she was away. She knew she could count on him.

Harvey enjoyed being retired, both from the Cincinnati Police Department and from private investigative work, although he still did a little of the latter. He was particularly fond of restoring antique automobiles. It had started a few years ago when he had a chance to acquire a 1942 Studebaker from an aging uncle. In his spare time, he'd completely restored it. He did such a good job on the Studebaker that someone offered to buy it, and he sold it for a tidy profit. Since that time, he'd restored and sold a few more vintage cars. A rare find had been a maroon 1948 Packard limo, which he restored and sold to a wealthy physician. Harvey's favorite project had been a 1929 Model-A Ford. The shiny black vehicle had been purchased by one of the local Ford dealers and remained on display in their showroom. A sign beneath the automobile read, RESTORED BY HARVEY A. CHAPMAN. The endorsement brought him several new clients. His passion aside, Harvey Chapman was fearless, street smart, and tough as nails.

Harvey answered his phone.

"Harv, this is Lynn."

"Lynn, what's wrong?" he asked. "I can hear it in your voice."

She said, "Harv, you offered to come to Budapest. I didn't think I would need you, but I was wrong." Then she told him about her and Morgan's ordeal. "I believe the police made those guys leave the house tonight. We were sure relieved when one of them came in and partially untied us, which allowed us to get away." Lynn asked Harvey if he could come to Budapest and said she could have him here tomorrow morning.

"Damn straight I'll be there," Harvey said. Lynn gave him his flight details. "By the way, I'm at your building now. Mr. Smith has this place shining. You'll be pleased. But I'll go get packed now so I can get to the airport. Reserve me a big car and I'll drive to the hotel. Make sure the girl stays in. I'm out of here."

Lynn disconnected from Harvey and felt great relief knowing he would be there in a few hours. She told Morgan about Harvey Chapman. "He's completely capable of ensuring your safety."

"Cool. Maybe if they catch those guys, my parents will let me stay till the end of the semester. It's just a couple more weeks," Morgan said.

"If they capture them, both of you will be safe. Even if you went home, if they are still out on the street, Ivona could be in danger."

Morgan said, "I am as concerned about Ivona's safety as my own. If anything were to happen to her, I don't know what I would do. It's strange, but this incident makes me think of the times I felt like I was being watched, especially in Paris. Now that I know they were after Ivona, I wonder if I was picking up on her vibes when these men were following Ivona around."

"I believe anything's possible," Lynn answered. "I've heard of twin telepathy, when one twin picks up on what's happening with the other, even if they are separated by great distances. Some say it's a myth, but there've been studies that have shown that things like this really do happen." Then Lynn remembered the night she felt someone was watching her at the restaurant. Now that she knew the kidnappers were the same people who had tried to run her down, she thought they might have seen her with Morgan and decided to get her out of the picture. They might have been surveying the situation for a while.

"That is so scary."

"We were lucky. That's why we can't be too careful. These men, at least one of them, seems crazy. I'll feel a lot better when Harvey gets here."

Morgan said, "Funny. Early this morning, after learning about my twin sister and my mother, I felt like I was floating on the highest cloud in the sky. That seems so long ago now. I still feel great about it, but right now all I can think about is our nightmare and that guy's slimy touch. I can't wait to get in the shower."

They said good night, and Lynn retired to her room. Ella had left her a dozen messages. *I know Ella's worried that she couldn't reach me.* Before jumping into the shower, Lynn dialed her number. "Where you been? I've been trying to get you all day. Needless to say, I was getting concerned. I'm glad you called. I was wondering if you found out anything about the girls being in trouble."

"Whoa, wait a minute, Ella. Let me answer your first question. You won't believe the story I have to tell *you* either." Lynn proceeded to tell Ella about the kidnapping and escape.

Ella's exclamations of shock interrupted her story several times. When Lynn was finished, Ella said, "Good grief! That's just awful. You had to be scared out of your wits. I'm so glad you managed to get away. Miss Walker was convinced the girls were in danger. You gotta wonder about that. One twin was kidnapped, but the other was the real target. It looks like she was right. Shoot, everyone talking about vampires over there. Seems to me you'd be safer around them. Maybe you should get Harvey over there."

"It's already done. He'll be here in the morning. Morgan needs a bodyguard."

"That's good. Who would have thought this case would turn into all this?"

When her call with Ella ended, Lynn removed her clothes and headed into the shower. *At last.* The hot shower was just what the doctor ordered. It had been an extremely harrowing day. With her bandaged wrist held high to keep it dry, she basked in the comforting spray of hot water washing over her.

Lynn somehow believed this would not be the last they heard of the kidnappers. And what about Ivona and Nicola? *They definitely aren't safe.* She wondered when and how the men would strike next. She had scheduled a meeting with Nicola before this all happened, but she would try to move her appointment to an earlier time. Her discovery in Bucharest that Ivona had been listed in the census as Nicola's sister now had her thinking the ringleader knew Nicola back then.

Exhausted, she climbed into bed. Even though her mind was still racing, she was practically asleep before her head hit the pillow. Lynn slept peacefully and arose early the next morning. There was much to do.

CHAPTER
26

Wednesday, November 27

NICOLA PALAKI RETURNED TO HER office that afternoon at two o'clock. Her secretary met her with a stack of messages. As she looked through them, several caught her eye. The first one was from Ms. Simón from the Office of Academic Records. Nicola trembled with excitement as she began to read what it said. However, Ms. Simón's message said, "We were unable to locate a file for a female student with the last name of Wellington in all our records. Please contact our office if we can be of further help to you." Nicola was profoundly disappointed. She immediately dropped everything on her desk and called Ms. Simón's number. She identified herself and said, "I know I asked you to look in the sophomore or junior files, but it is possible she could be in either of the other classes too. Would you please do another search? This time, look through the freshmen and senior records as well."

Ms. Simón said, "We considered that possibility, so my assistant, Ursola, checked all records for every class, but she did not find anyone named Wellington." Nicola was disheartened. She had promised Ivona that she'd look for her sister's file. *I hate to disappoint her, but right now I feel as let down as I know she will.*

If her daughter was a student at CEU and was not listed as a Wellington, the only other possibility she could think of was that she was married. And the only way she knew to get her married name was to place another call to the Wellingtons. She wasn't looking forward to that. The last time they talked, Mrs. Wellington seemed to know nothing about what was going on. However, she decided to call them anyway after she returned her other calls.

Nicola then looked at her other messages. *Curious.* Two were from someone named Lynn Davis from the United States. The first one read URGENT FAMILY MATTER. The second one from this Miss Davis was marked *Extremely urgent.* The message read, *I MUST SPEAK TO YOU AT ONCE!* The third message was from her mother. *Call as soon as you get in! What is all this about?* she wondered; her other daughter, Ivona's twin, came to mind. She dialed Lynn Davis's number.

When Lynn answered, Nicola said, "This is Dr. N. René Palaki. I am returning your telephone call about an urgent family matter. Can you please tell me what this pertains to?"

Lynn said, "Thank you for returning my call. We have a meeting scheduled for later this afternoon. However, the sooner we speak, the better. Can you move me up on your schedule? This cannot wait."

"I am afraid I'm just returning to my office, and I have a backlog of work. Can you tell me what this is about?"

"I don't mean to sound clandestine, but this is something that would be better handled in person. I will just say this concerns your daughter Ivona and another critical matter that involves the Wellington family from Cincinnati, Ohio, in the United States."

Hearing this made Nicola's heart skip. Her eyes grew wide, and her face was instantly drained of color. *How does she know my daughter's name? And what does she know about the Wellingtons? Who is this woman?* Whatever the urgent matter was, especially if it had to do with her daughter, she was anxious to know. "Can you come to my office in thirty minutes?" she asked. Lynn told her she could, and Nicola said, "I want my mother here too. If she is available, I want to invite her."

"Of course. I will see you both shortly."

Nicola called her mother. "Reeni, I know you called me, but you won't believe this. I just returned a call to an American woman who wants to meet with me about an urgent family matter. It has to do with Ivona and the Wellingtons, and I don't know what else. She is coming to my office right now. Can you get over here too?"

"That's strange; I'll definitely be there. Here's why I called you earlier. Ivona had a near breakdown yesterday."

"What?"

Corina filled Nicola in.

"Oh, Reeni, what brought this on? Vonni's been doing so well for so long. Maybe it's because the other night she came so close to meeting this girl she thinks is her sister."

"Well, she was convinced that her sister was in trouble. After awhile, she calmed down and was able to go off to class. Anyway, even stranger—today she called me and said that campus security was going to drive her home."

"Campus security! Why?" Nicola recalled that Lynn Davis said the urgency involved Ivona. She became very nervous.

Corina answered, "Maybe it's what this Miss Davis wants to talk about. Ivona said security told her that she might possibly be in danger. That's why I left that message for you. I'm waiting here until she gets home before coming to your office. I may be a little late."

"Now I'm worried about Vonni. If she's in danger, I don't want her at home alone. She should come with you."

"It's all right. Some members of her study group are coming along with her. They will be studying here a few hours tonight. So I'm sure she'll be fine until I get back. I'll get there just as soon as I can."

* * *

Lynn arrived at Dr. Palaki's office a little before three. She waited while Nicola finished a telephone call. Nicola then stepped to the door to ask her in, extending her hand and saying, "Miss Davis, I'm Dr. Palaki."

Lynn noticed that Nicola was studying her face and realized the bruise on her jaw from the kidnapper's blow was still evident. She remembered how her driver, Jozséf, had reacted when he picked her up to bring her here today.

"What happened to your face? Did you fall?" he had asked.

"I'm afraid I had a little accident." Lynn apologized for leaving him sitting outside the restaurant the day before. She told him something unexpected came up and told him to be sure to bill for his time. He didn't probe.

As she shook Nicola's hand, Lynn noted that, as the pictures revealed, Morgan looked a lot like her. She said, "I'm glad you were able to see me. As I mentioned, this couldn't wait." Then she asked, "Is your mother coming?"

"Yes, she should be here shortly," Nicola answered. "May I take your coat?" Lynn handed Nicola her coat and Nicola asked, "Would you like tea?"

Lynn declined the tea and said, "Shall I wait for Mrs. Moldovan before we get started?" Once again Nicola reacted when she heard her mother's name.

"Just before you arrived, she phoned and said she was parking her car. She should be here shortly, so, please, let's wait a minute," Nicola replied. "But I am curious how you know all our names."

At that moment, Corina Moldovan walked in. She greeted her daughter and said, "Good. I'm on time." Lynn observed that Mrs. Moldovan was a couple of inches taller than her daughter. Her short hair was still mostly black, with touches of gray around the hairline. She had an olive complexion and an attractive, mature face. She pulled off her overcoat and hung it on the coat rack. She was wearing a smart pale blue suit with beige stitching around the collar and lapel. Clutching a small purse in one hand, she extended her right hand to shake Lynn's and said, "Hello, I'm Corina Moldovan."

"Mother, this is Lynn Davis. Please help yourself to tea, and let's hear what she has to tell us."

The two women shook hands and sat down at a round table. "We are very anxious to hear about this danger to my daughter. And we're most curious what this has to do with the Wellingtons of Cincinnati," Nicola said. "What is this about my daughter?"

Lynn said, "I will explain everything to you. However, first, if you don't mind my asking, is your daughter home from school yet?"

Corina looked surprised at the question but answered, "Yes, she and members from her study team are all there."

Lynn felt a sense of relief. "Great. I did not know how to reach either of you, or Ivona either, so I contacted campus security and asked them to drive her home."

Both women looked surprised. "We were wondering why they needed to bring her home. So it was you who arranged that. Why?" Corina asked.

"Let me explain," Lynn said. She told them she was an investigator and that she was here in Budapest at the Wellingtons' request. Since she now knew from Ella's conversation with the midwife that Nicola and her mother knew about Morgan, she assumed they probably had an idea what the subject was.

"Mrs. Sara Wellington asked me to come to Budapest to check on their daughter, Morgan, who has been here since August. She is attending CEU this semester." Lynn noticed the two women glance at each other. She wondered just how much or how little they knew. She said to Nicola, "I am aware the Wellingtons adopted your daughter."

Nicola nodded. Again, Lynn saw the furtive looks Nicola and her mother exchanged.

"I'm excited to hear that she attends CEU, where I am a professor. However, we have not met. Do you know why Morgan came to Budapest?"

Lynn explained about the summer program in Paris, when a Hungarian roommate encouraged Morgan to come here and then said, "Morgan only learned yesterday that she has a twin sister and that both she and her biological mother are in Budapest."

Nicola and Corina looked puzzled. Lynn noticed their look and asked, "Is something the matter?"

"We wondered if she knew. We just learned of Ivona's twin earlier this year when we received a letter from the midwife who delivered them." She added, "It's a long story. We spoke to Miss Walker, and she told us she had also written the Wellingtons. After not hearing from them, we contacted Mrs. Wellington and asked her if she had received a letter from the midwife. When she said no, we were reluctant to broach the matter of the twins, since they apparently didn't know about them. Frankly, we didn't know what to do."

Lynn remembered that during their call with Morgan yesterday morning, Mrs. Wellington had mentioned that Nicola had called asking about a letter from the midwife.

"I can understand that. Of course, you're speaking about Miss Flossie Walker." The women both looked surprised to hear Lynn say the midwife's name. "But apparently, the Wellingtons never received that letter. And as much as this information came as a shock to you, you can imagine it was the same for the Wellingtons and for Morgan. But to be sure, Morgan was absolutely thrilled about it."

Nicola said, "I know how difficult it was for Ivona. Our hearts go out to Morgan."

Then Corina said, "Ivona has excitedly mentioned a young woman she saw here in Budapest. She said when she saw her, it felt like she was looking into a mirror. She was convinced it was her twin sister. Last week a friend of Morgan's tried to set up a meeting between the two of them. He told her the girl's name was Morgan.

"Nicola, when Ivona was having her episode yesterday, she was talking about her sister," Corina continued. Then she explained to Lynn, "Yesterday morning my granddaughter began to feel that her sister was in danger."

"It's pretty remarkable that the girls haven't met and yet your daughter sensed that her sister was in danger." It seemed yet another example of the amazing telepathy the young ladies seemed to share. "I will tell you something else. Even the midwife, Miss Flossie Walker, had sensed the same thing. She contacted my assistant to warn me to watch out." The women did not know what to think about that.

"Oh dear, I'm definitely concerned about Morgan. Do you happen to know where she is? I pray nothing has happened to her," Nicola said.

"Yes, I know exactly where she is, and she is fine now." Lynn answered. Corina and Nicola breathed collective sighs of relief.

Nicola said, "When you called, you said that Ivona might be in danger. Please tell me what kind of danger she might be in and why you requested that campus security bring her home."

Lynn pulled a short newspaper article out of her briefcase; it told about two American women who were kidnapped but escaped. She said, "This is why I needed to speak with you." She handed the article to Nicola. Mrs. Moldovan got up and read over her daughter's shoulder. When she saw the headline KIDNAPPERS ON THE LOOSE, she said, "Yes, I saw this article in this morning's paper." She reread it along with Nicola, who got to the names of the victims and froze: Lynn Davis and Morgan Wellington.

Nicola gasped and said, "This was you and Morgan. Dear God!"

Corina said, "Goodness! I saw the article, but the name never registered. My word!"

"Please tell us what happened," Nicola said.

"I did say Morgan is fine now. But this is what I wanted to tell you. She and I were together Monday morning. We were leaving a downtown restaurant when two men in a parked car asked us for directions to the Buda Castle. I thought there was something unusual about them." Then Lynn told them that, without thinking, Morgan had stepped over to their car to help. One of the men pulled a gun and ordered them into the car, blindfolded them, and drove away. "They held us in an old house. At one point while the men were away, we managed to escape, but they caught up with us. They were angry, but thank goodness, they didn't hurt us." Lynn noticed that the women's eyes went directly to her cheek and the black eye that she'd tried to camouflage with makeup. She lightly touched her cheek and said, "Well, one of them did strike me pretty hard. But the good thing is, we managed to get away a second time, and that time we made it. We then reported them to the police." She paused and said, "So far as I know, they've not been caught."

Mrs. Moldovan said, "That is absolutely unthinkable. We are thankful that you and Morgan weren't seriously harmed. That had to be a very frightening ordeal. We hear more and more these days about tourists being kidnapped. Sometimes I wonder what our world is coming to."

"Mrs. Moldovan, I'm afraid this was not a random kidnapping," Lynn said. "Which is why I needed to talk to both of you immediately. These men knew exactly who they were after. They planned to contact you, Dr. Palaki, for ransom money because they thought they had kidnapped your sister."

Nicola was astounded. "My sister! They were going to contact me! I don't even have a sister."

Lynn continued, "The men who abducted us knew who they wanted." Then Lynn looked from one to the other and said, "Dr. Palaki, your daughter Ivona was their intended target. That is why she is in danger. Those men will probably try again. I gave this information to the police but asked them not to release your names to the press. They said they would keep an eye on your house.

"These men were planning to extort money from you in exchange for our release. They said they would let us go when they got their money, but I doubt they would have released us." Lynn continued. "I realize that had the kidnappers succeeded in contacting you, you would have taken it as a prank, never even dreaming that it was your other daughter they were talking about."

"You are absolutely right," Nicola replied. "I would have known Ivona was all right and definitely ignored it."

Lynn said, "I told the men they had the wrong person, but they didn't buy it. I was hoping you might have some idea about who would think she was your sister."

Nicola searched her mind in earnest. "No one comes to mind right now. But many years ago when I was in Bucharest, my classmates believed Ivona was my sister. I cannot see any of them doing such a thing. But I'll definitely keep trying to think of possibilities."

"If you come up with any names, it might help the police identify and capture them."

Lynn gave Nicola and her mother a description of their ordeal, including how the men took all their money and about their plan to reach Nicola this morning at her office. "I realized very early that they thought they had kidnapped your other daughter. Morgan realized it too. They never believed her when she denied being your sister. So when they asked for your home telephone number, rather than anger them further by continuing to deny being who they thought she was, Morgan told them your service had been knocked out in a storm."

Nicola took a deep breath.

Corina said, "That was quick thinking. It is by God's grace that you got away from those men."

Lynn told them one of the men actually helped them get away, and she described how.

"We have much to be grateful for," Corina said.

"But they're still out there. We gave the police as much information as we could. We told them how to find the house where we were held. The police seemed confident they would find the men. But until they do, everyone needs to take extra precautions. You need to remember these men wanted money. The leader of the two said you were rich and famous. He knew this because he had read articles about you. He's the one who believed Morgan was your younger sister," Lynn told them.

"They failed the first time, but that doesn't mean they won't try again. That's why I think you should all be very careful, particularly Ivona. We don't know how they tracked Morgan down, but they may have been watching her at the university. With Ivona there too, they might move on her like they did Morgan. That is why I contacted campus security today," Lynn said, adding, "I have a bodyguard lined up to protect Morgan, and you should take all measures to ensure that Ivona is safe too. I'd say she definitely shouldn't be walking around campus alone."

Realizing how serious this was, Nicola said, "Thank you for your advice. We will take every measure to see that Ivona is safe."

Lynn said, "The reason for my first message today was to set up a meeting for Morgan to meet all of you. Are you interested in meeting her? And your daughter—will she want to meet Morgan?"

Corina said, "We absolutely cannot wait to meet her. We've all thought of little else since receiving the midwife's letter. Ivona desperately wants to meet her. Since Morgan now knows about us, I suppose the Wellingtons do too."

"They do now," Lynn said, adding, "In fact, they will be coming to Budapest to meet with you as well. This is a recent discovery for them too. I know you can imagine the shock and excitement involved for all concerned. Morgan is especially thrilled about having a twin sister."

Lynn said, "Let me show you a picture of her." She pulled out a photo, and Nicola eagerly reached for it. She studied it fiercely. Her eyes began to water.

"My God, she's identical to Ivona! It's incredible. I want to meet her as soon as possible. If she is available tomorrow afternoon, I could make that work." She passed the photo to her mother, who'd been straining to see it.

Lynn replied, "Since the Wellingtons want to be here too, they will need time to make their flight plans. They were just waiting to learn the date and time from me."

They settled on Sunday for the big reunion.

CHAPTER
27

Budapest, Hungary, Wednesday, November 27

AFTER LYNN DAVIS LEFT THE office, Nicola and her mother marveled at everything they had just learned, from the kidnapping to Ivona's twin, Morgan. Nicola said, "Ever since receiving Miss Walker's letter, I have somehow known this day would come. I am overjoyed at the prospect of meeting her on Sunday. I only hope she feels the same about meeting me."

"I know how you feel. It would be lovely to begin a relationship that will carry through the rest of our lives," Corina said.

"What I can't understand is how the Wellingtons just learned about Morgan. Remember, the midwife told us she had written to them. But, of course, Mrs. Wellington said she never received a letter."

Corina said, "I know that sometimes things get lost in the mail. Perhaps that's what happened to her letter."

"You could be right. I would rather believe that than to think they knew about Ivona and chose not to get in touch with us. Ivona was so hurt. The only thing that brightened her spirits was finally seeing her sister at the department store. Since that time, she's been excited. Still, this kidnapping frightens me to death. To think I could have lost my other daughter before ever even meeting her ..." Nicola paused. "Well, I'm just grateful that she's safe."

Corina felt the same way. But she was concerned for all of them. "We've got to do everything we can to ensure Vonni's safety, and yours, from these kidnappers."

"Don't worry about me, Reeni. I can take care of myself. I just don't want any harm to come to either of my daughters. I will see if Vonni can stay home tomorrow, but with final exams approaching, I know she won't want to."

"Tomorrow she's scheduled to be with her study group. They're meeting at an off-campus laboratory. I feel better about that. I can drive her in the morning and pick her up in the afternoon," Corina said. She added, "Speaking of which, I better be getting back home so I can make sure everything is okay."

As she put her coat on, Corina said, "Now that we know about the kidnapping, I still marvel at Vonni's intuition yesterday; she knew something was wrong with her sister. If it was mental telepathy, I wonder if Morgan has it too."

"Me too," Nicola said. "And if the girls really are picking each other up, that could explain a lot about Vonni's early years, like her imaginary playmate, Margo. I believe Vonni's life would have been a lot easier had she and her sister been together or, at the very least, known about each other. I will never get over the fact that Miss Flossie Walker did such an unthinkable thing to us."

"She did us a grave injustice. Every day I have thought about the girls not getting to grow up together. They missed out on so much. Besides, neither of us got to experience your other daughter either," Corina said.

Nicola agreed. As her mother was walking out the door, she said, "Just call if you need anything."

After Corina left, Nicola found it impossible to concentrate. The visit with Lynn Davis had nearly left her in a state of shock. She'd been thrilled to learn that her other daughter was here in Budapest and that they would all meet in a matter of days. But the kidnapping saga was unnerving. She had to protect Vonni. And she prayed for Morgan's continued safety.

As she thought about the upcoming meeting, her excitement turned to concerns she could not avoid. Would Morgan accept her into her life? What kind of relationship can they have? She certainly did not expect to replace Sara Wellington as Morgan's mother, but ... Nicola wondered how the Wellingtons were dealing with this after all these years. She found it interesting that she was now concerned about how they were dealing with it. Until a few minutes ago, she had harbored a deep resentment that they had completely ignored Morgan's twin sister.

Nicola was also trying to ward off the guilt she was feeling over putting her child up for adoption so many years ago in the first place. Would Morgan hold it against her? Nicola realized she would not get any work done today. She thought about Miss Davis. She had seemed very capable. *She could probably help me with this.* Nicola felt the need to talk to her some more. In fact, she wanted to explain things to her, get her perspective. She telephoned Lynn and told her there was more she needed to talk to her about. "Do you have any free time?"

"My driver is just arriving at the hotel. I will be meeting Morgan for dinner in a couple of hours. Is now a good time for you? I can have my driver bring me back to your office."

Nicola agreed, and Lynn told her she would be there in fifteen minutes.

* * *

When Lynn arrived back at Nicola's office, Nicola closed her door and invited her to sit on her sofa. Then she joined her and said, "Miss Davis, thank you for coming back. After you left, so many things were going through my head. I just wanted to talk with you some more."

"I'm glad I was available to come right back. What did you want to talk to me about?"

"Well, in spite of my excitement, I have to admit to also being nervous and anxious about meeting Morgan. I know she will want to know how she and Ivona came to be separated, and I will share everything with her about that. But I'm concerned she might resent me for putting her up for adoption in the first place. You have spent some time with Morgan. How do you think she will feel about me?"

"She has talked about this. She will probably want to know *why* you put her up for adoption," Lynn said. "Dr. Palaki, not to add to your anxiety, but you should know Morgan has spent all her life wondering about you, her father, and whether she had any siblings. I understand most adopted children never feel totally at peace until they know who they really are."

"I will tell her everything, and I pray she will accept what I tell her."

"Morgan was ecstatic to learn that you and her twin sister were here."

"I'm happy to hear that. How did she learn about us?"

"On my first day here in Budapest last week, I discovered your picture in the university records. Your likeness to Morgan was remarkable, and I wondered if the two of you were related. I sent your photo to Mrs. Wellington, and she confirmed that you were Morgan's biological mother. She believed Morgan must have come here in search of her roots."

"I know everyone is wondering why they were separated. That's one of the things I wanted to talk to you about. Until earlier this year, I had no knowledge that I'd given birth to twins nineteen years ago."

Lynn said, "I am aware of that. My associate, Ella Braxton, met with Miss Walker this week. Miss Walker explained everything to her."

"So then you know the story," Nicola said.

"Yes. Miss Walker told my associate about the letter she wrote you last spring explaining everything."

Nicola replied, "That letter was the biggest shock of my life. It truly turned our lives inside out. I am still stunned over what she did to us. At the time, I thought of her as such a kind-hearted woman. I question that now. At least she was decent enough to finally tell us the truth."

"I understand how you feel, but from what I could tell, she had your best interest at heart from the very beginning."

"That may be so, but I have to admit, we were all very upset. My mother wanted to write Miss Walker to give her a piece of her mind. Since there was no return address on her letter, we hired a private investigator to locate her, and that's when we called her. We needed to know how much the Wellingtons knew. Miss Walker said she had written them too. So we waited to hear from them, but we never did."

"That's unfortunate," Lynn said. "The Wellingtons must not have received her letter. I'm certain they had absolutely no knowledge that Morgan had a twin. Your daughter was correct that Morgan did come to Budapest in search of her, but she had no clue that she was searching for her own twin sister."

"That's amazing. I feel better knowing the Wellingtons might not have known. But I wonder what happened to their letter," Nicola said.

"We may possibly never know," Lynn replied. "Back to the twins—wouldn't you have known you were carrying two babies?"

"When Miss Walker listened to the heartbeat, apparently the hearts were beating in unison so she could never tell there was more than one child." She continued. "Even my mother never suspected I was carrying twins."

"Mrs. Walker explained you declined the ultrasound, which would have made that known to you. She said that since you were putting your child up for adoption, you didn't want to know anything about it. That's understandable."

"It's true. I believed the less I knew about the baby, the easier it would be to give it up."

Lynn said, "Mrs. Walker told Ella that you had a very hard time with your decision to give your baby up. When you had to go to the hospital, she worried that you might not be able to have another child and it would be her fault."

"In her letter, she said that was why she made the decision she did. So because of her decision, the Wellingtons got their baby and we got ours. Still, my mother and I couldn't understand how she could take it upon herself to hand out my babies like that. She did tell us that because my girls were identical twins, separating them was a hard decision since she, too, was an identical twin."

"I assume you don't remember anything about the birth process," Lynn said.

"No, I have no memory of most of that. When the pain became unbearable, she put me to sleep. After I was released from the hospital, my mother and I returned to Miss Walker's clinic to collect our things and prepare for our long trip to Bucharest."

"How long were you in the hospital?"

"Three days. When we arrived at Miss Walker's clinic, we got the surprise of our lives. She went into a room and came out with a beautiful infant wrapped in a soft pink blanket. We were keeping my baby, and I was thrilled. We collected our things, thanked her, and said good-bye. We did not hear from her again until this past May.

"As we were leaving the United States, my mother and I decided that when we got back to Bucharest, she would be known as my baby's mother so I could have a fresh start. We named her Ivona Kay and left Cincinnati without talking to the Wellingtons. We respected their decision to change their mind, and frankly, we didn't want them to change back. Now we realize that if we'd contacted them, while it would have been problematic, at least we would have known the truth."

Lynn said, "I can imagine what a shock this has been to all of you."

"When we never heard from the Wellingtons, we could only assume they had no interest in getting the girls together. Of course we were extremely hurt and disappointed, especially Ivona, that her twin sister did not get in touch with her. Weeks went by. Then one day back in September, Vonni spotted Morgan in a department store here in Budapest. She knew it was her twin, and she's been excited ever since. Vonni believed with all her heart that Morgan came to Budapest specifically to meet her.

"I wonder if the Wellingtons would have wanted to adopt both girls. Or if I would have permitted them to."

"That's something else you may never know," Lynn said. "You allowed them to adopt one of your babies, and for that, I believe they will always be grateful. At least realizing the girls are twins may help them understand a lot about Morgan's early behavior," Lynn said. "She went through some things that may have come from sensing her sister, even though she didn't know she had one. I have read about twin telepathy. It is said that even if separated at birth, they can still have strong feelings toward each other. I'll say there certainly does seem to be a very strong connection between your daughters."

"Yes, like what Ivona went through yesterday morning when you and Morgan were kidnapped. Now that I know about Morgan, I now think I understand some of the things Ivona went through when she was younger too, such as feeling that she was missing something from her life. I now believe what was missing was her sister," Nicola said. "As a scientist, this phenomenon is something I know nothing about, but I accept that anything is possible."

"Imagine how strange it must have been for both of them to have these feelings, without knowing about each other."

The two women began to wrap up the visit. "It was so kind of you to come back. I really wanted to explain what happened when they were born. Our conversation has eased my mind. And I'm particularly relieved to know that the Wellingtons may not have received Miss Walker's letter. Because the thought that they did not want the twins to meet was very painful. I look forward to telling Morgan the whole truth and hope for the best. I look forward to seeing you all on Sunday. I wish it could be sooner," Nicola added with a wistful smile.

Lynn said, "I know you will be thrilled to meet Morgan, just as she will be to meet you. Sunday will be here before you know it."

Lynn left Nicola's office and walked to her limo, thinking about the midwife's decision to separate the girls. It was her impression that neither the Wellingtons nor Nicola or her mother would have wanted to miss out on the joy of raising their daughters. Therefore, the midwife's decision, as unorthodox as it was, seemed to have worked out for all parties.

CHAPTER
28

Budapest, Hungary, Wednesday, November 27

"Get me another beer," Pista barked to Fane as he sat in his apartment reading a newspaper. Suddenly, he exclaimed, "Looks like we made the damned newspaper. Check this out. It says here that the girl we picked up *was* an American. So we did get the wrong girl. Those two kept saying we made a mistake. I still say they were lying."

"At least they were good for plenty of cash," Fane said, bringing him a beer and popping it open. "We got good money from them."

"For now. But I was expecting a whole lot more—I'd intended to clean out the black one's bank account. I tried to use one of her credit cards to get something to eat, but it didn't work, so I cut them up in case she'd already reported them. Now I'm sitting here wondering what the hell the police were doing out there that night. They sure screwed us the hell up. I've been working on this job for months, and then just like that it's over. Tell you one thing; I'm still shocked those two were gone when we got back to our house. We left them tied up good and tight, didn't we?" he said, eyeing Fane suspiciously.

Fane caught Pista's distrustful look and slyly tried to change the subject. He was sure that if Pista ever learned he'd helped those women, he'd be history. But he was more afraid Pista would have killed the women and dumped them in the Danube. They didn't deserve that. He responded, "Sure did. And they even took your *pisztoly*. Now what're you gonna do?"

"That's no problem. I can pick up another gun as easy as I can get a pack of *cigaretta*."

Pista read the rest of the article, relieved there was no good description of him or Fane. At least they had done a good job of hiding their identities. And they were sure they'd left no fingerprints. But they'd failed at everything else, and he was pissed! Even if the girl was from America, he could have figured a way to get her parents or someone to wire some money before he was finished with her. She looked like she was from money. But that black one bothered him the most. If she had just minded her own business, he would be rich right now and far away from this damn town. He couldn't let go his anger, and he made a commitment to himself to finish her off. He would succeed the next time. Plus, he still wanted to get the girl.

He said to Fane, "Since we got the wrong girl the first time, the right little sister is still out there. I say it's worth one more try. We'll go over to the campus where we used to see her and get the real one."

"How will we know if we get the right one?" Fane asked.

"I don't give a damn which one we grab. Way I figure, either of them is good for something."

Fane said, "But the police saw our car. Probably got our license number."

"Listen, whiny-ass, why don't you just shut your trap. Don't you know how easy it is to put some different tags on a car? I'm willing to take a chance that we got at least one good try left in that old piece of junk. We change the tags, throw a little spray paint on the car, and we'll be good to go."

* * *

On Wednesday afternoon, Morgan called Bela, who asked, "Where were you yesterday? I looked everywhere for you. Plus I tried to call you several times."

"You're not going to believe this, but ..." Morgan proceeded to tell her about the kidnapping. Bela was shocked and horrified.

"That scares me to death. I'm so glad you and that lady got away. If anything had happened to you, I would feel guilty for the rest of my life, since I begged you to come here. Now I'm thinking about how you've been feeling like someone was following you. Maybe that's who you've been sensing."

Morgan filled in the details of what happened. "So obviously, I'm not in class today either. Plus, with this ankle, I'm still using crutches. But it's getting better, and I'll have a bodyguard starting tomorrow. So I should see you tomorrow afternoon."

Then Morgan dropped the news about her and Ivona Palaki being twins.

Bela screamed, "No way!"

"You heard right. We are identical twins," Morgan said.

"I always said she looked like she could be. I never dreamed it was really true. I can't even imagine how you must feel. It has to feel strange to have a twin you never knew about."

Morgan told her they would be meeting each other soon. When she told Bela that her mother, Dr. N. René Palaki, was a professor at CEU, Bela exclaimed, "Morgy, this is absolutely nuts. I can't believe how physically close to your real family you have been all this time. I'm so glad you came to Budapest, but I'm still shocked that you were kidnapped." They talked until Bela had to go to her next class.

Next, Morgan called György. She knew he would be upset when she told him everything. She dialed his number and reached him at the club, rehearsing.

"Morgy, I've been trying to reach you. I left messages last night."

"György, listen," she said, and then she told him about being kidnapped in front of the restaurant where he had dropped her off yesterday.

György was so stunned by the news he could barely focus. "Are you okay now?"

Morgan told him she was fine and that she'd moved to a hotel. He said, "I should have gone into that restaurant with you yesterday, or at least waited until you were done. But I can come over now and stay with you to make sure you're safe. Would that be all right?"

Morgan convinced György she was in good hands. Then she said, "You're never gonna believe what else I have to tell you." Excitedly, she explained that she and Ivona Palaki were twins and her mother was a science professor at CEU.

György was speechless. He knew how much this meant to Morgan and he was happy for her, but it all was just plain unbelievable. Then he thought of Ivona's call yesterday and told Morgan about it. "She told me that she believed you were in trouble. When I couldn't reach you, I was scared as a turkey on Thanksgiving, speaking of which, is tomorrow. How could she have known?"

Morgan too wondered how Ivona knew. György also told her what happened to Ivona last Saturday night. "She wanted me to tell you she hadn't stood you up and still wants to get together as soon as possible. I was going to call when you got home from class today to tell you all this."

"That's awesome. I never understood why she didn't show up last Saturday, so I am so glad to know what happened. At least we both want to meet each other. I don't know yet if she is aware that we're sisters. Miss Davis is arranging for me to meet the whole family—Ivona, my mother, and my grandmother." Morgan told him her parents were also coming to Budapest; when they left next week, she would be going back to the United States with them.

György couldn't hide his disappointment, but given that her safety was at stake, he tried to be understanding. "I just hope we can spend as much time together as possible before you leave."

Morgan felt bad for dropping the news on him like that. She would miss him too. In fact, she hadn't wanted to think about how much she didn't want to leave Budapest, and György, just yet. But with what happened yesterday, it just seemed like the thing to do.

They agreed to talk later.

* * *

That evening when Lynn and Morgan met for dinner in the hotel restaurant, Lynn told her all about her visit with her mother and grandmother.

Morgan said, "I'd have given anything to see them. What were they like?"

"You look a lot like your mother. Dr. Palaki's very attractive and very professional, and I was quite impressed with her. You take after your grandmother too. Mrs. Moldovan is a little taller than your mother. They both seemed very nice."

"I can't wait to meet them."

"I'm sure. The big reunion is now scheduled for Sunday," Lynn replied.

"Sunday? That's four whole days away. I wish it could be tomorrow."

"They said the same thing, but we had to give your parents time to get here. I called your mother, and she said they can arrive Sunday morning." Lynn told Morgan how excited her mother and grandmother had been to learn that she was here in Budapest. "In fact, Dr. Palaki said she recently saw a young lady on campus that she believed was you. Now that she knows that you're here, she is certain it *was* you she saw. She was thrilled about that." Lynn could tell Morgan was pleased to hear that.

Lynn continued, "I had to meet with them to alert them to the matter at hand—our kidnapping and the possible danger to Ivona."

"I bet that shocked them too."

"Their major focus right now is keeping Ivona safe from those kidnappers. I know I'll breathe a lot easier when my associate Harvey Chapman gets here to help ensure your safety. He's scheduled to arrive tomorrow morning from Cincinnati. We'll all have lunch together so you can get to know him."

"Good, then after lunch I can go to my afternoon class so I won't have to miss my exam."

"Mr. Chapman and I will take you. By the way, how's your ankle? I noticed you're only using one crutch now."

"It's much better after icing it all day. I may not even need my crutches tomorrow at all." Then Morgan told Lynn she'd been wanting to tell her something. "I want to thank you for getting us out of that situation yesterday. I believed we were finished. And even if they didn't kill us, I was sure that guy was going to take me into the other room and force himself on me."

"I was going to do everything in my power to save us. I'm grateful we were able to get away. That woman who picked us up was a godsend," Lynn said.

"I agree, but I want to tell you something else," Morgan said. She paused a moment. "I'm not proud of how I've acted toward you—you know, like a prima donna. You've been nothing but kind to me, and I just want to thank you for coming here to see about me."

"You're more than welcome," Lynn replied, surprised by Morgan's attitude adjustment.

Budapest, Hungary, Thursday, November 28

TODAY IS THANKSGIVING DAY BACK home. I definitely have a lot to be thankful for, Lynn thought as the kidnapping incident briefly entered her thoughts. As she waited in the lobby to greet her friend Harvey, Lynn thought about how much she had to be grateful for, including welcoming him here to help them. Harvey had called her from the airport to say he was on his way to the hotel. Lynn was excited about seeing him. When he walked into the lobby, she hurried over to greet him with a huge hug.

"Hey, Lynn!" Harvey chuckled as he returned her hug. "I'm glad to see you too," he said. Then he stepped back to get a look at her face and said, "Whoa! What did those chumps do to you? You didn't tell me about this."

Lynn didn't need Harvey getting upset. She made light of her bruise by assuring him that it was just a little slap. "But my face isn't accustomed to that kind of brute force."

"So what's with the wrist? Why is it wrapped up?" he asked. She told him about her fall. Harvey studied her black eye and quietly mouthed a few choice expletives. Then he told Lynn that he'd slept on the plane, so after he freshened up, he'd be ready to go.

"We'll talk over lunch," Lynn said. "Morgan and I will be in the restaurant. Tonight we'll have to find somewhere to have a nice Thanksgiving meal."

Harvey checked into the hotel and went up to his room to unpack.

When Harvey came downstairs, Lynn introduced him to Morgan. Morgan seemed comfortable around him. The first thing he said was, "Is it Halloween or something over here? I saw a bunch of young people all dressed in black. Some of the girls even had on black lipstick."

"They're probably Goths," Morgan said. "Short for Gothic. Some people call it punk."

Lynn added, "It's just a style. You'll see people dressing like that in the United States too."

"Well, to each his own," Harvey replied, shaking his head. "They looked like a bunch of weirdos, if you ask me."

While they ate, Lynn and Morgan shared the details of the kidnapping. Harvey listened and frowned, occasionally cursing under his breath. Finally Morgan looked at her watch and jumped up, reaching for her book bag. Harvey said, "Taking you to school'll give me a chance to get the lay of the land. Ready, Lynn?"

"Sure. After we drop Morgan off, you and I can talk."

The trio continued to chat while Harv drove to Morgan's campus. "Harv, you're pretty good at finding your way around," Lynn said.

"The car rental place gave me a map, plus the car has a GPS system."

They agreed on a place where Harvey would pick her up at precisely five o'clock after she finished her classes. Then they dropped her off at her building and watched her go inside.

While they rode around after that, Lynn told him about her meeting with Morgan's biological mother and grandmother. Then she filled in more of the details about their ordeal, including the description of the house where she and Morgan were held. "They're probably long gone by now though," she told him.

Harvey agreed. "I don't think they'd be dumb enough to sit there and wait for someone to show up and arrest them. Getting Morgan away from her apartment was a smart move. But we'll operate as if those boys haven't given up yet."

They stopped at a coffee bar. While sipping her cappuccino, Lynn said, "You know, I'm wondering how those people found Morgan at the restaurant. I believe they knew she was at the university, and they probably knew where she lived. I'm betting they'd been watching her for a while. How else could they have known where she was? She's lucky they hadn't tried anything before then."

"That's a good question. If we can figure that out, we might find them looking for her there again."

Lynn said, "I don't feel like those guys are going to give up. It's important to keep Morgan safe. Ivona's family knows to do the same with her. At any rate, Mrs. Wellington and her husband are coming to Budapest to be with Morgan when she meets her other family. When they return to the United States, they're taking her with them so she can't be a target again. And with that, my job here will be done. But if the kidnappers haven't been caught by the time we leave, that would leave Nicola and Ivona in danger. I would hate to see anything happen to them."

CHAPTER
29

ALL DAY LONG, IVONA THOUGHT about yesterday's events, starting with the campus security van driving her home. Then there was that incredible discussion she had with Niko and Reeni, confirming what she knew in her heart— that her sister *was* in Budapest. Hearing about her being kidnapped was frightening. And the American woman saying that she and Morgan were still in danger was disturbing, as was the fact that she was the intended victim.

Ivona knew the kidnappers could have harmed Morgan, or worse. The very idea that they had the wrong girl and could have hurt her nearly made her sick. Sunday was three full days away. That's when she and Morgan would finally meet. What if she'd never had the chance to meet her? The thought of possibly losing her sister before they ever had a chance to meet pierced her heart like a dagger. Ivona was sorry she'd let her down by not getting into the club last Saturday. If only she could see Morgan just for a minute. She could explain what had happened that night and that she really had wanted to meet her.

Reeni had driven her to meet with her study group that morning, but when they finished in the afternoon, one of her friends had to return to campus to pick up some materials. She decided to catch a ride home with him and called Reeni to tell her not to come pick her up. After her friend collected his materials, she asked him to drop her by the Arts campus for just a few minutes.

Ivona had no idea what Morgan's schedule was or where she might be. All she knew was that György Novak said her classes were on this campus. She had a strong feeling that she might somehow run into her today. She left her friend in his car and walked toward the front of the Fine Arts building to get a better view of the passing students. Ivona could almost sense her sister's presence nearby. She desperately wanted to see her and hoped to catch her coming out of the building. If she didn't see her, she might just have to wait until Sunday.

The next thing she knew, she was being whisked away by two men whose faces were concealed by caps and scarves. *What's happening?* She was too scared to scream because one of them poked her in her side, claiming he had a gun. He handed her a pair of black glasses and made her put them on. Then they grabbed her by the forearms, one on each side, and led her to a car, telling her to walk naturally. She heard the car door open, and one of them said, "Get your ass in the car." Not knowing what else she could do, she climbed in. It happened so fast she could hardly get her bearings. Were these the same men who kidnapped Morgan? Niko and Reeni had said they were real bad guys. She was convinced these were the kidnappers, and now they had her. She was terrified. The worst part was that she knew she should have heeded Niko's warning and not been walking around campus alone. This was her own doing.

* * *

Morgan could hardly concentrate. She'd been preoccupied ever since learning two days earlier that she had a twin sister and that Miss Davis had located her real mother. But the kidnapping episode had prevented her from basking in that news. Her excitement had caught up with her and was now running high. She would see her sister for the first time on Sunday. Could she wait until then? Although she had been eager to return to her classes, these major recent developments occupied her mind. She went to her last class and hoped she did okay on her exam. Harvey was to pick her up in front of the Fine Arts building after her last class at exactly five o'clock.

Lynn and Harvey were there at the appointed time and place. Morgan spotted them, waved, walked over, and got in their car. Harvey pulled away from the curb. Morgan told Lynn she was surprised she'd been able to get through the test with her mind so preoccupied with her exciting family matters. As she said it, she happened to glance up the street. Something was going on. What she saw was surreal. At once, she knew exactly who she was looking at, and it practically scared her to death. She pointed and managed to stammer, "It's th-them!"

Lynn looked up and saw some people moving toward a car, a run-down old vehicle that she recognized at once, even though it was now dark gray. She couldn't believe her eyes. "Harv, it's the kidnappers!" she exclaimed. "That's their car." Harvey looked toward where Morgan and Lynn had pointed and saw the old car parked up the street.

"What are they doing?" Morgan cried. But she froze when she realized right away what was happening. A girl wearing dark clothing and black glasses was being hurried to the car. But it wasn't just some girl. It was Ivona! Morgan was seeing her sister in the flesh for the first time in her life.

"That's Ivona," she screamed. "That's my sister! They're taking her!"

Just like Morgan and Lynn's experience two days before, Ivona was being forced into the back seat of the same car by the same terrible men and made to put on those horrible black glasses. There was no telling what they were going to do to her. Morgan knew her sister's fate lay in her hands.

The men hurriedly got into their car and Lynn shouted, "They're about to drive away."

As the old car started up and slowly began to move toward them, Harvey stopped his car and reached for his gun. "Those bastards aren't going anywhere."

Fearing they might lose them, Morgan knew she had to take matters into her own hands. In a flash, she was out of the car running to the middle of the street where she began waving her arms over her head.

"Morgan, come back to the car!" Lynn yelled in a panic as she jumped out to get her.

Morgan wasn't moving. She had found her sister at long last, and there was no way she was going to lose her in the very same instant. She remained glued to the middle of the street as the car rolled toward her. How she was going to stop the car, she didn't know. Adrenaline gave her the courage to try. Then, in a strange voice that seemed to come from the very depths of her soul, she screamed, *"You there! Stop!"*

The car was getting closer. Morgan began waving her arms wildly as if to stop it, but it was not slowing down. With vehicles parked on both sides of the street, there was no way it could go around her.

Lynn couldn't reach Morgan in time, and it sickened her. She knew full well what these guys were capable of, having narrowly escaped being run down by them herself just last week.

Harvey was also in the street, his gun aimed at the car. Lynn screamed, "Morgan, get out of the street!" By now, Morgan, was paralyzed with fear, unable to move. "Shoot the tires, Harvey!" Lynn yelled.

A split second from reaching Morgan and before Harvey had a chance to fire, the car swerved sharply and rammed into a parked car, pushing it into the car in front of it, leaving room for the old car to jump the curb before slamming hard into a telephone pole. Wrapped around the pole, the vehicle hissed and sputtered. Steaming water spewed out onto the street; the windshield was cracked. The driver was slumped over the steering wheel, unmoving, his head bleeding.

The kidnappers were stopped.

Morgan was safe.

Ivona was safe.

Lynn saw the man in the back seat with Ivona open his car door and take off, leaving his door wide open and the other man to his fate. Lynn yelled, "I'm going after him." She knew full well that Harvey's knees and those dress shoes would never permit him to move fast enough to catch him. Harvey rushed over to the wrecked car to scope it out. The driver appeared to be knocked out; blood streamed from a gash on his forehead. As Harvey was calling the police, he saw Ivona yank off her black glasses and try to open her car door, but it seemed to be jammed. She quickly exited through the open door and started running back toward the Fine Arts building.

Harvey yelled, "Ivona, come back." Ivona glanced back at Harvey with a confused expression on her face, but she kept running.

Lynn continued to pursue the other man. She followed him past several tall buildings. He turned down an alley. Lynn could see he had a gun in his hand. Fortunately, she was carrying hers too, but until the kidnapping, she had not felt compelled to have it on her in Budapest. She pulled her gun out of its holster, continuing in fast pursuit. When Lynn saw the man look around and take aim, she quickly dropped behind a dumpster. He fired a shot, missing her. An excellent marksman, Lynn fired back, aiming low. She thought she saw the man flinch but didn't know if she got him.

He kept going and began climbing up a fire escape. As she got closer, he turned and fired again, this time grazing her left shoulder. The bullet slowed her down enough to allow him to slip into a doorway on the second floor. Lynn wished she had backup. The dull pain in her shoulder did not stop her from pursuing him. *This guy isn't getting away if I can help it.* She ran to the fire escape and, using her good arm for support on the handrail, tried to make her way up the metal steps. She quickly realized she wouldn't be able to move fast enough to catch him.

Just then, she heard the sirens and turned to see a police car coming down the alley toward her. She jumped down and ran toward them, pulling out her ID. She told them what happened and pointed to the door where the man had entered the building. One of the policemen headed up the fire escape, and the other one drove her back to the scene she had just left.

Harvey ran toward the police car and said to Lynn, "The ambulance got here in two minutes. They just took the driver to the hospital. Did you catch up with the other guy?" She shook her head just as he noticed the blood on Lynn's left arm. He exclaimed, "Dammit, you've been shot!"

"It's just grazed, Harvey. Let's not worry about it now. Where are the girls?"

Morgan was coming toward them. She had not approached the car. It was all just too much. Now she saw that Lynn was bleeding and screamed, "He shot you!"

"It's just a surface wound, Morgan. I'll be okay. Where did Ivona go?"

"I saw her run over toward the Fine Arts building. I was going to catch her, but Mr. Chapman told me to stay here."

A terrified Ivona had watched the scene unfold from across the street. She saw the police cars and watched the ambulance take the driver away. Feeling safer, she headed back to the scene so she could tell the police what happened. As soon as she got close enough to see what was what, she looked up and saw her sister.

At that same moment, Morgan turned and saw Ivona. Their eyes met for the first time in their lives, and for one glorious moment, with their eyes fixed on each other, their worlds stood still. That dreaded sense of something missing that had plagued both of them all their lives vanished forever, their greatest hopes fulfilled.

For Morgan, her reason for coming to Budapest stood before her, the answer to her lifelong quest to find her biological connection, fulfilling her yearning for a sibling. She stared into the eyes of not just an abstract look-alike but of her own never-before-seen, flesh-and-blood identical twin sister.

Ivona too stood immobile. Although she had only known of her twin since May, it seemed like she had always known her. In seconds, her life flashed before her eyes.

Suddenly, they found themselves running toward each other, and when they reached each other, they hugged. They cried; they talked. And they laughed with abandon. All at once, they were both filled with a long awaited mutual abiding love for the other. Truly, the moment was magical.

* * *

After lunch with Agnes and Beulah, Flossie suddenly started.

"What's the matter, sweetie," Agnes said.

"I just felt something," Flossie answered.

"Does it hurt? Are you in pain?" Beulah asked.

"Oh, no, it wasn't like that. It was just a feeling in my mind," Flossie said, slightly embarrassed to have jumped like she had. In her mind's eye, she had seen an image of those two young ladies. It was like they were hunting for each other and finally they both ended up in the same place at the same time. It was an incredible vision, dampened only by a nagging feeling that they were still in danger. Miss Braxton had called her yesterday and told her that her feelings were correct—her partner and one of the twins had been kidnapped, but fortunately they got away. She wished it was over, but something still told her there was more to come.

"How is your daughter?" Flossie asked Agnes.

"She's much better. She and her oldest daughter, Michellie, are coming by Saturday."

"Being around young people keeps you young at heart," Beulah said.

"When my Lonnie died back in 1945, I knew that even though I might not have any kids myself, I could still bring them into this world. You know that's one of the reasons I became a midwife. I must have delivered hundreds of babies over the years."

Beulah asked, "Did you ever wish you'd had any of your own?"

"I sure did, but in a funny way, my sister's children became like my own. Their father was a great dad, but when Mossie passed, I became like a substitute mother to them. You know I have identical twin grandsons named Barron and Byron. They're close, just like my sister and I were. I feel a special kind of kinship with them."

What Flossie didn't mention was that she also felt a very special kinship with two twin girls she'd delivered nineteen and a half years ago. It was unexplainable, but there was definitely something there. Of that she was certain.

* * *

Harvey and Lynn talked to the police while Morgan and Ivona spoke excitedly to each other. The policeman asked them to come by the station after Lynn went to the hospital to give an official statement. He told them where the nearest hospital was.

Lynn told Ivona she was the one who had met with her mother and grandmother last night, and she was surprised to see Ivona on campus alone, particularly on the Arts campus. Ivona said she had come here looking for Morgan and explained why. She'd never thought she was putting herself in danger because she had a ride nearby. But when those men grabbed her, she realized what was happening, and it was so frightening. "I can only imagine how you and Morgan felt the other day."

While they talked, a small group of student onlookers gathered, observing the scene. Some of them may have recognized one or the other of the twins; some pointed from Morgan to Ivona with questioning looks and comments. Morgan and Ivona were oblivious to the crowd.

When Ivona called home and explained what happened, Nicola and Corina both got on the telephone. They were aghast to hear of her near kidnapping. Corina asked, "What happened to your ride home?"

"My friend had to stop back over here, so I asked him to drop me by the Arts campus. He was waiting to drive me home. I really thought it would be okay."

Her mother and grandmother listened while Ivona told them about her ordeal. She detected their fear and assured them that she was safe. She said the whole thing was over in seconds and she had not been hurt. "But something extraordinary happened," she said. "I met my sister. It's been wonderful, Niko. She's even responsible for stopping the kidnappers. This is so awesome. I am now with Lynn Davis, the woman you met last night." Nicola told Ivona she would pick her up. "I can't wait to tell you everything, but first, we have to go to the police station to file an official report."

Corina exclaimed, "Thank God you are safe! And we want to hear all about Morgan."

Ivona said, "I know. I've got to go now. They're waiting for me, but I will call you later."

Before going to the police station, Harvey took Lynn to the emergency room, where they cleaned and patched up her shoulder. The wound was, as she suspected, superficial. Harvey looked at Lynn's bruised face and then at her shoulder and said, "I have to do a better job taking care of you too, Lynn."

Lynn smiled and said, "I'm just angry the maniac ruined one of my favorite coats." Then she added, "You just do your job and take care of Morgan. I'll take care of Lynn."

And Harvey Chapman knew she would.

They went to the police station and waited while the crime report was typed up. They reviewed it and signed. The police told them that the car the men were driving was not registered. When they asked about the driver, they learned that he had suffered a concussion when his head hit the windshield and would be kept at the hospital overnight for observation. The police would interrogate him in the morning.

Harvey said, "Apparently he claimed he was just driving his buddy and the buddy's girlfriend to the movies. I'm afraid he's in big trouble. It's only going to get worse for him, especially because Ivona told the police how she was forced into their car. They now have it on record that he and his accomplice grabbed you and Morgan a couple of days ago."

Lynn said, "That's twice now this guy has helped us. He could have easily struck Morgan with their car, but he didn't." She reminded Harvey he'd untied them the night they got away. "He's obviously not as coldhearted as the other guy. It's good he was the one behind the wheel. We included that in the incident report."

Then Harvey drove everyone back to the hotel. The twins went into the lounge to talk some more, and Harvey went with them. Lynn went to her room to make her second call to the Wellingtons, having previously phoned them from the kidnap scene to tell them what had happened. Now she filled in the details. Mrs. Wellington was pretty stunned at the new developments. But she was also relieved to know the kidnappers failed again and that one of them had been caught. She said, "Horace and I have been discussing this. Now that all this has happened, it helps put in perspective Morgan's sense that someone was following her, even when she was in Paris. If it was the kidnappers she was sensing, then we believe she was picking up impressions from her sister. In fact, all her life Morgan's had these inexplicable sensations. We now believe she may have always been picking up her sister, which had to be frustrating since she didn't even know about her."

Next, Lynn called Ivona's home. Dr. Palaki answered and thanked Lynn. She mentioned that Ivona had already called from the police station. Nicola told Lynn they were exceedingly grateful for her part in rescuing Ivona, adding, "She told us you will bring her home tonight. We appreciate that, but my mother and I would be happy to come to the hotel to pick her up. We can't wait to talk to her, and we would love to meet Morgan."

"I know you would. Right now, they're downstairs in the hotel restaurant. Morgan's bodyguard is with them. I'm sure you understand they want to spend a little time together."

"Of course, I can see that they would want to be together. If you think it's best, I guess we'll just wait for you to bring her," Nicola said.

"If you don't mind, I think that will be best. I'll tell you this; the connection between them was instantaneous. It's clear they were destined to meet," Lynn said.

"Picturing the two of them together warms my heart. It is wonderful that they have a chance to get acquainted."

Before hanging up, Lynn told Nicola that the kidnapper who had been caught was named Fane Dobos and asked if she had ever heard of him. Nicola knew no one by that name.

After her phone calls, Lynn found Harvey in the restaurant, keeping a watchful eye on the twins. "I could tell they were both on cloud nine," Harv said, adding, "Those two look so much alike, for a minute I thought I was seeing double."

Lynn said, "Me too. You know, it's incredible how determined Morgan was to save her sister. Nothing was going to stop her. Thank goodness she wasn't hurt."

Harv said, "Yeah, she would have tried to stop that car single-handedly. I was afraid I was about to watch her get creamed. All I can say is she's got a lot of grit. That young lady's had quite a day. Both of them have. In fact, so have you, my friend. So have you."

Lynn looked at Harvey endearingly. "Thanks for being here, Harv. I really appreciate you, and I'm sure the twins do too."

"All right now. Don't go getting all mushy on me," he said, pleased all the while.

When Morgan returned to her room, she called her parents and filled them in on the attempted kidnapping of her sister and their first meeting. Afterward, she knocked on Lynn's door to tell her about her unbelievable evening. "Miss Davis, this has been the most incredible day of my life. If I had lost my sister before I ever had a chance to meet her, it would have been the worst day of my life, and I don't think I would ever have gotten over it. But as it turns out, this day was the best ever! It's almost like Ivona's near kidnapping was not even important except for enabling the two of us to finally connect. You should have seen Ivona's and my reactions when we first laid eyes on each other. I think we just stared at each other, like this couldn't be happening, like this couldn't be real.

"I was absolutely speechless at first. It seemed like I was looking at myself in a mirror. Finally, we ran to each other and hugged. After that, frankly, I don't even know what we said. I know I told her my name and that I had just learned about her the other day. Ivona told me she learned about me earlier this year from the midwife. Isn't that something? I don't understand why the midwife didn't tell us about her. I just talked to my mother and told her what Ivona said about the midwife's letter. She also wondered why she never got one. Anyway, after spending our whole lives without knowing about each other, we were just plain overjoyed. We both talked at the same time, and it was that way all evening. Sometimes we said the same thing at the same time or finished each other's sentences."

Morgan continued, "We're majorly different in some ways. For example, Ivona loves science, even has a double science major, and I am completely baffled by it. But I found out that our grandmother, Corina Moldovan, is a dressmaker. I guess I took after her and Ivona after our mother. There's another thing—I love being out on the water but Ivona has never even been on a boat. Once when I was young, I fell off a boat and could have drowned. Ivona has repeatedly dreamed about that very incident over and over. In her dreams, she always thought she was the one who fell in the water, but now we know the person she saw in her dream was me. Isn't that strange? But I've done the same thing dreaming about skiing, when it is her who's been skiing since she was nine.

"Oh, and this was the most amazing thing. I was wearing my gold pendant. My mother gave it to me when I was a little girl. She said it was a gift from the midwife who delivered me."

Lynn said, "I've noticed you wearing it."

"I wear it a lot. I had mine on, and all at once, Ivona screamed. She said, 'I have this exact pendant. The midwife told my grandmother this would connect me to my heritage. I can't wait to see what the message says when we put our two halves together.'"

Lynn told Morgan how exciting that was, but otherwise Lynn couldn't get a word in edgewise.

"And this was strange. Ivona said that yesterday morning she experienced a panic attack. She told her grandmother I was in trouble. Our grandmother didn't understand what she was talking about. But now we know that was when we were being kidnapped. She said she felt like she couldn't move her arms or legs or see anything. I think that was because we were tied up and blindfolded. She even called to warn György. Isn't this whole thing amazing?"

Lynn was happy for the twins. She had read that according to statistics, identical twin births occurred only four times out of every thousand. In addition to the rarity of identical twin births, Lynn believed Morgan and her sister shared a rare telepathic connection.

CHAPTER
30

Friday, November 29

MORGAN HAD BEEN TOO EXCITED to sleep the night before and had lain in bed thinking the night away. This morning, she was still elated and excited. The memory of meeting her twin sister yesterday put a continuous smile on her face.

Lynn was nursing her gunshot wound, but other than a slight discomfort when she moved her arm, she felt pretty good. As she and Harvey ate breakfast together, they discussed the events of the day before. Morgan and Ivona's meeting seemed coincidental, but Lynn believed it was a foregone conclusion. The twins were destined to meet. There was no other explanation. When she rose from the table and stood, she suddenly felt a little woozy. She swayed, and Harvey grabbed her and held her firmly.

"Are you all right, Lynn?" he asked.

"I think I just stood up too fast. I feel fine now. It's probably a combination of everything that happened yesterday."

"And don't forget about the kidnapping ordeal on Tuesday. You've been through a lot. And maybe you lost too much blood yesterday," Harvey added.

"They checked that at the hospital. I never had any idea that when I took this case, I would be doing hazard duty. But I do feel fine, really. I may rest while you take Morgan to class."

"That's cool. I'll check on you when I get back. You should probably spend the day resting. Don't even think about going out. The doctor told you to stay put for a couple of days, didn't he?"

Lynn groaned at the thought of doing nothing all day.

"Don't worry," Harvey said. "I'll stay with you."

Later he drove Morgan to class and waited for her outside her building to pick her up after the class was over. When he brought her back to the hotel, Morgan took a much-needed nap. That evening at dinner, she told Lynn that she and Ivona wanted to go out. "Ivona and I want to be together as much as possible while we can."

"Morgan, I'm sorry but I'm still nursing my shoulder, and I have doctor's orders to stay in. Harvey thinks I shouldn't be alone, so if he stays here with me, he won't be able to take you and Ivona out."

"But we thought we could just go to György's club. He's not playing tonight, so he can watch out for us."

"I can understand that you two would want to be together. But I have to be a hardnose on this. With the kidnapper still out there, we can't take any chances. Can you invite Ivona over here instead? The two of you could hang out in the lounge and even get something to eat together. Harvey can keep an eye on both of you."

Morgan frowned. "I really think you're making more out of this than you need to. That guy is probably in the next country by now."

Morgan should understand the danger of being out. Lynn didn't want to sound impatient, but she replied, "Until we know for sure, I'm not willing to take any chances. That man may not stop until he gets what he wants, or until he is stopped." Morgan looked exasperated. She probably wasn't used to not getting her way. However, she saw that she wasn't getting it right now, so she exaggerated a sigh and rolled her eyes and turned and walked away.

So much for that new attitude. Although Lynn understood Morgan's disappointment, that certainly didn't justify her insolence. *Rachel Davis would have never allowed me to act like that. Times have certainly changed.*

* * *

Later that evening, Morgan phoned Lynn from the hotel lobby. Lynn was working on her computer in her hotel room. "Hi, Miss Davis. I am downstairs in the lobby with Ivona. She wanted to thank you again. Shall we come up, or will you be coming down anytime soon?"

"Sure," Lynn said. "I can be down in five minutes." She finished an e-mail message she was working on and headed for the lobby.

There were several people in the lobby, but Lynn spotted Morgan right away. Ivona's back was to her. Lynn walked up to Morgan and said, "Hey there."

The young lady who Lynn thought was Morgan said, "Hi, Miss Davis. I'm Ivona," and smiled.

Morgan giggled and said, "Hi, Miss Davis. Ivona wanted to see you again."

Lynn furrowed her brow and glanced from Ivona to Morgan, extending her hand. Shaking her head, she said, "Amazing. I obviously can't tell you two apart. It's nice to see you again, Ivona."

Ivona laughed. "Don't worry, we have been getting that same reaction from everyone. I just wanted to thank you for coming to my aid yesterday. I already thanked Mr. Chapman. I heard you were injured, but thankfully not seriously."

"That's right. I'm just relieved that things turned out the way they did," Lynn responded.

The three sat and chatted for a few minutes before Lynn said, "Well, I'll let you two visit."

"Perhaps I will see you again," Ivona said.

"You will," Lynn replied. "I am coming to your house Sunday afternoon with Morgan."

Saturday, November 30

ON SATURDAY, LYNN TOLD HARVEY she'd overheard the twins saying tonight was ladies night at the Blue Diamond. Knowing how disappointed Morgan had been that she didn't get to go out Friday night, Lynn told Harvey she was fine with staying alone this evening so he could take the girls out. She told him she would eat in the restaurant. Morgan had said, "This will probably be our last chance. I'll be taking one of my finals on Monday, and my dad wants me to talk to the dean about completing my other courses online. We might be leaving here as early as Tuesday."

That evening when Harvey, Ivona, Morgan, and Bela walked into the club, everyone seemed to stop in their tracks to stare. The place was filled to near capacity, with only standing room available. Most eyes were on the two dark-haired identical twin beauties; they had coordinated their outfits. Each wore white sweaters, matching gold pendants, black slacks, and boots. As the girls walked over to stand by the bar, the crowd parted, as if by magic, to let them pass.

Up on stage, György was playing. He saw the crowd turn suddenly in unison. When he realized who their eyes were following, he set his guitar down, signaled to his band to keep playing, jumped off the stage, and headed toward them.

"Hi, ladies. I'm glad you could make it. You all look great!" They greeted him cheerily. György was proud to be seen talking to the best-looking women in the club. "Now," he said smiling at the twins, "I am very serious when I ask you this. Which one of you is Morgan?" He really did not know. The sisters looked at each other conspiratorially and smiled but said nothing. He studied their faces, thinking he would be able to tell because Morgan had a beauty mark on the upper left corner of her mouth. *Or is it the upper right?* he wondered when he saw that they both had similar marks. However, one was on the right, and the other on the left. He was confused, and the girls weren't helping.

Feeling bold, György said, "Then I'm just going to have to greet both of you with a kiss." He planted a peck on their cheeks, even Bela's, and they giggled. "I'll be back in twenty minutes." Then he ran back up on stage. During the rest of the set, he could hardly keep his eyes off the twins. He hoped to watch them dance, believing he'd be able to tell them apart, since Morgan might not be moving too well with a sore ankle. But they didn't go out on the dance floor. Mostly, they laughed and talked and enjoyed fending off the onslaught of guys who kept coming up to them. Harvey Chapman stood at the bar, positioned where he could watch their every move.

* * *

That evening, Pista, obsessed with getting revenge on that black woman, was ready to pounce. Assuming she was still at the same hotel, he knew where to find her. He put on a good pair of jeans and a black shirt. Then he grabbed a quick bite to eat. He was feeling pretty good now that his butt wasn't as sore as before. But every now and then when he made a wrong move, he felt those stitches and was reminded he still had some healing to do back there. But he couldn't afford to wait too much longer; for all he knew she could be going back to the United States at any time.

He left his place and got into his car, enjoying driving his slick black convertible. On his way to her hotel, he spotted a lady of the evening walking toward him. She had flowing red hair, was voluptuously endowed up top, and had long leggy legs. Now that one definitely looked tempting, and on any other night, he'd have stopped his car for her. But he had business to take care of. Still, as he drove past the woman, he thought about the fun he was going to have with that *néger* woman before he finished her off. The thought made him hot.

Pista found a perfect parking place across the street from the hotel that gave him a full view of the hotel's entrance. His timing was impeccable. He couldn't believe his eyes when, just as he was turning his ignition off, the little sister came through the revolving door of the hotel. He was so shocked he could have pooped his pants. This was too damned good to be true. He started his car. But then, out walked another one who looked just like the other one! *What the hell?* Then he thought about that girl who stepped out in front of the car, making that dickhead Fane blow everything by wrecking his transportation. She had looked so much like their girl. This had to be the same one. *Who in the hell is she?* Bottom line, there were two of them. But what were they doing together? Pista was too confused to move.

Then, as the door continued to swing around, out walked that black dude who had jumped out of the car the other day and pulled the gun on them. *This is damn near surreal.* He watched the three of them get in the car the valet brought and pull away. For a split second, Pista wanted to follow them, but he instantly thought better of it. First of all, he didn't want to try to take on three of them. Secondly, in his present condition, he wouldn't be able to run if he had to get away fast. Besides, the woman hadn't come out with them. That meant she was probably still in the hotel. And the real truth was, she was his number one priority right now. He couldn't let himself get sidetracked. He figured he could easily take her on, sore butt and all. She might be able to handle a gun, but Pista knew she could never match him physically. He turned off his motor.

So he waited and watched. After thirty minutes with nothing to show for it, he decided to call the hotel and ask for Lynn Davis, remembering her name from the night they grabbed her and the American girl. "I am sorry, sir. I believe she is dining in our restaurant at this time."

Bingo! An evil smile crossed Pista's face. *This is it!* He had her now. He exited his car and walked into the hotel and into the restaurant. While waiting to be seated, he spotted Lynn Davis sitting alone, looking all high and mighty. *We'll soon see exactly how high and mighty you are.* He asked for a seat where he could keep his eyes on her. He didn't care if she saw him. *How in the hell would she know who she is looking at anyway?*

At one point, he thought she might have recognized him, but again, so what? Although he'd removed his coat, he still had the scarf around his neck, partially concealing his face. Under his jacket he had on a black tee shirt that revealed his well-developed arms, shoulders, and chest, which he was always proud to show off. He saw the bitch lean over and start piddling with something and wondered what the hell she was doing now. When the waitress came over at that moment, he shooed her away. As Pista observed Lynn, his sixth sense suddenly told him something wasn't right. He saw the light from something in her lap. *She's using her mobile phone? She's called the police!* He grabbed his coat and got up from the table. However, because of his wounds, he couldn't move very fast without passing out from the pain. He made his way out of the restaurant and hurried as fast as he could through the lobby toward the front entrance.

Lynn saw the kidnapper hastily leaving the restaurant, and she jumped straight up and followed him out. She had to stop him. It was now or maybe never. He never heard her coming.

Suddenly, someone grabbed him from behind. *The bitch!* Pista was strong. He instantly jerked himself free from her hold and swung around, hurling his fist at her, intending to land the deadly blow that would end her once and for all. He had an excuse. She'd attacked him first, so it was self-defense.

A karate expert, Lynn blocked the blow, and he struck her hard in her ribs with his other fist. She clutched her side and doubled over but managed to catch him by his leg, making him fall on his very sore backside. He screeched as his stitches ripped open, sending pain like he'd never felt before coursing through his body, all the way to his eyeballs. Hotel security was on him in a flash, grabbing him. Lynn struggled to stand upright, holding her ribs.

"Let me go!" he yelled. "This crazy woman attacked me. Someone needs to call the police!"

Lynn leaned against the wall, in pain. At that moment she saw the police coming through the entrance door toward them. She pointed to the guy who was now being restrained by hotel security, and cried, "Here he is. Here's the kidnapper!"

"What the hell! She's lying. That bitch jumped *me!*" Pista yelled as two policemen pulled him to his feet and slapped a pair of handcuffs on him. "I don't know what she's talking about. I'm no damn kidnapper. She's the one who jumped me from behind." The police ignored him and began to walk him out to their car. Lynn noticed his limp as they took him away and realized the shot she'd fired the other day in the alley might have hit its mark after all.

One of the policemen needed to take Lynn's statement. The hotel concierge came over to act as interpreter, as the policeman didn't speak English.

When he finished, the concierge noticed Lynn struggling and asked, "Madam, are you all right?"

"I'm afraid I may need a doctor," she said, trying to catch her breath. "It feels like my ribs are cracked." Lynn feared she may have also reinjured her shoulder, where her gunshot wound had been healing nicely. The policeman helped her into his car, turned on his siren, and rushed her to the nearest hospital.

* * *

At the Blue Diamond, Ivona spotted him first. "Look over there, Morgan. See the guy staring at us in the corner? I don't know, but could he be the kidnapper?"

Morgan jerked her head toward the corner and stared at a guy who was staring back. "I don't know. We never really saw his face, but he was about that guy's size."

"He's been looking this way for the last fifteen minutes. I first noticed him when he was way across the room. He makes my skin crawl."

"We'd better tell Mr. Chapman," Morgan said.

Bela was coming off the dance floor. "What's going on, you two?" she asked, and they told her as they headed over toward Harvey Chapman.

Harvey saw them coming and walked toward them.

"We wondered if that was the kidnapper over there," Morgan said. "His eyes have been glued on us for several minutes now."

Harvey studied the guy and asked, "Are you pretty sure it's him?"

"Well, neither Ivona nor I ever saw his face. But Ivona spotted him staring at us for the longest time."

Bela squinted to see the guy Morgan was talking about.

"Morg, that's Albert. He's Klementina's big brother. And believe me, he's harmless."

Morgan looked puzzled until Bela added, "Klementina Limbek. There she is." She pointed to a girl on the dance floor and said, "He's come here with her before."

"I'm sorry. I didn't realize you knew the guy," Ivona said.

"I didn't either," Morgan said. "But I do know Klementina."

When the song stopped, Klementina walked over to them and said, "*Szia*, Bela. I saw you beckoning me over."

"Hi," Bela said. "I think you know Morgan." Then, pointing to Ivona, she said, "This is her twin sister, Ivona."

"Hi, Ivona," Klementina said. Then she turned to Morgan and replied, "I didn't know you had a twin."

Before Morgan could comment, Bela said, "We were actually talking about your brother. He looked familiar. Then we realized who he was."

Klementina turned to Morgan and said, "That's funny, because he was just asking about the two of you too. He thought he remembered seeing you in here before, but not with your twin. And he's far too shy to come over and say hello."

When Klementina walked away, Harv said, "You all go on and have a good time. Don't worry, I'm keeping my eye on you." He went back to the bar.

Sometime later, the music stopped and the band announced a short intermission. During the break, Harvey heard his telephone signal that he had a voice mail. He listened and hurried over to gather up the girls. "Ladies, I'm afraid we have to go," he said discreetly. "Miss Davis just had an encounter with the real kidnapper. He's in custody."

"Oh no. Where is she now?" Morgan questioned.

"She's at the hospital."

* * *

"I should never have left you alone tonight," Harvey told Lynn as they left the ER after X-rays and an exam showed that her ribs were not fractured. "You are one brave, crazy, lucky lady, Lynn. You should never have tried to stop that raving fool by yourself."

"I knew it was risky, Harv, especially with my shoulder still sore, but I couldn't afford to let him get away. He knew where I was staying. He was apparently stalking me. This guy had already tried to run me over, so I figured if he didn't get me tonight, he'd try again. He'd probably never stop until he got me or one or both of the girls. I hoped the police would get there in time to stop him. I had to do it."

Harv asked, "How did you figure out it was him, anyway?"

"When I glanced over and saw that tattoo on his right arm, I knew right away who he was. Plus, I had gotten a gander at his slick black ponytail the day we were kidnapped. This guy strutted into the restaurant, shaking his hair as if he were God's gift to women or something. And he was giving off these evil vibes. My intuition told me he was up to no good. It's a huge relief that he was captured."

"It's good you noticed that tattoo. But then you always were observant. That was one of your best traits as a police officer. That, plus you could shoot!" Harv paused thoughtfully and then continued, "And you were pretty street savvy ... And of course you were a quick study. As you can see, I could go on and on." Harv smiled, and Lynn did too. "So you think you actually hit him in the rear end the other day?" he asked.

"Now I do. I thought I saw him flinch when I fired, but I wasn't sure. But tonight I could tell he was favoring his backside. It looked like every step he took was painful. And you should have heard him scream when he fell on his bottom. I could almost feel his torture. If the guy'd been able to run, I don't know if I'd have caught him. He sure outran me the other day."

"I can say it's a good thing you did what you did since it worked out. But it could have been bad, Lynn. Real bad. So how do you feel now?" Harv asked.

"The guy is strong, and his fist packed a wallop. My ribs are real tender, but thankfully the pain killers are kicking in. My midsection looks a mess. The good thing is, I saw the blow coming and was able to back up just enough to keep away from the full impact of his fist or he might have done a lot more damage. I'm just glad my ribs weren't fractured. This has been some ordeal, but at least it's over now. Where are the girls?"

"After I got your message, I drove Ivona home and took Morgan back to the hotel. I left her locked in her room and told her not to dare leave. After hearing what happened to you, I think she has renewed respect for sound advice. She won't leave. After she was settled in, I got here as soon as I could."

When Lynn got back to the hotel, Morgan was waiting up. She knocked on Lynn's door, and Harvey opened it. "How's she doing?" she asked. "Was she hurt badly?"

Lynn heard Morgan and said, "Are you still up? Come on in." Morgan entered and leaned against Lynn's dresser while she told Morgan what happened.

Morgan told Lynn she was glad she hadn't been hurt worse, but she was elated that the bad guy was now behind bars. She said, "When you tell my parents, they'll be so relieved that both of them have been caught. Can we call them now?"

"I was just about to call them, and Ivona's parents too. Maybe I can still catch them before they leave for the airport."

She called Cincinnati. Mrs. Wellington answered in a concerned voice. "Miss Davis, it's quite late in Budapest. Is anything wrong?"

"No, just the opposite. I called to tell you that the second kidnapper was captured tonight. He's now locked up."

"Oh, my heavens. That's just wonderful. Now we don't have to worry about Morgan. Of course, I realize Mr.

Chapman is there, but one never knows for sure what could happen. How was he caught?"

Lynn told her about the incident, including that she ended up at the hospital.

"Gracious! You poor dear. I'm grateful you're all right. You have suffered a great deal on our behalf. Thank you for everything you have done for us."

"You're very welcome. Morgan's waiting to talk to you."

Morgan took the phone and said excitedly, "Mom, now that the kidnappers are caught, if my professors will let me take my exams, could I stay? Please, please?"

Cincinnati, Ohio, Sunday, December 1

FLOSSIE WALKER LIT TEA CANDLES and thought about the special people in her life who had passed on. She went through this little ritual on each of their birthdays. She always lit a candle for Mossie, one for her mother, one for her father, one for her brother Hampton. *My goodness, Hampton would be eighty-four years old.* The thought of her twelve-year-old brother at eighty-four made her smile. Another candle was for Aunt Bea. And one for Lonford Harper. Today was Lonny's day. This would have been his eighty-eighth birthday. That morning, she sat at her dinette table and lit a candle and said a special prayer for him. Then she gazed at the flickering flame.

She turned her eyes away from the flame toward the photo of Lonford, looking so young and handsome in his military uniform. Although she was tired of explaining to anyone who came to her room that he wasn't her grandson, she still kept his photo on display giving her ready access to her sweet memories. Flossie had loved Lonnie since she was sixteen. They started as friends, but it wasn't long before she realized she had a huge crush on him. She was happy when he began to take more than a *friendly* interest in her too, and soon their relationship blossomed into genuine love and pending marriage. Then one day he was gone.

Flossie relived that fateful time in December 1944. She was twenty-five years old.

On the last evening of his military leave, Lonford had taken her to dinner. They talked about their future together. Where they would spend their honeymoon; where they would live; how many children they would have; the names of their children, and anything else they could think of. After dinner, they went to the movies to see the musical *Anchors Aweigh*. Lonnie had wanted to see the *Story of GI Joe*, but Flossie didn't particularly want to have to think about military service. Lonnie would be returning to that life soon enough.

It had been a night to remember, because he had proposed that night. She'd always known they would marry, but now it was official. He placed the little diamond engagement ring on her finger, and she felt her life was complete. They had a wonderful time that evening, but Flossie found the enjoyment of the evening bittersweet since Lonford was leaving for Europe in the morning. Oh, how she would miss him.

That night when she got home, she awakened Mossie with a phone call, telling her about her engagement. Her sister was thrilled. The next evening, she went to see her father. Dr. George Walker checked out her ring and gave her a big hug. He told her about the baby he'd delivered that day, weighing in at nine and a half pounds! Flossie told him how much she wanted to have children. "When Lonny returns, we want to give ourselves a year, and then start a family. We hope to have four children, but I hope they're not nine-pounders," she'd laughed.

"I can't wait to see which of you will give me my first grandchild," George Walker said.

"I'm just sorry that our mother isn't around to see us get married, and to one day see her grandchildren," Flossie said. Her mother, Gertha, was a devoted woman whose family had meant everything to her. She was proud as the dickens of her twin daughters, and she also had a younger son, Hampton, whom she treated like royalty as the baby of the family. When Hampton died during an asthma attack at the young age of twelve, his sisters were sixteen at the time, and his death was rough on all of them. George Walker took his son's death particularly hard because he felt as a physician, he should have been able to protect his family from illness. But Gertha Walker suffered the most; Hampton's death turned out to be more than she could bear. Her health began to suffer. Two years after Hampton's death and just after Flossie and Mossie started nursing school, their mother passed away in her sleep. The family suspected she'd died of a broken heart.

"I'm sure Gertha and Hampton are smiling down on us right now," Flossie's father said reverently.

Two months later on a wintry December day, Flossie, Mossie, and George Walker were seated in the living room of Dr. Walker's home. Dr. Walker dreaded sharing the news he had summoned his daughters to his home to pass on. Grimly, he said, "Mrs. Harper phoned me to give me some terrible news."

The twins looked at each other. Mrs. Harper was Lonnie's mother. At the mention of her name, Flossie's heart stopped. She wondered if Lonnie was all right. She soon found out. Their father looked at Flossie tenderly and said, "Daughter, Lonford was killed in battle yesterday." Flossie passed out in Mossie's arms. When she came to, her father gently told her that Lonnie's segregated infantry had volunteered to go into battle. Unfortunately, they'd suffered several casualties. Lonnie had been the first of his infantry to die.

He died a hero, but it broke Flossie's heart. She couldn't believe he was gone. He was so young. They'd had their whole lives ahead of them. He was her soul mate. It was Mossie's strength and support that got her through that difficult period. She often said that without Mossie, she would not have made it. Their closeness was her salvation. She looked to Mossie for the strength to carry on. Their mother used to tell them about how, even as infants, they could hold extended *conversations* with each other in their playpen long before they could talk.

All the immediate people in my life are gone. Thank goodness I have extended family.

Mesmerized by the flames, Flossie now thought about her long-deceased father. George Washington Walker was a well-loved general practitioner who made house calls several nights a week, treating everything from chicken pox to broken bones and delivering babies. Even in their teens, the girls used to wait up for him to come home so they could hear all about his latest deliveries. Flossie remembered one special evening.

"Girls, I'm home. Come, let me tell you the news," their father called out. He placed his medical bag down and hung his hat on the hall tree. Flossie and her sister came running out to greet him, both giving him a hug. They went into the living room, and Dr. Walker said, "Tonight, I delivered my first set of triplets!"

They squealed with delight. "Three babies?" Mossie asked.

"Yes, and the thing is, everyone thought the mother was just having twins. She'd already picked out twin names for both boys and girls. So the third one came as quite a surprise."

"Did she have boys?" Flossie asked.

"What were their names?" Mossie wanted to know.

"She did have boys, but remember, that third one was a surprise. Their names were Martin and Barton, and the surprise baby was named ..." He paused to let them guess.

"Carlton?" Flossie guessed.

"Partin?" Mossie answered.

"Carrie Ann," answered their father. "The third one was a girl." And they all enjoyed a good laugh. He went on to explain that the other twin girl's name would have been Mary Ann.

Dr. Walker was an inspiration to both of his daughters who, following his path, decided to pursue medical professions. Flossie and Mossie even went to work at the same hospital where he sent his patients. Dr. Walker passed away when the twins were thirty-two years old.

With Lonnie gone, Flossie had never married, but Mossie had. She and her husband, Howard Eugene Jackson, had two children, Hazel Irene and Billy Ray. Today, Hazel was married, with no children, but Billy had identical twin boys. Although Flossie never became a mother, her nephews and niece became like her own children, and she came to love them as if they were.

Two years after her sister's tragedy, Flossie recalled making a major career decision. Further inspired by memories of her father racing out in the middle of the night to deliver babies, she decided she wanted to deliver babies too. She became a certified nurse-midwife, delivering hundreds of babies to grateful mothers over the course of her career.

Thinking about her family brought Flossie back to that fateful night, nineteen years ago. Being brought up a Christian and taught to never tell a lie, Flossie knew that when she did tell one, it had been a doozy. The dilemma she faced today was a doozy too. Identical twin girls, separated at her hands—one growing up in America and one in Europe—each one never knowing about the other. And now both of them were in danger. Flossie was fearful for them but didn't know what she could do to save them. She wondered if the Wellingtons had ever contacted Corina and Nicola and her daughter.

Back in May on the night of Mossie's *last* visit, she'd finally found the long-lost address. By writing that letter to both families, at least she had begun to right the wrongs. Thinking about it took her to her closet; she pulled out a copy of the letter from a shoe box and read it silently.

> *May 12*
> *My dear Mrs. Moldovan,*
> *I have put off writing this letter for far too long, but I must wait no longer … It is high time you knew what happened the night your daughter gave birth nineteen years ago …*

Flossie slowly read the entire three-page handwritten letter. Reading the words stung as the awareness of what she had done hung over her head. If there was any relief, it was in knowing that at least now the women knew the truth. Flossie wondered if it would have made a difference to the mother had she known there were twins. It would have been so much better for all concerned if they had been able to make their decision from a fully informed position. Nicola Moldovan could have chosen to go ahead with the adoption, or she might have decided to back out of the adoption so she could keep both of her babies. At least, it would have been her decision. *Not mine.*

When someone knocked at her door, she placed her copy of the letter back in the shoe box. The nurse came in to dispense her morning medicines. After taking her meds, Flossie walked over to her window and looked out at the cold, blustery day, finding it relaxing to watch the leaves swirl outside while she felt warm and cozy indoors with her memories.

CHAPTER
31

Budapest, Hungary

TODAY WAS THE BIG DAY.

Before going down to meet Harvey and Morgan for breakfast, Lynn received a call from the Wellingtons, who told her they were now in Paris and that their plane from Paris to Budapest had been delayed. Sara Wellington said she'd already called her daughter. Although they would be arriving an hour later than planned, she told Lynn they didn't want things to be held up. "Go ahead with the meeting. We don't want Morgan to have to wait any longer to meet her biological family. She is ready for this. Horace and I will get there as soon as we can."

At breakfast, Morgan was beside herself with excitement. In a few hours, she would meet her mother and grandmother. "I'm sorry my parents are going to be late, but I can hardly wait."

"I can feel your enthusiasm, and I'm excited for you. By the way, how's your ankle?" Lynn asked.

"Practically good as new. This is the fifth day, and I hardly feel any discomfort. My crutches are history."

"Just take it easy so you don't injure it again."

"And how are you feeling this morning?" Harvey asked Lynn.

Lynn said she was doing well too. Her gunshot wound no longer hurt, and the pain pills gave her great relief from the soreness in her ribs. The wooziness she'd experienced the other evening and the bruises on her face were gone. She told Harvey all that.

"And Morgan, I never asked you how your night was," Lynn said.

"We had a really great time. Ivona and I find that the more time we spend together, the more we find how much alike we are. Oh, and guess what—we both even bite our fingernails."

"Your similarities continue to amaze me. I think it's really terrific that you two are so much alike."

"Me too. I can hardly wait to see her again in a few hours. Oh, and did Mr. Chapman tell you we thought we spotted the kidnapper at the club last night, around the same time he was actually stalking you?"

"I told her all about it," Harvey said.

"That was quite a coincidence."

Lynn knew that Morgan was going to ask her parents if she could stay a few extra days, and Lynn wondered if they would allow her to. If they did, she would probably be asked to remain behind a little longer as well, but there would be no need for Harvey to stay. She said, "Harv, I was thinking. Before you fly back to the United States, if you get the chance, you might want to look around at antique cars while you're over here. I've heard you can get some pretty good deals here."

"Great idea, Lynn. In fact, I saw a couple of vintage cars advertised in the weekly English newspaper that looked interesting," Harvey replied.

* * *

"Morgan, we're ready to go," Lynn said, tapping on Morgan's door.

Morgan came to the door and asked, "Hi. Can you come in for a moment?"

"Sure," Lynn replied as she walked into Morgan's room. "Are you about ready?"

"I'm so nervous, I've changed clothes a dozen times. Does this look all right?"

"You look very nice. Why so nervous? At breakfast you were excited. Are you getting anxious about meeting the rest of your family?"

"I think so. I've been waiting all my life for this, but suddenly, I'm into the *what ifs*. I can't wait to see everybody, but I really want to know why they gave me away. I may not like what they have to tell me, but I have to know."

Lynn understood Morgan's dilemma. She also knew that everything Morgan needed to know would come out in a very short time. "I believe it will go well. Remember, your parents will be coming in shortly after we get there. So they can help you process this too."

Morgan continued. "I'm sure I'll feel better in a little while. After all, if Ivona's at all like her mother and grandmother, then they're probably pretty neat people too."

Lynn's phone rang. It was Harvey, telling them he was waiting for them outside the lobby.

* * *

Lynn and Morgan arrived at the Moldovan home right on time at one-thirty in the afternoon. "I'll give you a call when I'm ready for you to come back and get me," Lynn told Harvey.

As they exited Harvey's car, Morgan stared at the yellow house. She had seen it just last night when Harvey brought Ivona home, but now, getting a better look at it, she said, "This is the house I've seen in my dreams." Lynn remembered the dream Morgan had shared with her and understood.

The two walked up the short sidewalk and across the wooden porch to the front door. "Are you ready for this?" Lynn asked. Morgan nodded, took a deep breath, and smiled. Lynn rang the doorbell.

"They're here!" they heard Ivona call out.

When the door opened, for the first time in her life Morgan found herself standing face-to-face with the woman who gave birth to her. She was speechless. Lynn watched as Nicola gazed back at Morgan, seemingly mesmerized by her as well. Standing in the doorway, the two looked into each others' eyes. Lynn could tell Morgan's emotions were running high. After a few awkward moments, Nicola blushed and said, "Forgive me. For a moment, I was too excited to move. Hello, Morgan. I am Nicola Palaki, and I am so happy to see you." Then she reached for Morgan's hands and held them a moment.

Morgan said, "I am very happy to meet you too." Nicola put her arms around Morgan's neck and gave her a very long hug, which Morgan returned. Then Nicola greeted Lynn Davis and they stepped inside. Morgan found it hard not to stare at her mother as they walked into the living room. Nicola looked so much like her and Ivona. And she almost looked young enough to be their sister. Morgan fleetingly wondered how different her life would have been had she grown up, like Ivona, in Bucharest, Romania, with her mother and grandmother and twin sister. She experienced a swift pang of regret for not having had that opportunity.

Ivona hurried up to Morgan and greeted her with a big hug. "Hello, Morgan! I'm so glad you're here. You just met Niko, our mother. So come. Let me introduce you to our grandmother."

Morgan greeted Ivona warmly and then took her hand and walked with her over to Corina, who was coming toward them. "Morgan, this is our grandmother, Corina Moldovan."

As she looked at her identical twin granddaughters, tears moistened Corina's eyes. She smiled and said, "Hello, my darling. This is a great day. It's so wonderful to meet you at last. May I give you a hug?"

Morgan responded by opening her arms. She tried unsuccessfully to hold back her own tears as she experienced her grandmother's embrace. She could feel the warm outpouring of love, and it felt extremely special.

When they separated, Corina dabbed her eyes with a handkerchief. Morgan used her hand to brush away her tears and responded sweetly, "I'm very happy to finally meet you too."

Ivona's eyes were also moist, for this was a moment to remember. She had never seen Reeni cry and was touched by her grandmother's tears. Nicola looked poised, but she too looked to be on the verge of tears. She was thrilled that Morgan had accepted her hug as well as Reeni's.

After the greetings, Lynn told them the Wellingtons' flight was delayed and that they would arrive within the hour. Nicola invited everyone to have a seat in the cozy living room.

Morgan looked around the house. She took in the curtains, the colorful rug on the hardwood floor, the pictures on the walls. Her eyes were particularly drawn to photos of the happy family. Mother, daughter, and baby. *Shouldn't it have been mother, daughter, and two babies?* And was that distinguished-looking man with Ivona her father? *My father?* The twins sat side by side on a window bench. Seeing Morgan's interest in the family photos, Ivona took a photo album from the bookcase to show her. She identified each picture. Morgan laughed when she saw Ivona's baby pictures. It was as if she was looking at her own photo album.

As they sat, Morgan and Ivona's warm expressions of affection seemed to set the tone for the gathering. To observing eyes, the two sisters looked like they had been together their entire lives.

Nicola said, "Morgan, I understand that you attend CEU too. What are you studying?" When Morgan answered, "Fashion design," it opened up the subject of Corina's being a seamstress. "Perhaps you inherited your interest in fashion from your grandmother."

The small talk went on for a while. And it was pleasant, but it was not quite what Morgan needed to hear. Meeting her biological family was what she had always wanted. And the pressure was mounting inside of her to know the thing that she most wondered about. "May I ask you something?"

"Yes, of course, Morgan," Nicola said.

Looking from Nicola to Corina, Morgan continued. "I always wanted to know who you were, Dr. Palaki." She noticed her mother start, probably at being referred to as Dr. Palaki, but she didn't know what else to call her. Certainly not Mom or Mother. Ivona called her Niko, but that didn't feel quite right either.

Even though Morgan had always yearned to know about her biological roots, she had been plagued by the notion that her real parents hadn't wanted her. This was compounded by the fact that all her life people had noticed the physical differences between her and her adoptive parents. She would sometimes hear whispers about being adopted. She hated that people focused on that so much. But the thing she needed to know more than anything else was, "Why did you give me up for adoption?" The burning question was finally out, and with it came the tears. Ivona put her arm around Morgan and handed her a tissue. When Morgan dabbed her eyes, she raised her head, ready for an answer.

Here was the moment of truth. Nicola had anticipated this question, and she was ready to explain. As much as she would have liked for her and Morgan to slowly work up to it, it was not to be. Nicola had to address her daughter's question honestly, just as she and Reeni had done with Ivona. She hoped Morgan would accept her answer. Speaking softly, she said, "I will explain everything." Corina waited, ready to help her daughter if necessary.

Nicola said, "My mother and I lived with your parents. She was their housekeeper. Unfortunately, I got pregnant at fifteen. It was very devastating. I'd had big dreams, but I thought I would have to drop out of school. Your father had often encouraged me to pursue science. I loved science and had aspirations of following in his footsteps.

But I believed there was no chance of that then, and without an education, I knew I would never be able to give my child the kind of life she deserved.

"Looking toward the future, my mother and I did not know how we were going to make it. I hadn't even finished high school yet, college seemed out of the question, and the future looked bleak. I was too ashamed to go back to my school or to face my friends and teachers. I didn't even want to face my boyfriend. Fortunately, I didn't have to go back. It was arranged for me to finish out my year at a private boarding school in another state, where I lived in a dormitory."

With everyone's attention focused on her, Nicola continued. "The Wellingtons suggested that after the baby was born, I might want to return to my old school. My mother could keep my baby while continuing to work for them. Even though I was very young, I knew that would have proven to be a real hardship, if not an impossibility. Besides, I felt too ashamed to return to my school again. So my mother suggested that after my baby was born, we go back to Bucharest, where I could finish high school. However, we both felt my child deserved so much better than the life we would be able to provide, so we had to talk of alternatives. I never even considered ending my pregnancy, but I did have to consider the difficult choice of putting my baby up for adoption. Meanwhile, the Wellingtons, being childless, expressed an interest in adopting my unborn child."

Nicola knew she still had to answer Morgan's tough question. "Agreeing to the adoption was the most difficult thing I had ever done. I went back and forth on this. In the end, I gave in because I truly thought it would be best for my baby. I felt the Wellingtons could give my child so much, whereas I could promise nothing. So as much as

I hated the idea, I began to accept it. Furthermore, it felt right that if anyone were to adopt my child, it should be them. They had done so much for my mother and me."

Morgan sat in rapt attention as her mother talked about her life and her pregnancy. Yet her biggest surprise came when Nicola said that Miss Walker, the midwife who handled her delivery, told them that at the last minute the Wellingtons had changed their minds about adopting her baby. Therefore, they would get to keep their baby after all. "When Miss Walker told us that, we were ecstatic. I'd never fully embraced the idea of giving up my child, and I was so relieved. I knew we would manage somehow."

Morgan looked perplexed, as if she was unable to comprehend what she was hearing. "I don't understand. Why would the midwife tell you they changed their minds about adopting me when I sit here, living proof that they did adopt me. And what about the fact that I was a twin?"

"I understand your confusion. What I just told you is what we believed all these years. We only learned earlier this year what really happened the night you were born." Then Nicola proceeded to tell Morgan about the midwife's letter. Morgan learned about the problems with the birth of the second baby, Ivona, and that Nicola had to be hospitalized for several days. Morgan was completely perplexed when she learned that neither her mother nor grandmother had known that Nicola was carrying twins. Nor did they ever know that the Wellingtons had adopted one of her babies after all.

How can that be?

"Did the midwife send my parents the same letter? I never got the impression they knew anything about any of this," Morgan said, bewildered and somewhat disbelieving.

Nicola said, "We phoned Mrs. Walker and asked her that same question, because we wanted to set up a way for Ivona and you to meet. And of course, your grandmother and I wanted to meet you too. The midwife said she had sent Mrs. Wellington a similar letter to ours. She also gave her our contact information, but unfortunately, we never heard from her. We were reluctant to contact your parents without knowing for sure that they'd received the midwife's letter. Your telephone number was unlisted, so I finally phoned your father's office. That's when I learned he'd had a stroke. We chose not to bother them at such a critical time, although we desperately wanted to. Some weeks later, Ivona thought she saw you in a department store here. We tracked down your unlisted home number in the States, and I called Mrs. Wellington to ask if you were in Budapest. But when Mrs. Wellington told us she had not received a letter from the midwife, I didn't feel comfortable bringing up the subject of your being a twin if she knew nothing about it."

Morgan was more confused than ever. She said, "My mother never received a letter from the midwife. If she had, she would have told me."

"We'll have to discuss that with her when she gets here," Nicola said, not knowing what else to say about the letter.

Nicola told Morgan she and her mother had been thrilled to get to keep their baby. Soon after the birth, they returned to Bucharest to make a fresh start. "I never knew about the part of me I had left behind. When I learned about you a few months ago, I was devastated."

Tears welled up in Morgan's eyes, but she had fought them back long enough. Finally she succumbed. Nicola came over and sat beside her and took her hands.

CHAPTER
32

MORGAN COULDN'T HELP BUT THINK about how different life might have been for everyone had the adoption never happened. Right now she had to wrestle with her feelings about her mother's decision. Why had her mother given in to juvenile peer pressure? She asked herself, *What would have been so bad about being pregnant and staying at her same school?* Morgan knew girls who had gotten pregnant but continued right on as if nothing had ever happened. She'd even heard that some schools provided day care for their students' babies. If her mother had never decided to give her baby up for adoption, none of this would ever have happened. Besides, they'd kept Ivona and everything turned out all right. As it was, all their lives were all affected because of that decision. Even though Morgan had been adopted by the Wellingtons, she somehow still felt cheated.

"I would never have dreamed it was all so complicated. But I would like to ask you another question."

Nicola nodded and waited.

"What about my father? Would you tell me about him?" Morgan asked.

Nicola said, "Yes. Of course you would want to know about him too. His name was Randolph Edward Parks. He was a junior in high school when I was a sophomore. Randy was tall and good-looking and smart. He was also captain of the football team, and very popular. All the girls were crazy about him. I was quite proud to be his girlfriend. In my mind, the sun rose and set on him. He dreamed of becoming an astronaut."

"I called Randy once when I was away at boarding school. I had thought a lot about our baby and was considering telling him about it after all. He told me he thought my family had moved out of state and that he was dating another cheerleader. Anyway, I never told him I was pregnant. I didn't want him to think he had to marry me and ruin his college plans. And I definitely didn't feel ready for marriage myself. Like I said, I was far too immature. In any event, I never spoke with him again."

Corina added, "Your mother never told me who her baby's father was. She was afraid I would call his parents and make him take responsibility. No doubt I would have done just that."

"So what happened to him? Where is he now? Maybe I can meet him one day too," Morgan said.

Nicola shook her head and took a deep breath. "Randy did accomplish his dream of becoming an astronaut. However, I am very sorry to tell you—" again she took a deep breath and sighed—"that he was one of the astronauts on board the Rover—the shuttle that exploded in space five years ago." Morgan's hand flew to her mouth and she gasped in shock, remembering watching that explosion on television over and over. Everyone had perished. She had felt horrible for all of them. Now she was learning her natural father was one of those who died in that horrible accident.

Morgan pointed to the family photo on the mantel on the sideboard and asked, "Is that him?"

"No, that was my husband, Adam Palaki. He passed away eight years ago." Nicola got up and walked to the bookcase to pick up a high school yearbook. She leafed through it and found Randolph's picture and handed it to Morgan.

Morgan took the yearbook and studied the photo of her father, rubbing his face with her fingers. She said, "My real father is dead, and I will never get to meet him. That makes me very sad."

Nicola nodded and answered, "When Ralph died, he left a family. He was survived by his wife and two children. They live in Texas."

Two children! Now Morgan was finding out she even had two half-siblings. She wondered about the ages and genders of her father's children, but by then she was just too overwhelmed by it all to ask any more questions.

When Ivona was just a little girl, Nicola had told her about her real father. Otherwise, she knew little more than Morgan was learning right now. Ivona herself had lost two fathers: Randolph Parks and the only one she knew, Adam Palaki. Listening to her mother talk about her biological father brought back painful memories of her adoptive father's death. *But this is Morgan's moment,* she thought, resolving to stay strong. Still, she wiped a tear from her eyes every now and then.

Nicola cleared her throat. It was apparent this conversation had been difficult for both her daughters. Corina suggested they take a break for refreshments. That must have struck the right chord, for they all stood.

A sudden chime at the door gave everyone pause. Lynn looked at her watch. It was a quarter to two, and she realized it was probably the Wellingtons. They'd arrived in Budapest at half past noon and had taken the limo directly to Nicola and Corina's house.

Everyone remained standing, and Corina went to the door. She opened it and looked into the faces of her former employers, Sara and Horace Wellington.

Sara looked back at the woman who for years had been her housekeeper. The years since she'd seen her had been kind. "Hello, Corina," Sara Wellington said. "You're looking very well."

"My heavens, Doctor and Mrs. Wellington. It's so nice to see you again after all these years. You look wonderful too. Please, do come in." Corina took the wheelchair handles from the driver and maneuvered Dr. Wellington into the room.

Mrs. Wellington told her driver, "Thank you. Please wait for us." He tipped his cap and walked back to his limousine.

Morgan heard familiar voices and was excited that her parents had arrived. She rushed to them. "Mom, Dad, you made it! I'm so glad to see you!" She hugged them both. "How do you feel, Dad?"

Dr. Wellington said, "Hello, Princess. Your old dad is doing pretty well. I'll be a hundred percent in no time. How are you feeling?"

"Good. I'm glad you're here. Come see everyone. We were about to have some refreshments. We've been talking a little. I've learned so much. I want you and Mom to know what really happened."

Corina went to hang up the Wellingtons' coats.

Suddenly, Mrs. Wellington's gaze fell on Ivona, who was standing slightly behind Morgan. Seeing the lovely young woman, the very vision of their daughter, nearly caused her to sway. At first, she could not speak. However, after a long pause she murmured, "Dear God."

Morgan saw her mother's reaction and motioned to Ivona to step forward. "Mom and Dad, this is Ivona. Ivona, this is my mother and father."

Seeing Morgan's identical twin sister, Horace Wellington said, "As I live and breathe … It is remarkable that God made two of our Morgan."

Recovering her composure, Mrs. Wellington said, "I am pleased to meet you, my dear. How lovely you are!"

Ivona extended her hand to shake Mrs. Wellington's and say hello. Then she bent down to shake hands with Dr. Wellington. "Young lady," he said. "You are a sight for sore eyes. I'm very pleased to meet you."

"I am very happy to meet the both of you too," Ivona replied, unclear what he meant by that strange phrase.

Mrs. Wellington, noting Ivona's expression, smiled and said, "That means he is happy to see you," and Ivona smiled.

Nicola said, "Hello, Doctor and Mrs. Wellington. It is wonderful to see you both again. It feels like practically a lifetime."

"Hello, Nicola," Mrs. Wellington said. "It is good to see you all grown up. We understand you've done very well for yourself, and we congratulate you on your accomplishments."

"Thank you, Mrs. Wellington. My mother and I owe you and Dr. Wellington a huge debt of gratitude for all you did for us."

Sara Wellington nodded.

"My star scientist," Dr. Wellington said, greeting her pleasantly. Then Mrs. Wellington said hello to Lynn and introduced her to her husband.

"I am honored to meet you, Dr. Wellington," Lynn said. "I'm glad you're doing well." Horace Wellington acknowledged Lynn's words, and Lynn asked, "How long will you be staying in Budapest?"

Mrs. Wellington responded, "We only plan to be here two or three days."

She studied Nicola and detected nervousness. *If she is nervous, is it because she is seeing us for the first time since they'd left Cincinnati. Or is she uncomfortable at what she has to tell us? Feeling guilty perhaps? I suppose so after what she's done.* It had surprised Sara Wellington when Morgan said she was eager for them to hear what really happened.

To Corina and Nicola, Mrs. Wellington said, "Miss Davis has been keeping us informed of these very unusual developments, including the kidnappings. We were so relieved to get the phone call yesterday that the kidnappers have both now been captured. We feel much better now. I'm sure you feel the same."

"We feel so much better that they are now behind bars," Nicola said. When Miss Davis had called her late last night and told her about the kidnappers' capture, she'd recognized his name, Pista Valdú. She knew Pista as a young truant back in Bucharest. He was the cousin of her classmate Vilmos, who was now a physician, but Pista was a habitual criminal. The last she'd heard, he was serving time in prison.

"More importantly," Mrs. Wellington continued, "Horace and I wanted to come in person to understand how this happened."

"Of course," Nicola said. "We are eager to share the truth with you."

"Very well, then," Mrs. Wellington said, glancing at Morgan with an endearing look. "Of course, we also wanted to see our daughter's twin sister with our own eyes." She looked from Morgan to Ivona and smiled. "Your resemblance is truly remarkable."

After learning about Morgan's twin, Sara had not known what to think. Furthermore, she honestly couldn't imagine what Corina and Nicola could possibly tell her that could make the situation tenable. She assumed they had deliberately kept from her and her husband the fact that another baby had been born. Although it would have been more challenging, she would gladly have adopted both the girls. But even if she had chosen not to do so, at least the twins would have known about each other. How unfortunate that they had been separated. She thought about how badly her daughter had wanted a sister, so much that she'd actually created an imaginary one named Eva. She instantly connected the two names. *Eva and Ivona? How ironic.* While not exactly the same, the names were certainly similar. She looked firmly but quizzically from Corina to Nicola.

Nicola said. "Mrs. Wellington, won't you and Dr. Wellington come and join us in the living room? We have refreshments. And then we will share with you what we just told Morgan."

"Mom, Dad, it's pretty unbelievable," Morgan said.

Everyone went into the living room and sat down. Corina brought in a tray of refreshments and set it on the coffee table. Mrs. Wellington poured two cups of tea and handed one to her husband.

"Would you care for anything else?" Corina asked the Wellingtons.

"Thank you, Corina, but right now, we just need answers," Mrs. Wellington said. "Horace and I traveled here, in part, to learn the truth. Obviously none of us knew Morgan was born a twin. We are eager to know what happened." The coolness in her tone was not lost on Corina or Nicola.

Nicola said, "I understand. The circumstances surrounding Morgan and Ivona's birth were only made known to us earlier this year by the midwife who handled my delivery, Miss Flossie Walker."

Sara Wellington looked surprised at hearing the name. "Yes, I remember Miss Walker very well. In fact, I recommended her to you. But what do you mean that you just found out the circumstances of their birth?"

Nicola said, "We received a letter from Miss Walker back in May. She told us exactly what happened the day I gave birth." Mrs. Wellington looked perplexed. Nicola then proceeded to tell them what had happened, as she had told Morgan. Sara Wellington looked as though she doubted the story, and then something crossed her mind. She thought of that unusual phone call from Nicola recently, asking if she had received a letter from the midwife. But she continued to listen, and she was horrified when Nicola told her about the second baby being choked during childbirth. Her husband looked empathetic.

Even though Mrs. Wellington was prepared to doubt the story, it was believable. She remembered when Miss Walker had rung her doorbell the evening of May 11. "I have a beautiful surprise for you," she had told the Wellingtons, who beamed with joy at the bundle in the midwife's arms.

When Dr. Wellington told her they would have picked their baby up, she had said, "It's quite all right. My patient and her mother are gone, and after I cleaned this pretty little girl up, I didn't want you to have to wait any longer than necessary." They'd invited Miss Walker inside. She immediately handed the baby over to Mrs.

Wellington. She set a diaper bag full of essentials on the hall table. Sara and her husband always wondered why the midwife had delivered the baby herself. They'd dismissed it after awhile. Now it made sense that she might not have wanted them to come to her clinic.

Mrs. Wellington still had a questioning look on her face. "I'm sorry, this just isn't adding up to me." She was ready to say more, but at that moment, Corina, who had stepped out of the room momentarily, returned with a letter in her hand.

CHAPTER
33

"PERHAPS THIS WILL HELP. I think you should both see this. It tells everything. In fact, we were of the understanding that you had received a similar piece of mail," Corina said of the envelope in her hand. "This is the letter we received in May from Miss Walker. It is dated May 12 this year." She handed the envelope to Mrs. Wellington so she could see the postscript and the return address. Mrs. Wellington examined the envelope and noticed its authenticity. She nodded at her husband.

Corina said, "I would like you to read it. If you still have questions afterward, we can discuss them."

Mrs. Wellington handed the letter back to Corina and said, "Please, just read your letter."

Corina read.

May 12
My dear Mrs. Moldovan,
  I have put off writing this letter for far too
long, but I must wait no longer. I'm getting old
now and when I'm gone, I can't let my secret die
with me. It is time you knew what happened the
night your daughter gave birth.

The room was so quiet everyone could have heard a pin drop. Mrs. Wellington glanced at her husband. She rubbed her hands together nervously.

  When Nicola was about twenty weeks along,
  I recommended that she have an obstetrical
  ultrasound so we could get a better look at the
  development of her baby. But since she was
  giving the baby up, she declined. She did not
  want to know anything about it, even its gender.
  She even wanted to be asleep when the baby
  was born.

Hearing that, Nicola again thought of how unwise she had been not to have had the procedure. The Wellingtons glanced at her and then back to Corina. Sara Wellington tried to quiet her nerves. Corina continued reading.

  The baby's birth was easy. I handed her to
  my aide, who left the room to clean her up. Your
  daughter was still asleep. You were in the next
  room, for as I remember, you did not want to
  see the baby. I didn't know it was not over yet.
  Within a few minutes, Nicola started moaning,
  and that's when I realized she was having

another baby. None of us had known she was carrying twins.

Unfortunately, that second baby got tangled in her umbilical cord, so I had to act fast to save it. After the second baby was out, Nicola started hemorrhaging. You rushed your daughter to the ER. In all the turmoil, neither of you knew she'd had another baby.

Young Nicola had been crying herself to sleep over the impending adoption. I was very worried that with the problem she'd had during her delivery, she might not be able to have more children. And if she was unable to have more, it would be my fault. Since no one else knew twins had been born, I decided to take matters into my own hands to ensure that she would have a child too.

Lynn observed Dr. Wellington pat his wife's arm. She realized how emotional it probably was for them to hear this account. She was moved by hearing it as well. For although Nicola had told her the story, Miss Walker's words gave additional insight. Lynn thought about how Miss Walker had carried the burden of this decision all these years.

After the two of you left for the hospital, I took Nicola's firstborn to the Wellingtons. I also gave them a gift for the baby—a little gold pendant in the shape of half a heart.

Morgan gasped softly and reached to touch the pendant around her neck.

I took care of the other baby until you returned from the hospital to pick up your belongings a few days later. Then I presented that baby to you, along with the other half of the gold pendant. I told you the Wellingtons had changed their minds about wanting to adopt. Of course, that was not true.

Seeing how happy you both were when you took the baby in your arms made me feel I had done the right thing. Your reaction made it worth all the risks. I am so sorry for the lies I told. I have despaired so over having separated those girls. I had no right to play God and tried not to let myself think about it again. I told myself it was best no one ever know the truth. It would only hurt everyone.

Yours were the last babies I delivered. I closed my practice, and after a six-month break I went back to work as a private duty nurse until I retired.

And now, Mrs. Moldovan, I want to tell you about those gold half pendants I gave each of your granddaughters. I had an identical twin sister named Mossie. We were very close. Your granddaughters were born on Mossie's and my birthday, May 11. Mossie died nearly fifty years ago in a tragic accident. However, even in death, we have remained close, for she is in my heart. I felt her urging me to write this letter.

Those pendants were mine and Mossie's, obtained on our thirteenth birthdays. After Mossie died, I kept her half with mine. It meant so much to me to have something personal that had belonged to her. The evening you and your daughter went to the hospital, I felt Mossie compelling me to give our pendants to those babies. When the two pieces are put together, they have a very special message. One day your daughter may learn just what that is.

Morgan and Ivona looked at each other. Morgan grabbed her pendant and held it fondly.

So that is the truth of what happened that day, nineteen years ago. I have told you everything. I cannot turn back the clock, but I pray that everything turned out fine. Please forgive me.

God bless all of you,
Flossie Walker

The room was deathly quiet when Corina finished reading the letter. For a few moments, everyone remained eerily quiet, their minds filled with the amazing revelations that letter contained. Even though no one could have ever conceived something like that, the explanation set forth in the letter made sense. Mrs. Walker's honest confessions were heartfelt and believable. And the letter left not even a shred of doubt in anyone's minds about how the twins came to be separated. Hearing the midwife's words helped everyone completely understand and even accept what had happened. Amazingly, hearing this letter being read also seemed to remove any inclination to cast blame, even on the midwife herself.

The Wellingtons were silent and thoughtful. Finally, Dr. Wellington spoke up. "This is an incredible story. We're actually speechless. It seems that both of our families have been both victims as well as benefactors of the midwife's actions. Benefactors since because of her, we both had a beautiful daughter to raise."

Corina let out a deep breath. She folded the letter and placed it back in its envelope. Mrs. Wellington looked at her daughter and said, "Morgan, dear, how are you feeling?"

Morgan and Ivona had been absorbed in listening to the letter, Ivona for the second time. It was Morgan's first time hearing the actual words from the midwife's own pen.

"I'm really okay, Mom," Morgan said. "Dr. Palaki already told me all this. The truth is, at first I was upset at what I learned. I needed to work it out. But after hearing the midwife's words, I believe I can now accept what happened. Lifelong questions have been answered for me. I feel bad for what I have put you and Dad through with my secrecy." She hugged both her parents.

Then Morgan looked at Nicola and said, "At first I was angry and hurt that you had agreed to adoption. But now I think I can understand it. You were so young. And you never knew about me. Somehow that letter put everything in perspective for me." She and Nicola hugged.

Then Ivona spoke. "Thank you, Reeni and Niko. I know this whole thing has been so difficult for both of you, and for all of us. But I want to say to you, Morgan, that we may not have grown up together, but we'll definitely grow older together. Well, maybe not physically, but we'll always be in touch with each other." The twins hugged.

Lynn sat, quietly watching the developments. Mrs. Wellington turned and said to her, "Miss Davis, it seems the girls were destined to meet each other. That would probably have led to Morgan meeting the rest of her biological family anyway. But your tenacity uncovered information that enabled us to have this special gathering. And if you hadn't been so protective of our daughter during the kidnapping, there's no telling what would have happened to her or Ivona. We absolutely cannot thank you enough. It is unfortunate you suffered the injuries you did. We're grateful you're on the mend."

Dr. Wellington looked at Lynn and said, "I completely agree. We appreciate everything you've done."

Lynn smiled and nodded.

He continued, "Corina, I must apologize if my wife or I came across as if we thought you and Nicola had deliberately misled us."

Sara added, "I'm afraid we unintentionally jumped to conclusions. I hope you can forgive us for thinking the worst. Now I can imagine how shocking it was for you to receive this news after all these years. Our hearts go out to you for what you have both endured."

Corina said, "Nicola and I were worried that you would think we'd kept this from you. We're glad you can accept the truth."

Lynn told Mrs. Wellington, "My associate, Ella Braxton, met with Miss Walker in Cincinnati last week to ask her about the situation with the twins. Miss Walker told her that several weeks after mailing those letters, she received a phone call from Mrs. Moldovan and Dr. Palaki asking if she had written to you, since they hadn't heard anything from you."

Nicola explained how they desperately wanted to contact the Wellingtons. Sometime later, she'd called Dr. Wellington's office and learned he'd had a stroke. "Even though Ivona was dying to know about her sister, we hadn't wanted to bother you at such a delicate time. After a few more weeks, we called you again to find out if you had received a letter from Flossie Walker."

"It was indeed a surprise hearing from you after all these years. However, as I told you I never received Mrs. Walker's letter. Now I understand you wouldn't have wanted to spring this on me out of the blue. I trust Miss Walker wrote the letter, but I guess I'll never know what happened to it," Mrs. Wellington said. Then, looking directly at Corina, she said, "Had we known, we would definitely have gotten in touch with you about this. I'm sorry you had to go for so long thinking we knew but didn't contact you."

Suddenly Sara Wellington thought of something. The envelope Corina handed her from the midwife was framed by a lovely lilac pattern. She remembered seeing that pattern before. Her hand flew to her mouth. "Oh my goodness," she said. Everyone looked up as she relayed the story about the day their housekeeper had dropped some mail in the pool; one letter ended up completely unreadable. "I remember, because it was in an identical envelope and written with a fountain pen, just as yours is. All the words had run together in a blur. I know now that letter was from Flossie Walker, and I so regret not getting the chance to read it. I can assure you we would have contacted you immediately and made arrangements for the girls to meet."

Lynn said, "According to Ella, Mrs. Walker had always felt torn because she separated the twins, and yet she felt connected to them at the same time. Here's something you might find hard to believe. Last week, on the very day we were kidnapped, she phoned my associate and insisted that she get a message to me that the girls were in danger." The news surprised everyone. "Of course Ella called her back the next day to tell her what had happened. Miss Walker said it wasn't over yet. And at that time, she was right," referring to the effort by the kidnappers to grab Ivona the next day.

"But thank goodness, now it is," Sara Wellington said. A strangely calm mood filled the room as everyone digested what might have been different had the Wellingtons read Miss Walker's letter.

Morgan had to bring up something Miss Walker said in her letter. She said, "It was so exciting to learn the story behind our pendants. I always felt this pendant somehow connected me to my biological roots. I just never dreamed it connected me to an identical twin sister. Mom, remember you gave this to me on my ninth birthday. It has always been special to me, and I still wear it often," she said, touching it. "Like now."

"You treasured that little piece of jewelry," Sara Wellington said. "We held it until you were old enough to appreciate it."

Ivona pulled hers out from underneath her sweater and said to Morgan, "Remember how excited I was the other day when I saw yours around your neck? I also wear mine sometimes. My mother gave me mine when my dad adopted me. Niko, you told me this was a special heirloom that pertained to my heritage. For some reason, that always made me feel good." Then Ivona said to Morgan, "After we received the midwife's letter back in May, I have been eager to see what the two pendants say when they're put together." She removed her necklace.

At the same time, Morgan was reaching behind her neck to unfasten the clasp of hers. Then she said, "Mine says, *I am as you are together always.*"

"And mine says, *Like you, like me we will be,*" Ivona added. "Let's put them together."

Morgan and Ivona hurriedly placed their gold pieces together on the table in front of them. The two halves formed a perfect heart. The inscription had grown quite faint from wear and age, but the twins were completely transfixed by the two-sided message the pendant bore. In fact, everyone sat riveted when the twins read one side aloud together: *"I am like you as you are like me."* Then they turned it over and read the other side: *"Together we will always be."*

Ivona said, "I love it!"

"Ivona, finding you has been the best thing that ever happened to me. Meeting each other was our destiny," Morgan said, smiling as she clasped Ivona's hands. "I know that together we *will* always be."

Ivona smiled back at Morgan and said, "Because *I am like you as you are like me.*" The twins hugged and wiped happy tears from their eyes.

Lynn noticed that even Dr. and Mrs. Wellington's eyes glistened as they watched the girls. Nicola and Corina's eyes were wet too. It was such a special moment, even her own eyes were threatening.

The room was quiet for what seemed like a long time. After a long moment, Corina broke the silence. "Nineteen years ago, Miss Walker prophesied that there would be a day when this little broken heart would bring our little baby great joy. Her prophecy has been fulfilled."

* * *

Back in Cincinnati at the Felix House, at the precise moment the two golden heart pieces were joined to reveal their message, Flossie Walker felt a movement in her soul so powerful, she knew something wonderful had happened. It was not like the potent force she experienced the moment her sister died. This time, her intuition immediately told her it was the twins. They are not only together; now they know that together *they will always be*. She'd waited such a long time for this, and her heart rejoiced. The danger the twins had been in seemed a thing of the past.

* * *

Lynn had observed the amazing reunion unfold before her eyes. Everyone agreed it had almost felt like Miss Walker had been sitting in the room, telling her story. And even though the twins had missed out on the experience of sisterhood, Lynn felt they would quickly make up for what they lost. She was witnessing firsthand the incredible bonds of identical twin relationships.

With the meeting over, picture- and video-taking came next. Everyone got their fill of pictures and movies of the twins and everyone else. Then Nicola said, "Can we all go to dinner together? It would be a shame to end such a perfect day now."

"Horace and I were hoping the same thing," Sara Wellington responded.

Lynn declined the dinner invitation, but the rest of the group agreed to go. When Harvey picked her up, he asked, "Why didn't you go to dinner?"

"Harv, this was a private family reunion. They wanted to continue bonding. I'm glad I got to see it come about. Their story is so unusual, I wouldn't be surprised to see it turned into a made-for-TV movie."

Over dinner, the conversation between all was free-flowing and enjoyable. The twins sat next to each other and sometimes held their own private conversations. Nicola and Corina told tales of Ivona's early years, and the Wellingtons shared some of Morgan's first adventures. Nicola watched her twin daughters and smiled. At one point, the girls were asked about their kidnapping ordeal, and they both gave graphic details, entrancing everyone who listened and admired them for their courage to survive.

Mrs. Wellington said, "If anyone had ever told me we would all be sitting here like this, I would not have believed them. Seeing Morgan and Ivona touches my heart, and I am grateful that things turned out as they have. Girls, I believe your lives have been changed forever. Indeed, all of ours have."

Dr. Wellington raised his glass in a toast. "Here's to friends and relations that will only grow stronger."

"Hear, hear," everyone roundly chanted. Then they clinked their glasses, and each took a sip to seal the deal.

CHAPTER
34

Monday, December 2

Morgan was excited "Miss Davis! Today, I got permission from all my professors to take the rest of my finals this week. They moved them up a week for me. My dad told me to make arrangements to complete them online, but my dean suggested I try for early exams, and all my professors agreed!"

"That's super. Are your parents going to stay too?"

"That's just it. They have to leave tomorrow. But they aren't completely comfortable leaving me here by myself, so my mom is going to talk to you to see if you could stay just a few more days. Please, please!" Morgan smiled, crossed fingers on both hands, and held them up for Lynn to see.

"No problem, Morgan. I can stay. Harvey will go ahead and leave tomorrow, but since the kidnappers are off the street, you and Ivona are much safer now."

"Oh, thank you, Miss Davis! Ivona and Bela and György will be so happy I'm staying."

Lynn asked, "Can you be ready for all your finals this week?"

"Oh, sure. I'm pretty well prepared. I'll go let Mom and Dad know," Morgan said, preparing to race out of Lynn's room.

"Oh—do you have everything out of your apartment?"

"I have a few more boxes to pack up. Mom and Dad were going to take me over there tonight, but Dad isn't feeling too good today, so my mother said that if you were able to stay here, perhaps you can go over with me to pick up the last of my things."

"Sure thing," Lynn said.

Morgan hurried out to tell her parents the news.

A few minutes later, Sara Wellington called Lynn. "Morgan told us you are willing to stay here with her this week. That means a lot to her, and we really appreciate it."

"You're quite welcome. I'm perfectly fine with staying."

"We hoped you would be. Morgan really wants to finish her semester here. I expect Mr. Chapman will be returning to Cincinnati right away."

"Yes, he's leaving in the morning."

"We've already checked the flight schedules. You can leave this coming Saturday and be back early Sunday morning." Lynn assured Mrs. Wellington that was satisfactory. "Even though the kidnappers are now locked up, after everything Morgan's been through, I would like you to continue to keep a close eye on her. We wouldn't want anything else to happen. The two of you have been through more than enough. Call me after you get back so we can settle up with you."

"Will do," Lynn replied.

Then Sara expressed her gratitude. "Horace and I don't even want to think about what could have happened had you not been with Morgan the day those criminals abducted you both. I believe it wouldn't have been pretty. Undoubtedly your quick thinking and actions saved you both from a terrible fate."

"You're most welcome," Lynn said, adding, "It's what you hired me for, after all."

"Oh, that was far beyond the job we asked of you. There's no question about that. The way Horace and I see it, you could have returned to Cincinnati after two days in Budapest, and you would have done what we expected of you. But your pursuit to find answers ended up giving us more than we could have ever hoped for. We're so fortunate that you were on the case for us. I am going to tell Elizabeth Remington she gave me an excellent recommendation, and if the opportunity ever presents itself, I will be happy to do the same."

Lynn thanked Mrs. Wellington for her comments and said, "Have a safe trip home."

Lynn made arrangements for Jozséf to transport Morgan to and from school. Morgan called for room service and stayed in Monday night to study for Tuesday's exam.

When Harvey returned from his outing, he called Lynn. "I've had the damnedest day. Bought me a car and arranged for it to be shipped home."

"That was quick. What did you buy?"

Harvey cleared his throat boastfully and said, "A 1934 Rolls Phantom V two-door coupe. Gray and black."

"You bought a Rolls Royce? That sounds fantastic! Congratulations," Lynn said.

"Well, that's not the half of it. I'll tell you about it over dinner." They arranged to go to a nice restaurant on Harvey's last evening in Budapest.

"I'll be waiting downstairs at seven."

At dinner, Lynn told Harvey she'd be staying the rest of the week so Morgan could finish her final exams.

"I gotta tell you about my experience today." Harvey proceeded to tell her a long story about how he went to an antique auto dealer in a small Mediterranean-style village. "It was pretty quaint. Had cobblestone streets and museums. You'd have liked it."

"Sounds like it. So what happened?"

"I saw this Rolls on display and liked it right away. Let me tell you what happened. The dealer gave me some cockamamie story about how the first owner, a rich landowner, had eight wives. But half of them died one day when lightning struck a tree and the tree fell on them during their annual harvest picnic."

"That's pretty morbid," Lynn said. "Didn't know they had polygamy here."

"Yeah, and I don't know that they did. But like I said, this was the guy's wild story. Anyway, he said the car was parked only inches away from where the tree fell and didn't get a single scratch, but the wives died. Then the man began telling me that legend had it the car held magical powers, and some pretty incredible things happened to the next few owners. One obtained massive wealth; another lived to be 110 and was said to have been driving the car the day he died. So there are supposed to be some big miracles for the next two owners. See, there were four miracles in all: one for each of the wives who died."

"Come on now, Harvey."

"Course, that didn't sway me, because I didn't believe a word of that nonsense. Anyway, when I went out to look at the car, some guy slipped up to me and gave me the skinny. Turns out the dealer had a gambling problem and had to sell the car today or the car's owner, some rich woman, was taking it to another dealer. He needed the profit from this sale to pay off some serious debts. So he tried to charm me into buying it by making me think it had special powers. Guy could have saved himself the trouble. I was pretty sure I was gonna buy it anyway. But at least, the guy who gave me the straight scoop made me realize how desperate the dealer was, so I made the guy a puny little offer, and after a little back and forth I got myself a real deal. Check it out." Harvey pulled out his smart phone and showed Lynn the picture he took.

"That's a beaut, Harv. What are you going to do with it? Sell or keep?"

"I'm not a Rolls Royce kind of guy. I'm selling this baby. I'll make a tidy profit." Then Harvey winked and said, "Or ... I'll see what kind of miracle I'm entitled to."

* * *

After leaving the restaurant, Lynn and Harvey came upon a huge old Gothic-style church. Lynn saw the name and said, "Say, Harv, I saw that church in the tourist guide in my hotel room. It said it is believed that those soaring arches were built to draw one's spirit up to heaven. But most importantly, it said that if you stand directly under its central dome and speak a quiet prayer to a deceased relative, the spirit of that person will answer you."

"I'm happy to let the departed rest in peace. I don't need to speak with them."

"Oh, come on, Harvey," she said. "Let's go in."

Harv found a place to park. They climbed the stairs toward the church entrance. Outside, they studied the building's decorative stone work for a minute. Much of the stone was black with age. The heavy, dark, ornately carved wooden doors were massive. The huge arched windows were filled with bright stained-glass painted gold, with a large black crucifix in the center. A plaque identified the church as being over seven hundred and fifty years old.

Lynn and Harvey entered. Inside, they waited until their eyes adjusted to the dim light emanating from lighted candles and the stained-glass windows. They could see a few other people quietly milling about. The dark wooden pews were empty except for a couple of women who sat several rows apart. Both were dressed in dark clothing, and one's face was hidden behind a black veil. The other's head was covered with a black hood. "That looks a little weird," Harvey whispered when he glanced at the women.

Lynn spotted the miracle dome and looked up to see a colorful stained-glass painting in its center. They watched as a woman stood under the dome, apparently listening closely. Another was standing by. All at once, a wide smile crossed the first woman's face. She whispered something excitedly to the other one, who rushed to give her a hug. The other woman eagerly took her chance under the dome while her friend stood by for support.

"Look. The first one must have gotten a response. I wonder how they know when they've heard from their dear departed. Do you think they actually hear their voices?" Lynn whispered.

"Watch out now. Sounds like you're starting to believe that stuff," Harv said.

"I just might. There is something to metaphysics, but it's perfectly harmless. Mostly, though, I'm just curious what happens under that dome. Want to try it?" Lynn asked.

"I don't even want to be in here. In fact, I'd say, let's get out of here now. You ready?" Harvey answered.

"Okay, spoilsport. We'll walk back along the other side and then we'll leave." Lynn and Harvey studied the perimeter church walls, which were made of marble and contained several wall tombs, some topped with elaborate marble effigies. The article she'd read had said that the highest officials of the church and certain others were buried in those tombs.

Harvey leaned over to Lynn and whispered, "This place is nothing but a veritable high-rent cemetery."

Suddenly they both had the strange feeling that something was brushing lightly against their faces. Lynn looked startled.

"Do you feel that?" she asked.

"I feel something all over my face," he said. "What's going on?"

Lynn said, "Don't know. Maybe it was one of the spirits they conjured up. But when it started crawling behind my collar, I figured I'd had enough." They hurried out of the church. Driving back to their hotel, they laughed about both getting spooked back there.

When they returned to the hotel, Harvey packed while Lynn waited and watched. When he was finished, he told Lynn he'd be leaving at six in the morning. Lynn said, "You have been such a huge help. Things might have turned out much differently had you not been here. Thanks for dropping everything to come look after us. I'm glad you got yourself a Rolls Royce out of the deal."

"You know I'm always here for you, Lynn. Don't get yourself into any more trouble this week, kid."

Back in her hotel room, Lynn thought about the sense that something had brushed across their faces in the church. She decided to look it up online and read some comments from people who had toured it in the past. One comment in particular caught her attention. It said that a tour guide had told his group that because the building was so old, there was no way to control the spontaneous drafts throughout the church that occurred at various times. It said that the movement of the air sometimes startled people, who felt like they were actually being touched by a feather. *That works for me.*

* * *

With Harvey gone and Morgan in class, Lynn decided to shop. She checked with the concierge, who recommended Hero Square for buying souvenirs, but he also highly recommended that she see one of the city's most famous tourist attractions in the same area—a historic medicinal bathhouse for men and women. He told her, "Budapest is known for its many public baths, but this one is quite something to see. It was the first spa built in the city and has some fifteen pools and can accommodate several thousand people at a time. You may even want to tour the facility. I can assure you it is well worth seeing." Lynn thought she would check it out.

She went to Hero Square, where she found several souvenir shops. She enjoyed taking her time as she looked around for gifts for the folks back home. The array of artifacts was interesting. She found models of famous structures, such as the Buda Castle and Parliament building, and beautiful pictures identifying Budapest as the Pearl of the Danube or Paris of Eastern Europe. Lynn had seen enough these last two weeks to understand why this lovely city would have such flattering nicknames.

She selected a few items for her mother and aunts. For her uncle, she found a meerschaum pipe for his occasional indulgence, and she found the perfect Hungarian stacking dolls for Ella and Janet. She ran across a variety of Count Dracula figurines and wondered if the legends of those supernatural creatures were perpetuated to cultivate superstition and increase tourist fascination and the demand for such souvenirs. She resisted the whimsical urge to buy a Count Dracula figurine for her uncle.

Lynn spotted the bathhouse, situated in a park just across from where she had been shopping. It was the lone building situated picturesquely among neatly manicured gardens, a large decorative fountain, and marble statues. The huge, ornately carved, baroque-style building had copper domes and tall steeples guarded by bronze warriors on horseback. Lynn decided to at least walk over and have a look.

The minute she opened the large, carved wooden door, she knew she wanted to see more. Stepping into the building felt almost like she had stepped right into an ancient world. Looking down a long corridor beyond the entryway, she could see what appeared to be ancient ruins with marble pillars and lifelike statues. It reminded Lynn of how ancient Rome must have looked. She purchased a self-guided tour pass and was told to follow the arrows.

Even though it was November, the heat emitting from the saunas, steam baths, and thermal pools brought warmth and humidity to the corridor. As she walked, she admired the life-sized colored frescos, intricate wall carvings, suits of armor, and thick marble columns. Through the columns she could see pools and saunas, each one nestled in its own separate wing. The pastel-colored walls against the blue waters were an appealing sight.

Lynn walked up and down the various wings and saw units where exercises were being supervised by trained therapists. She passed a station where the unprepared could rent swimsuits and towels; she remembered seeing a sign saying swimsuits were mandatory. Lynn had read somewhere that not all bathhouses in Budapest required swimsuits. She walked by separate pools for men and women. The pools were situated under huge domes through which light streamed in, giving the sensation of being outside. She could detect a light smell of chlorine. A sign said the temperature of the indoor pools ranged from 21 to 43 degrees Celsius. Next, she came upon a large pool where some women chatted in small groups in the water while others exercised. Beyond that was another large pool, steam rising from the water. It was full of men, most of them elderly. Chess players sat on stools at tables in the water and quietly pondered their next moves. She passed several young women sitting in a sauna, and young men played volleyball in another pool.

Just as Lynn passed a group of massage rooms, a door opened and she got a pleasant whiff of the lavender fragrance coming from inside. Soft spa music was playing in the background, creating a nice ambience. Next, she glanced through a set of double doors to the outside, where there was a huge heated pool. Through the steam, she could see both men and women enjoying the water. *How big is this place?*

Finally, after admiring a lovely interior garden, a theater that looked like a smaller version of the Roman Coliseum, and a library, Lynn found herself at the end of her tour. It had been a great way to spend an afternoon in this fabled land.

That evening, Morgan came to Lynn's room and said, "I have something for you." A few days earlier, Morgan saw the fabric Lynn had purchased and had secretly decided to design an evening dress for her. She looked on as Lynn opened the envelope and removed and thumbed through the sketches, studying different sides of the sophisticated, off-the-shoulder gown with enthusiasm.

Lynn was impressed. "Morgan, these are fabulous. What a great designer you are," she said, picturing her new beaded fabric becoming this elegant dress. "It'll be my pleasure to wear this authentic Morgan Wellington original one day." Lynn even had the perfect occasion in mind. One of the e-mail messages she'd received while in Budapest was from Yale's Alumni Committee, advising her of the upcoming biannual alumni ball.

CHAPTER
35

Wednesday, December 4

LOCKED UP AND WITH NOTHING to do, Pista had plenty
of time to think. Over and over, he tried to figure out
why his venture had failed. He had done everything
by the book as Alphonse had taught him to pull off a
successful kidnapping. But that bonehead Fane had
screwed up. Worse, here he was, bound for prison yet
again. Since he was a repeat offender, he'd probably
get a heavy sentence. He thought about what could
be one last attempt and hired himself a lawyer, a Mr.
Daniel Carp.

On Wednesday morning, Daniel Carp phoned Nicola
Palaki. He told her Pista was requesting a meeting with
her. At first, Nicola couldn't believe she heard the lawyer
correctly. Pista Vladú had abducted and brutalized one
of her daughters and almost succeeded in kidnapping
the other one.

She answered, "After all that man as done, what could he possibly have to say to me except 'I'm sorry' a thousand times?"

"I understand," Mr. Carp said. "Mr. Vladú does seem sincerely remorseful and wants very much to apologize."

"I am not interested," Nicola said adamantly. "Please do not contact me about this again. Tell Pista Vladú to leave me and my family alone."

"I will tell him, but from what he has said, it could be in your best interest to see him. From what I understand, he wants to warn you of a future threat."

"What!"

"Yes, he seems to know of some impending developments concerning you and your family. Will you agree to a short meeting with him? It will probably take no more than thirty minutes of your time."

"Absolutely not! I want nothing to do with that man. Why doesn't he just tell the police about this alleged threat?"

"That's what I recommended, but he will not do that for fear that if he returns to prison, he will become a target of those inmates who don't care much for snitches."

Nicola thought about what the man was saying. As much as she detested the idea, she felt she needed to meet with Pista. If what his lawyer said was true, her family's safety could still be in jeopardy. She couldn't risk that. They made an appointment for ten o'clock that morning.

Nicola didn't want to stand before this criminal alone and thought about Lynn Davis. She'd been so involved in the case and in saving her daughters, Nicola wondered if she would possibly go with her. She called and told Lynn about her meeting with Pista and asked if she would accompany her. She told Lynn, "If what the lawyer told me is true, my family's safety could still be in jeopardy." Lynn agreed to go.

Pista sat in his cold gray cell. He had asked his lawyer to get Nicola over there. He needed money and figured it was worth one more try. He was depressed about failing because of that meddlesome black woman. He so wished he'd taken care of her that night when he missed running her over in his car. Once again, he cursed himself for failing.

He wasn't sorry he had gone for the big money. Nicola Moldovan was worth plenty. His had been a good plan. But because of it, he needed money more than ever. He had legal fees to pay; he didn't have enough of the money left from what he'd taken off the women to pay his lawyer's retainer. He wasn't ready to sell his sports car. If Fane hadn't wrecked his old car, he could have sold it and gotten a little cash, but he was ending up with little more than what he had when he started. So the way he saw it, Nicola Palaki was his last shot.

If he faked an apology, maybe she would fall for it. Then he would tell her about Alphonse, his former cell mate, who had talked about getting in on the action. Of course, he knew that Alphonse was just talking big, but she did not have to know that. If he could convince her that Alphonse was coming after her and her sister, she might go for his offer. Pista needed to pay his lawyer, who could hopefully keep him out of prison. Or at least get him a shorter sentence.

At ten o'clock, Nicola Palaki and Lynn Davis arrived to see Pista Vladú.

Pista gave a startled look when he saw Lynn Davis. *What the fuck is this bitch doing here?* He looked at his lawyer and then quietly demanded to know why she had come along.

Mr. Carp told him, "Dr. Palaki asked Miss Davis to join her."

Pista was pissed. This bitch was the very reason he had all these problems. "Why didn't Nicola Palaki just come alone?"

Carp continued, "She will speak with you only in the lady's presence."

Pista grunted. He didn't like it, but at the moment he had no other choice. Trying to look innocent, Pista said, "First, I want to say I am sorry for what I did to you and your family. I didn't intend to hurt anyone. It's just that I was drinking, and the alcohol made me do something stupid."

Nicola looked at Lynn, who shook her head subtly. She turned back to Pista but said nothing.

Pista couldn't read either of the women. *Is she buying this or not?*

Then Nicola asked coldly, "Why did you ask to meet with me?"

Pista tried to soften her up a little. He said, "You must remember me, don't you? You lived up the street from us in Bucharest. You remember my cousin, Vilmos, don't you? He's a doctor too. By the way, I never knew you had two little sisters. They sure look alike."

"If you don't get to the point, I will leave."

"Okay, okay. Now I know what I did was all a big mistake. I never should have bothered your family. Apology accepted?"

Nicola felt no need to respond.

"Have it your way. So here's the deal. There's this guy I know back in the slammer. He's a pretty bad man. I had told him about my plan to kidnap your sister. He always said if you had anything left when I finished, he'd come get the rest. And he meant it too." Pista added cagily, "He's getting out in a couple of weeks. I can make sure he never bothers you, or anyone else, if you get my meaning."

"So far you've said nothing that interests me," Nicola said.

"Well, now, that's where you're wrong. See, the job was really supposed to be me and him, but he didn't get out on schedule, so I got Fane to work with me. Now this guy is pissed, and he's gonna want his cut, or he'll come after you himself. All I need to do is send him a little money, tell him I cleaned you out and I'm sending him a cut. Tell him you left the country or something so he'll back off and go away."

Watching Pista squirm and listening to him change his story, Lynn waited for Nicola to respond.

"I would never give you even two cents," Nicola said.

This bitch can't be serious. He continued, "The way I figure, you give me a thousand for my troubles. I'll send the guy his half, and your problem will be kaput. I'm planning to go straight. Going to get a real job."

Nicola said, "I thought this was important. We're leaving."

Pista threw his hands up in a gesture of defeat and said, "Your mistake, lady. Don't say I didn't warn you."

They stepped outside the room. Mr. Carp joined them a moment later. Nicola said, "Do you think there really is someone out there who's coming after me and my family?"

Lynn said, "He's probably just trying to hustle you."

Daniel Carp said, "I think I know who my client is talking about. Fellow is about to be released after serving nine years. I understand he and Vladú were cell mates at one time. So I guess it's possible there could be something to his story, but I doubt it. The guy I know about wouldn't be dealing in small amounts like that. Sorry I cannot be of more help."

Lynn said, "The police told us that the other kidnapper, Fane Dobos, said there were just the two of them but that

Pista was so determined, he'd probably try something else. This sounded like a weak, last-ditch effort to get some money."

Mr. Carp listened and said, "Dr. Palaki, I'm really sorry for your troubles. I don't believe you will be bothered by Mr. Vladú again. The guy's a real case. Some, you just cannot rehabilitate."

After Morgan got home from class, she went with Lynn over to the American Embassy to make a final report. Then they went to the police station where Lynn told the officials how Pista's accomplice, Fane Dobos, had come to her and Morgan's aid to prevent them from being harmed. She and Morgan told them Fane had definitely helped them escape. Although he had a criminal record, he had probably saved their lives, and they hoped putting in a good word would bode well for him when he got sentenced.

Thursday, December 5

No good Ringyók! Pista paced the floor of his cell and then kicked the wall in anger, instantly feeling the pain shooting through his backside. He regretted the move. When he'd been arrested the other day, they first took him to the hospital to attend to his wound. His behind seemed to heal quickly after being properly treated. The pain that just shot through his rear end was a reminder that he still wasn't 100 percent.

He'd been in jail six days and found it tolerable compared to being behind prison walls. But he'd learned that later this morning he was being taken downtown to be arraigned. His holiday might be coming to an end. He thought about his meeting yesterday morning with Nicola and the other one. *I hope they're in court. I'll tear them apart with my bare hands, especially that black one.* He was certain that if she hadn't come along with Nicola, Nicola might have taken the bait. Ever since Pista had gotten his butt kicked by an African inmate in front of everybody during his first prison stint many years ago, he'd had no use for blacks. In fact, this was the man Pista had killed a few years later. He'd made it look like the *Néger* came after him. Far as he was concerned, they were all worthless.

After breakfast, he was handcuffed and put into the back seat of a police car for the short ride downtown.

Pista considered his plight, especially the part where he might be going right back to prison. He hadn't even been out a year. He almost wished he'd never come back to Budapest. He could have gone back home to Bucharest, or even headed down south to Slovania and made a new start. He could be living a normal life, like everybody else, though somehow that idea repulsed him. Pista was not like everybody else, and he knew it. He believed he was destined to make something out of his life.

In fact, he'd be living the good life right now if it hadn't been for that *kurva Afrikai-Amerikai*. Pista was full of rage and hatred for her. First she'd meddled with his girl and even managed to dodge his car when he was about to run her down. Then she escaped from the house, shot him in the ass, and got him arrested. *I'm going to get her if it's the last thing I do.*

The policeman was driving down a one-way street toward the courthouse. Suddenly, the officer in the passenger seat yelled, "Watch out. That fool's coming right at us." Pista looked up to see a car coming toward them at a high rate of speed. *Oh, hell!* The one driving couldn't swerve because cars were tightly parked on both sides of the narrow street. They realized the safest bet was to stop the car and try to jump out. But their hands never even touched their seatbelts before the oncoming car smashed into them, nearly pushing the vehicle's engine into their laps. Pista was thrown around in the back seat. When he got his bearings, he saw the two policemen both slumped forward. They weren't moving. This was his chance! He had to get those keys.

Pista turned around and strained to use his handcuffed hands to lift the keys off the driver's belt. It was an awkward struggle that hurt like hell, but a desperate man finds ways. He grabbed the keys and then sat up and reached for the door handle to get the hell out of there before people started arriving. But there weren't any door handles. *Shit!* He leaned back on the seat and kicked the window with his feet, knocking it out with one attempt. Then he turned around and reached with his handcuffed hands out the window to open the door. He grabbed the keys and was running down an alley when the first police car showed up. Several bystanders saw him running, but they were more concerned with the two policemen who were still out cold and the driver in the other car, whose head was completely bloodied, caved in by his windshield.

Pista ducked into an alcove in the alley and managed to get his handcuffs off, which was very hard because He had to work with his hands behind his back. He realized he couldn't be running down the street in jail clothes and handcuffs. When Pista got to his flat by way of the back alleys, he entered through the side door of his building. For a moment, he wondered how he'd managed to get away. *It was obviously destiny*, he thought. He clearly was not supposed to spend the rest of his life rotting behind bars or he'd be standing in front of a magistrate right now. He also took what happened as a clear sign that he was supposed to carry out his revenge against that woman before getting out of town.

He changed clothes, collected his money from a hole inside in his mattress, packed his few belongings in a sheet, and hurried to his car. The car was registered in his friend's name, not his own, so he didn't worry about being ID'd by his vehicle. He bought himself a telephone, called the hotel, and asked for Lynn Davis, whose name was permanently seared on his brain. The operator told him Lynn Davis was out, so he found a place to get some sandwiches and beer and then drove over to the girl's apartment to see if the black woman was there. *Hell, if I see the girl, I just might grab her again. Why not?* He thought about Fane Dobos. *Who needs that chump? If I ever see his sorry ass again, I'll kick it too.*

But Pista decided he would do best to stick with his plan to get the woman first and then get the hell out of town. He ate his sandwiches and drank beer while he waited. It wasn't long before he saw a taxi pull up to the door. He wasn't even surprised when both the woman and the girl went inside. By now, Pista knew fate was clearly on his side. *I'll wait right here and get her ass when she comes out.* Pista got out of his car and stood near the entrance behind some tall, thick hedges. He figured she could be coming out anytime now and was prepared to take her by surprise. Every time the door opened, he prepared to lunge.

Earlier that morning, Lynn said, "Morgan, we need to go over to your apartment to get the rest of your things."

"I was thinking tomorrow would work, but now that you mention it, maybe today is better. That way, I'm free to hang out with Ivona tomorrow night, our last night together. I get out of class around three today, and we can go when I get back."

Lynn's driver was not available, so she arranged a taxi for three thirty that afternoon, and they went to Morgan's apartment. Zaka, the attendant, greeted Morgan. "I haven't seen you in a while," he said pleasantly.

Morgan told him she had been away. "We're gathering my things, so we'll need you to call us a taxi. We would like a minivan that can carry large boxes and suitcases, to arrive in about thirty minutes."

The ladies went up to Morgan's apartment. The place was small but light and airy. It was minimally furnished and had a nice view of the park situated next to it. Morgan's bed was unmade and clothes were strewn around, but in no time, she'd gathered her suitcases and boxes and began throwing clothing from her closets and dresser drawers into them. Lynn helped her and sealed the boxes with tape she'd brought along. Morgan collected the rest of her personal articles.

When everything was packed, Lynn said, "This'll take a couple of trips downstairs. We can leave some things with the young man while we come back up here for the rest."

On their first trip down, Lynn carried a heavy box and Morgan her suitcases. Then they went back upstairs for the other two boxes. Before going out the door of her apartment, Morgan took a final look around and said "Good-bye, Budapest." She didn't look unhappy.

When they arrived downstairs, Zaka told them it would be a few minutes before their taxi arrived. Lynn said, "Maybe we can go ahead and set this stuff outside. Then, all the driver'll have to do is load them in his vehicle." She and Morgan each grabbed a box and headed for the door.

Zaka hurried over to Morgan and said, "Here, let me take this." He grabbed Morgan's box, and Morgan stayed inside, holding the door. When he set it on the ground, he announced, "I'll get the other one," and went back inside.

Pista was getting tired of lying in wait, but his need for revenge was stronger than his impatience. So he waited, and when the door opened, he braced himself to pounce. But it was just some guy with a large box. He watched as the guy set the box on the ground and stepped back inside. Next, out came the black woman carrying another large box. Lynn was going to stack her box on top of the other one; Morgan held the door for her to come back in.

Pista didn't know what the hell was going on, and he didn't really care. He had the woman.

He pulled out his gun and quietly came out from behind the bushes. Lynn's back was to him. "Okay, bitch," he said. "Drop the box. You're coming with me."

That voice. Lynn recognized it immediately. She was stunned. *Isn't he supposed to be behind bars?* She dropped the box and whirled around.

"Don't try anything or I'll kill you right here!" he snapped.

This fool is crazy. "Just calm down. I'm not trying anything," she said in a raised voice as she put her hands in the air.

Morgan heard Lynn talking and poked her head outside to see what was going on. "What's happening?" she asked.

Lynn shouted, "Morgan, get back inside!"

Momentarily distracted by the girl, Pista jerked his head in her direction. Somehow, he hadn't expected to see her at that moment.

In a swift move, Lynn knocked the gun out of Pista's hand. "Call the police!" she shouted, and she quickly grabbed her own gun from its holster.

As Pista's gun skidded away, he lunged for it, fully intending to finish Lynn off right there. He grabbed it and turned it toward Lynn. She pulled the trigger. Pista yelled and fell to the ground, where he writhed in pain from the shot to his thigh. Lynn quickly bent over and grabbed his gun then aimed her gun at Pista. A stunned Morgan opened the door and ran out. "Are you all right?" she asked Lynn, who nodded.

Zaka looked excited when he stepped out and reported, "The police are on the way."

Lynn continued aiming her gun at Pista. People going by in cars noticed the commotion and slowed down to observe the action.

As Pista lay on the ground squirming, Lynn wondered how he'd gotten out of jail. *That was a close call.* Within minutes, the police arrived and summoned an ambulance. They took Lynn's statement. Morgan and Zaka shared what they had witnessed. The ambulance took Pista away. It was finally over.

Friday, December 6

FRIDAY NIGHT, JOZSÉF TOOK MORGAN to Ivona's house to say good-bye to her birth mother and grandmother. All firmly promised one another that they would stay in touch. Then he took the twins to the Blue Diamond, where Morgan and Ivona hung out for the last time. On Saturday morning, Ivona, Bela, and György came to the hotel to see Morgan off. György gave Morgan a friendship ring, and they pledged lasting friendship. Jozséf loaded his limo and waited, as did Lynn. After a short visit, bittersweet good-byes were said. Lynn looked around one last time and said, "Morgan, this is it. Let's go home." *And none too soon!*

"An invisible thread connects those who are destined to meet, regardless of time, place, and circumstance. The thread may stretch or tangle. But it will never break."

~Ancient Chinese proverb

Epilogue

Cincinnati, Ohio, May 11, Twelve and a Half Years Later

ALONG WITH ALL HER FAMILY, Flossie Walker sat at the dinner table, where she nibbled lightly on her meal. It was early afternoon, and her family had just celebrated with a birthday dinner for their favorite aunt, along with her friend, Beulah. Dear Agnes had passed away six years ago. This was a landmark day, for today Flossie had turned one hundred years old. Her mind was still as sharp as it had always been, but her body was weak.

When asked what she wanted for her birthday, she'd said, "Don't you all get me a single thing. I have everything I need. I'm just happy to see another birthday. Don't expect to have too many more."

Over dessert, the family sang "Happy Birthday" and made merry chatter. When the celebration was over, everyone gave Flossie Walker a hug and a kiss. Miss

Walker found herself gazing from one face to the next. She was trying to etch every fine detail of their faces into her memory. At four o'clock, her niece, Hazel, who had recently turned seventy-two, drove her and her friend back to the Felix House. It had been a long day, and Miss Walker had much more to look forward to before the day was over. When she stepped into the dining hall and waved to everyone, they shouted back, "Happy birthday, Flossie!" One of the Felix House attendants jumped up from his table to escort her upstairs. She told Hazel, "Don't come up, baby. I'm pretty tired."

Back in her room, Flossie prepared for her evening by following her nightly regimen. One of the nurses' helpers came in to help her wash up. Even as a new centenarian, she still used only plain water on her face, which was still virtually wrinkle-free. Next she applied her trusted Vaseline to her cheeks and forehead, after which she rubbed herself down using that good-smelling lotion that nice young lady Lynn Davis had given her some time ago. The fragrant lotion was expensive, and Miss Walker saved it for special occasions. This day was certainly a special occasion.

Miss Davis was that private detective who had gotten those twins together in Budapest, Hungary, years ago. When she had come to visit her here at the Felix House the year it happened, it had been something special. Miss Walker had truly enjoyed hearing about Morgan and Ivona and their discovery that they had that telepathic quality that she and Mossie had shared. She had been tickled to hear Lynn Davis tell about how everything had turned out, as well as to learn how Nicola and Corina Moldovan were doing.

Flossie remembered how gratifying it had been to learn that both Mrs. Wellington and Nicola Palaki had said they would not have wanted their lives to have been any different. Everyone realized that had the twins stayed together, one of the families would have been childless; each had been happy to have raised their wonderful daughters. While the twins would love to have grown up together, Miss Davis told her that they understood what had happened and were both appreciative of the parents they had.

The most special thing about this birthday so far was the surprising birthday card Miss Walker had received yesterday from Budapest, Hungary. It read:

Dear Miss Walker,

Ivona and I obtained your address from Miss Lynn Davis and did not want to miss the opportunity to congratulate you on your one-hundredth birthday and to wish you a very happy day. We are proud to share a birthday with you and your twin sister.

Ivona and I are doing very well. And we are together. I moved to Budapest seven years ago and am now married, with one son. I am a fashion designer and worked with my grandmother, Corina Moldovan, for three years to perfect my craft. Now I have my own designer label and many famous customers. Ivona is a successful scientist and is not yet married. But she is doing very well and she has a very nice beau.

My sister and I remain amazed at the decision you made thirty-two years ago when we were born. We know you acted from your heart to do something that turned out to be good for everyone concerned. We want to thank you for the courage and wisdom of your decision. The two of us get

along famously. But then, I am like Vonni, and
she is like me. And together we will always be. ☺
We wish you everlasting happiness.

The letter was signed Morgan Wellington Novak and Ivona Palaki.

Miss Walker shook her head and smiled at the thought of those young women, who were nineteen years old when they first got together. She was pleased that they managed to remain in each other's life. Somehow she had felt they would.

She donned her long pale-blue nightgown and housecoat, slipped into her terrycloth booties, and pulled her nightcap over her head. It had been a great day, and the best part was yet to come. Today, as had happened for the past sixty-two years, Mossie would come to her in her dreams. Flossie wanted to stay awake until 7:02 p.m. in anticipation of her sister's visit. It always felt so much like the real thing.

She plopped down in her rocking chair and slung the throw Hazel had given her across her legs. Cinderella was pretty old now, but she could still manage to jump onto Miss Walker's lap and cuddle warmly against her. Flossie stroked her cat, who in turn purred contentedly. Then she began to hum "Precious Lord," another of her favorite spirituals. It was only 5:30 p.m., but extremely tired after her big day, Flossie decided to close her eyes just for a minute. First she set her alarm for 7:02 p.m. and rested her head on the back of the headrest. She fell fast asleep but awakened with a start when the alarm sounded.

Mossie was sitting on the weathered brown leather ottoman. Like every time before, she was dressed in her white nursing outfit. Flossie was instantly wide awake, her mind crystal clear. Her vision was sharp, the colors she saw bright and vivid. As she looked into her sister's face, she could see the soft glow surrounding her countenance. Very happy to see her, Flossie said with a big smile, "Mossie, girl, this is our big day. One hundred years old! I never thought I would still be around this long."

"Well, someone had to prove that our family has longevity. Since Aunt Beatrice, so far you're the oldest. Congratulations and happy birthday, my dear sister!"

"And happy birthday to you too, Mossie! I have been waiting all day to see you."

"Flossie, I must tell you something. This is my last time coming to see you. For this time, you're coming with me. Your work here is done."

A big smile broke across Flossie's face. She was good and ready.

She sprung up from her chair, tossed the throw across it, gave Cinderella a final pat, and took Mossie's hand. This time, Flossie did not need her cane. Holding hands, the sisters walked out into the bright sunlight and into the fields of tall grass and wildflowers. Lilac bushes offered a sweet aroma. The blue sky was dotted with pure white clouds. Birds chirped gaily, and the sun smiled down on them while the warm breeze caressed their faces. Flossie looked back only once, happy to leave all earthly concerns behind. She smiled.

Swinging their clasped hands, Flossie and Mossie began to skip gaily. They skipped and laughed until it seemed they should be out of breath, but they kept going and going until they came upon their little brother, Hampton. He joined hands with them as they skipped happily off into the horizon. Flossie saw her parents just up ahead beckoning to them. This beautiful day was one to celebrate. And all was truly right with the world.

* * *

The continuous sound of the alarm clock brought the evening nurse, Ruby McIntire, to Miss Walker's room at 7:10 p.m. Flossie Walker was one of Ruby's favorite people. In fact, she was an inspiration to all around her and a role model for anyone who wanted to stay keen while growing old. To keep her mind sharp, Miss Walker had surprised everyone by taking up a new language and had nearly become fluent in Russian. She was current, witty, and wise. She and Ruby McIntire had had many conversations on topics ranging from politics to music. When it came to music, Flossie could discuss the rapper 50 Cent as easily as she could Benny Goodman, the King of Swing.

After knocking on the door and getting no response, Nurse McIntire let herself in with her master key. "Hello," she sang out. Cinderella, Miss Walker's cat, was pacing fitfully around the room. The nurse thought the alarm was probably agitating old Cinderella. She noticed Miss Walker sleeping in her rocker. She walked over to the nightstand and shut off the alarm clock, noticing that it had gone off at 7:02 p.m. The nurse was surprised to see it had been sounding for eight minutes. A stiff white nursing cap with bobby pins clipped to both sides was perched on the ottoman. Nurse McIntire hadn't seen one of those except in old photographs. She picked it up for a close examination and figured that Miss Walker must have pulled it out while reminiscing about the past.

The nurse looked around to see if Miss Walker had awakened yet, and she immediately observed that Flossie Walker was far from awake. Indeed, it was apparent she would not awaken again. Somehow, though, Nurse McIntire wasn't startled by what she saw. She felt for a pulse she didn't expect to find, for she already knew. Flossie Walker was gone. Nurse McIntire sat on the bed facing Miss Walker and rubbed her hands together. She knew that if anyone had been at peace with her life, it was Flossie Walker, who had told her many times that she had reconciled all the loose ends of her past. She'd often told her how she looked forward to the day when she and her twin sister would finally be together again, even though they'd never truly been apart. She'd had a long and fulfilling life, and although her eyes were closed, the sweetest and most tender of smiles radiated across her face, so compelling as to warm the hearts of any beholder. Flossie Walker's passage seemed to have been a welcome one, and her smile was full of rejoicing over her transition into eternal life. Nurse McIntire was so moved by Miss Walker's blessed life, she felt tears of joy well in her eyes.

The two women had often sung hymns together, and at this moment, the words to one of their favorites crossed Nurse McIntire's mind. She began to sing softly.

Precious Lord, take my hand,
Lead me on, let me stand,
I am tired, I am weak, I am lone.
Through the storm, through the night,
Lead me on to the light,
Take my hand, precious Lord,
Lead me home.

Afterword

In Budapest, Hungary, at exactly 1:02 a.m. (7:02 p.m. in Cincinnati, Ohio), Morgan and Ivona were celebrating their thirty-second birthday with a night out on the town. They had already enjoyed dinner with family and friends and were sitting around telling funny stories and jokes.

All at once, both twins were gripped by a sudden feeling that something significant was happening. Within seconds, though, they knew that *it* had just come to an end. They looked at each other with knowing eyes and then gave a quick nod, for they knew what had happened and what they needed to do. And so, in keeping with what was in their hearts, they raised their glasses high to toast a very special person. They toasted to honor the life and death of Miss Flossie Mae Walker, age one hundred, a woman whose name was known to everyone in the group, thanks to Morgan and Ivona. For they had told her story many times.

After the toast, all present shouted, "Hear, hear." Then they clinked their glasses and took a sip to honor a midwife—a woman with whom the twins had an inextricable connection. Flossie Walker was indeed honored for having had the courage of her convictions and the strength to follow her own mind.

English Translations of Hungarian Words Used in this Book

Hungarian	English
Afrikai-Amerikai	African-American
Balfasz	Jerk
Bűvös óra	Magic hour
Cigaretta	Cigarettes
Fogas	A type of fish
Igen	Yes
Ki ez	Who is that?
Kuss	Shut up
Korhadt	Punk
Köszönöm	Thank you
Krumplileves	Potato Soup
Kurvával	Whore
Kurva	Bitch
Lúzer	Loser
Meleg fuzzies	Warm fuzzies

Mia fasz	Prick
Nagyon sajnálom	I am very sorry
Naturaqua Mentes	A brand of bottled water
Néger	The N-word
Nem na gyon	No Trespassing
Paprikash	Paprika
Pisztoly	Gun
Ringyók	Whore
Segíts minket?	Will you help us?
Sürgős	Urgent
Szalonnás	Bacon
Szia	Hi
Szilveszter	New Year's Eve
Szuka	Bitch
Szukák	Bitches
Segélyhívó	Emergency
Tervezz	Plan
Tudna segíteni?	Can you help?

Message from the Author

THE CONCEPT OF TWIN TELEPATHY, when identical twins share a special bond that enables them to mentally communicate with each other, is but a theory and not yet a proven science. Still, no matter what it is called, over and over we hear examples of the unexplained, extraordinary connection between twins. For example, we hear that some identical twins complete each others' sentences or know when something is wrong with the other one. Some even feel the other's pain, and many times, one will know what the other one is thinking.

Two of my sisters were identical twins, but both passed away at an early age. I know their bond was strong, and for reasons of my own I believe they shared this *one-mind* connection although I never got to explore the notion of twin telepathy with them firsthand. Thanks to an in-depth conversation with a young friend who had an identical twin sister, I gained additional insight into some intriguing aspects of this "telepathic" relationship. This woman, who lived in China, vividly described the close connection between her and her identical twin sister, who lived in Europe. From her, I heard some amazing things, the most bewildering being that she and her sister sometimes shared each other's dreams. Discussions with other twins corroborated these exceptional stories. One identical twin told me, "Everything you've ever heard about twin relationships is true."

This book has been about the separation of identical twins at birth. It presumes that this phenomenon called twin telepathy exists and is shared by some of the characters in this book. The separation of the twins across cultures and continents added what I felt was a unique dimension to their bond.

At the heart of this story is the midwife. You got to know what her life was like from her early years until the end. You could see how her actions on one fateful occasion created the premise for this story. Perhaps you could understand why she did what she did, just as the characters in this story came to understand it.

And then, of course, we had to have some bad guys, but thank goodness Lynn Davis just *happened* to be on the scene at the right time. And for those who are wondering how Lynn is doing after all she went through, well, she's all better now and ready for her next big case.

I hope you enjoyed it.